For my friend Stewart Wieck, who left us far too early. He lived like a warrior-poet, always dedicated to his family, friends, and fans—in that order. And he died with a sword in his hand.

Also, as always, to my wife, Ann, and our kids: Marty, Pat, Nick, Ken, and Helen. No matter where life takes us, you're all forever in my heart.

LEGACY OF ONYX

MATT FORBECK

BASED ON THE BESTSELLING XBOX® VIDEO GAMES

TITAN BOOKS

Halo: Legacy of Onyx
Print edition ISBN: 9781785656750
E-book edition ISBN: 9781785656767

Published by Titan Books
A division of Titan Publishing Group Ltd
144 Southwark Street, London SE1 0UP

First Titan edition: November 2017
10 9 8 7 6 5 4 3 2 1

A CIP catalogue record for this title is available from the British Library.

Printed and bound by CPI Group (UK) Ltd, Croydon, CR0 4YY

HISTORIAN'S NOTE

While this novel begins in 2549, a few years before the end of the Covenant War, the bulk of *Halo: Legacy of Onyx* takes place in 2558 and steps into the average lives of those who are trying to normalize and rebuild. Its tale comes to full stride alongside the *Halo: Fractures* short story "Lesson Learned," which follows a pair of Spartan-IIIs who are suddenly requisitioned for a highly classified assignment in the most mysterious location in the galaxy.

CHAPTER 1

Memory fades.

Especially memories from childhood. The older one gets, the further they recede, until it almost seems as if there were no childhood at all. Molly Patel was not *that* old and she could barely remember anything from before she was seven.

She could, however, remember some things that happened when she *was* seven. There was one thing in particular she would never forget. Nine years ago, back in 2549. The day her homeworld—Paris IV—died.

She remembered the sky burning.

Monstrous alien starships scudded through the blazing clouds, glowing with unearthly power. Gargantuan machines hung in the sky, spitting out smaller craft that swarmed among them like angry hornets, hurling down destruction on everything below.

Wave after wave of those vessels brought hell to the surface of her planet. The invaders spilled out the sides of their transports, violent energy blasting from their weapons as they cursed her people in strange alien tongues. Their sole purpose was to attack the humans on Paris IV, to destroy their homes, to kill every single one of them.

The only thing that kept Molly and her family alive during the global assault was, simply, that the invaders hadn't yet caught up with them on their terrified attempt to escape.

"We're not going to make it," her mother, Brigid, mouthed as their vehicle raced down an empty road that wound out of their neighborhood, tracing the shoreline and leading toward the nearest evacuation point. In a moment of panic, Molly's mother had slipped into unveiled honesty. Had she given it thought, she would probably have said something different, at least for Molly's sake.

Before Molly's family had left their house, her mother had frantically strapped her into the seat as if Molly was an Orbital Drop Shock Trooper—one of the legendary Helljumpers who would launch down from a perfectly good UNSC ship into the heart of war. Those were the good guys. The ones who were battling in the streets to save Molly's homeworld—and failing miserably.

Molly remembered the lines of worry on her mother's face as she peered back from the front passenger seat. That expression had been deepening for hours, ever since the first signs of the invasion, and now those lines looked as if they might actually crack, causing her to crumble with them.

Molly wanted to say something to her mother to make her feel better, but she was seven. She didn't have the words. If she was being honest, she maybe still didn't.

Somehow, her mother stayed strong.

"We would have been killed going the other way for sure," Molly's father, Gotam, had said with a slight quiver in his voice. "You saw what they did to the highway back there."

The family was heading for the spaceport, just as the emergency broadcasts had insisted, but they had gotten a late start. Molly's parents had been trying to contact her older sister, Grace, who had spent the night at a friend's house. When they tried to call, they found that the comm lines had all been completely overloaded with traffic. They couldn't get through to her, no matter how hard they tried.

Eventually, her parents had given up and driven as quickly as they could to the house where Grace had been. When her mother dashed through the open front door though, no one was inside. The family Grace was staying with had already abandoned the place. They'd taken Molly's sister with them—or so Molly had hoped.

That was when things started to come unglued for Molly. She started to cry, just a little, as softly as she could. She was missing Grace already. The horror of losing track of her sister at such a crucial moment had marred her mom's face when she returned to the car. Another thing that Molly still remembered, and quite clearly: that look.

Her dad had assured both of them that Grace would be fine. That she had probably left in the first wave of evacuations. They just needed to get off the planet themselves now, he told them. Eventually they'd find her.

Of course, they never did.

By the time they got close to the highway that led to the spaceport, even Molly could see they would never be able to even reach that road. Vehicles just sat there, stacked in either direction as far as the eye could see. They moved but in almost imperceptible increments.

Molly's dad stopped the car and got out, scanning the road every which way to see what their options might be.

That's when things really fell apart. The aliens, who had been a remote threat entirely out of sight, suddenly became very real.

A gigantic, unnervingly strange ship—larger than any building Molly had ever seen—descended from a dark cloud and came thundering in over the highway. It loomed there ominously for a long moment, casting its vast shadow over the thousands of vehicles clogging the road for kilometers ahead, as if it were waiting for something.

Orders?

A word from their alien gods?

Then the ship fired a massive beam of energy from its belly. It lanced straight down to the ground, several thousand meters in front of where the family's vehicle had stopped.

Molly's mom shouted at her to shield her eyes, but the pull of her own curiosity was stronger than her mother's voice. She stared at the staggering destruction stretching before her for as long as she could. She was simply too stunned to blink, much less turn away. It was unlike anything Molly had ever seen in her life—or had seen since.

The beam was so bright it physically hurt her eyes, but she couldn't tear her gaze from it. Although it struck the road more than a kilometer away, she could still feel its scorching heat on her face, as vehicles exploded and the earth below the beam completely gave way. Even through the hundred-meter waves of dust and debris the ship's weapon kicked up, Molly could see what the aliens were doing to the surface of her planet—the place she had called home. The beam melted everything it touched into a bright, glowing slag that flowed like torrents of lava, churning out and away from the beam's impact before it shifted from white to red to black as it cooled.

Molly's dad wasted no more time. He leaped back behind the wheel and spun the vehicle around, taking off in a new, desperate direction as he hunted for another route to the spaceport. He didn't have a plan, and he had no time to come up with one. This gut reaction was the best he could muster.

But so far, that hadn't done Molly's family much good.

"We're still ten kilometers from the evacuation site," her mom said. "We should have left sooner, Gotam. We shouldn't have let Grace—" Brigid stopped herself. "I wish we lived closer."

"Stop. How could we have anticipated this?" Molly's dad said, as they darted past an abandoned car on the side of the road. "And Grace will be fine, Brigid. She *has* to be."

Molly craned her neck as they bolted down the highway. She was trying to watch a cluster of people who had gotten out of their vehicle. They were on their knees, praying.

Some part of Molly, even at the age of seven, had wondered if those people had the right idea.

She had seen the ship. She had seen what the aliens were capable of. *Who can escape that? And if we can't get away, what is the point in running now?* Maybe it would have been better to pull off to the side of the road as well and make their peace while they waited for the end to come.

In the end, Molly was glad it wasn't her decision to make. She was just a kid back then, but even when she recalled this moment years later, she wasn't sure she would have kept on going.

Another vehicle suddenly hurtled past them, headed in the other direction. On this road, they hadn't seen anyone going *away* from the evacuation point all morning. That car was headed *toward* the destruction. *Why?*

"Not a good sign," her mother remarked.

"That's insane," Gotam replied, shaking his head. "They go back that way, they're going to run straight into the Covenant."

"What could be so much worse in this direction?"

"At this point? Nothing."

Without thinking, Molly instinctively reached over to the empty seat next to her, the one where Grace should have been. She'd done it hundreds of times before—it was like second nature—but this time, Grace wasn't there to comfort her. Molly's heart sank, and she bit her lip.

In the far distance, the city of Mímir suddenly came into view, its towers defiantly spearing up into the sky. Molly's family had chosen to live on the outskirts, farther from the spaceport. She'd often wondered if that decision had cost them precious time.

Without warning, another huge Covenant ship descended from the clouds and ignited its own ground-melting weapon, ripping into Mímir's skyscrapers as if they were paper. It was humbling to see such majestic human structures tumble to the ground in seconds. For a long moment, the car was filled only with silence. Nothing could have prepared them for what this day had brought. It was too awful for the imagination. Then the silence was jarringly broken, drawing Molly's attention back to the road ahead.

"There's another one," Molly's mom said, as a second car passed theirs going the opposite direction.

Her dad cursed. "And there's more up ahead of us. What's going on?"

From the backseat, Molly peered between them, trying to figure out what the other drivers were doing if the evacuation site was their only chance for survival. Stumped, she looked past them and toward the spaceport as it came into view. It still seemed so far away, like a cluster of tall buildings emerging from the sea.

One after another, ships—human ships—rose stridently up into the sky on tails of fire and smoke. They weren't alone though. Smaller Covenant craft suddenly burst from within the clouds and chased the escaping ships as they fled. Some of the refugee shuttles managed to soar straight past the aliens, whisking their passengers from the grim fate of Paris IV to the safety of invisible stars.

Other ships weren't so fortunate. The swarm of Covenant fighters caught them, unleashing a barrage of white-hot energy at their hulls, transfixing each for a moment like a moth in a flashlight's beam—until it exploded in a flash.

Like thunder that came after lightning, the noise of their destruction didn't reach Molly's ears until seconds later, a series of low thuds punching through the air, synced with the precise order of destruction. The impulse to weep over those who had died followed almost immediately, even though Molly had likely known none of them.

But they were humans. Fellow citizens of Paris IV.

For a brief moment, Molly wondered if Grace was on one of those ships. For a seven-year-old who loved her older sister, there wasn't much that could be more painful than that. The vision of the falling debris still choked Molly up when her mind went back to that day.

At the time, she didn't think she was making that much of a commotion in the backseat, but her mother noticed soon enough. She reached back and held Molly's hand to comfort her, but her father didn't respond at all. He was too focused on something up ahead. Molly wiped the heavy tears that had welled up in her eyes and tried to see what her father was fixated on.

The road rising before them led toward a bridge that extended over a river flowing into the nearby ocean: the location of the spaceport. Molly followed the structure of the bridge with her eyes and spotted a tremendous gap in its center. It had been severed completely in half. Long, twisted bits of rebar stuck out of the ends of the shattered concrete like broken fingers reaching for the other side.

"Well, that explains why everyone was turning around," her dad said. His voice sounded distant, unreal, as if in complete disbelief. "Dammit. The nav system should've reported that."

Her mom grimaced. "If the Covenant hadn't taken down all the comm networks, it would have."

Her dad punched the dashboard with his fist and cursed

again. He looked down at the readouts for what seemed like a long time and then, without warning, stomped on the accelerator. The engine growled like a starving beast, and the vehicle suddenly launched forward.

Molly's mother somehow held back her surprise and managed to gently put her other hand on his arm, clearly straining to be as calm as possible. "The bridge is gone, Gotam. We can't make it across."

"Do we have any choice?" Molly's dad glared down the road ahead as the vehicle rocketed onto the actual bridge. He showed no sign of stopping. "Isn't it better to die trying?"

As the car veered around a handful of abandoned vehicles and shot toward that horrifying gap, the weight of what her father said hit Molly, and she screamed in terror. She couldn't help it any longer. Her mind started imagining the feeling of falling.

They were only seconds from tumbling headlong into the open sky past the bridge's shattered edge and from there straight down into the water below. Maybe that would have been better than being melted to death, but by how much?

"Hon. We can't make that jump." Brigid's grip on Gotam's arm tightened, but her voice remained steady and even, as she refused to look ahead.

Molly couldn't keep her eyes off the road.

As the vehicle rushed even closer toward the edge of the bridge, her dad suddenly blinked as though he had finally snapped out of a trance. He switched feet and stomped down on the brake pedal instead. The sudden change in momentum thrust Molly forward against her seat restraints until they bit into her shoulders, and the car swerved back and forth, struggling desperately to come to a stop. She could smell the stench of burning rubber, and she wondered if maybe he'd changed his mind a little too late.

The car violently came to a rest though, just shy of the last possible moment. The horrible fall Molly had expected never came. The empty space beyond the broken steel and concrete stretched before them. They sat only meters from the edge.

"Okay . . . okay. You're right," Gotam said, his voice shaking. Molly had never heard him like this. Beads of sweat rolled down the side of his face as his hands gripped the wheel. He took a deep breath, trying to steady himself. "We have to go back."

"And then what . . . ?" her mom asked.

"I . . . really don't know." He swallowed hard, then put the car in reverse, hit the gas, and wrenched the wheel around, spinning in the opposite direction. "Maybe we can make it to the tunnel at Cochineal Pass," he said.

"You think that's going to save us?" Brigid asked in disbelief.

The car lurched forward again as Gotam leaned on the accelerator and wrestled it back into the middle of the road. "Has to be better than standing underneath one of those ships with nothing between you but empty sky."

Like the cars they'd seen before going in the opposite direction, the family now raced back as fast as they'd come. Soon they passed once again the same people praying on the side of the road.

More of them stood gathered there now. A few new carloads had joined, probably seeking solace in one another's company for what they knew would be their final moments.

Molly caught a flash of them that she never forgot, an image imprinted in her mind. They were standing there clutching one another's hands. Even years later, she could still make out their faces.

Some of them hugged their loved ones tight. Most wept.

Once their car zipped past the roadside supplicants, Molly turned forward again and peered through the windshield. One of the Covenant ships a dozen or so kilometers away—probably the same one from before—was slowly canting toward their car. Its unrelenting beam continued destroying everything in its path like a tornado of light.

For a second, Molly wondered what had happened to the traffic they'd seen ahead. Before she could give it much thought, it quickly grew warmer in their car. Her skin went moist with sweat. The ship was still far from them, but its blindingly white beam was slowly drawing closer, causing a swift ascent of the temperature, like that of a heating oven.

Molly's mom reached back and held her hand. "It's going to be all right, Molly."

Even then, she could tell how much of a lie that was—that her mother was saying it simply to help her feel better. Still, Molly couldn't blame her.

"I know, Mommy." Molly could lie too.

As her dad squeezed every bit of speed he could muster out of the car, the enormous ship edged toward the vehicle from the right, and the vicious sound of its weapon grew impossibly loud. Just over the guardrail, stretched out below, Molly could see the valley where the beam had launched its approach. It bore a long, jagged trench of scorched earth.

"Hang on. We're going to make it. I promise you that," her father said through gritted teeth, as he slung the car around a corner toward the mountain pass.

The mouth of the tunnel suddenly appeared up ahead, and the road snaked into it. Even as it grew closer, it still felt so far away. At the same time, the dark purple starship loomed toward their car, drawing nearer by the second.

The nose of the vessel disappeared over the roof of the car. All Molly could now see was white light from its destructive beam plunging out of its gut toward the earth below and blotting out most of the sky.

Molly finally had to turn away. It was too close to bear.

"Gotam . . . ? Are you sure?" Her mother gave voice to the doubts that had been growing in Molly's own mind. She wanted to believe her father's words, but an unshakable fear had already gripped her heart.

"Giving it everything we got," he replied, struggling to keep his voice composed.

There was no traffic. The road was vacant. To Molly, it felt as if they were the only ones left on Paris IV, the only ones still trying to survive. All the others, it seemed, had either made peace with their impending doom or had already met it.

But for some reason, her family had held out hope.

The car roared on, and Molly kept her eyes fixed ahead.

The bright, lethal light now blanketed everything on the right, crushing all of the shadows in the car and filling it with a searing heat. In front, the dark, safe tunnel rushed toward the vehicle. Molly's fingers dug deeper into her seat's armrests as waves of grit and debris from the beam's impact on the valley below pummeled the side of the car.

The Covenant ship was right on top of them.

At any second, the blaze would consume them.

Her family's desperate quest to reach the mouth of the tunnel felt so achingly slow, as though time had nearly stopped. Molly would later remember vividly how the vehicle hurtled toward the gaping maw, a dark and chilly refuge that promised to swallow them, to protect them from the fatal touch of the Covenant's scorching light.

Molly began to bounce up and down in her seat, screaming as the overwhelming light forced her to close her eyes. She felt so full of unbridled terror that her seven-year-old self was trying to will the car to go faster by shaking the seat with all of her might.

"Go, Daddy!" she shouted. *"Go, go, go, go, go!"*

Her mom squeezed her hand so tight it hurt, but Molly didn't complain. The pain meant she was still alive.

"Hold on!" her dad shouted. "Almost there!"

"Don't stop, Gotam!" said Brigid.

Even with her eyes shut tight, Molly could see the melting beam's wall of light through her eyelids, as it flooded into the car. It felt as if a tsunami of blinding heat were reaching out to devour them.

As they drew close to the tunnel, their back now to the ship, Molly risked opening her eyes. She could see trees and large boulders from the surrounding area being swept across the road directly in front of them, as though they were caught up in a cyclone.

The vehicle was just seconds away from the tunnel when the inside of the car suddenly became superheated, forcing Molly to gasp for air. In an instant, she felt as if she had been physically placed on a sun, her skin beginning to burn, her throat and eyes immediately going dry, as if being cooked alive. She could no longer see even the blackness of the tunnel's mouth. The heat and light had blown everything out.

Molly closed her eyes again, expecting the end.

An instant later—

They emerged from the blinding nimbus and bulleted into the tunnel, miraculously swallowed by the darkness. Her eyes had trouble adjusting at first. Slowly, things came into focus, but her ears still pulsed with the beam's churning cacophony, even as it grew farther away.

The rapid change in temperature was as if she'd jumped into an icy lake on the hottest summer day. As much as she welcomed it over the deadly heat, it shocked the air from her lungs. She couldn't breathe. She couldn't do anything but look into her mother's face. Molly could faintly see a small smile of relief from the front passenger seat.

She also saw what lay ahead and couldn't warn her father to slow down. She didn't have the breath or the words. All she could do was point ahead when she saw the taillights racing toward them at full speed.

Her dad's eyes hadn't adjusted in time, and he spotted the problem too late. He slammed on the brakes again, but the vehicle's momentum was simply too great.

Molly didn't remember the impact, but she knew what happened.

Their car rear-ended a truck at full speed, the front end of their vehicle crumpling like a paper bag. The vehicle's air bags must have instantly inflated, enveloping her in a cushioning cocoon, even as it tore her mother's grip away.

The last thing she remembered was hearing her mother shout her name.

Then everything went completely dark, and she didn't know anything else. Not for a while at least.

Sometime later—she couldn't tell how long for sure—Molly awakened to find herself still strapped in her seat but unable to see anything in the pitch-black.

For a moment, she wondered if she was dead. *Maybe this is what it's like?*

Molly's parents weren't religious at all, and they hadn't done much to prepare her at such a young age for thoughts of the afterlife. For all she knew, a person's body just stopped working, and the person was stuck inside it, unable to do anything else ever again.

But she was in too much pain for that to be the case.

Molly ached from head to toe, and her mouth felt as dry as a desert. She was exhausted and in agony, but most of all she needed water. She reached up to touch her face and had a moment of horrible panic when she realized that she couldn't feel her hands.

Soon she figured out that the car had stopped and pitched forward at a sharp angle, and she was hanging from her seat's safety restraints. The harness had cut off the circulation in her arms. Her hands were still there, though, and they worked, even if they felt clumsy. She brushed her hair from her face and felt something rough crusted on her skin.

Molly knew it had to be blood.

Then through the darkness came an awful stench, like rot mixed with spilled fuel and vomit. She wanted to plug her nose, and for a moment, she tried breathing only through her mouth. The scent was indescribably awful, but she tried to focus on other things.

How long have I been out? Is the Covenant ship still blasting the ground just outside the tunnel? What happened to my parents?

The cold silence from the front of the car answered the last question. Only when Molly was older would she realize that the smell had come from them.

She fumbled with the catch on her seat's safety straps, but she couldn't seem to work the release. Her fingers were just too numb, and she couldn't make them function properly. She tried for as long as she could manage before giving up and letting them drop slack again.

As Molly hung in the car, feeling frustrated and hopeless, memories of what had happened began to flood back. She began to cry, softly at first, then in big sobbing gulps. She was tired, but somehow she had enough energy left for tears.

She pleaded with her mother and father to wake up. To be alive.

All she wanted was to give up.

For some length of time, Molly just hung there and let her mind be drawn into a black hole of grief. Then, without warning, the back window of the car shattered, showering her with broken glass.

The sudden noise startled her to the core, and she screamed in response, thinking that the Covenant had finally found her. It wasn't enough that they had leveled her entire world. Now they had to find her here and finish her off too.

Molly bit back her cries, realizing that she should have been quieter. But it was already too late. They'd found her.

She took a deep breath and cringed as she waited to die.

Flashlight beams shone down into the car from behind her. She could now see that the car had tilted forward on impact. Its nose had jammed deep under the truck it had barreled into, lifting the entire back of the car off the ground.

That was when she saw them: the barest glimpse of her parents, still in the front. They didn't move. They just hung against their seat belts. Limp. Gone.

"I found one!" a man shouted above her. "She's alive!"

A wave of relief washed over Molly. She'd been convinced that it was the Covenant who'd discovered her, thinking she'd be hauled out by a giant alien with jagged teeth.

Instead, this was a human. She'd been saved.

Then Molly really began to weep, not from terror but from a chaotic mix of emotions she could barely understand. There was relief for certain, but it was blended with the overwhelming loss of her parents, as well as what she'd later come to know as survivor's guilt.

She was alive and they were not.

Her parents hadn't been alone in that. Most of Molly's home-world hadn't made it either—including Grace, as she would only later discover.

"It's all right," the man said to her. "I got you."

He reached in and cut one of her car seat's shoulder straps with a large knife. Then he wrapped his free arm around her so she wouldn't fall and gently sliced through the other strap. Once she was free, he sheathed the weapon and with his strong, callused hands pulled her backward and up through the car's rear window, lifting her as if she were little more than a doll.

Molly heard other people, shouting, tramping in her direction, but she didn't pay any attention to them. She just curled up against her savior's broad chest and cried quietly into his uniform. When she opened her eyes, she saw the name stenciled on his shirt.

The image of it burned into Molly's brain. It read: SGT. JOHNSON.

CHAPTER 2

The sky over Aranuka was bright and blue as Molly Patel strolled home from school. In the five years that she had lived in the vast city-platform, built above the original atoll that had long since vanished under the waves of the Pacific Ocean, Molly had come to love how new it seemed compared to anywhere else she'd ever been. It was almost as if it had been pulled fresh from a package and dropped right onto the water.

It may have seemed a bit *too* fresh to some. It still had a new-city smell—mostly because not enough people had moved back here after the war ended.

But Molly knew that's what was bound to happen after the Covenant finally found Earth and attacked the ground anchors of the planet's key space tethers in their invasion. Aranuka housed one of those spots, and the Covenant had nearly taken the tether there down. It made sense to her that people might be somewhat reluctant to shoot roots in a place that had been almost entirely removed from the map just a few years ago.

The tragic part was that the Covenant hadn't been all that interested in the tether to begin with. Humanity had plenty of other ways to get into space, so a giant freight elevator wasn't that vital a target for the invaders. According to records released shortly after the attack, they had apparently thought an artifact was hidden under the platform, something of incredible value to them, left behind by an ancient race of beings known as the Forerunners—a civilization that had long since disappeared from the galaxy.

They had been willing to tear the entire area to pieces to find it.

Not much had been left of the original Aranuka platform after the United Nations Space Command drove the Covenant off, though the space elevator itself had survived. That was probably why the Unified Earth Government had set to rebuilding the city so quickly. It was part of their global Project Rebirth, an ambitious drive to plaster over the gaping holes the alien ships had clawed out of the planet in places such as there and New Mombasa.

For the most part, it had worked. The Aranuka platform and elevator looked better than they ever had, a sparkling jewel strung on a glittering chain set in the center of the Pacific, thousands of kilometers from anywhere else. The only trouble was that not too many citizens were eager to move back in.

Besides, of course, the folks Molly referred to as her Newparents—the people who had adopted her after the destruction of Paris IV.

Back when the Covenant invaded Earth, Molly and her Newparents had been living in Wisconsin, seven time zones to the east of Aranuka—somewhat removed from much of the battle. But for a xenolinguist—Yong Lee—and an honest-to-God archaeologist—Asha Moyamba—the lure of properly exploring an archaeological dig such as the one the Covenant had started right beneath Aranuka proved far too appealing. Even though Molly had tried to deter them, no force on Earth could keep them from taking advantage of that opportunity.

Despite her objections, Molly and her Newparents wound up on the city-platform of Aranuka, and Molly was now slated to be part of one of the first graduating classes to attend all four years at Admiral Harper High School.

After finishing there, Molly had only one goal: she planned to join the UNSC.

This time, the decision would be entirely hers, and it would most certainly be over and against Yong and Asha's objections. The tables would finally turn.

Yong had lost a sister who'd been a tough-as-nails Orbital Drop Shock Trooper, which had been tragic for everyone who was close to her. By all accounts, though, she'd known exactly what she'd signed up for, and she would have been the first to admit it. But because of that loss, Yong refused to risk losing anyone else in action. That included his adopted daughter.

Regardless, after how the military had saved Molly's life back on Paris IV, she felt a deeply rooted obligation to serve in some capacity, no matter how dangerous a career it might be. Marines such as Sergeant Johnson were her heroes. And if she was completely honest, Molly wanted to be a hero for someone like her seven-year-old self too. Especially now that the future of the galaxy seemed as uncertain as ever.

The war might have come to a close, but rumors of chaos continued to abound. Apparently human insurgents had started to take up a lot of the slack in the terror department, a problem humanity had known well before the Covenant War had interrupted it.

And the Covenant wasn't quite dead yet either.

Back in Wisconsin, Molly had felt fairly safe—at least until the Covenant had figured out the location of Earth. Wisconsin just felt so far away from anything that had to do with the war.

Here in Aranuka, though, the ghosts of the thousands of people who had died at the Covenant's hands seemed to haunt every street corner. And in the years since, not too many of the living had showed up to crowd them out.

The UEG had rebuilt Aranuka—and a number of other Earth cities hit hard by the Covenant—in an effort to help the planet heal, but this remote island paradise still stood so hollow and lifeless. Businesses and the military continued to use the tether to move freight to outer space and back, but most of that had become automated long before the Covenant showed up.

Molly's history teacher said that this tiny atoll had never really held a large population to begin with. Only about a thousand folks had lived there before its beaches had been swept under the waves. Maybe about ten times that many had called it home a few centuries later, just before the Covenant's vicious invasion.

Still, the small population wasn't all that bad for Molly. It meant that even on the salaries of a couple of academics, her family could afford a penthouse apartment in one of the nicest sections of town, with wide windows that opened onto the Pacific Ocean to the north and west. Maybe Molly didn't see anyone else in the lobby when she entered the building, and maybe the elevator didn't stop a single time on her way to the top, but the view at sunset was gorgeous. It was like something from a dream, even if a quiet and uneasy restlessness clouded most of her days.

But today was different.

The moment Molly walked into their apartment, she knew something was wrong.

Both of her adoptive parents' briefcases sat next to each other on a bamboo bench near the door. Given the dedication they had to their respective professions—especially since moving to Aranuka—this was disturbingly odd. They shouldn't have been home this early.

Despite the circumstances of their arrival in her life, Molly loved them both. She didn't have any other living relatives—or at least any willing to raise an orphan in the middle of a war. Asha and Yong had been college friends of her real parents, and after she'd survived Paris IV, they'd taken her in without hesitation.

Despite everything else that was going on in their lives, they'd graciously made room for Molly in their hearts, which even now gave her reason to pause and be thankful. If she hadn't been utterly traumatized by the glassing of her homeworld, everything would have been picture-perfect. Looking back at the first few years after Paris IV, Molly realized that she had been a handful for them. At the time, she'd just wanted her real parents back. It didn't matter to her how wonderful the substitutes might be.

Early on, her Newparents had even helped Molly look for Grace. Molly had fantasized that if her sister was somehow alive, Grace could have taken custody of her instead. Grace would have only been twelve at the time, but somehow that hadn't mattered to Molly.

Grace was actual flesh and blood: family. At least the two of them would have had each other, Molly rationalized. That would have been enough.

Instead, within weeks, Molly and her Newparents had learned that the escape ship Grace and her friend's family had filed onto was incinerated on the launchpad before it could take off. Molly remembered the day she found out. She even remembered exactly where she was.

They had been in Wisconsin. Asha and Yong had come home from work early to give her the news the moment she came home from school. They sat Molly down on the couch in the living room and broke the news to her as gently as they could.

It didn't matter. It felt as if the Covenant had murdered Grace all over again. Molly cried for weeks, refusing to talk to anyone.

Despite the early struggles of their new relationship with

Molly, Asha and Yong had never tried to take the place of Molly's parents. Not entirely.

Even though they were the ones raising her, they sincerely wanted to remember their old friends just as much as she did. They kept a framed picture of Molly's parents in the living room and often told her about the wonderful things they had all done back in college. It was vividly clear to Molly that they'd genuinely cared about one another.

Asha and Yong didn't have any children of their own, and for the most part they seemed pretty thrilled to have Molly around. But they worked long hours, something she'd come to appreciate over the past few years. After Molly would get home from school, she had complete freedom until they got back from work, and that buffer had helped her cope with a lot of the pain she'd wrestled with.

Molly eventually came to prize that solitude, that freedom. It was the one time of day she didn't have to deal with peers or anyone looking over her shoulder. It was her time alone.

Though she now fought it, memories of the day Asha and Yong had come home early with the news of Grace began weighing down in the pit of her stomach. She wondered what other kind of information could possibly drag them both away from work.

Asha greeted Molly from the couch in their living room with a wide, toothy smile. Asha had long, sleek hair, dark and shiny as her eyes, which glinted with curiosity and kindness. She liked to wear long, flowing clothes, and since the move to Aranuka, she'd adopted most of its native Polynesian styles because of how much they delighted her. Embracing this new culture was one of her newfound joys.

"Hi, Molly!"

Molly crinkled her brow. "You're home early."

"Yes, well . . . Yong and I have something to tell you," Asha said, completely ignoring Molly's suspicions.

Molly cocked her head and sauntered into the living room, which was filled with wicker furniture on a bamboo floor and slanting sunlight—also part of Asha's efforts to embrace the local culture. The hopeful look in her eyes only made Molly more nervous. Something was off, but this clearly wasn't bad news.

Then Yong strode into the living room from the kitchen and stood beside Asha. Yong was tall and rangy, his dark hair cropped in a sharp and stylish cut. He'd recently started wearing half-moon, gold-rimmed glasses with which he could pull up data at will for his job, but he had them folded up and stuffed into his blazer's breast pocket. He clearly didn't want to be distracted. Whatever this was, it was big.

Yong leaned over the back of the couch, which faced toward the sea, and put a hand on Asha's shoulder, presenting Molly with a united front. When they were both standing, Yong towered at least a foot over Asha, but despite their vast differences in style, height, and temperament, to Molly they always seemed like a well-matched pair.

"It's huge news, sweetie," he said, wearing the same fragile smile as Asha.

This sounded familiar to Molly.

The two had pulled the same trick when they'd announced the family was moving to Aranuka. To Molly, it had turned out all right in the end, but at the time she'd done a great job of making them all miserable. She'd absolutely hated moving—especially being uprooted. She did not share her Newparents' excitement over novelty and change.

Molly dropped her chin and stared at the floor for a moment. She thought for a split second that maybe if she waited long enough, they would see how upset the whole thing had already made her and forgo spilling whatever it was that would wreck her world.

That didn't happen. They were far more patient than Molly, so she eventually gave up and raised her eyes to meet theirs, forcing the words out of her mouth.

"Okay, guys . . . what is it?"

"We got new jobs!" Asha's smile spread even wider.

"*Both* of us, as a matter of fact." Yong came around from behind the couch and sat down next to Asha. He gave her a proud sidelong hug.

Molly sighed. A stab of fear hit her insides, validating all of the dread that had built up since she'd stepped through the front door and seen their briefcases. She wanted to be happy for them, but a change of employment wasn't what this announcement was about. This was just the prologue.

"Don't fret." Yong held out a hand as if that would allay Molly's fears. "We're *all* going."

That answered *that* question. Molly tried to put on a serious face and handle this with maturity, but everything in her fought against it.

"So . . . that means we're moving? Again?" She sat down next to Asha. "I was just starting to like it here."

Asha reached up and put a gentle hand on Molly's shoulder. "Yeah, I know it's another move. There have been a lot of them, haven't there?" Asha said, echoing Molly's concerns. "After this, though, I don't think we'll be moving again for a long time. Maybe never."

Never? The thought had rarely entered Molly's mind, as she just assumed all homes were temporary. She wasn't sure how she felt about something permanent.

Molly didn't have too many friends in Aranuka. There weren't all that many others her age here, at least not yet.

But she hadn't made a lot of friends back in Wisconsin either. That was for an entirely different reason. Many of the kids there had family in the UNSC. A number of them had even lost someone they loved in the war.

But none of them had survived the glassing of a planet.

Except for Molly.

The media had made such a big deal out of her survival that some had taken to calling her "the miracle child." Molly was one of only a handful of people to have lived through the destruction of Paris IV, and the story of her unexpected rescue in the tunnel had been blasted across the newsfeeds. The real miracle was that anyone had been looking for survivors at all. Most of the UNSC was, by that point, pulling out of the star system, abandoning what little was left of the planet.

That Molly was in a tunnel when the land around her was glassed had made a huge difference. If not for the accident that had lifted the back of her car off the ground—above the liquefied material that surged into the tunnel—she probably wouldn't have made it either. In some weird twist of fate, the glassing of Paris IV had ultimately kept Molly alive long enough for her to be rescued.

Molly had wound up in a military hospital for almost a week, and it had taken the UNSC another week to get her on a transport headed for Earth. She had only been seven at the time, but she still remembered desperately trying to find out what might have happened to Grace the whole time she was there. No one could tell her.

In the years that followed, Molly had found herself slowly becoming obsessed with news about the war, and with the UNSC in general. Part of it had stemmed from a genuine interest in humanity's survival—the Covenant threat was real and needed to be stopped—but the other part was that she desperately wanted to find and thank Sergeant Avery Johnson for hauling her out of that mess.

She never got the chance to see him again. Apparently, he'd died helping the legendary Spartan super-soldier, the Master Chief, stop the Covenant, once and for all . . . or so the *declassified* version of the story went.

By the time Asha and Yong had brought Molly home, news of the arrival of "the miracle child" had reached their town in Wisconsin. Because of that, people treated Molly differently. She wasn't an average little girl to them, but a conversation point over dinner. Given her loss and the spectacle surrounding her survival, it took a long time for her to start feeling like a normal kid again. Therapy helped in the early years, but eventually her psychologist said she'd done all she could, and Molly would have to continue her journey on her own.

So she did.

Shortly after that, they'd made their way to Aranuka.

Although Molly had been against it at first, coming to this isolated place had helped in ways she had not foreseen. Many of the people who lived alongside them had lost family to the Covenant, just like her. Even though the war was over, some people would still be fighting the pain it had brought till the day they died.

So they had that in common at least. It may have been mostly empty, but over the years Aranuka had slowly become home.

And now that was going to end.

"You're going to love it," Yong said, veiling some of his enthusiasm. "Where we're headed . . . it's not what you think. There's nothing like it in the galaxy."

At sixteen, Molly knew hyperbole when she heard it, but she wasn't ready to respond. She'd let Yong continue before mounting her defense.

"The place we've been assigned to is . . . well, it's a whole new world to explore. To be honest, even that doesn't do it justice! And we'll have a real house with a real yard in a brand-new town made specifically for researchers like us—"

"It almost sounds too good to be true," Molly interrupted, only partially attempting to restrain her sarcasm. If she didn't know him so well, she'd have guessed that he'd made the whole thing up. "Where exactly is this paradise?"

His face took on a stern grimace. "Well, that's the thing, Molly. It's top secret. So you can't tell a soul."

Asha gave Yong a tug on the shoulder. "Take it easy, hon. Molly's been with us for years now. You know that she's able to keep a secret."

"I'm being serious," he said, going several shades colder. "Molly, where we're headed is a matter of Naval Intelligence. You know ONI, right? They're hardcore folks, and they keep their cards very close. Even casual conversations about what we're about to tell you could end . . . badly for everyone."

The Office of Naval Intelligence. That piqued Molly's attention.

Since her Newparents were now working on a site that had been the target of the Covenant during the war, Asha and Yong were sometimes involved in highly classified projects. Over the past few years, that had become business as usual. Once in a while, they told Molly briefly about things they were working on, always using the vaguest terms and only after swearing her to complete secrecy. Molly knew that if she didn't keep this information safe, it could destroy them all.

So no, the Office of Naval Intelligence did not play around.

Molly narrowed her eyes at Yong. "Now I'm actually intrigued."

"Oh, honey," Asha said in a hurry. She'd seen that light in Molly's eyes before, and Asha wanted to rein her in before she got too excited about the wrong thing. "This new project doesn't have anything to do with the war. Not directly, at least."

"It's better than that," Yong said, struggling to restrain his excitement. "It's the most *intriguing* place in the entire galaxy."

"So . . . what is it?"

"You know what kind of work we do, right?" Asha asked.

"You study alien cultures. Like the Forerunners."

"That's right," Yong said.

"None of that's classified, though," Molly said. It was hard for anyone to hide the news about the Forerunners, since the Covenant had dug up one of their artifacts in Kenya before the end of the war. Rumor had it that they excavated an enormous machine built a hundred thousand years ago, a structure over one hundred kilometers wide. Specific knowledge about the Forerunners was still sketchy, at least to the public, but Molly had managed to fill in some of the gaps with what she'd gleaned from Asha and Yong.

"What you might not know, though, is that ONI funds our research of the Forerunner culture and technology. We're private contractors for them with the UEG," Asha said. "So our work ultimately helps the government reverse engineer the ancient technology in order to help build better tech for humanity in the future."

Molly recognized this had to be true on some level, but she thought if ONI wanted this technology, it was probably for a specific purpose. "Why? Do they want to use it to fight someone?"

"What? No." Yong's face filled with concern. "Why would you think that?"

He always bristled when Molly talked about fighting. He was determined to show her just how awful he thought it was. Sometimes he even seemed to take it personally, as if he were angry that she didn't want to become an academic like them.

Molly didn't mean to insult their professions, but she'd watched them at work for years. While she could see why their careers were both important and interesting—especially to them—if she had to sit in an office and try to grok alien tongues or even go out to a dig in the middle of nowhere and unearth dusty old artifacts, she knew it would drive her mad.

All of that was stuff done behind the scenes. Molly wanted to be on the front lines, right in the thick of things.

"Well, they were powerful, right?" she asked.

"We study the Forerunners because their understanding of the universe was so much deeper than ours," Yong responded patiently. "Like Asha said, if we can decipher the things they left behind and then reverse engineer them, we can make massive leaps forward in our technology and our knowledge of the way things work. It's hugely valuable, not just to the UNSC, but to all of humanity. Everything from medicine to urban infrastructures and things like faster-than-light transportation . . . their technology touches every aspect of our lives."

"But can't you just do that from here? I mean, *haven't* you been doing that?"

"Yes"—Asha smiled wanly—"but that was a while ago. Years even. We've finished what we came here to do and exhausted most of what we were brought here to research. We're done with our core research now, and others will pick up where we left off. This next thing . . . that's what we're being tasked with again."

"Oh." A tragic picture spontaneously entered her mind. She could see where this was heading. The rest of her life on some backwater dustball of a planet where she'd be lucky to find enough oxygen to breathe. Somewhere that would have even fewer people than Aranuka, if that was possible.

"The Office of Naval Intelligence has made some astonishing finds over the years since the war ended," Asha continued. "And, as it turns out, Yong and I happen to be at the top of our fields with regard to researching Forerunner technology, especially in our respective areas of specialization. There aren't really any researchers out there with our specific skillsets, at least not readily available."

"So what?" Molly tried to rein in her frustration. "Why does this immediately mean another move? You just said they sent you the artifacts to research before. Can't they just do that again?"

"They do, honey," Asha said, "with *some* of the assets we research. But other artifacts are simply too big, even for the largest ships we have. There are Forerunner installations out there as massive as an entire world. The bottom line is that the UNSC needs every expert out in the field, doing this research in person. In particular, they need *us*."

"Something we've worked on in the past . . . well, we have really intimate knowledge of it," Yong said. "In fact, no one understands these things as well as Asha and me. This is why ONI's reassigned us, and it's why we have to leave Aranuka. We need to be on-site and doing the initial research in person. There's just no other way."

The writing was on the wall, and Molly's fear began setting in. This was going to happen, no matter what she said. *What is this place going to be like? Will it be dangerous? Will it be exposed to the Covenant?*

Asha and Yong immediately sensed her palpable shift from fight to flight. "Listen, Molly. Where we're going is *entirely* safe," Yong said. "When it comes to avoiding the threats that are out there, like whatever's left of the Covenant, this place . . . it might be the safest place in the galaxy."

Molly had a hard time buying that. "What's safer than Earth?"

Yong smiled and looked at Asha, before turning back to Molly. "Imagine living inside an immense hollow sphere, heavily secured from any and all outside forces. Something that enemies can't attack from above. And then imagine that it's classified and completely off-limits to most of humanity, and so large it would actually take a full battalion of researchers several lifetimes to even come close to exploring it all.

"Honestly, Molly, the site I'm talking about here . . . there's so much room that we could lose the entire population of Earth in it and not even notice." Then he leaned in close with complete seriousness etched on his face. "Hundreds of times over, even."

"The fact that it exists at all is proof of just how unimaginably far ahead of us the Forerunners were from all other civilizations, even the Covenant," said Asha. "It's the largest and most profound single archaeological find—alien or otherwise—ever recorded. There's just nothing like it."

The Newparents were not prone to exaggeration, but Molly couldn't help but be filled with skepticism. It didn't sound like reality at all, but something they'd lifted from one of the stories they used to read her at bedtime. "So where exactly is this archaeological marvel?" Molly asked, expecting more hyperbole.

Yong leaned back with a slightly conspiratorial grin. "It's a place called Onyx."

CHAPTER 3

What the hell is that?!" Spartan Tom-B292 shouted as the UNSC Pelican he was riding in arced high over what had become a full-on battle zone inside Onyx. He pointed down at a massive structure looking something like a giant stainless-steel skull that had been flattened out with a hammer to the size of a small town. It sat half-buried in the top of a once-grassy hill that had been decapitated as part of an archaeological dig.

A dozen smaller figures cast in the same metallic style stood arrayed around it, blasting away at a scattered pack of archaeologists, who were cowering behind whatever cover they could find. Tom recognized them right away as Forerunner armigers, robotic soldiers programmed by a long-dead alien race to protect their artifacts from other people—which apparently included the archaeologists. The armigers carried energy rifles powered by the same high-tech source that emitted a reddish glow through their eyes.

"That's a lot of our people getting their asses kicked!" Spartan Lucy-B091 shouted in response.

Tom had to admit she was right. If they didn't get down there fast, there wouldn't be any civvies left to save. He hated leaping into an environment he didn't understand though.

"Not them! The big guy!"

"The sculpture?" Lucy asked, confused.

"If that's what it is!"

"According to the briefing—which you clearly didn't read—"

"How did *you* have the time?"

The ramp opened up on the back of the Pelican, and Lucy started edging toward it. Tom followed right behind her.

"That's part of what the researchers call Project: GOLIATH," Lucy said. "They've been cropping up all around the galaxy lately, and a couple have even come alive and started moving around on their own!"

Tom popped on his helmet and squinted at the one below them. "This one looks pretty damn buried!"

"For now! But that's not our problem at the moment! These armigers crawled out of the ground earlier today and have been trying to shoo our researchers away. With their weapons."

Tom hefted his assault rifle. "We have a solution for that."

Lucy smiled at him and then fitted her helmet on and checked the action on her assault rifle too. "We *are* the solution for that."

She leaped out the back of the Pelican and let the jump jets embedded in the back of her Mjolnir armor slow her fall. Tom went right after her.

They hit the ground running and started taking down armigers straightaway. They had fought such machines here before, more times than Tom cared to count. That went all the way back to the first time they'd been stationed inside Onyx with Spartan Kurt-051, training the Spartan-III Gamma Company.

Back then, the machines had outnumbered the Spartans by exponential numbers. This time around, although there were six armigers for every Spartan, the odds didn't bother Tom a bit. This they could handle.

The Forerunner soldiers seemed to have come to some kind of tacit détente with the UNSC forces inside Onyx over the past few months, almost as if they'd simply agreed to ignore the people who'd taken up residence there. Something about getting too near the Project: GOLIATH site, though, had apparently set them off. Fortunately, it hadn't triggered the appearance of a full-fledged army of them.

"Watch your nine!" Lucy shouted.

Tom spun to his left and gunned down a pair of armigers who'd been charging straight at him. She spun to her right and did the same.

Although Tom didn't talk about it much, he actually enjoyed this sort of dance. He and Lucy had performed this choreography so often over their years working together—since they'd been kids—that little felt more natural to him. The rhythm of their feet, the bullets, and even their reloads all seemed in perfect sync.

Behind his helmet's polarized face shield, he smiled.

In a handful of moments, it was over. The armigers had all been blasted to pieces, and Tom and Lucy had sustained little more than a few scorch marks on their armor.

Lucy scanned the horizon for more trouble on the way while Tom motioned for the grateful archaeologists to head for the Pelican, which had landed a short walk nearby. As they filed up the ramp and into the safety of the aircraft, Tom reported in.

"Chief," he said into his comm. "All clear. Looks like we got here in time. The diggers had no major casualties."

"Glad to hear it. Good work," Director Franklin Mendez said on the other end of the comm. "And that's *Director* Mendez these days."

"Right," Lucy chimed in. "Doesn't look like the armigers damaged it at all. If anything, it seems like they were trying to protect it."

"Any sign of life in that damn thing?" Mendez asked.

"Negative, Chief," said Tom.

The old man breathed something between a weary groan and a sigh of relief. "For all our sakes, let's hope it stays that way."

CHAPTER 4

Not long after Yong dropped the name Onyx and provided a handful of new details, Molly's Newparents received an important call over the comm from their director, probably connected to the relocation. Molly retreated to her room for the rest of the afternoon, trying to process what they had told her. Beyond the name, she didn't have any details, but . . . if she was honest, she wasn't sure she wanted to.

Molly was not exactly thrilled about moving, especially off-world, and she wasn't planning on being shy about telling Asha and Yong. Most of her life had been about adjusting to a move. She was tired of it.

But *where* they wanted to take her? That was what caused Molly the most concern. The idea of living at some UNSC research site inside an enormous Forerunner sphere the size of an entire solar system? *That* part was worth her revulsion alone.

Even if Earth wasn't the safest place in the galaxy, at least it wasn't a hundred-millennia-old Forerunner installation, where you walked on the interior surface like the inside of some strange alien shell and thousands of scientists were trying to figure out what it actually did—in case it went completely bad and killed them all.

At first Molly objected that there wouldn't be any place for her there, but Asha and Yong assured her that wouldn't be the case. In fact, there'd be more residents in their research site at Onyx than in all of Aranuka. ONI had been there for years and had already constructed a large-scale research colony that had all of the workings of a major metropolis—something Asha referred to as "state-of-the-art in civil engineering and urban infrastructure." This new city would apparently house thousands of researchers and their immediate families, all in brand-new homes as fine as those in any urban colonial site.

It had shops, restaurants, gyms, and all the other trappings of civilian life—even if the city was set on an artificial world holding a star at its center, something Molly had a hard time conceiving. From what Asha and Yong had told her, the city inside Onyx had only been around for five years and existed alongside remarkable Forerunner living facilities and structures—something that had never before been managed in human history.

They even had a school with others Molly's age, with larger classes than those she'd grown used to on Aranuka. This came as a shock, albeit a pleasant one . . . but that's when her Newparents dropped a bombshell. This one was the most difficult to fathom, and it made Molly livid.

Humanity wasn't living there alone.

Onyx had aliens too. Sangheili. Unggoy. Both ex-Covenant species.

This wasn't a complete surprise, but it didn't feel right to Molly and probably never would. The logic was pretty straightforward: who better to help ONI research the Forerunners than former members of the Covenant? After all, the Covenant had evidently studied and worshipped the Forerunners as gods for generations. That had been the whole premise for their war against humanity, or so the story went. Ultimately, the Covenant had been entirely wrong about the Forerunners, which had led to a massive civil war in their ranks. According to the newsfeeds, they called it the Great Schism, a shocking split that helped the UNSC win the war against the Covenant.

In any case, the facts were pretty straightforward: these species had spent more time researching and reverse engineering Forerunner artifacts than any human ever had. To ONI, working alongside them was a necessary evil.

But the thought of living next door to such creatures—much less actually going to school with them—made Molly sick to her stomach. Their kind had been responsible for nearly thirty years of brutal warfare, some of which she had experienced firsthand.

Some of which she still had nightmares about.

This would be different, Asha and Yong had tried to assure her. There were supposedly "good" Sangheili who had worked under the leadership of the Arbiter, the alien warrior who'd formed an alliance with humanity to put an end to the Covenant after discovering the truth about the Forerunners. A number of other alien species had evidently flocked to his banner, and—along with the legendary Spartan, the Master Chief—helped overthrow the Prophets, the group of aliens who had led the Covenant.

This band of Sangheili eventually became known as the Swords of Sanghelios, the name of their homeworld. These Sangheili warriors now worked alongside humanity for the purposes of peace . . . or so the Newparents had explained.

To Molly, though, all that background was irrelevant. The fact that she'd have to live alongside aliens was enough for her to outright refuse to go. She would most definitely put up a fight.

And after what had happened on Paris IV, who could blame her?

Molly and her Newparents ate dinner in silence that night, in part because she was still trying to absorb everything Asha and Yong had told her. Also, in part, because there was no way in hell she was going to live next door to the monsters who had murdered her family. Once the meal was over, though, they adjourned to the living room again.

"Okay." Molly readied her opening salvo. "You said it was safe. How do you figure that? Especially with ex-Covenant there?" She tried to hold back any frustration in her voice, although she was pretty sure she'd failed. "If it's the most important Forerunner asset in the entire galaxy—and ONI's classified it and is doing everything they can to understand it—then someone else is sure to want it, right?"

Yong spoke first, with an even tone. It was the linguist in him. He would try to socially engineer the situation because he thought if he could find the right words, he could make any problem go away. "Molly. You don't have to stay there any longer than you want. After you turn eighteen, you're legally an adult and can make your own choices about where you live. Until then, we're your legal guardians . . . so you have to come along with us."

"Legal guardians?" Molly shot back. "What about what's *right* for me? What about what's *fair*?"

"Would it be fair for Yong and me to give up the greatest professional opportunity of our lives?" Asha said. "Would it be right to walk away from the chance to help do humanity some serious good? Potentially even save millions of lives?"

"Can't I have a normal life without constant changes for once?" Molly didn't care if she was raising her voice. "What about something normal for *me*? It seems like every single time I get settled somewhere, something falls apart. I'm so tired of it. I just want things to stay the same! I want them to be normal!"

"Look, Molly, we know our careers have taken a toll on you," Yong said, still maintaining his composure. "Change isn't easy, and you've seen more than your share of it, especially *painful* change. If this wasn't important, it wouldn't even be on the table. One of the main reasons this is the best possible opportunity for *all* of us is that, unlike our current positions here, which are very temporary, this would *not* be. This would be a permanent and lifelong investment for me and Asha—and for you it would be a life without having to worry about any more changes. This is what you need, Molly. And we obviously can't leave you behind. We need to do this—and you need to come with us."

"What if I found a family to take me out here? I'm sixteen, I'm not a kid anymore. I could come visit you. Or you could come see me."

"Molly, it doesn't work like that, okay? You can't just zip in and out of Onyx like it's a run-of-the-mill spaceport. This place is serious. The research facility is top secret and under the complete control of the UNSC. It's the only way they could guarantee the researchers' safety. People are *not* free to come and go as they please."

"So what you're saying is that, if I go with you, I'm effectively just stuck there?" Molly shrank into the couch she was sitting on, falling more into despair about the whole idea with each passing moment. There seemed to be no way out. Once again, her life was being completely uprooted by circumstances beyond her control—and it seemed as if no one really cared about that. Worse, she'd be forced to live around creatures whose kind had less than ten years ago been bombarding the surface of Paris IV.

"You make it sound like you'd be a prisoner," Yong said. "But it wouldn't be like that."

Molly folded her arms across her chest and suppressed a sob. "How so?"

Yong shrugged. "Onyx is a wonderful place, Molly. There's

nothing like it in the galaxy. It's filled with things no one on Earth has ever seen before: machines, creatures, technology, and many worlds' worth of uncharted, unexplored territory. You would be one of only a handful of humans in all of history to have ever set foot on this world. That's a big deal. Sure, you can't just leave at the drop of a hat, but that seems like a small price to pay for an experience like this. It's the single greatest discovery of our species. Period."

"You're not getting it. I don't want to be a linguist or an archae-ologist," Molly finally snapped. "I don't want to be what you two are. I have other plans for my life."

"We know," Asha said solemnly. "You've been quite clear about that for a long time now."

"Just leave me here then," Molly said through gritted teeth. "Can't you just release me into the foster-care system or something? I'm sixteen now. I could survive fine. Then I'd be in line to become a soldier when I turn eighteen. That's what I want anyway."

"Molly, that's *enough*. It's out of the question, so I don't want to hear that kind of talk," Yong said with an edge she'd rarely heard in his voice. "We're not going to abandon you. Ever. And I really wish you'd drop this fantasy about becoming a soldier."

"Why's that?" Molly spread her hands wide. This wasn't the first time they'd had this argument, and it wouldn't be the last. "Didn't soldiers save us all from the Covenant? In fact, the only reason we're still here—and *you* can do the kind of work you do—is because soldiers fought those aliens off this planet. The only reason I'm *alive* is because a soldier came and found me."

Asha and Yong exchanged sad and frustrated glances for a long moment. Then Asha finally sighed and said, "Humanity needs all sorts of people to protect it. Not just soldiers. *Our* work on Onyx, for instance, could unlock secrets to help protect everybody.

Maybe even put an end to war completely. Think for a minute about the kind of power required to *build* something like Onyx. This is an installation the size of a *solar system*. There are secrets there that could keep humanity safe for thousands of years."

"Or consider the alternative," Yong said. "If people like us don't try to figure these things out, imagine if some hostile group with a vendetta managed to unlock the secrets of a facility like Onyx first. Where would that put us then?"

"The fact is that science is a vital part of humanity's efforts to defend itself," Asha continued, "even if we still have soldiers. That's why the Onyx research project is being sponsored and overseen by the UNSC. The Office of Naval Intelligence knows this and they intend on using Onyx and its secrets to prevent anything like the Covenant War from ever happening again."

"That's what I don't get," Molly said. "ONI and the UNSC exist to fight wars. If they find a weapon on Onyx, they'd use it if they needed to, and you know that. And so you're just going to dig these things up for them?" It was a fair question given ONI's reputation as a shadowy government organization with mercenary activities, but Molly knew she was crossing a line, effectively accusing her peaceable Newparents of working for the people most inclined to leverage any discoveries they made in hostile, war-oriented ways.

"ONI may be pulling the strings on our projects," Yong said, "but we don't work for them directly, nor for the UNSC either. We're going to Onyx on a peaceful mission, for purely academic purposes. It has to be this way, especially given the different kinds of people we'll be working alongside."

"The UEG-contracted researchers actually occupy a different territory inside Onyx, entirely separate from the ONI facilities," Asha said. "We'll obviously be working *with* ONI, but not *for* them. Like we mentioned earlier, we'll be working alongside the Sangheili and other species, and the UNSC is obviously reluctant to give them any of kind of direct access to its own bases."

"That right there sounds like a perfect reason for me to *not* go then," she said, trying desperately to make her Newparents see the light. "To you guys, this is just another job. To me, it's a nightmare. Think about it for a second. This isn't just another project. You're asking me to live next door to the same monsters that killed my family!"

Molly shocked even herself with how raw it felt to say that. Most days, she didn't think about the destruction of Paris IV at all. She'd buried it deep in her heart, in a place that could only be reached by her. Asha and Yong's proposition had reopened wounds she'd wanted to keep locked forever.

To live with the same kinds of aliens who'd taken away her mother, father, and sister—that was too far. That should have been enough for them to say no to ONI, or to just let Molly do her own thing. They were being selfish after they had made the commitment of raising and taking care of her. Given all of the things that had happened to her, a move like this should have been completely out of bounds.

After a moment with her head down, Molly looked up and could see that Asha and Yong wanted to come over and hug her, but they kept their seats.

"These are not the same beings who did that horrible thing," Yong said in an even, yet sympathetic, tone. "Do you think ONI would ever let anyone like that into Onyx? Trust me, Molly, the people we're working with here are safe and like-minded, no matter their species. Every single one of the aliens who will be there comes highly recommended by the Arbiter and his Swords of Sanghelios first. ONI's got dozens of security filters to weed out any and all threats. They've likely been scrutinizing even our family for months as well."

"He's right, Molly," Asha said. "No one gets in without ONI's sanctioning. Onyx is effectively impenetrable from the outside. And even if you're worried that some ex-Covenant terrorists might somehow find a way in, the UNSC has installed the toughest security protocol ever created. We've been told that they may even have an actual fireteam of Spartans there."

Spartans?

Molly let that sink in for a moment.

That news was a potential game changer for her. If Spartans were there, that meant a level of safety she could rely on. Even among aliens.

Everyone knew about the UNSC's Spartans, the unstoppable super-soldiers who had fought against the Covenant for nearly thirty years. Spartans were one of the only things that could stop the aliens during the war. They were the stuff of legend, and Molly's Newparents knew—despite their reservations about soldiers—that if the Spartans had anything to do with Onyx, it would directly affect how she felt about the move.

Molly took a deep breath and worked hard to get ahold of herself in the wake of her cathartic venting and this new information. After a long moment, she exhaled, forcing out as much of her fear as she could.

Spartans did make this different, as much as she didn't want to admit it.

"All of this is beside the point," Asha said with welling eyes. "We love you, Molly, and we're going to take care of you and protect you until you're old enough to live on your own. So this discussion effectively is over. You're going to come with us because we couldn't live without you. Everything is going to be fine. I promise you that."

Molly stared out the window at the encroaching dusk and frowned, taking in that promise as the sun sank to the horizon. As much as they said they wanted to hear her out, she knew that ultimately she had no say regarding what happened to her life, and that made her angry and frustrated. This had been her story since she was seven, and it wasn't going to change anytime soon.

"Do we really have to live side by side with aliens?" Molly asked wearily.

Asha slid off her chair and sat down on the couch beside Molly. A moment later, Yong followed suit and slipped in on the other side. Together, they leaned in and gave Molly a gentle hug. She fought the urge to embrace them in return, even though she wanted to . . . but she couldn't, not yet. It still hurt too much.

"Yes, in a way. Perhaps not as neighbors, but there will be Sangheili there," Asha said soothingly. "They're allies now, Molly. And they're all experts and scientists too, not soldiers. They won't be a threat. I promise you."

"I can't just forget Paris IV."

Yong gave Molly a grim nod. "Of course not. But even if the Sangheili were on the wrong side then, Molly, they're on our side now. These Elites don't *want* war, just like us. That's why this research facility exists."

Yong had used the term the UNSC had dubbed the Sangheili after their first encounter, the same one most often heard in newsfeeds: *Elites*. Outside a few exceptions, the Elites were the most effective warriors the Covenant had to offer, so it had been a fitting nickname at the time—especially since the two species had been introduced by way of weapons rather than words.

Molly leaned into Yong. "I don't know if that makes me feel a whole lot better."

Asha squeezed her shoulders. "You've read the reports. Without the Arbiter and the Elites who pledged to help him, we'd have lost the war."

"But what about the rumors of there being another Covenant—like the group that attacked New Phoenix last year? Or *any* of the other hostile alien groups out there?" Molly asked. "The newsfeeds keep saying how dangerous they are. What if *they* found a way in?"

Yong waggled his head slightly from side to side, half conceding the point. "You're right. There are elements that still exist, like the Servants of the Abiding Truth, who continue to see the Forerunners as gods—and they're certainly a problem. That's probably why they've stationed Spartans on Onyx. ONI's not going to take any chances at all."

"What Yong said earlier isn't an exaggeration, Molly," Asha said. "Onyx is the safest place in the galaxy. There's no question. You're more at risk here in Aranuka than you would be on Onyx, and that's a fact."

Molly sighed. If she was serious about not going with them, the only real option she had was to run away, but she couldn't see how that would work. Maybe she could disappear in a normal metropolis, but here on the empty and secluded Aranuka platform—surrounded by nothing but thousands of kilometers of open ocean on every side—there wasn't any place for her to go.

On top of that, she knew how much leaving her Newparents would hurt them. Despite the pain she felt today, there was no way she could bring herself to inflict that on them. No matter where they wanted to take her, she couldn't just abandon them like that. Especially not after all they'd done for her—all the love they'd shown her.

That was it. She'd have to move with them to Onyx, and she'd have to be a good soldier about it.

Molly would follow orders and go along with their plan—for now, at least.

But they couldn't make her like it.

And they couldn't make her stay past her eighteenth birthday. So she would count the days and do the time. But the moment she got her proper, legal chance to get free and clear of Onyx? On that day, Molly would leave without a second thought. And nothing they could say or do would keep her there a moment longer.

CHAPTER 5

ural 'Mdama had long ago promised himself that he would avoid backwater planets like Hesduros if he could. The Sangheili warrior had spent enough time in such places during his short years, trying to avoid being captured by the Arbiter and his traitorous kind. And all along, Dural had wanted nothing more than to take the fight straight to them on his homeworld, Sanghelios. He also had no desire to become like many of his uncles: either to flee his keep in their ancestral homeland in Mdama or to be slaughtered like a herd of helpless *colo* in their pens.

The young Sangheili had come of age in the dying days of the war with the humans, and he had survived those days only to watch his proud people become fractured, broken, and ultimately beaten. Dural vowed that he would not end up like them. Instead, he would do everything in his power to lead them back from the brink of irrelevance and to reclaim their glory.

Yet Dural found himself on *Song of Wrath*—a heavily armed barque bearing down through the dense atmosphere of Hesduros—about to meet with a lowly kaidon who was only valuable to him because of a simple accident of fate.

But perhaps fate knew nothing of accidents.

From his seat at Dural's left hand, Shipmaster Buran 'Utaral—a battle-tested commander—signaled for his attention. Buran might have gone soft around the middle from spending too much time on a ship rather than on the field of battle, but he had lost none of the edge in his steely eyes.

"We are on our final approach to the province Panom," the warrior announced. He added discreetly, "Are you sure this is our best course of action?"

Before Dural could answer, Ruk 'Nuusra snarled at Buran from the seat on the right. "How dare you question the Pale Blade's judgment in front of the crew? We have been over this a dozen times. This may be a bold and daring choice, but if Dural 'Mdama declares this to be our path, then may the gods bless it."

Dural quieted Ruk with a sharp gesture. As the one they called the Pale Blade, he appreciated Ruk's support, but he was more than capable of dealing with Buran himself. "Do you doubt the judgment of Field Master Avu Med 'Telcam?" Dural asked the shipmaster.

"Never." Buran put a fist to his chest in a sign of respect for their former leader's memory. "But he is not the one who put us on this path."

"No, that was my decision," Dural said. "But he named me his successor as the leader of the Servants of the Abiding Truth. If you doubt my judgment, then you doubt his."

That 'Telcam had chosen one as young as Dural 'Mdama over such stalwarts as Buran rankled the shipmaster, but not enough for him to ever challenge the Pale Blade over the leadership of the Abiding Truth. At least not yet.

The field master's decision had surprised Dural as well. The Sangheili youth had loyally served him and the Abiding Truth since the day 'Telcam had taken him in more than five years ago. The field master had been one of the last to see Dural's mother alive, as a passenger on his own starship during their failed siege against the Arbiter Thel 'Vadam—the battle that had launched what the Sangheili had come to call the Blooding Years. She had died while in 'Telcam's charge, and out of a sense of responsibility, the field master had taken Dural on as his apprentice.

'Mdama knew who was really to blame for his mother's death however: the Arbiter himself, who had betrayed all of Sanghelios when he led so many of its people to join forces with the humans against the false Prophets. If he had not sundered the Sangheili so, they might still have been victorious over the humans in the end. Instead, Dural's once-proud people now found themselves so terribly reduced to weakness. For such sins—along with the death of his mother—Dural had long ago vowed that Thel 'Vadam would pay.

This was the next step upon that quest.

Buran looked away, unable to meet Dural's eyes. "As the Pale Blade commands," he said sullenly, using the name the young leader had earned on the field of battle.

Some might have thought the designation an insult, a derogatory reference to Dural's pale skin, something that set him apart from many of his fellow brethren of Ontom, Sorovut, or Kaloabyn—the lineages that formed the bulk of the Servants. Dural, however, knew that it marked him as one not from the compromised lowlands and coastal city-states, but from the province of Mdama, proud and indomitable since its birth. Dural 'Mdama was not simply different from the others among the Servants though. He was better.

Because of that, he had embraced the name, transforming it from insult into honorific, weaving a legend of terror into the hearts of all those who heard of his deeds. Many of the warriors of the Abiding Truth wore armor cobbled together from their time serving with the Covenant, improved with whatever pieces they could pick up along the way. They looked like militia soldiers, similar to those from the early days of Sanghelios. Most of them were too preoccupied with the function of their armor to see the practical advantage of instilling fear in the hearts of one's enemies as well.

For himself—and at the urging of the field master—Dural had painted the pieces of his own armor all in a pale blue, the color of an energy blade. His helmet and harness were of an anchorite-warrior sect, a fierce and ancient variety he had recovered from the vaults of the Ontom temple, where the Servants of the Abiding Truth were stationed. In many ways, Dural had fully become the Pale Blade. With his former history largely forgotten, others now spoke only of his skill on the battlefield. They easily set Dural apart from the rest—exactly as he had desired.

The Sangheili rode in silence the remainder of the way down to the keep at the center of Panom, a small and remote township slung out across the edge of a densely forested region of Vakkoro, a supercontinent in northern Hesduros. The detachment of warriors landed the barque just outside it and disembarked in formation. After their vanguard fanned out in advance of those in command, the Pale Blade took the lead, with Buran and Ruk at his sides.

A grizzled Sangheili, who somehow made Buran look like the peak of fitness, hobbled through the front gate of the keep to greet their command. He led a congregation of browbeaten, poorly armed warriors from within the town. This was the kaidon Panom—the Sangheili leader of the city-state of the same name—and as he limped toward the Servants, Dural wondered why none of his own people had stepped forward to wrest control of the keep from him, upholding the ancient traditions. It was the noble thing to do to this old creature. He must have done much for them in the past to command such respect even now.

Or, perhaps, they were merely all weaklings.

"Greetings, Dural 'Mdama." The kaidon tilted his head to the side to get a closer look at the young commander. "I would like to say I am pleased to see you here, but I think I have had enough of warriors from the line of 'Mdama for a lifetime."

Dural favored him with an understanding nod as he surveyed the walls of the keep. Several sections had been obliterated with what appeared to have been plasma fire, recently enough that the people of Panom had not even had time to properly clear the rubble. "The Arbiter's arm has fallen heavily upon you."

"True, but we would never have attracted the traitor's attention if I had not permitted Jul 'Mdama and his allies within my walls. He may call himself the Hand of the Didact, but he has only drawn the hand of destruction to our people. His campaign against the Swords of Sanghelios brought the Arbiter's wrath down on us."

"I understand this is why my uncle decided to abandon his many redoubts on this world—or what's left of them since the assault—and take the battle to the Arbiter's doorstep. He prepares for his assault on the contested states of Sanghelios even as we speak."

Dural had called Jul his uncle, for that is how he had long known him—just as all the fledglings on Sanghelios called their older male relatives *uncle*. They might each know their mothers, but to prevent nepotism, they were all denied the knowledge of their fathers. Mostly.

Panom scoffed. "Much good that will do my people, we few who survive." The warriors around him all nodded in grave agreement.

"We have all lost much to the Swords," Dural said. "And even more to their allies."

Panom grunted. "I heard about the death of Avu Med 'Telcam. To be cut down like that by one of the demons . . ."

"He is sorely missed." Dural appreciated the sentiment, but he had not come here to commiserate with Panom over losses.

Panom sensed Dural's eagerness. "You have other concerns, I

know." Panom craned his neck to see Dural's warriors continuing to pour out of the starship. "I'm afraid, though, that you've come here ready to start a war with a missing foe."

"We are actually not here to fight on this world. And we do not need your help. We simply need access to the ancient portal that lies within your land."

Panom scowled. "The same portal that brought Jul 'Mdama to our home? What good would that do you? Are you fleeing from the Arbiter's forces yourself?"

Ruk huffed at that, clacking his mandibles together.

"Such efforts will do you no good," Panom said, irritated. "Do you think we would not have used the portal ourselves if we could have escaped the Swords' assault on our keep in that way? It has not been active since the day Jul 'Mdama arrived years ago. On our side, at least, it remains sealed."

Dural shook his head. "To you, certainly. But not to me."

Panom peered at the young warrior, now suspicious. "What fool's errand are you on, fledgling?"

Dural didn't care for the condescending tone. He stretched up to his full height and did not seek to hide the anger building in his voice. "I aim to bring the fight to the Arbiter's clan and his human allies so that we can avenge the death of our former leader, the esteemed Field Master Avu Med 'Telcam."

Panom shook his head at Dural in amazement. "I admire your ambition, but you have already run headlong into the first wall of your plan. The portal you seek will not open for you, for me, or for anyone else on this world. Your uncle had to coerce a Huragok—one of the very servant-tools of the gods—into opening it for him when he was on the other side. And, as you can see, fledgling, I don't have any of those rare creatures in my employ."

Panom's warriors growled in assent.

Dural motioned toward *Song of Wrath*'s open bay door, and a squad escorted a blue-and-purple creature down the boarding ramp. It was roughly the size and shape of an *okadoth*—a Sanghelios-native soft-bodied aquatic animal, similar to the humans' jellyfish—hovering a meter off the ground. Four prehensile tentacles dangled from its sides, languorously squirming about. Its head snaked out from the front of it on a sinuous, long neck, and its eyes stared out from its glowing blue face, devouring every bit of its new environment.

"How fortunate then, Kaidon Panom, that I do."

CHAPTER 6

"I'd like to personally welcome you all to Onyx," said the holographic projection at the end of the passenger cabin on board the UNSC *Milwaukee*. "I'm Director Hugo Barton." He was communicating through some kind of real-time comm system, the attendant had advised earlier. Apparently, he was speaking from his office on Onyx through a faster-than-light dimension called wavespace.

Admittedly, Molly was a little disappointed to see him appear there. Her family was on a UNSC starship heading for their new home inside this mysterious and ancient Forerunner world, and she'd been hoping to be welcomed by someone or something a bit more . . . exciting.

It was not as if she were expecting to have someone such as the Master Chief greeting them, but her heart sank a little when a man who looked like an antiquated scientist or a midlevel bureaucrat popped up, rather than a war hero clad in a set of battle-scarred Mjolnir armor. For Molly, one of the only silver linings in moving to Onyx was the possibility of seeing a Spartan in person. She'd been nursing the hope that she'd run into at least *one* of them, maybe even on the way there.

Nevertheless, Molly knew the director was probably more important than any particular Spartan in the grand scheme of ONI's operations, especially as it related to Onyx and its research facilities. Molly had never heard of the man, but that might have been a reflection of just how good he was at his job. The word about ONI was that one never heard an employee's name mentioned publicly unless the person was in public relations or was dismissed, something that rarely happened.

According to other more sensational rumors, *termination*—in the most lethal sense of the word—was how ONI usually let their employees go. Once you were ONI, you were ONI for life, whether you liked it or not.

Director Barton was balding and pale, worn but determined. He wore a dark suit and tie but seemed uncomfortable in both. This was clearly not his favorite part of the job.

The man chose his words carefully as he spoke to the assembled passengers on the *Milwaukee*, a large *Poseidon*-class carrier that had been repurposed for shuttling facility personnel, civilians, and goods back and forth between Onyx and the rest of the galaxy. Yong, Asha, and Molly were on board, along with a few hundred other people. Altogether, the passengers barely filled out half the transport's main cabin, which had been fitted with comfortable, roomy stadium-style seating that let them all have an unobstructed view of the large display at the front of the cabin.

When Molly had been rescued from Paris IV and transported to Earth, all she remembered was being strapped into a soldier's jump seat in a much smaller craft, and it had taken what felt like forever to get there. Part of that had likely been because she hadn't been allowed to go straight from Paris IV to Earth due to travel protocols. Taking the direct route would have left a trail in the ship's nav system and made it far too easy for the Covenant to follow them back home and launch an attack directly against Earth, and no one wanted that. Not until a few years later did the aliens finally track down humanity's homeworld.

The *Milwaukee* had been fitted with the latest slipspace drive technology, something reverse engineered from some machines recovered on Onyx, Yong had explained to Molly earlier. This would cut down on the ship's travel time substantially, which meant that the transport didn't need large stasis bays for cryo-storage or even private berths for the passengers. Instead, *Milwaukee* had been fitted with enough comfortable seats for the several-hours-long trip to their new home. This was a sharp departure from decades of extremely long space travel that had demanded harsher measures.

Yong and Asha, sitting on either side of Molly, each reached out to give her hands a gentle squeeze. She was not sure how, but they knew immediately what she was thinking. Evidently, she didn't mask her disappointment well.

"I got confirmation from our contact back in Aranuka. There's actually a full detachment of Spartans stationed on Onyx," Asha said with a knowing smile. "You'll probably see them around all the time. They gave all authorized employees an extensive briefing on what to expect when we got there. This one is for everyone else."

Molly sat back and took a deep breath to mask her excitement. She was going to see Spartans after all!

She tried to focus her attention on what Director Barton said as a number of holographic spheres representing a solar system rose in front of his own projection. Even though he was speaking to many high-level academics, Molly could tell that Barton was keeping his explanation fairly simple so that the rest of the people aboard the ship would be able to understand it.

"You've reached the Zeta Doradus system, which puts you about thirty-eight light-years from Earth. The fourth planet here was known as Onyx for decades, and the UNSC eventually used it as a large-scale research site and a training ground for Spartans."

Training? Molly wondered.

Obviously she knew the Spartans didn't just spring into existence, and she had read much of the published information about their augmentations and armor, but she hadn't given a lot of thought to how they had been educated or field-tested. It made sense that they would be trained for years in a classified location, forged into an unstoppable breed of soldiers before being deployed into the wild. A lot about their origins was kept shrouded in mystery, likely part of ONI's design, both to keep their cards close to their chest and to create an aura of formidability around the legendary heroes.

"As we investigated further, it turned out that Onyx wasn't a normal planet at all," Barton continued. "Many years ago, when it was first discovered, Onyx was simply a remote but habitable world and was even considered a good candidate for human colonization. When a number of Forerunner structures were discovered on the surface, however, it was quarantined, and it underwent extensive research—that has only recently been declassified for you and your research teams."

Molly knew this wasn't the full story. Even though everyone aboard the ship had been aggressively vetted with a dozen background checks and granted top-secret clearance to this realm of UNSC jurisdiction, she was completely confident that ONI still tailored everything it revealed to anyone, even its own employees.

In fact, she would have been disappointed to learn otherwise.

"Toward the end of the war," Barton continued, "the planet ended up tearing itself apart for reasons we have yet to fully understand. As it disintegrated, however, Onyx revealed that its physical mass had been composed almost entirely of Sentinels—the automated Forerunner drones that many of you have already interfaced with in your research."

In front of Barton's own projection hovered a holographic representation of a strange alien-looking machine with robotic sensors and grapplers, including a glowing series of lights on its central mass. Three large, booming arms were connected to a larger chassis, with what appeared to be a firing mechanism fixed to its undercarriage. Molly wondered if that was intended to be its weapon.

"All that remained of Onyx after this cataclysmic event was a twenty-three–centimeter object that had housed a secret slipspace enclosure for over a hundred thousand years. This enclosure was like an invisible pocket in realspace, where things could exist completely outside reality . . . literally. Within the enclosure was a massive Dyson sphere with a diameter roughly the size of Earth's orbit around Sol. All of this had been spatially compressed in slipspace and then buried at the center of the world of Onyx since the time of the Forerunners.

"The sphere is called a shield world, as some of you already know. It was built by the Forerunners as a refuge: an immense shell-like construct, the interior surface of which resembles the surface of natural worlds—but this one spans two full astronomical units from one side to the other. It has some fascinating elements within it—at least, now that the sphere has transitioned into realspace."

A scruffy-haired boy a few rows ahead gasped at this information, but his father shushed him before he could start asking questions about it. Molly had felt the same exact impulse, but she'd been able to control it. Whatever Onyx was, her Newparents' description had not accurately painted the picture. She found it strange and slightly frustrating to begin feeling a genuine curiosity about something she had so vehemently protested, but there she was, looking forward to seeing this new place.

"We actually had UNSC personnel inside the sphere when it

transitioned to realspace. And while they were inside, due to a time-dilation effect of the slipspace container, what had only been days and weeks for them passed as full months for those of us on the outside. That all changed when the sphere left the slipspace enclosure and physically entered realspace with the rest of the galaxy. Actually, a number of other amazing things happened all at once."

The previous hologram vanished, and a new one took its place. This one showed the Sentinels that had formed Onyx dissolving away from the planet like a cloud of dust, and then it zoomed down to an impossibly small sphere that coursed with energy. It hung there in empty space for a moment, and then began to grow so fast it almost seemed as if it were exploding.

"First, of course," Barton explained, "the sphere expanded out into realspace, fully enveloping the star system it was in, Zeta Doradus. Obviously, it actually didn't change its size at all, just its spatial *location*. To give you a rough idea of what we're dealing with in terms of size, its interior surface area is the equivalent of half a billion Earths. Not all of it has been terraformed—in fact, evidence indicates its construction was never fully completed by its original architects—but a substantial percentage of the interior surface appears to be habitable."

The image changed then to show the sphere swallowing the rest of the system's planets as it spread out rapidly to take up most of the star system. Molly realized that this wasn't how it had actually happened, but just a computer simulation. What really took place would have been too far beyond human comprehension for it to be clearly conveyed through images.

"Second, during its expansion process, the sphere gathered Zeta Doradus's three inner planets through a complex kind of gravitic system. It wove them into the vast space inside itself, and they now orbit around the Dyson sphere's own internal sun. Yes, you heard that right. It has its own sun, although we're not quite sure if it's artificial or was somehow pulled from another system. The data we have is inconclusive. Either possibility is plausible for the Forerunners, as some of you know, despite our inability to understand all of the mechanics at play."

The sphere that represented Onyx now hung there in space, and a smaller star hovered next to it. Molly gasped at this. It was incredible to see an artificial structure utterly dwarf a star that had fed an entire system of planets with heat and light.

"Third, the sphere's expansion path, precisely anchored to Onyx's original orbit, put it right alongside the system's real star, Zeta Doradus, in a stable and consistent orbit. Though significantly smaller than the sphere, the sun sits just outside the exterior of the shield world. We're not exactly sure why or how this happened either, but one of the results is that Onyx is able to gather energy from the sun from a fixed siphon located on its outer surface. It's a pretty remarkable feat of engineering, even after years of seeing it in action."

A thin, red-haired woman raised her hand to interrupt but spoke before Director Barton could even acknowledge her. "Doesn't it seem miraculous that putting these two massive objects into such an orbit didn't somehow tear one or both of them apart?"

"When it comes to the Forerunners," Barton said, "miracles are a normal, everyday thing. Spend enough time on Onyx, though, and you'll quickly come to the conclusion that there's really no such thing as a miracle. Just science so advanced we can't currently comprehend it. But that's obviously where you fine people come in."

Molly glanced around the cabin. Her family was seated toward the rear, so she could only see the backs of people's heads. Of the couple hundred people assembled, most were adults. But there were plenty of children too, ranging from infants all the way up to teenagers her own age.

She'd been watching some of them throughout the trip. Picking a researcher out of a crowd wasn't all that difficult, although this group was heavy on that vocation. Still, they stood out from the ship's crew and from the military personnel for all the reasons one would expect, generally because they weren't quite as fit, having spent most of their time on academic studies. They often seemed to be ruminating about something rather than paying attention to anything directly in front of them. They were obviously preoccupied with what lay ahead of them metaphorically instead: whatever they had been called to Onyx to do. And they always wore this look of wistful, dreamy anticipation, something Molly frequently saw with Asha and Yong, especially recently.

The researchers' companions, however—the *normal* people, as Molly thought of them—weren't quite as serene about all of this. To them, and to Molly in many respects, this voyage to Onyx was clearly less of a grand adventure and more like an ominous mystery. For most people, the Forerunners were a concept they had only recently become aware of, and they hadn't given much contemplation to advanced alien races doing *good* things, especially in the wake of the Covenant War. The idea that a species had existed a hundred thousand years ago and had created machines the size of worlds was understandably frightening on a lot of levels. Despite this, all of these people had been at least dedicated enough to their loved ones to accompany them on this voyage.

But just like Molly, what choice had they?

Many of them had probably been through knockdown, drag-out arguments like the ones she'd had with her Newparents. *How could they not have?* Molly thought. That was a lot of misery and second-guessing to bundle into a single transport, but they all seemed to be managing it for the moment.

She began to wonder how well that would last once they had all settled into their new houses—homes situated next to the same aliens whose species had spent the better part of the last three decades trying to eradicate humanity from the galaxy. No one would have even thought of such a thing during the war, and for some people—apparently only those rational and logical such as Molly—the basic concept still seemed insanely dangerous. She was curious if anyone else in this room had ever seen a planet being glassed up close, as she had.

"Are there any other questions?" the real-time projection of Director Barton asked.

With that, at least a hundred hands shot up, including Molly's.

"I mean about the sphere itself," Barton said. The majority of the hands went down. "And I further mean, anything that I can answer quickly that might be of interest to the entire group." Most of the remaining hands slipped away this time.

But not Molly's. She was one of only a few who persisted, and she realized she might actually get to ask the ONI director a question. She might finally get the answers she wanted—the ones she deserved.

And then Director Barton nodded toward her.

Molly almost choked. She had so many queries clashing in her head that she could barely figure out where to begin. For a few seconds, she just sat there in silence, before Yong gently nudged her in the ribs with an elbow. She finally gave up trying to parse all of the different things she wanted to ask and just blurted the first one that came to mind.

"Why is the sphere called Onyx?" She blushed as soon as the words left her lips. It seemed like such an inane question. "I-I mean . . . wasn't that the name of the planet that was already here?"

"An excellent point. What's your name?"

"Molly. Molly Patel."

"Well, Molly . . . when the Dyson sphere expanded into real-space, the planet Onyx had already been destroyed. Remember it disintegrated as the Sentinels sheared away from the planet's original superstructure. Since the sphere occupies the space where the planet once was—and since it was at the heart of the planet to begin with—most people called the sphere Onyx by default, and since then the name has just stuck.

"Officially, the Office of Naval Intelligence named the sphere ONI Research Facility Trevelyan, after a Spartan by the name of Kurt Trevelyan. He gave his life to single-handedly prevent Covenant forces from entering the sphere and taking control of it, at the same time saving the lives of all who were with him. In fact, that number actually includes a couple of the Spartans stationed inside Onyx right now. If you run into them, maybe they'll be willing to share more."

Now *that* was a story Molly desperately wanted to hear—especially if she could get it from the Spartans who were involved.

"The Forerunners called this place Shield 006. And, yes, that implies that there are at least *five* other shield worlds out there somewhere. Most of you know, however, that evidence points to there being literally hundreds of these installations of varying shapes and sizes. Onyx is the most significant—in both scale and scope—that we've found, and I'd personally wager that this is the single greatest discovery humanity has ever made."

An older woman with silvery hair and skin like old leather raised her hand. "What does it look like? Onyx. The sphere. From the outside, I mean."

"Another excellent question, although it's hard to explain something like that in words. Instead, I think you're at the point in your journey where I can just show you."

The director reached forward and pressed an unseen button outside the holographic projector's range. The roof of the cabin depolarized, turning transparent. As one, everyone in the cabin craned back their necks to take in an unobstructed view of outer space stretching out before them.

Or at least they tried. Molly only saw utter darkness.

"I don't see anything at all," the old woman said.

"That's because you're looking directly at the outside of Onyx. If you turn to look *behind* you, you might be able to see a field of stars."

Every one of the passengers that could manage it twisted in his or her seat and looked through the aperture toward the stern of the ship. Molly saw just what the director had noted: a black sky blazing with unblinking dots of light. But when she turned back toward the space in front of them, everything was entirely dark once again.

She followed the massive shape up and noticed a faint line that stretched across the rear edge of the cabin's ceiling, at which point the stars seemed to disappear. The passengers around Molly started to murmur in amazement—including Asha and Yong— and they all began piecing it together at the same time.

"That's right," Barton said, anticipating the collective reaction. "You're close enough to the sphere now that it blocks out a large portion of your view. From this distance, the surface's material actually has a deep brown hue. Think dark chocolate, but since we're approaching Onyx from its dark side—opposite Zeta Doradus—it's practically impossible to distinguish from absolute blackness surrounding it.

"Even on the opposite side of the sphere, you can't see much of it either at this distance. This place is so large and lacks significant detail, and its dark color tends to absorb the light from *any* angle.

Generally, the only way to tell it's there with the naked eye is the fact that you actually can't see *anything else* where it is. No stars, no sun, nothing else, because it's completely blocking them out. From a far enough distance, the sphere would, of course, seem like a point or perhaps a small globe with dimensional imaging. From here, though, it looks like an immeasurable wall that takes up most of your field of view."

Another hand went up. This one was attached to a boy about Molly's age. He had dark hair cropped short and large, brown eyes, and he was sitting next to a couple who bore such a striking resemblance to him she assumed they were his parents.

The director acknowledged him with a nod.

"What does it look like from the *inside*?"

"Well, if you can wait just a few more minutes, you're going to find out." Barton flashed a welcoming smile. "I could try to prepare you for it, but there's really no good way to do that. I've attempted that a number of times with previous arrivals, but . . . I just can't seem to do it justice. How about I let Onyx speak for itself?"

A light flashed to the right of the director, and he glanced at an image on a panel in front of him. "Talk about timing. If you all would care to watch, I'll leave the cabin's hull depolarized so you can take in your first view of this world in all its glory."

Every head in the cabin lifted to gaze through the starship's transparent roof. The lights inside the ship dimmed almost to blackness, which made Molly uneasy at first. It almost seemed that suddenly nothing at all protected them from the vastness of space, other than maybe the faith that the ship's hull would hold. *How close are we to Onyx? Have we already passed into the sphere itself?* She could no longer see the stars behind them, which had to mean they were almost there.

Directly ahead of the *Milwaukee*, a faint blue glow appeared, and it grew both in size and brightness at an increasing pace as the ship approached it.

"To those who have seen similar Forerunner technology in the past, that may look like a force field growing within the Dyson sphere's shell, but it's actually the shield world's physical doors over the access point," Barton said. "The blue color you see there is a hard light barrier that shrouds the entire entrance, imperceptible until you are at this range. Once you get a bit closer, automated security systems will disengage, and you can move through it unhindered."

As confident as the director sounded of that, Molly wasn't quite as certain. It was one-hundred-thousand-year-old alien technology. *How can he be so certain?* As they drew nearer to the brightening swath of blue light, she found herself gripping Yong's hand so hard he squawked in mock pain just to make her ease up. The wall of energy towered upward like an impossibly large gate until they were so close that Molly could not see anything else. The scale was bewildering and took her breath away.

Just as it seemed that the hard light barrier might swallow the entire ship, it suddenly faded out of existence. A moment later, complete darkness once again enveloped the *Milwaukee*, as though the energy shield had never even existed.

"And so, you're in," Barton announced. "As you might imagine, a structure as large as Onyx has a rather thick skin. However, you're traveling fast enough that you should be through it in a matter of seconds. We've worked closely with Onyx's native Huragok population to ensure that everything we do here is by their existing protocol and entirely safe. Keeping Onyx secure from outside threats is the highest possible priority."

"Huragok?" Molly asked, unaware that it was out loud. Yong responded only by putting his finger over his mouth and smiling. Apparently, Molly would have to find out exactly what that was later.

Molly noticed that Barton hadn't mentioned how *many* seconds it might take, and she found herself fighting the urge to count every single one of them. It was extremely difficult to tell what the interior of the sphere's skin looked like, but buried in the thick darkness Molly thought she could see lattices and spires, vast trusses and gantries that crisscrossed like an endless web—or perhaps her eyes were only tricking her and it was completely empty. As their ship sailed through the blackness, another blue hard light barrier appeared before them, and this one grew even faster than the last.

As the *Milwaukee* approached the second field, it too disappeared, revealing a massive square of light so bright that initially it hurt Molly to look directly at it. The blinding square grew larger and larger until it occupied every centimeter outside the vessel. She had to raise her hand to protect her eyes, but a moment later, the ship was through. Everything began to slowly come into focus under the sudden, brilliant midday sun that broke through the carrier's transparent hull.

"You're now officially inside Onyx," Barton said. A smattering of applause sounded throughout the cabin. "From here, *Milwaukee* could just head directly for the spaceport, but I've asked the captain to take the opportunity to rise up a bit higher so we can show you a small fraction of the place where you're going to be living."

Molly craned her neck backward to see the massive aperture fade away behind them, as though they had risen from the unseen depths of the world. A few large structures climbed upward on all sides, surrounding the enormous hole in the ground that they had come through. From this angle, she could tell that the ship was rising out of the ground much swifter than it had initially appeared to be. The *Milwaukee* ascended, and the towers quickly fell back behind the carrier, rapidly shrinking as the ship gunned by them.

"The thing about standing on the surface of Onyx is that it immediately appears to be flat," Barton said. "Just like if you stood on Earth or any other habitable planet. While Onyx curves upward at the horizons—which is the opposite of what you would expect, of course—the distances involved are so great that you can't actually detect this from any point on the surface. Not without specialized equipment at least.

"To fully appreciate that, you'd actually have to go much higher. In fact, you would have to leave behind the atmosphere that lines the interior surface of Onyx. Even then, it would still require long-range imaging systems to capture just how large this structure is."

As Barton spoke, the sky around the ship began to fade, this time from blue to black. Molly assumed there would soon be nothing around them but utter darkness once again, with the exception of Onyx's sun, which stared down at her from the direction of the *Milwaukee*'s nose.

"There aren't any other stars inside here," Molly said, somewhat stunned by the seeming emptiness of the space inside Onyx. That this world was entirely artificial . . . the very concept was almost unbelievable.

"Of course not," Yong said. "Except for the sphere's sun, that is. All the other stars are outside this place."

Barton interrupted the crowd's sustained awe. "If you look off to the starboard side, you'll see Mackintosh looming out there, which is Zeta Doradus III, the closest of the three planets that now orbit Onyx's stellar core. It's at the point in its stellar orbit where it gets impressively close to the inner surface of the sphere and our research facilities directly below. According to our understanding of its path, this phenomenon can only happen once every few thousand years, so"—he grinned—"you're welcome."

As the *Milwaukee* rose higher above the surface, the entire vessel canted slightly back, probably both to block the brightness of the sun, which was dead ahead, and to give those in the cabin a better idea of the land spreading out below. The effect was disorienting: they were looking through the transparent ceiling of the ship at the ground they'd soon be walking on and calling home . . . but it was now absurdly far above them.

The ship continued to rise farther from the surface, cresting upward like a whale launching out of the water, and the breadth of the terrain below seemed to grow faster than any eye could follow. Soon the surface of Onyx consumed half the sky, the face of the world coming into full view. Not too long after that, with the top of the ship now facing downward, all they could see was Onyx's surface sprawling out in all directions, seemingly infinite.

Molly's mind struggled to make sense of it all. It was simply too big, too majestic, incomprehensible—it felt like something humans were never intended to process. Unable to absorb the immenseness of it all, she tried to focus her attention on smaller, more digestible things.

Through scattered clouds, Molly could see vast landmasses sprawling out far below the *Milwaukee*. Some of them featured rivers and lakes, while others included bodies of water so large she could only think of them as oceans. In other areas, there seemed to be no land or water at all, nothing but an unremitting darkness. *Maybe these are places the Forerunners hadn't quite gotten around to finishing?* There was no way to tell, not from that distance, and Molly had no clue what it *should* look like outside of the little she had already seen.

Strangely, it appeared to be nighttime on some parts of the

sphere, while others basked in full daylight. One or two areas seemed to be in transition, bathed in a golden twilight. Molly knew there had to be some rhyme or reason to it all, but she couldn't parse it. *Perhaps it's a shadow cast from Mackintosh or by some machine in the upper atmosphere that simulates quasi-normal daily cycles?* Much as she hated to admit it, some things were just beyond her, a sentiment she was confident many of the people on the flight shared with her. All of this was more than she could have ever been prepared for.

For the first time, Molly could see what had drawn her New-parents to this place—as well as anyone else on the transport, and all of those who'd come to Onyx before them. As she'd been told over and over, these researchers could literally spend their entire lives trying to explore Onyx and only scratch the surface. There was nothing else this vast or immense in all of human space.

Molly thought back to the worlds she'd lived on: Paris IV and Earth. Even though she had spent her entire life on those two planets, she knew so little about them beyond the cities and the streets she'd explored. She'd seen just fractions of these planets, even though she'd called them home. Places such as those felt insignificant next to the unimaginable scale that now spread out before her.

Onyx was the equivalent to half a billion of those worlds. That was more habitable living space than humanity had ever discovered anywhere—no, *everywhere* else combined.

Molly had never felt so small.

Asha reached over and squeezed Molly's hand just when she needed it the most. That tiny bit of human contact brought Molly's mind spiraling back down into her seat, and she gave Asha's hand a grateful embrace right back.

Then Molly smiled.

Coming to Onyx was suddenly no longer just about potentially her meeting Spartans or even grinding through her last couple of years with the Newparents. Instead, she found her heart filling with excitement for *everything* this amazing world might offer.

Onyx would be an adventure. She knew that for sure now.

CHAPTER 7

ompared to any of the homes Molly had lived in before, her new house was at least four times as large. Most of the military-style buildings in Trevelyan—the ONI settlement that had grown up around the main entrance into Onyx—looked as though they had been slapped together in a single day by immense automated machines. They were those typical pale green prefabricated structures that the UNSC manufactured en masse. Molly assumed that they were easy to build and maintain over long periods, accomplishing what they needed to, but no one except perhaps a Spartan could ever have called them home.

Molly's house, in contrast, had the architecture of a twenty-fourth-century colonial dwelling, at the dawn of the *Domus Diaspora*—when humanity began leaving the Sol system and its interplanetary colonies. The house had been built out of the same kind of material as most of the quarters in nearby Trevelyan, but instead of pale green, here the structures were mostly white with blue trim. They also sat on lush green lawns that lined freshly paved black streets.

Molly's part of the city had probably been an open field before the UNSC arrived and began building what appeared to be a typical human subdivision on a completely artificial, alien world. The area humanity occupied sat on the outskirts of a Forerunner city that had apparently once been called the Citadel. Intriguingly, some people actually lived and worked in the Citadel, using the existing structures that had been an empty ghost town when the first human explorers had arrived here years ago.

Despite the handful who braved living in the place they were researching, most of those who had come to Onyx only worked in the Forerunner sites and then came back out to the human city to live. The UNSC had gone to great lengths to make this portion of the Citadel's outskirts seem like an idyllic town in a nostalgic view of Earth's past. That approach contrasted sharply with the ancient city, but it helped remind everyone of the awe and respect they should have as they worked to unlock Forerunner secrets. The name for this unlikely merging of human settlements with impressively tranquil, physics-defying Forerunner structures was Paxopolis.

According to Asha, that meant "city of peace."

With all of the paradigm shattering Molly had experienced on arrival at Onyx—and her finally seeing the majesty of this installation firsthand—she desperately needed to take a step back and explore something normal and familiar. She decided to survey her new home.

Their family had three bedrooms on the upper floor. Asha and Yong had their own master suite, complete with an attached bathroom. Molly's room was possibly twice the size of her room in Aranuka, but she wasn't entirely certain if she liked that yet. On the first floor was a dining room, a kitchen, and a massive living room that took up the entire front side of the house. It all sat on top of a basement with plenty of storage space. To Molly's surprise, the basement was built out of reinforced permacrete that was at least a meter thick and seemed to serve as a safety shelter too.

For some reason, that thought gave Molly a tinge of nervousness. Their nearest neighbors on either side were at least ten meters away. While people lived across the street, her backyard let out onto a rolling field of grass that tumbled away into a pleasant forest in the distance. Molly wasn't quite sure she wanted to explore any of that space yet. Her neighborhood and the surrounding terrain seemed so big and daunting, part of her immediately wished that more people would come so that there would be less open space everywhere. After living in Aranuka for years, the scale of even this small community was overwhelming.

To complicate things further, Molly had no idea what local wildlife coexisted with the community. This was an alien world with alien ecosystems—probably billions of them—so fauna of various kinds was certainly guaranteed, and even threatening predators seemed likely. Before Molly boarded the tram that took her to her family's street, she overheard a conversation between two men about something large and mean, but she couldn't be sure exactly what they meant. What little she'd gleaned made her think that even Paxopolis wasn't entirely safe.

What catalyzed her uneasiness was that they hadn't yet met anyone outside of the people at the spaceport and those who'd joined them on the ride out to Paxopolis. Even then, talk had been brief and fuddled, as most people were still recovering from the trip to Onyx. Now that she was in her new home, though, Molly began to feel lonely. She wondered if this place, despite all of the promise it held, would be worse than Aranuka.

Then a chime sounded.

Someone was at the door.

Molly could hear her Newparents stop unpacking and move toward the main living space to respond, but Molly was the closest, so she just answered it.

Three people stood on the front porch.

At least one of them was a Spartan. The man didn't have armor on, but it was clear just from the size of him—he towered over everyone else—and from his confident mien. Though young, he bore in his eyes the look of an experienced hunter.

All three of them stood like soldiers though. The Spartan stood well over two meters tall, with broad shoulders and short black hair. He gave Molly an easy smile that told her she was safe.

The woman who stood next to the Spartan was slightly shorter than Molly. She looked strong and had shoulder-length dark hair and bright blue eyes. She seemed to be in her midtwenties, roughly the same age as the Spartan, and had a gritty concreteness about her. She seemed as if she could tear someone apart with her bare hands.

The man who stood in front of the other two was much older and entirely bald. He could have been their grandfather, although there was nothing soft or inviting about him. Although he wasn't wearing a uniform, he was clearly UNSC to the core. The man stood at parade rest as if he were ready to snap his heels together and salute at a moment's notice. Despite his rough veneer, though, Molly thought she saw something elusively kind about him too.

"Hello," the older man said in a gruff voice that completely matched his look. "I'm Director Franklin Mendez, and I manage the infrastructure and security of this research community and the facilities that exist in this part of Onyx. You must be Molly Patel."

Molly could only nod. *How do they know my name?*

Director Mendez gave her a warm smile. "These are two of my finest people." He gestured to the other man. "This is Spartan Tom-B292."

"You can just call me Tom," the Spartan added with a thin smile. "No need for such formalities out here."

Mendez turned to the woman. "And this is Spartan Lucy-B091."

Molly was dumbstruck and remained silent. Her first day here and she had already seen *two* Spartans. But when she looked again at Lucy-B091, she was even more shocked. Molly couldn't believe someone so small and compact could be part of what she had envisioned as Spartans, yet here she was. Lucy gave Molly a gentle nod of acknowledgment, but she was still speechless and could only blush.

"Are your parents around?" the director asked.

Molly nodded again, still silent, but didn't move.

He smiled. "Can you tell them we're here?"

"I'm so sorry," Molly finally said. "Yes, please, come in."

She stepped back from the door and turned to call for Asha and Yong, but they were already there.

"Oh, hello!" Asha said with a fragile smile, slightly mortified by the state of the house. "Sorry. We're still pulling things out of boxes."

The adults all shook hands and introduced themselves to one another. "I hope you're settling in well," Director Mendez said. "If you find you need anything here that is missing, don't hesitate to put in a requisition for it. We have large stocks of just about everything, and we can place orders for anything unusual to be brought in on the next transport."

"Thank you so much," Asha said. "We really don't want to be any trouble at all. We're just thrilled to be here."

Yong chuckled. "As she says, yeah, we're excited to join you, and we're looking forward to getting to work."

"We're pleased you two decided to join our team," Director Mendez said. "Our mission here has immeasurable value, as I'm sure you are both fully aware. The three of us"—he included the two Spartans—"barely survived the Covenant War. If this place offers any hope of stopping another conflict like that, it's obviously worth every effort we can possibly muster. You two are incredibly important to that end."

Lucy cleared her throat and shot a glance toward Molly.

"My apologies." Director Mendez fixed Molly with his steely eyes and smiled. "All *three* of you. Paxopolis isn't just a collection of the greatest Forerunner experts in the galaxy. It's a community of families too. That's actually central to what this city was designed for: not just research, but for all our citizens to build their lives alongside each other, together."

"Are you going around and checking in with every group of new arrivals?" Asha said.

Director Mendez shook his head. "No, unfortunately not. It's a big city with a lot of folks moving in right now, and we don't have the staff to manage that. We're here because of your *particular* expertise. The work you've done in the past has been revolutionary. Director Barton is eager to get you into the field and get your eyes on the asset, so we wanted to come by personally to welcome you and make sure everything was taken care of."

"Is that safe?" Molly interjected. "The field, I mean."

There was a brief pause as the three traded looks.

"That's a bit of a loaded question," Tom said with a wry smile. Then his voice became serious. "In a sense, all of Onyx is 'the field,' and most of Onyx is far from safe."

"But Paxopolis itself *is* secure," Lucy said reassuringly, "as is Trevelyan and most of the outskirts in this part of Onyx. And that's mainly because our team works hard around the clock to keep it that way."

"Technically speaking, everything within three kilometers of a paved street is fine," Mendez said. "We've actually widened the perimeter far beyond that, but it's a good rule of thumb to stick within those borders. If you bring up a map on one of the service pylons, the latest safety boundaries are updated automatically. We are constantly in the process of pushing out those borders and securing more and more of Onyx, but unless you have a UNSC escort with you at the time, you're required to stay within the specified perimeter. We also have a strict curfew. No children allowed outdoors after dark, unless accompanied by an adult."

"This includes teenagers of your age," Tom added.

"Out of curiosity, what's the point of that?" Molly asked, surprising herself with boldness. She was mildly insulted that she wouldn't be trusted to be out on her own, and partially concerned with why that might be.

Mendez nodded at her with sympathy. "Much as some of the people living here would like to pretend otherwise, Onyx isn't exactly a civilized place, even in our sector. And it won't be for some time. We're living inside an almost entirely unsettled frontier, populated with all sorts of strange creatures, many of which we've never seen or catalogued in any human database. According to the records we have here, most of what we see in this sphere was gathered from across the galaxy over a hundred thousand years ago. Put your eyes on some of the critters in this place for even a second, and you'll see very quickly the wisdom in curfews and perimeter fences."

"Not to mention the Forerunner technology and automated machines that are scattered everywhere," Tom said. "This place is untamed in many ways. If you stumble across anything you feel threatened by or can't make sense of, you probably need to report it to us immediately. Humans have been here for years, and we've accomplished quite a bit, but there's so much about this place that we still don't know. And not all of it is harmless."

"Which is why we're here," Asha said, as she put a comforting hand on Molly's shoulder. "To help further that understanding with our research."

"Exactly," Lucy said. "Our goal in providing security is to

keep you happy and healthy while you do it."

Mendez glanced at Molly for a second before leveling his gaze at Asha and Yong. "Permission to speak privately?"

Molly's Newparents exchanged a look before nodding for her to go upstairs. She wasn't thrilled by this, but she didn't want to look stubborn or childish, especially in front of the Spartans, so she quickly obeyed. This wasn't the first time this kind of thing had happened, and Molly knew the importance of keeping secrets.

Well, somewhat . . . Molly climbed the stairs but remained within earshot, now very interested in what they might discuss. She could see the group through the gaps in the stairwell's banister.

Mendez began speaking in hushed tones as soon as he thought Molly was gone. "I'd like to give you folks more time to settle in, but we may need to accelerate your onboarding. ONI is getting more reports from our local comms relay of signal tremors on colonies spread out across human-occupied space, just as your research a year ago suggested might happen."

Asha's brow furrowed in concern. "You're referring to Project: GOLIATH? You think the Forerunner machine we discovered last year has something to do with that?"

Molly had heard Asha and Yong use that word—*goliath*—before, but she had never understood what they were talking about. The two of them had spent long periods together last year researching something, but she'd mostly ignored it. All that she'd been able to glean from her Newparents' conversations about it was that this artifact was huge—possibly larger than any other they'd researched—and mysterious. And it had apparently been hidden on some remote world, deep underground.

"Some analysts are seeing a pattern with these events," Mendez continued. "And there seems to be a connection to the one we found on Onyx. Many of the planets that fit the parameters you folks established are now pinging a long-range communication signal that matches the one you proposed we'd see during your time on GOLIATH. It *could* be a coincidence . . ."

"But it probably isn't," Yong finished. "We completely understand, Director. We'll get right to work."

"As soon as we make sure Molly's settled in," Asha said.

"Of course," Mendez said with a measured smile. "We'll clearly need your full attention on your work, and that means making sure you're not worried about any issues at home."

"We're glad to hear that," said Yong.

"That's where my security team comes in." Director Mendez motioned toward Tom and Lucy. "Honestly, I'm just an old soldier who knows a thing or two about operating large-scale projects, especially classified ones in remote parts of the galaxy. I help manage security, but most of my work keeps me behind the desk. Tom and Lucy are part of our boots on the ground here. They're directly in charge of security for this sector of Onyx, and they roam wherever they're needed."

"We're peacekeepers here," said Tom. "Our team is mainly composed of personnel from the Corps. We generally patrol the perimeter, keeping the community safe from outside threats and also making sure everyone gets along. We're obviously trying out something very new with this place and its . . . population. We want to make sure that everything remains copacetic and operable at all times."

"Have you had many problems with that?" Asha asked. "Internal issues, I mean."

Tom and Lucy glanced at each other so fast Molly didn't think anyone else noticed, but Director Mendez didn't flinch. "Some," he said. "They've mostly been between humans and the Sangheili. A lot of people on both sides are still haunted by ghosts from the war."

For Molly, that was worth an interruption.

She headed downstairs casually, as though she were getting a drink. The others were so deep in conversation that no one seemed to notice at first. Molly sidled up to Asha, who gave her shoulder a squeeze and a knowing look.

"Yeah . . . it's hard to blame them," Molly said sympathetically. "You don't get over things like that easy."

"We understand that as much as anyone," said Lucy.

Molly believed her. As Spartans, both Lucy and Tom had to have fought against the Covenant for years. She didn't know their personal history, but they'd probably lost more friends than either could count. Molly wasn't naive; she'd done her research and knew what the war had cost every soldier who'd been involved. She'd seen it with her own eyes.

Toward the end, Molly had believed in the mantra "Spartans never die." She'd been younger at the time, but she'd wanted it to be true.

Most details about the Spartans hadn't been known until the very end of the conflict, but by then ONI was going out of its way to release vids and stills of them from the front lines. These messages showed Spartan after unstoppable Spartan plowing through enemy lines.

Later, when all the shooting finally stopped and people started counting up their losses, Molly just knew that part had to be a lie: Spartans do die. Even the Master Chief had gone missing for a while and was presumed dead for a few years. That he'd eventually come back didn't change the reality that many Spartans—and countless other UNSC soldiers, including Yong's sister—had not.

Still, Molly couldn't help but wonder if any of them had lost their entire family to the Covenant—not to mention their home planet—as she had. She imagined that it might actually have happened for soldiers like Tom and Lucy—and probably with remarkable frequency. People like them might risk their lives to stop a threat from killing innocents, only to return home and discover that everything they'd personally fought to protect had been destroyed.

"I want to reassure you that we've checked out everyone here," Director Mendez said. "On top of that, we're keeping everyone under a watchful eye. We don't expect any trouble, so you shouldn't either. Rest assured, you will be protected by our people."

"And to help ease any internal tensions," Lucy said, "ONI's designed cross-cultural-encounter training lessons. You can tap into those from any network terminal, either here in your home or elsewhere. Once you've completed those, you're welcome to attend cross-cultural events too, where you can meet and get to know your new neighbors—human or otherwise."

Molly sighed deeply, looking away from the guests. She still had no desire to meet any aliens or have training lessons on what to do around them. She didn't plan to be around them at all. When she saw the sheer size of this place—and even the area they'd be calling home—she genuinely hoped that she might somehow manage to avoid them altogether. To Molly, that still seemed like the right path, no matter what assurances for her safety the director or the Spartans gave.

"The war's over," Director Mendez said. "We aim to make sure it stays that way."

As he said this, Molly saw some movement behind him, back in the street he and the Spartans had entered from. She craned her neck around to see who it might be. When Molly finally spotted the stranger in the road, she stiffened in horror.

It was a Sangheili.

The revulsion Molly felt at seeing such a creature in person was so overpowering she had to physically will herself not to scream. She turned away and braced herself, refusing to run for the safety of her bedroom. The glimpse she had of the monster, though— even at this distance—was enough to make her stomach turn.

Director Mendez squinted at her for a moment, then glanced back toward the street and frowned. "You have sharp eyes there, Molly. I take it that's the first Sangheili you've seen?"

Molly wanted to respond—to somehow explain—but she couldn't. She just gave him a solemn nod, not daring to put her eyes back on the alien for an instant. Asha gave Molly a sideways hug, and Yong stepped next to her to hold her hand.

"It's all right, Molly," Asha said in a low voice. "No one's going to hurt you here."

With all her heart, Molly wanted to believe that, but that same muscle began hammering in her chest. Flashes of her past came thundering to the fore of her mind. That creature was one of the things controlling the ships that killed her homeworld.

The rush of emotions that came with those memories was almost too much for Molly to bear. It was all that she could do to fight back tears of panic.

Lucy leaned over to gaze into Molly's eyes, giving her an understanding nod. "You don't have to worry, Molly. That's Kasha 'Hilot. She's the headmaster at our school."

"Given our accelerated timeline for your work, she would like to personally introduce herself," Tom said to Molly's Newparents, "but she obviously has some concerns about how that might affect Molly. That's why she's been hanging back so far."

"I'm sure it would be all right," Yong said, eager to see such an alien up close for the first time.

Asha shot him a sharp frown. *No.*

Molly disagreed too. She didn't think that meeting a Sangheili outside her new home, or anywhere else, would be all right. *Why would I?* It was bad enough that this Kasha 'Hilot already knew where Molly lived, but now the thought that she would be running the school Molly had to attend made her stomach flip. All of the excitement for Onyx that she had built up on the way to this house suddenly vanished, as if a storm cloud had scudded over the place.

Yong looked down at Molly with determination in his eyes. "It has to happen sooner or later. Better here and now, while we're with you, than on your first day at school, right?"

His comment reminded Molly that she had agreed to steel herself to attend school here—even though she was pretty confident there would be Sangheili students with her. She wouldn't be able to ignore the aliens in this place. Still, she had thought she would have a little more time to prepare herself and possibly find a way to keep her distance.

But here Kasha 'Hilot was, and Molly had no place to run.

Director Mendez cocked his head to one side and looked at Molly's eyes while he spoke. "Part of the philosophy behind this little town of ours—really the main purpose that Paxopolis exists the way it does—is that we want to show people how it might be possible for humans and other intelligent species to coexist. We can't manage that if we all stay huddled in our own little segregated groups. So the school is a natural place for this community to learn more about each other and how we can live together.

"It's also critical for us to see each other as equal partners in this venture. That's why ONI insisted we have a Sangheili in charge of our school. We've been working with Kasha for about four years now to get it operational and working like clockwork. Despite the many challenges with how to educate a variety of different species and cultures at the same time, she's done a fine job. Remarkable, actually."

"We believe you, Director," Asha said, "but perhaps now's not the right time. For Molly's sake."

Molly knew that Asha was trying to protect her, but something inside Molly now rose to the challenge, stronger than her fear. The bottom line for Molly was that she couldn't stomach the idea that she might dishonor her parents' memories by cringing in front of a member of the race of aliens who'd killed them.

Perhaps Kasha 'Hilot hadn't destroyed Paris IV. She hadn't tried to kill Molly or her parents. But she probably hadn't tried stopping the aliens either, not while they were wiping out human worlds one by one.

Then Molly realized something.

She could make this argument for humans in the different wars they'd fought in the past too. Not every one of the same people were responsible for the acts of their government or even for the actions of their fellow citizens. Why was this argument so hard for her to make for a Sangheili?

Although Kasha 'Hilot had been part of a civilization that had caused horrific destruction for thirty years, she might never have lifted a finger to help the Covenant. Maybe her mate had been on one of the warships Molly had seen? Or her father, or a sibling? Maybe she'd been training her own children from the earliest age to kill humans, right up until the very moment the war stopped.

Or maybe none of that was true at all.

"No," Molly said, preparing herself for the inevitable.

All of the adults focused on Molly. She fought the desire to turn around and flee.

"You don't have to do this," Asha whispered. She was still trying to protect Molly, but Molly knew everyone could hear at this point. Maybe even Kasha 'Hilot. And that made her less okay with backing down. Molly would rather face a Sangheili now to prove to everyone there—especially the Spartans—that she wasn't afraid than cower back in shame.

"It's okay." Molly hoped no one else could detect the quiver in her voice. She took a deep breath. "I'll be fine."

With that, Director Mendez, Tom, and Lucy stepped aside, revealing the gigantic Sangheili now standing at the end of the sidewalk. Molly took a step forward, out onto the porch, determined to overcompensate for any fear. Her Newparents recognized that and fell in behind, one to each side. Molly could feel their presence, and it somehow gave her the strength to open her mouth.

"Hi."

"Hello." The alien's voice was much deeper than Molly had expected, especially for a female. "I am Kasha 'Hilot. You may call me Kasha."

She spoke a human language—and surprisingly well.

But that wasn't all. Molly could hear a kindness in the Sangheili's tone that surprised her.

"I'm Molly Patel. Molly."

Kasha stood at least a full head over everyone else present, even Tom. As the alien stepped forward, she crouched down on her strange, muscular legs to get a better look. Her posture and gait were unnerving, too strange to even describe, as she leaned forward and dropped to eye level with Molly.

Yet, that Kasha even felt inclined to lower herself made Molly feel more comfortable. She appreciated the gesture. It would have been easy for any adult—much less a school headmaster—to put herself in a position of authority, but Kasha had actually taken pains to avoid that. It was surprisingly selfless.

Molly stared openly at Kasha, taking in all the strange details of her form. Molly had seen stills and brief vids before with Sangheili in them, but they'd always been hidden inside armor. Kasha was a saurian biped with ashen leathery, reptilian flesh—lean and strong but still quite large. She had a flat face on the end of a long, thick neck, and her eyes were a golden color, with the slightest black pupil slits. The Sangheili had no perceptible nose, just nostrils at the center of her face, but the oddest part by far was her mouth.

It had sharp, pointed teeth that lined not only her upper jaw—which was shaped roughly like a human's—but her *four* lower jaws as well. These were longer than a human's, hinged like mandibles that could splay out. When Kasha pressed them together, she could form words in Molly's language, but when they separated, they looked terrifying and strange.

Kasha's hands each had two fingers in the middle and an opposable thumb on each side of them. Both her arms and fingers were long, but not fragile. They looked as if they could rip Molly to pieces if Kasha was so inclined.

The Sangheili reached one hand out. Molly started to flinch away but then realized that Kasha was offering to shake hands.

Despite the alien's effort at courtesy, Molly didn't reciprocate right away. To her, the notion of shaking this creature's enormous hand seemed bizarre. *Why should I?*

Molly must have hesitated for too long, unsure what to do or how to possibly get out of touching the Sangheili at all. But it was too late.

Yong gave Molly a nudge from behind, and she finally stuck an open hand out toward Kasha and accepted her greeting. Molly's hand disappeared into Kasha's odd and massive claws, and she gritted her teeth behind what she hoped was a smile.

To her surprise, Kasha's skin was warmer and much softer than Molly would have guessed. She imagined it would have felt like a serrated vise, but the headmaster shook hands with a gentle grace Molly would have thought impossible.

"I am pleased to meet you, Molly," Kasha said. "I look forward to seeing you in school very soon."

Molly gaped at her, entirely unsure how to respond.

"She's excited too," Asha chipped in for Molly. "It's just been such a long journey for us all to get here."

"I understand." Kasha's facial expression may have been intended to be a smile. "It is all right. You should have plenty of time to adjust before you report for classes."

"I will," Molly said, almost as a question, but unsure why. Then, before she could stop herself, she blurted out, "Are there a lot of Sangheili children there too?"

Kasha gave what seemed to be a kind sound, which told Molly that Kasha must have understood the impulse behind the question, maybe even better than Molly did. "Not *many*, but some. Most of the students are human, but we have several Sangheili fledglings at the school, in a wide range of ages. There are a number of them in your class, in fact."

"Are there other aliens too?"

Kasha's mandibles pulled back a bit, just barely exposing her rows of teeth. "Yes, there are . . . but we do not like to rely on the term *alien* when referring to those in our school. Although we are all different species, we believe that there are no aliens in Paxopolis."

Molly cringed at the response, concerned that she'd already done something to offend the alien—*being? creature?*—in charge of her education. She felt a slight measure of shame, but at the same time she wondered why she even cared. "I-I actually didn't mean anything by it."

"Of course not. It is not a slur to call someone an alien. But it is not especially useful in this place. Remember, to a Sangheili fledgling, *you* are the alien, correct?"

Molly shrugged. "I suppose so. But what other kinds of *children* are at the school then?"

"As I said, we have many humans and a good number of Sangheili. We also have a few of the Unggoy. None of the other races from the Covenant are here, since they are not part of the alliance between our people and yours. Only those who were committed to mutual peace between our kinds joined us here, most belonging to the camp of the Arbiter. Rest assured, Molly, there is no one here that is fond of war."

As she spoke, Kasha softly touched Molly under the chin with the tip of one of her thumbs. Despite Molly's best efforts to remain wary and guarded, she had to admit that the Sangheili's actions were strangely affectionate, and they threatened to bring a smile to her face. Unwilling to grant that yet, Molly stopped the impulse in its tracks.

"It was a pleasure to meet you, Molly," Kasha said as she stepped back from the porch and stood up to her full, towering height. "And you too, Asha Moyamba and Yong Lee. It is my hope that we are all going to be good allies on this world."

"I hope so too," Asha said, as Molly stepped backward alongside her Newparents.

Molly, however, still wasn't entirely convinced.

CHAPTER 8

Are you ready?"

"Yes, Pale Blade," Ruk said. Buran responded with a silent nod.

A contingent of the Servants of the Abiding Truth prepared to enter the Forerunner portal near Panom's keep. The Huragok—which had apparently called itself Even Keel during its time in the Covenant—had for some time been fiddling with a series of interfaces hidden on the side of the portal, and finally the creature indicated it was ready to activate it.

Dural and his Servants were fortunate to have found the Huragok on the Sangheili fortress world of Bhedalon, the water planet the Covenant had used as a seat of power, naming it Tide of Celebration. Even Keel had been alone, trawling the vast debris fields that floated on the surface, repairing what it could of the carnage that remained in the wake of the Great Schism. It took little convincing to retain Keel's services. Most of what held value on that world had long since sunk to the bottom its dark oceans.

The portal Keel had activated was a large, circular aperture set into a wall nearly five meters in height. The site had fallen into disrepair over the long ages since its construction, not un-like Panom's keep. The wall stood atop a circular dais three wide steps high. The structures, though dilapidated, were all obviously of Forerunner make, but over the centuries they seemed to have been altered, both by the vast passage of time and likely the people of Panom, who had added their own touches. One of those was a wide flagstone patio that fanned out from the now-roiling energy field framed in the wall. Dural imagined that the rustic Sangheili on this backwater planet had likely gathered here for centuries to offer up their prayers to the Forerunners, as well they should have.

"No one has used the holy gate since Jul 'Mdama employed it to escape from human custody." Panom shot a grim glance back toward his modest keep and the scores of Abiding Truth warriors gathered nearby. "Things are bound to have changed on the other side over the past five years. You cannot know who or what might be waiting there."

"Has your defeat at the hands of the Swords of Sanghelios stripped you of all courage?" Dural asked.

The kaidon flushed at the insult. "We did not bring the forces of the Arbiter down on our heads. They came here to destroy your uncle and his damned ghost of a Covenant. We should never have let him and his people use Hesduros as their base."

"The foolish suffer the consequences of their actions."

Panom spat on the ground. "Jul not only despoiled our lands as he built up his factories of war so he could pursue his own ends, he commandeered our people! Now he is gone, off to take the battle to Sanghelios in some desperate plan, and he has left us defenseless despite all his promises. Were he here right now, I would show him the consequences of his betrayal."

Dural put a hand on Panom's shoulder. "The Servants of the Abiding Truth *are* here now, and we shall not abandon you, Kaidon. As a show of gratitude for your permission to use this gate, I am leaving behind a complement of vehicles and weaponry that your warriors can employ to defend your homes should the Swords of Sanghelios ever return."

The Servants of the Abiding Truth had no need to strike such a bargain with the kaidon, other than out of respect for his faith and sympathy for his situation. Dural had heard that his uncle had become faithless and mercenary in his actions, despite his promise to resurrect the Covenant. And Dural personally knew how ruthless Jul 'Mdama could be with those who thought they had every reason to trust him.

Another factor for Dural's offer to Panom was the regrettable fact that they had only now discovered through Even Keel that the portal on the receiving end was far too small for the Servants of the Abiding Truth to move much of their heavy equipment through. While there was space enough for even the largest of Dural's warriors to pass, the ingress juncture proved too narrow to navigate even a Banshee, much less something as large as a Wraith or a dropship. If the Servants attempted to take one through, only the gods knew what kind of damage they might cause to the portal . . . or themselves.

This complicated Dural's plans for their invasion of Onyx, in that they would have to proceed there by foot, until they found a receiving portal large enough to accept some of their smaller craft. Nevertheless, it did not hamper his determination in the least. All obstacles were only a proving ground on which to test his faith and courage. He would not falter on the path like Jul 'Mdama.

If Dural was forced to leave such things behind with Panom, better to leverage them to protect the keep and the portal in case the Arbiter himself or even Dural's uncle felt the need to return to Hesduros. If what was written of this place called Onyx was even marginally true, Dural did not anticipate ever needing to come back to Hesduros. Even so, it would be foolhardy to cut themselves off from their only avenue of retreat.

Although some of his own warriors might have balked at such a transaction, it was practical and necessary given the decisions they had already made. It might also grant the Servants an exit strategy if their efforts proved unfruitful, though Dural refused to doubt that they would. He had always planned to leave the vast majority of his complement here for the time being, while only a handful of his most trusted men scouted ahead with him.

Deep within, something told Dural that, if Onyx was what had been prophesied, then it might have other means for getting the vehicles safely through the same portal on Hesduros. He would risk keeping the vehicles here while leveraging Even Keel's talents on Onyx. Panom likely knew the real motivation behind Dural's show of kindness was self-serving, but the kaidon was cunning enough to not turn such resources down, no matter the motivations behind them.

"You have our thanks," Panom said, and Dural turned away.

The Pale Blade had accomplished many feats in his relatively short career as a leader among the Servants, but he had never been through a portal such as this before, and the idea of using it slightly concerned him. Stepping through this field of light—the writings claimed—would somehow transport him to a location countless light-years away, but for Dural, the journey would seem to take only an instant. That violated everything he knew about how the universe worked, but much of what the Forerunners had created seemed to occupy that category. That was a key tenet as to why the Servants continued worshipping this ancient race, even after the revelation that the San'Shyuum, who had once led the Covenant, had been false prophets. As Dural's former mentor had often remarked, *A god who creates tools is still a god. It is not for us to impose qualifications upon the divine or presume to guess its intentions.*

With a dozen of the Pale Blade's warriors at his back, Dural took one last look at Hesduros on either side of the wall and deeply breathed in the air. Then, gripping his carbine tightly, he pressed forward and threw caution aside, putting his fate in the hands of the Forerunners.

Dural turned to Ruk and Buran as he approached. "May I see you on the other side."

The light swallowed him whole, its brightness drowning out all else. It felt like millions of fingers—or perhaps cilia like those at the ends of the tentacles of a Huragok—were pressing into his flesh and then tugging it apart. The sensation was somehow not painful, although he could not say he cared for it.

A moment later—unsure how much time had passed—Dural emerged inside what was clearly a Forerunner structure, an interior that looked much like many of those he had visited on other worlds: smooth gray walls, floors, and ceilings formed into vaulted spaces with long lines of lighting embedded throughout. Dural could have been anywhere, on any of the countless planets the Forerunners had visited and left their inscrutable mark, but it certainly resembled the place Jul 'Mdama had once described as the temple through which he had escaped the shield world.

The place the humans called Onyx.

After a long moment, the others eventually came filing in after Dural. Ruk came first, and Buran followed close on his heels, both shivering briefly as they recovered from the effects of the journey.

Ruk glanced around the area and shook his head in disbelief. "Tally yet another victory for the Pale Blade and his bravery! To think we have made it all the way to this most glorious facility! The one the ancient texts spoke so highly about!"

Buran hissed. "And without the humans being made aware of our presence. Let us see how long we can keep it that way."

"Do you fear taking on the humans, Elder Buran?" Ruk said.

"I fear us giving away our hard-won advantages without cause."

Dural stepped between the two of them. "Which is precisely why I asked only a dozen more warriors to come through with us for the time being. We must scout the area before we send back for the others."

"Gods preserve us," Buran said as he peered around the chamber. "Are you certain coming here was right, Pale Blade?"

Buran glanced about as if the ceiling might suddenly come to life and fall on him. Then the older Sangheili became transfixed by the ancient symbols that glowed on the walls. He stumbled toward one in particular, taken by its beauty—yet fatally distracted and open to attack.

"Good to see an old warrior like that give himself over to the faith," Ruk commented.

"His preoccupation with mere machines exposes him to injury," Dural said, checking his own armor to ensure it still functioned.

Ruk looked at Dural sidelong. "Are you giving voice to doubts in the gods? After having traveled through *that*?" Ruk pointed back toward the gate, through which the remainder of the advance strike team was still streaming one at a time.

"I have no doubts about our mission, our warriors, or our gods," Dural said in a loud voice. "I only have doubt in blind faith. The Servants of the Abiding Truth hold a faith that is well-founded because we have seen what the Forerunners left behind. They did this for the benefit of those who would follow, so we should not doubt what we have seen. Yet we should take care to not be overwhelmed in the present at the cost of the future. We all know how well such foolishness among our people served the Arbiter when he sought to set Sangheili brothers against each other."

Buran snorted at that and turned from studying the symbols, seemingly freed from his trance. "Would you have refused to withdraw from the Covenant then, when the Prophets betrayed us?"

"We did not leave the Covenant," Dural said, his voice a low growl. "The Covenant left us."

If Dural was honest, however, he knew there was truth to Buran's remark. Many of the people of Mdama had already begun to give up on the Covenant late during the war. By the time Dural's mother, Raia 'Mdama, had died, the ancient rites outlined by the San'Shyuum had meant nothing to him anymore. Following the Prophets had been the epitome of blind faith for his people, which is perhaps why he despised it so.

Still, Dural wanted a reason to believe, even as a child—and his mother's death had led him to that.

It happened at the start of the Blooding Years, when Jul 'Mdama—both Dural's uncle and the kaidon of Bekan keep, where Dural was hatched and raised—plotted with the Servants of the Abiding Truth. Their efforts were simple: a full-fledged naval attack against the Arbiter and his native forces on Sanghelios.

During the days leading up to their strike, though, his uncle was lost, and when Jul went missing, Dural's mother, Raia, left the keep, following in his wake, hoping to find him. Instead, she found Field Master Avu Med 'Telcam and then demanded to follow the Sangheili leader as he initiated the assault. Raia was on the frigate *Cleansing Faith* when it was shot down during a battle with the *Swordsman*, the personal cruiser of the Arbiter himself.

Only later did Dural discover that Jul had survived, but the Sangheili leader never returned to Bekan keep. Naxan, an elder and great-uncle in Dural's clan, was forced to take over in Jul's absence. The moment Dural could manage it, however, he went looking for Jul himself. He refused to be abandoned by the only true leader his keep had left.

Reflecting, Dural wondered if he should have simply stayed at Bekan keep, but the Swords of Sanghelios knew of the connections between the Servants of the Abiding Truth and his family's estate. It would have been foolish for them not to make an example of Bekan once they had the chance. And after the death of his mother, Dural only had one other family member he trusted: his brother, Asum. But even he stayed only for a time.

Distraught over their mother's death, Asum went off into the fields around Bekan keep to grieve, and that was the last time Dural saw his brother. Asum never returned, though Dural did not stay long enough to know his fate for certain.

In the end, it mattered little. Dural had already made his decision.

Left alone in those moments to contemplate his purpose, Dural pledged to follow in his mother's footsteps and try to finish the task she had begun: to find Jul 'Mdama, wherever he might have gone. But after the failure of the Servants' initial assault on the Arbiter, there was no way to tell what had happened to Jul. Only the barest of clues existed: Jul had reached out to Naxan in the days after the passing of Raia, sending a message from a remote world. Where that had been and what his ultimate plans were, Dural still did not know.

In the years that followed, Dural searched the outer lands for his uncle and asked about Asum as he did, but he never found any trace of either. It was as if they had both been plucked from Sanghelios by the gods.

It was in those days, however, that Dural found his purpose: to join and fight alongside the Servants of the Abiding Truth.

While under the guidance of Field Master Avu Med 'Telcam, learning the path of the warrior, Dural still kept an eye out for Jul 'Mdama and for Asum. Jul did not resurface until years later, now at the head of what he referred to as his Covenant—a burgeoning reformation, but now without the San'Shyuum's oversight. By this time, Dural had already been blooded in battle several times over, fighting on the front lines of the Servants' inexorable push against the Swords of Sanghelios.

The rumors that flooded in from the field master's sources indicated that Jul had spent a great deal of time on Hesduros, far from the eyes of the Arbiter, building up his resurgent Covenant one ship at a time. When Dural first noted this, he contacted Naxan, who then told Dural something his mother had never shared with him, something that would irrevocably shatter his world.

Dural was Jul 'Mdama's birth son. And not only that, but Jul already possessed this knowledge. Jul *knew* that Dural—whom he had left in Bekan—was his child.

In the Sangheili tradition, children were all raised together by the keep's females, who never let the fathers know who their fledglings might be. This time-honored practice was meant to keep the parents from showing their children any bloodline favoritism, giving them an egalitarian society in which people had to earn any reward on their own merits rather than having anything granted. For the most part, it worked extremely well, but Raia had loved Jul so much that she had broken the taboo and shared the identity of his sons with him.

It was a foolish choice, and one that had wound up causing Dural great pain.

Yet, with this new light came new choices.

Should he abandon the Servants of the Abiding Truth and Avu Med 'Telcam and set out for the redoubts his real father had built on Hesduros? Or should he remain loyal to the one Sangheili who had played the role of father to him during his most formative years?

It did not take long for Dural to measure the scales. . . .

Jul 'Mdama had knowingly abandoned both Dural and Asum to rot in Bekan keep while he hid from the Arbiter's wrath and dishonored Raia's death. When Dural finally realized this, he became enraged. If he did set out to Hesduros, it would not be for reunion, but for revenge. Only the field master was able to persuade Dural to not hunt Jul down and demand blood satisfaction for his dereliction.

Instead, 'Telcam placed Dural on the path to where they now stood: Onyx, the great refuge of the Forerunners.

Today had been the culmination of long years of pain and anger, and now—finally—Dural was here.

"Yes," Dural repeated. "The Covenant left *us*. Do you think Jul 'Mdama and his forces—which he foolishly refers to as the Covenant—would have had the vision or the resources to come here? They were *on* Hesduros for years, and yet they spent their days in hiding, fighting over scraps rather than returning here into the embrace of the Forerunners' greatest treasure."

Buran huffed to the side. "I still think there is wisdom in leaving well enough alone. Your uncle was the only one to have seen what was on the other side of this portal. Perhaps there was a good reason for him to have refused to return."

"This shield world houses more Forerunner machines—both weapons and vehicles—than any other place in the galaxy," Dural responded. Buran's testing grated on him, although he had grown used to it. "You've read the script, Buran. Yes, the humans have infested it, and their numbers here grow daily. What better reason to act quickly? They are already desecrating all that the Forerunners left behind, many of them working alongside the Arbiter's own clans to do it! And if they are not stopped, what do you think they might do with the machines they find here?"

Buran appeared bewildered at this. "Our people have a head start of centuries on their efforts. We have been exploring the majesty of the Forerunners for ages, before the humans even knew they existed."

"Perhaps." Dural approached Buran's face to exert his authority.

"According to what the field master himself learned before his death, the humans have gathered their best researchers here and unleashed them to this very end. They are pulling apart this world stone by stone, defiling the temples of the Forerunners in order to deliver the very weapons and ships of the gods into the hands of our enemies."

"What heresy and blasphemy!" Ruk spat. "How much longer must we be forced to stomach such treachery? The Arbiter and his allies must die!"

Dural was about to voice his agreement when Even Keel finally came through the gate. With the Huragok now here, the Servants' advance team was complete.

From what the field master had told Dural—which he had heard from contacts close to Jul 'Mdama himself—the Forerunner temple they had accessed stood within twenty or so kilometers of the humans' main base within the shield world. This intelligence, however, was from roughly five years ago.

Who knew what the humans have done since then?

In any case, this location lay far too close to the human base, not in the least because the humans might be monitoring the place at that very moment. As far as Dural was concerned, it had been a matter of sheer providence that no humans had been in this temple upon their arrival. The Servants needed to set up their own camp soon, but in a different area, somewhere from which they could safely stage their scouting efforts.

Dural beckoned the Huragok forward, and it floated to his side. The bizarre creature communicated natively with its sign language, but with the Servants it employed an older technology recovered from Covenant vessels, which simultaneously translated its signs. Via the circuits built into Dural's armor, Even Keel could understand him, and he could interpret its sign language through the collar he wore.

"We need to set up a base on this shield world," Dural said.

"Can you alter the portal to have it bring us to a defensible site within the sphere, one far enough from the humans who have infested this place?"

"It is possible," Even Keel's surrogate voice chimed in Dural's collar. "I must evaluate this side of the gate."

"See to it, Huragok. I want to keep it within a safe striking distance, though, for when the time of our attack has come."

Even Keel set to work immediately.

"I do not like this," Buran said, nodding at the Huragok. "We are far too dependent on this single Engineer. What happens if he is injured?"

Or killed, Dural heard in Buran's voice. Dural would have also added: *Or betrays us.* Either was a possibility in this place.

"Once we set up camp and ferry in the rest of our warriors, our singular goal is finding *other* Huragok within the sphere and taking them for our own. They are the key to the Forerunner prize we seek."

"And what if the *nishum* already have those Huragok in their employ?" said Ruk, using the Sangheili invective for the human species. "If the humans have been here as long as you say, they must have captured some of the creatures and put them to work."

"I hope for that to be true," Dural said. "That would mean they likely have more than one together at a time, which makes them easier targets. Also, stealing their Huragok would not only help us, but would hurt them as well."

Ruk made an affirmative grunt. A moment later, Even Keel indicated that it had found a safe location. It surprised even Buran, who seemed to be losing his grit in this place. It was likely too much for the old Sangheili to process.

As Dural approached, Keel gestured for him to enter the portal once more. Dural moved quickly toward it without hesitation, motioning for the others to follow. "You are in charge of the

Huragok," Dural said to Ruk, turning his back to Buran. "Stay here until I send someone to fetch you."

"And if you do not return?"

Dural barked a harsh laugh at him. "I do not plan for failure, Ruk. Stay vigilant."

As Dural walked through the portal, the sensation this time was not nearly as unpleasant, perhaps because he was not traveling quite so far. It felt as if he were moving through a thick veil of webs, but the feeling quickly passed . . .

And Dural emerged inside another Forerunner facility. In many ways, it resembled the one he had just left but was far wider and taller, vaguely similar to some of the Forerunner structures back home, in the city of Ontom. It seemed to be a vast containment facility of some sort, but no doubt had spiritual significance. He sighed when he examined the portal and realized that this machine was also too small to transport his vehicles through. He would have to wait for that victory.

Then Dural heard a rumble: the muffled sounds of battle. This was not the comforting sound of elegant Sangheili weaponry launching blasts of superheated plasma, but the discordant rattle of automatic gunfire, the kind the humans produced in war.

Somewhere outside the large structure, humans shouted at each other in a tongue Dural recognized as one of their primary languages. He could not speak it, but the translator in his armor untangled their unseemly babble into something coherent.

Some of them shouted orders. Others cried out in terror and panic. For a moment, Dural worried that they had somehow detected the Servants' arrival at the temple site and were headed to his warriors' position, but the situation was not about him or the Servants who remained at the other site. It was about something entirely different.

Somewhere outside the structure—among the shouters and

shooters—a massive creature bellowed in agony until its voice trailed off into nothingness. The warriors of Dural's splinter team finished appearing behind him, and he signaled for each of them to take cover and keep silent.

If the humans were occupied with another foe—perhaps a native animal of some sort—then this presented the Servants with a prime opportunity to strike an unsuspecting enemy. The humans might never be so distracted again.

On the other hand, whatever the humans were fighting could also pose a problem. It might well be such a dangerous animal that Dural would be risking his entire scouting team. Despite his eagerness to engage the wretched human foes as soon as possible, he had no desire to bury his entire operation in the ground during their first hours here in the shield world.

After he quickly surveyed their surroundings, Dural noticed that, apart from the portal, the room had only one entrance. He signaled for his team to fan out to either side of it, a large aperture that was far enough away so that anyone coming down the long, wide corridor leading into the chamber could not see them.

At that very moment, Dural heard a pair of voices coming toward the far end of the hallway. Even without his translator, he could understand their tone and inflection because the field master had forced him to learn it, despite his natural aversion to their speech. These humans were clearly scared.

Avu Mel 'Telcam had allied himself with humans in the past—faithless ones eager to betray the Arbiter—and he expected Dural to be able to do the same when 'Telcam was gone. He had no love for the frail and sickly mammals, but communicating with them had ultimately proved a necessary evil. Dural had bucked against the learning of the language, but he knew enough to understand it, with the translation device filling in the gaps.

It would have been a far worse sin to avoid the humans and let the Arbiter and his allies triumph over all Sanghelios. Though, in the aftermath of 'Telcam's death, Dural often wondered if the field master had been mistaken about the necessity. After all, a demon—one of the soldiers the humans called Spartans—had finally hunted down and killed him.

"What the hell was that?" a female of the human band said. "Some kind of land-shark?"

How odd that the humans let their females fight beside them. *How desperate for help must they be?* Yet Dural had heard rumors of female Sangheili fighting within the Arbiter's own ranks—another blasphemy the traitor had picked up from his human allies.

"It wasn't friendly, whatever it was," the male replied. "The creatures here were harvested from other planets across the galaxy. They could have come from anywhere."

"Why don't you give that coldhearted lecture to Trevor?" the female said. "Better yet, you can tell his wife and kids once we get back to Pax!"

Dural leaned in to listen closer. The humans spoke of *families* rather than *forces*, and Dural wondered exactly what kind of humans had been brought there to explore this world. Perhaps there were far more researchers than even he had considered . . . and far fewer warriors.

That might explain why these people had apparently struggled so hard to defeat the beast that had attacked them. It also meant his forces could make easy work of them.

"They knew the risks when they came here," the male said, irritated. "We all did."

"Risks?" The female let out a bitter laugh. "We came here to explore alien archaeology—not to get torn to pieces by a face full of razor-sharp teeth."

"Nobody wanted Trevor to die. Sometimes when you're wandering around a strange planet and not following protocol, really bad things happen. Inside a place like Onyx, that's bound to be even more true."

"That's the best excuse you can come up with? 'Things happen'? I can't wait for you to try to sell that to your superior officer."

Dural wondered if the male, at least, might be a soldier.

That would make more sense, even if Dural could not understand why he would bring a female along. They did not belong anywhere near the field of battle.

Dural's mother served as hard proof of that. Raia should have stayed at the keep with him and his brother. If she had, she might still be alive.

"If you and the rest of your research team want to get out of here in a better condition than Trevor, I suggest you fall in line and head for the portal back to the Repository before that thing's friends come back looking for it."

"We're not leaving Trevor's body here for the animals," another male voice called from farther back.

"Then you need to grab it fast," the soldier said. "Those portals aren't always stable for long, and the clock's ticking on our window to get back."

If the humans had come here via the portal, then Dural and the Servants clearly stood between them and their only means of escape. Dural motioned for his warriors to ready their weapons.

Buran put a hand on Dural's shoulder and gave him a wary look. "No need to alert the humans to our presence quite yet," he whispered. "We can be gone before they even know we are here." Dural shrugged off the elder with a glare that told him the next time he presumed to put his hand on the Pale Blade, it would be returned broken.

The sound of footsteps coming down the corridor toward the Servants echoed into the chamber, and Dural nodded toward the others. When he judged the pair to be halfway toward the main contingent of their splinter group, he gave the signal to attack.

Dural gripped his carbine and led the charge down the corridor, firing upon the pair of humans, who had frozen in their tracks. They might have been wary of more monsters attacking them outside, but they had not suspected they might run into a troop of fully armed Sangheili warriors within the structure.

"Cut them down!" Dural shouted as one of his bolts struck true and felled the female weakling. Although he had briefly fought humans in the past, the bulk of his engagements had been against fellow Sangheili. Technically, she was the first human Dural had ever killed in battle, and he swore in that moment that he would always remember that.

She would not be the last on this campaign. Countless others would fall before him, but she would not be forgotten.

"Make sure no human escapes!" Dural shouted as his warriors mowed down the soldier and charged up the corridor to seek out any other prey. "Tonight marks the end of their dominion over this shield world. We shall take it for the Servants of the Abiding Truth! We shall take it for the field master!"

CHAPTER 9

With Asha and Yong's expertise on the mysterious Forerunner machines attached to Project: GOLIATH—whatever that was—the two were in high demand by ONI analysts. This meant Molly didn't get to spend too much time adjusting to Onyx from the comfort of her new home. Within a few days after the family's arrival, her Newparents sent her to the school, and she was bored enough by then that she decided not to fight it.

But boredom, she soon discovered, was the lesser of two evils. Molly almost immediately hated the school in Paxopolis, also known as the Pax Institute. This was not Aranuka by any stretch. For example, when she surveyed the dining hall, which one expected to be innocent enough given the overarching purpose of the city and its peaceful researchers, Molly instead found it packed with hundreds of angst-riddled, mercurial kids who seemed to be perpetually in unruly moods. Despite the allegedly idealistic purpose of Paxopolis, its school had all of the bad ingredients of a normal school on any other human planet—possibly even more so.

Then again, Molly didn't care for most other schools she'd attended either. It wasn't that she didn't get good grades—she actually performed remarkably well—but she just couldn't stand most of the teachers or the others. She could never connect with them, and that frustrated her to no end.

When Molly lived in Wisconsin, she was only seen as the refugee, the kid who'd survived the glassing of her planet. Everyone who found out about Paris IV would give her the same sad, pitiful look, as if the person knew her and her story. But Molly didn't want special attention or sympathy. She just wanted to fit in, to blend in with the crowd, to be normal, whatever that meant.

Molly liked most of the people she knew there, but it seemed that they were so cut off from the war that it didn't mean much to them. To most of Earth before the Covenant showed up, the war was out of sight and out of mind. True, some of them had volunteered to fight against the Covenant, and Molly applauded their bravery for that. Yet, the people she knew in Wisconsin, of course, were the ones who'd stayed home, who knew the least about what was going on in the colonies as the Covenant wiped out one world after another.

Maybe they did what they could to support the war effort, but as far as Molly was concerned, it was hard to know what you were supporting unless you saw it firsthand. To most of Earth, the war was both literally and emotionally light-years away. It was always someone else's problem.

Plus, by the time Molly started living in Wisconsin, the war had already been going on for twenty-four years. An entire generation had grown up under the looming shadow of an interstellar invasion by an alien force armed with superior technology. That was all they had.

The adults who knew about the time before the war would never understand Molly's generation. Not truly. The war was the backstory of their entire lives.

But Molly was the only one in her Wisconsin town who'd actually experienced it in person, for whom war wasn't just background but the darkest chapter of her life.

When Molly moved to Aranuka, she'd hoped for a better time at school. Unlike in Wisconsin, she had something vital in common with her neighbors there. They'd been through a Covenant invasion and survived. The sudden and traumatic attack of Earth had put them all on a level playing field. Molly hoped there would be some kindred spirits she could connect to and relate with. But that never happened.

Many of the kids she went to school with hadn't been in Aranuka during the actual invasion or even seen the Covenant's destruction outside of newsfeeds. Like Molly, they'd come with their families from relatively secure locations to fill the massive hole the attack on the space tether had created. Many places on Earth had remained untouched by the Covenant, and the majority of these citizens had come from such locations.

At the time, Molly figured she could at least bond with the ones who *had* been somewhere directly attacked during the Covenant's invasion, even if that was on Mars or Luna, both of which were also ravaged during the assault. But a crucial difference kept cropping up. While even those people had all survived alien invasions, Molly hadn't been around for *their* experience.

They already had plenty of friends they'd formed a trauma bond with in the aftermath of their particular Covenant attacks, and despite her hopes for friendships, they never welcomed Molly into their groups. Some even showed animosity when she tried to find her way in. Their differences in experience had created even more challenging barriers than before.

Ironically, Molly found herself more alone in Aranuka than she had been in Wisconsin. In Wisconsin, the people had tried to bring her into the fold, even if it was out of some kind of botched effort toward sympathy. In Aranuka, everyone immediately expected her to be part of a *different* group because of where she'd come from and what she'd been through.

But *no one* had been through what Molly had, which meant she didn't have a group. She just had herself.

Molly didn't know how that was going to work in Onyx. But given all of her apprehensions about the place, she didn't have high hopes. Still, she would put on a brave face for her Newparents, mostly because a large part of her had abandoned any hope for a normal life the moment she'd met Kasha 'Hilot. Also, it had become clear over the past few days that her Newparents had enough to deal with, adjusting to their new jobs and the urgency that seemed to attend Project: GOLIATH.

Fortunately for Molly, she'd arrived near the start of a new school session, so she didn't have much catching up to do. It was October back on Earth, and although Onyx's natural calendar—if such a thing could be conceived of—didn't match up with Earth's, the research community's policy was to observe Military Standard Time, which was, at least in theory, universal across all UNSC sites.

Pax Institute featured an odd mixture of architectural styles drawn from humans, Sangheili, and Forerunners. Parts of the education facility seemed to be designed to make all species feel at home, which Molly admitted was a strangely impressive task. The building complex featured large spaces with high ceilings. Many of them had no ceilings or roofs at all and stood open to the sky, or so it seemed to the naked eye.

The colors of the school tended toward neutral: pale grays and purples with highlights of glowing blue lights that seemed to suffuse every room. The interior doors were made of a kind of transparent barrier that activated and deactivated when someone approached them, and the walls—even the interior ones—had long windows so one could see people moving all about one at any time. Some of these qualities may have simply been for aesthetic purposes, or to present a comfortable, egalitarian atmosphere in which very different species could coexist.

Knowing ONI probably had a hand in the school's design, Molly suspected other motives, such as security. ONI would want to lock down quickly if something went terribly wrong.

Much of the school's design—and scale—allowed her to circumnavigate any interaction with the other species, which was her biggest concern. In fact, she could have minimal interaction with *all* of the other students, largely due to the class sizes and the general scope of the campus. She had seen several groups of aliens milling about the buildings and in a few of her classes, but she easily avoided them, finding the farthest possible seat in a class, even if it was in the front row. Molly fantasized that she might be able to complete the rest of her education and even leave Onyx without talking to or even having eye contact with another species.

The thought gave her some measure of relief.

During the last of her morning classes, Molly heard the word *Huragok* again, the same creatures Director Barton had mentioned on their approach to Onyx. Paxopolis—and the larger Trevelyan research facility—had a small team of Huragok. They worked alongside the researchers, giving them an opportunity to control and manipulate Onyx's native environments and even to improve and repair the new structures the humans had built here.

Molly had never seen a Huragok in person, but she had spent the better part of the previous night learning about them from the Onyx briefing vids Director Mendez had mentioned. They were living machines the Forerunners had designed millennia ago to maintain their technology. These jellyfish-like creatures of tech-imbued flesh were filled with some kind of gas that made them float. Instead of arms and legs, they had prehensile tentacles that could wield just about any tool—whether human or otherwise, according to the vids.

The Covenant had apparently enslaved the Huragok, referring to them as Engineers, while to the Forerunners they were apparently known as *servant-tools*. To Molly, however, the images and vids made the Huragok look like something that belonged deep underwater. She would be perfectly fine if she never saw one in person, and part of her hoped that she wouldn't.

When her grade broke for lunch, Molly made her way to the campus dining hall. As she expected, the hall was just as architecturally and technologically impressive as the rest of the school, but that didn't make it more inviting. Most of the students eating in the hall sat at round tables in groups of up to eight. Even though Molly could see pockets of friends, she was too new to identify any of the cliques she expected to find here, but she didn't suppose it mattered. None of those groups were likely to want to have much to do with her.

And that was fine by her. She didn't want anything to do with them either. Her plan wasn't to make friends. It was to just get through the day, hopefully without having to interact with any other students . . . especially the aliens.

Molly stood in line with the rest of the students to get her food, but when she looked for a place to sit down, it seemed as if every table she spotted was already occupied or spoken for. Most of the people sitting at the tables were human, but one corner of the hall seemed to have been set aside for aliens—the *other species*, as Kasha 'Hilot had reminded her. About half those were filled with Sangheili, while the rest overflowed with the smaller Grunts. Glancing at them, Molly felt a familiar revulsion and anxiety rising in her stomach, just like when she'd met the Sangheili headmaster.

Molly found it incredibly telling, and even alarming, that despite all of the positive ideals that had been lauded during her initial meeting with Director Mendez and his team, this room—in the middle of the most social activity of the day—told a completely different story. Part of this made her feel vindicated: Molly wasn't the only one who didn't like this idea.

The aliens seemed to share her apprehension. She certainly wouldn't have been comfortable with humans and Sangheili commingling at the same tables, and the hall showed her that—at Pax Institute—little effort had likely been made at uniting the different species on Onyx.

They looked as divided as ever.

As Molly surveyed the hall, she spotted plenty of seats open at one of the tables at the far end of the room, right at the border between the human side and everyone else. After closer examination, however, she saw that a single Sangheili sat there, eating alone. That made Molly's decision easy. She wasn't about to sit next to him, even if that meant her skipping a meal altogether.

Eventually, after navigating the full hall, she spotted an entirely empty table a little farther along that same borderland. She claimed it for her own: Molly Patel, nation of one. This might not be a bad lunch experience after all, she dared to hope.

Ignoring the other tables, Molly made quick work of her food and was just about to start her dessert when a human boy— roughly her age—came up to her table with his tray and cleared his throat. He was thin and lanky, and moved as if he'd just hit a growth spurt and didn't quite know how to handle his frame. The boy had curly dark hair, deep-set brown eyes, and a crooked smile that told Molly that he was probably more uncertain than happy at the moment.

"Do you mind if I sit here?"

Molly didn't care what he did. She gestured to the open seats at the table. "Do you think there's room?"

"Thanks." He sat down with an empty chair between them, careful not to get too close. "You're new here, right? I saw you on the transport from Earth."

Now that he mentioned it, Molly had seen him there too but had completely forgotten about it. So many people had been on the vessel, and she'd done her best to ignore most of them. "Ah, that explains it."

He cocked his head at her, confused. "What do you mean?"

"Why you don't have any friends here either."

"Well . . . I actually started here three days ago, which I guess means that I have a head start on you in that department. Doesn't look like you're doing too great either." He let out a nervous laugh. "My parents keep telling me it's only a matter of time. We haven't even been here a full week, right?"

"Did you have a lot of friends at your last school?"

The boy hesitated for a moment, apparently unsure how much he should divulge about his past life with a total stranger. Then he shook his head.

Molly had to admit that it took some guts to tell a complete stranger that you didn't have friends anywhere at all. He could have lied—he could have told her whatever he wanted—but he didn't. She realized she probably couldn't have done that right out of the gate. And she hadn't exactly been the most cordial of strangers.

Maybe there's more to him than meets the eye, she thought. *He's not an alien, so at least he has that going for him.*

"Me neither," Molly finally said. "Let's make that the basis of our table."

His eyes lit up, and he smiled. "The thing that binds us together?"

"Exactly. Outsiders-only table. Insiders not welcome."

It happened in an instant: Molly didn't feel so alone anymore.

The two introduced themselves and chatted over lunch and then went outside into the school's courtyard for the rest of the hour. The sky was a bright blue, and the planet they called Mackintosh loomed like a solemn visage spread above them. The courtyard sat out to one side of the school, behind the main building. The area right outside the school was paved with concrete, but it eventually gave way to a wide field of trimmed grass. Benches had been scattered all around it, along with a few repulsor courts on which to play gravball sports, such as slingshot or ricochet.

The boy, Kareem El-Hashem, had been living on Luna when the Covenant had first invaded the Sol system. Although Luna had been attacked by the Covenant, Earth and Mars had taken the brunt of the assault. Kareem's mother was apparently an expert in Unggoy culture, and when she'd gotten the invitation to join the researchers in Onyx, they'd picked up stakes and moved the entire family, rather than try to rebuild what had been taken from them.

"Unggoy?" Molly said, as they strolled out into the courtyard with the rest of the students. "You mean Grunts?"

Kareem shrugged, apparently not approving of the pejorative. And he didn't seem worried about whether Molly approved of his mother's career. "They'd probably prefer *Unggoy*, right?" he asked, correcting her. The two finally found a spot in the shade of a large oaklike tree overlooking a pickup gravball game not too far off. "She's been studying them for years."

"Seems like we've got plenty of live specimens for her in this place." Molly cast a glance to a group of Unggoy at the far end of the repulsor courts.

"During the war they were part of the Covenant. They may have been small but they were still warriors. Maybe they're not as intimidating as the Mgalekgolo." Kareem offered a knowing glance. "But there are a lot of them out there. More than most people realize."

Molly suppressed a shudder at the mention of the Mgalek-golo. She hadn't given them a thought in months. They were crea-tures that had served in the Covenant during its prime, known to humans as Hunters. Massive, heavily armored bipeds with an immense shield on one arm and an assault cannon on the other, Hunters apparently traveled in what was referred to as bonded pairs—which meant they fought in packs of two. The most in-triguing and somewhat horrifying thing about them was that they weren't actually biped aliens, but rather vast colonies of intelligent eel-like creatures that had tightly woven together to form a body. Or so the terminal vids had informed her.

"Hold on," Molly interjected, as a horrible thought occurred to her. "We don't have any Hunters here in Onyx, do we?"

Kareem shook his head. "Not as far as I can tell, but I just got here, like you."

"No. It's mostly humans," a nasal, high-pitched voice said im-mediately behind them. "Plus they have a bunch of Sangheili, of course. And a few of my kind too."

Molly spun around in shock. Though it spoke with their words, whatever had snuck up behind them was *not* human.

The thing stood about four feet tall, not including the large pack it wore on its back, out of which a tube snaked around to clamp over where its nose should have been. The alien's body was covered in a rigid shell, much like that of a crab, except it was a vi-brant purple running toward blue. Its skinny arms and legs ended up in somewhat oversize hands and feet, and the smaller creature stared up at them with unblinking eyes set over a lipless mouth filled with jagged teeth.

It was an Unggoy.

The UNSC soldiers had called this species Grunts because they were forced to do much of the scut work of the Covenant during the empire's rampage across human space. Unggoy were often used as cannon fodder, the first line to soften the enemy before the other troops were deployed. Molly didn't feel the need to have sympathy for any part of the Covenant, but she'd noted more than once that there always seemed to be so many Unggoy in combat stills. That wasn't surprising, she supposed. The Covenant probably had a constantly replenishing supply, forcing each generation to give their lives for the cause.

And for thirty years that cause had been the extinction of humanity.

"Hello," the Unggoy said with eerie clarity. "My name's Gudam Keschun. I'm a student here too."

Molly just stared for a second. She could barely think of what to say to this creature that had caught her completely off guard. After about five awkward seconds she blurted out the first thing that came to her mind. "Are you in our class?"

Molly didn't know why she had asked that. She didn't care and didn't want to talk any further, but it was the first thing that came to her instinctively.

But Molly also found that it didn't seem to bother her to be this close to an Unggoy. Unlike the Sangheili she'd seen on Onyx, this little Unggoy seemed relatively harmless. For a moment, she had to remind herself: this was a kind of creature that had been at war with humanity not so long ago. They might even have crewed the ship that killed her parents back on Paris IV.

"Of course," Gudam said. "That's why I'm here, right? They don't let the little ones interact with the big ones. By age and maturity, I mean, not size, right? Or I'd never be allowed anywhere near aliens as big as you, much less the Sangheili students. I think they're even *born* taller than the adults of my species!"

That must have been a joke by how much Gudam seemed to

laugh at it, though it was difficult for Molly to tell if the creature was joking or simply struggling to breathe. The thought of an Unggoy finding itself funny was intriguing enough for Molly to crack a smile. It was such a human thing to do.

"Gudam's in our math class," Kareem said. "She's the teacher's pet."

What? Molly was trying to parse what she'd just heard. Gudam was a *she*, which had not been obvious to Molly at all.

"You're only saying that because she's my mother, but she doesn't favor me more than any of the other five in my clutch."

Other five? Again, Molly had a hard time comprehending. "Your mother's the teacher? And there are *six* of you?"

"In my clutch. And another four in the younger clutch. Plus another dozen from my other mother's clutch, but they're all grown and gone now. They didn't come with us."

"You have two mothers?" Molly didn't know anything about Unggoy sexual preferences or mating habits. Everything Gudam was telling her was brand-new.

"Yuh-huh, and three fathers, but only one of them came with us to Onyx. He works as an explorer, just like my other mother, Momma Beskin, but the mother who's here, Momma Aphrid, she doesn't know anything about stuff like that. You know, Forerunners and the things they built. But she didn't want to just sit around all day long being useless, so she teaches here instead. She's the best!"

"How come I didn't see you in math class?" Molly said, slightly confused. She'd suffered through that first thing in the morning but didn't remember seeing any Unggoy. "Or your mother, for that matter?"

"The man who's been teaching us the last couple days was a substitute," Kareem said. "Teacher Aphrid should be back in school later today."

"She was home taking care of me this morning." Gudam dug her strange foot into the grass and twisted it about, as though slightly ashamed—another surprisingly human mannerism. "I decided to try running around outside without my breathing kit on." She pointed at the pack on her back. "I need methane to breathe. If I don't have any, it really gets to your head after a while, you know? Well, I suppose you don't, breathing all that high-powered oxygen the way you two do!"

Gudam coughed a couple times after that, and Molly wondered if Gudam's voice was always that wheezy, or if it was an effect of her messing with the wrong gas in her lungs. She struggled for a moment to catch her breath, grabbing on to Kareem's arm as she did.

Then something happened.

Molly couldn't believe it at the time, but she found herself actually beginning to feel sorry for this creature. The Unggoy. Molly tried to remind herself that this thing was part of the Covenant—or, at least, she would have been had the war continued. And, to Molly, Gudam was as genuinely ugly as could be, almost offensively so, but even still . . . something about her intrigued Molly. She found Gudam strangely adorable, but couldn't explain why.

"How old are you?" Molly asked, again not quite sure where the question came from. It seemed entirely logical despite the completely illogical nature of the conversation's participants. *What kind of small talk is one supposed to have with an alien?*

"I just turned five!" Gudam said brightly. "As humans count years at least. We had a big party for me and all my clutchmates."

Gudam again started laughing loudly, attracting the attention of other students. She would have probably continued if another fierce coughing fit hadn't stopped her again.

"Just five?" Molly could hardly believe it. Gudam seemed to be about the same size as the other Unggoy Molly had seen in the dining hall.

"Unggoy grow to maturity rather quickly," Kareem said. "I think Teacher Aphrid is actually only ten years old."

"That's right!" Gudam said. "But she doesn't look a day over eight!"

Molly had a hard time reconciling Gudam with what she'd known about Grunts before coming to Onyx, the little she'd learned through newsfeeds and Waypoint articles. She zeroed in on a loose fact, something obscure that had frightened her when she first heard it: some Grunts would make suicide runs, charging into a group of humans and activating plasma grenades. The Unggoy may have been cannon fodder, but they'd killed a lot of people.

But Gudam didn't seem dangerous at all.

Had there been Unggoy on the ships that had destroyed Paris IV? Molly wondered once more. *Almost definitely. And they'd likely murdered millions during the war—including my sister and my parents.*

The thoughts were sobering, but it was where Molly's mind went.

Gudam hadn't been on one of those enemy vessels, but if the war had still been going on, she could have wound up on a ship like that, doing what those who came before her did: trying desperately to kill more humans.

Maybe even trying to kill me.

But instead, this strange alien was cracking jokes and acting friendly, and that strange shift made Molly's stomach twist.

"So who are you?" Gudam stuck her hand out to Molly. "Any friend of Kareem's is a friend of mine." Gudam lowered her voice in confidence. "I hear that's the kind of thing humans say to each other. I've been reading on the side to catch up."

Molly hesitated for a moment, but then she took the little creature's large hand and shook it. At first, Molly was nervous. The Unggoy had thick clawed hands that vaguely reminded Molly of a crab's pincers. She wondered if she'd even get her hand back in one piece. Yet, despite the roughness of Gudam's shell, her touch was surprisingly gentle and light. She shook Molly's hand with what seemed to be sincere glee.

"I'm Molly."

"Hello, Molly! You're only the second human I've done this with! Most people get uncomfortable, you know. I don't blame them. I mean, you humans are so soft and fleshy, you need to protect your skin, but I think I see why you do this among yourselves—shake hands, I mean. It's fun to make contact like this, isn't it?"

The Unggoy's mouth spread into a wide smile, showing every one of her vicious teeth. Molly did her best not to think of what it would feel like to have those things sink into her soft and fleshy skin.

"I suppose so." A slight grin appeared on Molly's face without her intending it.

The three turned at a sound, hearing someone snarl behind them.

"Damn hinge-heads," an angry boy said. "We ought to space the lot of them. One at a time."

Molly tried to assess what she was seeing. A trio of large boys were stalking toward a single Sangheili who was standing off to one side of the courtyard by himself. She didn't know how well Sangheili ears worked, but she could easily hear the boy's words and was twice as far away from him as the alien. Still, the Sangheili didn't acknowledge the human. He just kept his head down and seemed to ignore the kid.

Molly recognized the Sangheili as the same one she saw sitting by himself in the dining hall. The one she'd refused to sit with. Most of the Elites were challenging to tell apart here, shades of browns and grays. This Sangheili was different though. Its skin was paler than that of most of the others, almost white. The alien definitely stood out from the other members of its species, at least on Onyx.

Some humans who had been near the Sangheili moved away from him as the three boys approached. The one in the lead was buff and burly, with short-cropped hair. He looked as if he could be a marine in training. The two who followed in his wake were cut from the same mold. They were each shorter and smaller than him, though not by much, and they wore the same dark scowls.

"Uh-oh," Kareem said in a low voice meant only for Molly's ears. "That's Karl Zakovksy, and that's his brother Zeb, and their friend Andres Malez."

"They're trouble?" she asked.

"Biggest bullies in the school, from what I can tell. They haven't picked on me yet, but I've been steering clear of them."

"That's not easy to do in a school this size," Gudam said. She stared openly at the troublemakers as they went by a few paces away. "Eventually, the people who want to find you will find you."

Karl strode up to where the Sangheili stood with his back to them, looking out across a field and into the forest just outside the school grounds. The boy reached out and shoved the alien in the shoulder, almost knocking him to the ground.

"Watch where you're walking," Karl said to the alien. Instead of moving past him, though, Karl stopped and cackled as the Sangheili staggered forward and then caught himself.

"Yeah," Zeb said, echoing his brother. "Watch where you're walking!"

The Sangheili turned around slowly and gave each of the boys a dead-eyed stare. He stretched out to his full height so he could look each of them in the eye. They were older than him, maybe, and taller, but he easily outmassed each of them.

Molly's apprehension about the aliens aside, she knew how this could end. In a fair fight, the Sangheili could probably take down any one of those boys, even Karl. But they clearly weren't interested in making this a fair fight. She scanned the courtyard to see if any faculty were around to stop this, but not a single adult was in sight.

"I was standing still." The Sangheili's voice was higher than she expected, but she hadn't heard too many voices from his species before. She wondered if he was a younger fledgling.

Kasha was the first Sangheili who had ever spoken to Molly in person. Before that, the most she'd ever heard came from news-feeds with Sangheili such as the Arbiter, the leader of the Swords of Sanghelios, giving a speech. His own Elites had claimed to be humanity's allies since the end of the war. He often spoke in delegations and peace conferences between his government and the UEG. As intimidating as the Sangheili were, the Arbiter had a magnificent voice, deep and resonant.

The Arbiter and his Swords of Sanghelios stood out as the shining example Molly's Newparents often used to prove the Sangheili weren't inherently evil. Even if they'd been deceived by the Prophets into attacking humanity for nearly thirty years.

To Molly, that made little difference. She understood her Newparents' interpretation of the events, but she didn't think that being fooled into murdering millions of people got you off the hook for *murdering millions of people.* They were still responsible for what they had done.

With the war stopped, are we supposed to just act like it never happened? Molly's parents and sister were still dead. *How am I supposed to deal with that?*

"Then watch where *we're* walking," Karl said. The other boys sniggered at that.

"Are we to do this again?" The Sangheili shook his head on his long stalk of a neck in a weary way.

"Do what?" Zeb said. "Put you in your place?"

"I am where I am meant to be, human."

Karl smirked at that and glanced about as if looking for something. "Really? This doesn't look like a hospital to me."

"Or a graveyard," Andres said darkly.

His tone was more unsettling to Molly than Karl's or Zeb's. The other boys were being cruel, but Andres sounded as if he didn't want bruises, but blood.

"We have been through this ritual several times," the Sangheili said. "What will it take to put an end to it?"

"That's simple." Karl leaned in toward the Sangheili. "All we have to do is put an end to you."

That's when Gudam appeared between the two boys. "Hey, Karl! What's up?" she said in a dangerously happy voice.

The boys had been too focused on each other to see the Unggoy slipping up until the last second. She was so small and slight in her movements that it was easy to lose track of her. Both the Sangheili and the human boys edged back, completely off guard.

Karl didn't just move back though. He must have seen the Unggoy as a threat, and he lashed out with a punch. His fist caught Gudam on the right side of the tube that covered her nose. With a horrible crack, it went flying off to one side, along with a spatter of glowing blue blood.

Molly was stunned. She looked around the courtyard for someone, a teacher—*anyone*—who could help. There were only students, all of them staring at the scene, frozen.

Gudam spilled backward, her limbs splayed out in every direction. The pack on her back slewed off at an awkward angle and began leaking methane. She started coughing, clearly unable to properly breathe the oxygen all around her.

This had suddenly become very serious.

Kareem ran to Gudam and knelt down next to her, checking to see if she was all right. Molly wanted to do the same, but for some reason didn't. She just stood there, feeling helpless.

"You attack a little Unggoy?" The Sangheili stabbed a long finger at Karl. "For the crime of greeting you? This time you have gone too far."

The Sangheili was angry, this much Molly could clearly see. As much as she didn't like him or his kind, she couldn't blame him. Molly may not have had a long list of friends inside Onyx, but Gudam was about the friendliest creature Molly had ever met. It didn't matter to her what grievance Karl might have against the diminutive creature; she didn't deserve to get laid out like that. No one did.

"You think so?" Karl said. He had reeled back for an instant when he'd seen how badly he'd hurt Gudam. Now he stepped forward again, owning the attack and evidently hungry to mix it up with the Sangheili. Karl thought he had finally found something that pissed the alien off enough to drag him into a fight. "Let's see just how far we can take this."

Karl reached out and pushed the Sangheili. To Molly's surprise, the alien didn't stop him. He didn't raise a hand at all.

Molly scanned the courtyard again, hoping to find an adult this time. She saw other Sangheili fledglings. They were watching too. For a second, she thought they would step in to defend one of their kind. Yet . . . none of them even moved in the direction of the fight. Instead, once they discerned what was happening, they all turned away, completely uninterested. Molly didn't understand. *Are they going to let one of their kind get pummeled?*

"Some hinge-head you are," Karl growled, pushing the Sangheili again. "You going to just let me shove you around like that? Don't you have the guts to do anything about it?"

The Sangheili flexed his big fists. "I do not care to fight you, human."

"I didn't ask you that." Karl shoved him with both hands this time, much harder than before. "Did I?"

Still, the Sangheili only staggered back, regained his footing, and did nothing. He just glared at Karl as if he might snap at any moment and bite the boy's head off.

Karl sneered at the Sangheili. "You don't care what we might do to you?" Karl turned toward Gudam. "Or your little pet here?"

That was it for Molly. She couldn't just stand there and watch anymore. Not with Gudam lying there, hurt and struggling to breathe. *Someone has to stop this,* she thought. Then . . . without her recognizing it, her own anger suddenly took over and moved her feet for her.

Her instincts had kicked in again.

Molly barreled toward the conflict and came between the Unggoy and Karl. "Knock it off, all of you!"

Molly hated bullies. She always had. Especially the kind who picked on people smaller than them. It probably had something to do with her having had to fend for herself in the last two schools, or perhaps it was because of what had happened to her family on Paris IV.

The bottom line was that she didn't let anyone push her around. Not ever.

As Asha often told her, *It's not the size of the dog in the fight that matters. It's the size of the fight in the dog.* And Molly could fight big if someone pushed the right buttons.

Karl stepped back and gawked at her audacity. "Are you kidding me? *You're* going to stand up for that *thing*?" He clearly hadn't processed the possibility of a human defending an alien. Molly didn't blame him for that. She hadn't foreseen it herself until just a second before doing it.

"I don't care about *him* or *her* or *whatever*!" she said as she got up in his face. "*You* don't get to step up to someone minding their own business and start knocking them around!"

Taken aback momentarily, Karl recovered and glared at Molly, raising his hand to her much as he'd done to Gudam. Molly hadn't surprised him though. He wasn't about to smack her down out of some mistaken instinct of self-preservation, or out of some anger he'd held over from the war. He was just furious at her for having dared to try to stop his bullying. This time, he was going to hit a human being, and he was going to mean it.

Molly cocked back her leg preparing to kick him, but Karl knocked her flat before she could even strike. He had backhanded her across the jaw, and she felt a sting of pain as her lower lip split open against her teeth.

Molly fell to the ground, clutching her mouth. Although she'd been through a war and had dealt with all sorts of bullies in other schools, she'd never been in a real fistfight before. It wasn't the pain that shocked Molly, at least not at first. It was the idea that someone would actually hit her.

"Damn hinge-head hugger," Karl spat at her.

Molly pulled her hand away, and it was covered with blood.

Kareem launched himself at Karl. He came at him from the side but didn't get far. Zeb and Andres grabbed Kareem before he laid a hand on their friend. Together, they slammed Kareem to the ground, flat on his back. Molly heard the air escape his lungs as the wind was knocked out of him. Kareem was struggling to breathe now too.

Molly quickly recovered. She jumped to her feet and lunged at the boys, who'd begun kicking at Kareem. Just before she reached them, Karl stuck out his leg and tripped her. Rather than tackling Andres, she stumbled into him.

Andres shoved Molly back and took a step toward her, his fists up and ready. His knuckles darted out and slammed into her face before she could regain her balance. Molly stumbled backward, howling and holding her eye, trying to figure out what the hell had just happened and hoping he hadn't blinded her for life.

Someone's hands caught Molly and kept her on her feet.

She looked up to see Andres moving above her, his other fist cocked back to hammer at her again. Molly braced herself for the blow. This one was probably going to knock her out cold. These jerks would actually hit a girl.

Then a voice from behind her boomed out. "Hold it!"

Andres froze, his arm still back and ready but his eyes flung wide. He took a huge step back and put his hands in the air to show he had stopped.

Molly took a moment to blink the pain from her eye and watched her vision slowly clear. Satisfied that she hadn't gone blind but still wincing from the pain, she looked up to see who'd saved her.

It was a Sangheili instructor Molly had glimpsed earlier that day, the first male Elite she had ever seen in person and without any armor, unlike in the war vids she'd watched. The label outside his classroom had said that his name was Dinok 'Acroli, and apparently he specialized in xenolinguistics. This meant that he taught Sangheili how to speak to the humans, and vice versa.

Molly hadn't signed up for any of his classes. She had no interest in learning Sangheili or being taught by a giant monster. He was tall with deep indigo skin, and he very much fit the mold of the Elite warrior.

The Sangheili instructor approached with a powerful confidence and disciplined movements, towering over all of the children in the fight. Even the Sangheili youth—who turned out to have been the person who had caught Molly—was taken aback in Dinok's shadow. Despite not being dressed for war, the appearance of the massive Sangheili instructor had proven enough to subdue the entire crowd. Molly found herself legitimately scared for her life.

Then she realized the young Sangheili was still next to her. She jerked away, glaring at him through her swelling eye. She couldn't help but recoil sharply at the realization that he had *touched* her. She didn't need any help in this fight, certainly not from a Sangheili.

Dinok glowered down at each of the seven children in turn and shook his head in dismay. "You are all in a world of trouble."

For Molly, this was now officially her worst first day of school ever.

CHAPTER 10

Molly's Newparents weren't impressed by her getting into a fight on her first day at Onyx's school. They grounded her for the week. Since she had no social life, the punishment didn't mean all that much to Molly, but she decided not to point that out. She didn't need to give them a reason to come up with something worse.

In actuality, they weren't that upset by what had happened. Asha even congratulated Molly on standing up to a bully, while Yong got her a stim-adhesive to bring down the swelling on her eye and lip. She explained to him that she'd already used two in the school infirmary, but he insisted.

Asha and Yong cared less about Molly's getting in trouble at school than they did about her putting herself in danger, especially given the nature of the altercation and the clear tension between the species at Pax Institute. This was not the picture of tranquility Director Mendez had painted for them, but school scuffles probably didn't rank high on his list of security concerns.

Molly's official punishment at the Pax Institute was a one-day suspension, which Kareem got too. Karl, Zeb, and Andres were each sent home for a week. The two aliens involved weren't punished at all. That rankled Molly a bit because they were both at the center of the conflict, but since neither of them had thrown a punch, she couldn't argue with it.

The bullies all accused Molly of attacking them out of the blue, but the three weren't the most clever kids. They must have known the school's security cameras would vindicate her. However, the fact she had attacked Karl before he hit her had forced Kasha to punish her as well.

"You're getting off easy because you have only been at school a few hours and this is, of course, all new for you," Kasha told Molly in her office, a strange hybrid of human and Sangheili design that somehow felt both open and claustrophobic. "Because of this, however, your record is no longer clean. So do your best to stay out of trouble from here on out. Understood?"

Molly didn't feel that she deserved any scolding at all. She'd been trying to stop three bullies from beating the life out of two aliens—at least one of whom she should have left out to dry. But in the end, Molly understood. The headmaster had to deter fighting somehow.

It probably was just a rumor, but she heard Karl and Zeb's and Andres's parents took them out to dinner that night for "standing up to aliens." She found it hard to believe: *Who are these parents? How do people like that get picked to be part of this project? Aren't there intensive screenings to root those kinds of people out?*

Molly could rationalize her own fears. She had good reason to be nervous about the aliens, but she still wasn't about to start picking a fight with them. On top of that, she wasn't one of the adults hired to do research here. If this baffling rumor about the bullies' parents was true, it told a far bleaker story about Paxopolis than the city's name implied.

When Molly had a chance to unpack all that had happened that day with her Newparents, she found herself somewhat embarrassed by the whole thing. She hadn't intended to wind up on the side of aliens, even ones as harmless as Gudam. She'd been doing everything she could to avoid them until just minutes before the fight. But what made her even more uncomfortable was that the Sangheili fledgling had helped her.

Molly hadn't needed his help, and she certainly hadn't been looking for it. The last thing she wanted was for people to think she was incapable of fighting her own battles and so had to enlist the help of a Sangheili instead. She could take care of herself, especially with a bunch of jerks like those three. If she could have done it over again, she would have just ignored the whole incident and walked away.

"So why'd you do it then?" Asha asked. Asha had this annoying way of cutting through all the emotional clutter around any issue and getting right to the heart of it.

"Are you saying I did the wrong thing?" Molly asked, confused. Asha had seemed pretty supportive up till that point.

"Not at all. I'm asking why you stepped in to protect that Unggoy."

"I already told you about that."

Asha gave Molly a weird, soft smile. It told her that Asha knew the answer to her own question already. She was just waiting for Molly to catch up. "I didn't ask *what* you did. I asked *why*. Just give it some thought."

"You'll have plenty of time for that during your suspension," Yong said. He seemed to think the idea of Molly being punished was hilarious. Yong knew what Molly was capable of in academics, and how she'd spent the last few years as a hermit within her old school, never being involved in anything controversial. She'd finally done something of note in a social context—a fistfight—and he found it too comical to consider it anything more than an extended joke.

Unfortunately for her, Molly was the butt of that joke.

"I'm not going back to that school," she told them flat out. "You can't make me."

"You're just upset," Yong said. "Give it some time."

"We're sorry if we pushed you too fast," Asha said. "It's just that you have to take this first step at some point. You staying home isn't going to make this any better. And our work is ramping up."

"How can that be?" Molly asked. "Everything the Forerunners made has been lying around for more than a hundred thousand years. What's the sudden rush now? Is it that GOLIATH thing that you were talking about with Director Mendez and the Spartans?"

Yong frowned and exchanged a serious look with Asha. Molly had made a momentary lapse in the heat of the moment. She'd completely forgotten that she had been eavesdropping on that part of the conversation and wasn't supposed to know what they'd been chatting about. Yet another knee-jerk reaction of hers had gotten her into trouble.

"You shouldn't have been listening to that, Molly," Yong said, his eyes intensely serious.

"I'm sorry. You're right. I shouldn't have," Molly said plaintively.

But Yong didn't scold her. After Asha nodded, Yong spoke to Molly in a hushed tone with a stern look on his face. "Can you keep a secret?"

"What do you mean?" Molly asked.

"Look, you've been through a lot today. We know this move wasn't exactly what you wanted. I feel bad; Asha feels bad. This transition was tougher on you than either of us, and we're only days in. We want to level with you about why we're here."

"At least," Asha said, "to help you understand why this is so important. But you've got to keep this under your hat, Molly. If you don't, we can get in a *lot* of trouble."

"Not the kind of trouble you want us in either," Yong said, with a cold stare. "The kind that lasts forever."

"Okay, okay," Molly said. "What's the big deal?"

"Project: GOLIATH was focused on a large Forerunner machine Asha and I explored extensively years ago, hidden belowground on a colony world. Apparently it's not the only one. They've discovered more of them recently, these enormous and ancient machines. They're actually cropping up all over the galaxy. On inhabited worlds even."

"And this time it's different," Asha added. "They're not all just lying unresponsive below the ground anymore, which is how we found that one in the past. Something's happening to them, something potentially *bad*. The reason we're here is that ONI needs our help to figure out what that thing is."

Molly understood the facts logically, but she didn't see how any of it was relevant. "What does this have to do with me coming to Onyx and going to a school where I get beat up for defending aliens who I don't even like? If I don't want to go to the school again and I can learn from the networked tutor system at home—what does *that* have to do with your work?"

"We need you in school, Molly," Yong said, not beating around the bush. "You need to be around others your age, and you need to learn in a context like Pax Institute. You're not leaving the school. If it gets too difficult, we'll talk to the headmaster."

"We love you, Molly," Asha said with a concerned but sincere look on her face. "We're here for you. But we can't have you at home all day looking after yourself. We need to know that you're safe and someone's keeping an eye on you. And we want to impress upon you the importance of this project. Our work here on Onyx—it's not a game. It's really *that* serious. These machines, if they awaken . . . it's a matter of life or death for the people on those worlds."

"Fine," Molly said flatly, realizing that their tip of the hand was to show her she wouldn't get her way. "Just leave me alone."

She stormed upstairs and locked herself in her room. Perhaps she should have been happy that her slip of the tongue hadn't resulted in a more severe punishment, but she was done. Molly didn't want any excuses from them, or to have to relive the fight or her motivations, or any of that. She just wanted the day to end.

For the next few days, Molly's Newparents actually left her alone.

Molly didn't know if they thought that a kind of benign neglect was the best way to deal with her at the moment or if they were just too busy with their own work. Or maybe they realized how angry she was about having to go back to that school, that they didn't want to engage her on that topic again unless they had to. Sometimes Molly questioned their parental abilities, but taking her in had been a bit of a surprise for them. As she grew older, though, her questioning became more frequent. At the age of sixteen, it happened most of the time.

But if what they were saying about these incidents on other worlds was actually true? That this was a life-or-death situation? That certainly put a different spin on things.

As Molly came down from the frustrations she'd felt immediately after the fight at school, she recognized that her squabble with those kids was insignificant against the backdrop of what was taking place on Onyx. The things that Yong and Asha were dealing with were far more critical, and it was irrational for Molly to think otherwise.

She decided that she'd cut her Newparents some slack next

time they had a conversation, but she still wasn't sure when she'd be ready to go back to school. Without the Newparents at home to make her return, she'd been able to get away with hunkering down at home—at least for now.

Molly took advantage of her free time by soaking up as much as she could from the newsfeeds. What she saw confirmed her suspicions. Asha and Yong hadn't been joking about things heating up around human-occupied space. A litany of crazy rumors were coursing through the feeds, mostly about entire colonies going dark and the military being deployed in response.

Was another war brewing? Or was this connected to the machines Yong and Asha had mentioned? Seeing glimmers of the things her Newparents had mentioned being reported on Waypoint was both eerie and sobering.

Whatever's going on is real and scary. Real scary, even.

Molly suddenly realized that living inside a gigantic Forerunner shell surrounded by military personnel did make her feel a bit safer.

It didn't surprise her when Asha and Yong sent a comm message on Friday night saying they had to work through the weekend on-site. Molly wondered what that meant: *Where exactly is "on-site"? Exactly how connected is what they're working on here in Onyx to all those events out there?* Maybe they weren't as safe as they had told her they would be.

Molly figured that at least they wouldn't bother her about school during the weekend, but Monday still rocketed toward her like a maglev train. They clearly didn't want her to miss another day, but she wasn't sure she was ready to go back.

"We'll talk about this tonight," Asha told her when leaving the house on Sunday morning. From that, Molly knew that her self-enforced suspension from school was about to come to an end, so she began steeling herself for what lay ahead. Seeing those same kids: the ones she'd fought against, the ones who'd just gawked as it all went down, and even the ones she'd fought alongside . . . she just wanted to forget it all happened and never talk to any of them again.

That afternoon an unexpected visitor stopped by.

Molly went to answer the doorbell and found Spartan Lucy standing on her doorstep, dressed in her UNSC fatigues. "Permission to come inside?"

"Of course." Molly stepped aside and let her in, genuinely surprised. She hadn't seen Lucy—or Tom or Director Mendez—since the day she and her family had arrived. It was a big shield world, after all.

Lucy glanced around and then strode straight into the living room and sat in Asha's beat-up chair, which the family had brought with them from Aranuka. Molly offered Lucy something to drink, but she declined.

Molly found herself strangely calm, despite having a real-life Spartan sitting in her living room. A few weeks ago, she would have fainted.

"I'm here on unofficial business."

"Asha and Yong won't be back until tonight," Molly said. "They've been working around the clock on something."

Lucy nodded. "They have an important mission. But I said *unofficial*. I'm not here for them, I'm here for you. I'm here to encourage you to go back to school."

Molly sat down in Yong's chair and folded her arms across her chest, taking a deep breath. "Yeah, well, I don't want to."

"We all have things we don't want to do, Molly, but we do them anyway. Your mission while you're here in Onyx is to get an education."

"I can do that at home."

"At the Pax Institute."

"Why?"

"You already know why, Molly. Part of Paxopolis's purpose is to show that humans and other intelligent species can actually live and work together—in a real and authentic way. That's one of the main reasons for this whole thing."

Molly gently rubbed her eye, which still ached. "And what if we can't?"

"That was a human who gave you that shiner, not an Elite."

"Because I was dumb enough to step between him and an alien."

"That alien's name is Bakar. And it happened because you were brave enough to step in and help."

"For all the good it did me."

"I said you were brave. Not smart."

Lucy came across as so serious that it took Molly a moment to realize she was joking. Spartans had an extremely dry sense of humor, apparently. At least this one did.

Molly wondered if that had something to do with their training. Some rumors alleged that the Spartans had been raised from childhood to be soldiers. It had always seemed far-fetched to Molly, but not so much now that she'd met a couple of them.

"Well, how could I help that?" Molly said, growing more offended as she thought about what had been said. "There were three of them, and they were all bigger and stronger than me."

Lucy smiled at her. "You're about the same height as me, Molly."

"Yeah, but I'm no Spartan. You probably could have taken those boys down blindfolded."

"Yeah, well, they *were* boys. But honestly, it's not because I'm stronger than them."

"Well, that doesn't hurt. They were—"

"It's because of my training and my experience. I've taken on plenty of opponents much larger and even stronger than me, and I laid them out when I needed to."

"With a weapon, yeah."

"Not always. Working as a Spartan often isn't about charging in with guns blazing. For most of our operations out in the field, it's much more efficient to get the job done quietly. And trust me, I've done *that* many times."

Molly shrugged at her. "I don't see what good that does me—unless you're going to sign me up to become a Spartan."

"That's not what I had in mind. But maybe I can help you out with some training."

"Are you kidding?" Molly was genuinely shocked. "You're going to teach me to *fight*? What about the headmaster? Wouldn't she have a problem with this?"

Lucy pursed her lips for a moment. "It was Kasha's idea, actually. And it's not teaching you how to fight. If you're up for it, I can teach you self-defense—how to protect yourself and others. This isn't something you would use against the kids at school, but a way for you to help hone some of that fierceness you've got coiled up inside. It's pretty obvious you're not cut from the researcher cloth, like your parents. You've got a warrior in you."

Molly's breath caught in her chest. A Spartan was offering to give her combat lessons? She couldn't believe it. It was almost too good to be true. She tried to compose herself before responding.

"I'd love that, actually."

Lucy smiled. "Excellent. Tom and I have actually been talking about this with Director Mendez for a little while. You'll technically be our first student."

First student? This told Molly that they had bigger plans for this class of theirs, but that somehow she had been selected to go first. That was profound, almost too much for her to take in.

"Our goal is to teach you discipline and defense, not to make you into a weapon. We'll hold classes at the Pax Institute, right after school."

"Ah." Then Molly saw the catch. She'd been trapped into going back to school. "So this class is only for kids going to the Pax Institute? That's the kicker?"

Lucy shrugged. "I'm not trying to trick you into this, Molly. But if you're going to stay home the entire time you're with us in Onyx, are you really going to need self-defense lessons? This is for kids who are willing to come out of their shell and learn what it looks like to be a soldier—even though I'm guessing your parents won't be terribly thrilled about it."

Lucy was completely right. They wouldn't be thrilled about it at all, but the opportunity had come directly from a Spartan and involved Molly's peacefully agreeing to go back to school. They'd at least see it as a worthwhile compromise, she hoped.

"Fine. I'll go back to school. For now."

"That's all I ask." Lucy got up to leave. "If your parents are okay with this arrangement, we'll see you tomorrow after classes."

"I hope this will be worth it."

Lucy gave her a wry smile. "Molly, that is the last thing you have to worry about in the universe."

CHAPTER 11

When Molly finally returned to school the next day, she went with the benefit of knowing that she wouldn't have to deal with Karl, Zeb, or Andres for the time being, since they were still on weeklong suspensions. The same wasn't true of anyone else there, of course.

If people had ignored Molly on her first day, now they treated her as if she had the plague. She'd never been shunned before, but at first she didn't mind it much. In fact, it made things a lot easier. Molly hadn't come back to make friends. All she could think about all day was just how much she wanted to get through her time inside this stupid sphere and blast the hell out of there as soon as possible.

As far as Molly was concerned, she was living in a prison. She didn't need to associate with the other inmates. She just needed to serve her time and then get out at her first chance to do so. Moving from class to class with her head down, she tried desperately to focus on the training that awaited her at the end of the day.

When math class came around, she saw Kareem and Gudam. Teacher Aphrid—whom she'd never before met—greeted her at the door. Without inhibition, the Unggoy sprang toward Molly with a spontaneous hug that she couldn't deflect.

"Thanks so much for helping out my little Gudam," the Unggoy said in her high-pitched voice. The teacher's grateful embrace was cold and scaly and *very* unpleasant, but Molly could tell that it was sincere.

The Unggoy looked much like Gudam, though to Molly all of their kind looked similar. The teacher was about a hand span taller than Gudam, though, with a shell a bit more vibrantly blue in parts. Unsurprisingly, Aphrid seemed to have the same aggressively optimistic attitude that marked Gudam.

Molly had a hard time comprehending that. Aphrid's child had almost been seriously harmed by another student who hated aliens. To Molly, the strange glee about the entire circumstance was the most alien thing about her.

At first blush, Molly found that unappealing. She even hated it. Aphrid's "little Gudam" had been attacked and probably wouldn't ever truly be safe in a school with kids such as Karl, Zeb, and Andres.

Who knows what would have happened if Gudam hadn't been able to get to her methane in time? Who knows what might happen once those punks come back? Molly started to wonder if this attribute of Aphrid's was one of the reasons the Covenant so easily put down Unggoy and used them as expendable soldiers by the thousands.

But Molly also found something about the Unggoy's demeanor— a happiness that seemed unshakable—vaguely infectious. It seemed impossible to remain irritated with Aphrid, even for the length of class. Apparently the Unggoy teacher refused to let her joy be controlled by others. There was something heartening in that.

In the meantime, Gudam seemed perfectly fine and was just as talkative as ever. Molly hadn't given much thought to her since the event but found herself relieved that the Unggoy hadn't been seriously injured.

"Momma Beskin patched me right up as soon as I got home," she said, pointing to her jaw, which to Molly didn't show any sign of injury at all—or perhaps she just couldn't tell. "Poppa Marfo was angry about it, but Momma Aphrid managed to smooth the rough parts out of his shell. By the time I finished telling him everything, he insisted that we invite you over for dinner!"

Gudam looked up at Molly with wide, expectant eyes, suddenly quiet, which caught her completely off guard. *Has an Unggoy family just invited me over to their home?*

"That's very kind," Molly said, trying to find a way out of the invitation. "But I'm not even sure what foods Unggoy eat."

"Oh, we eat all sorts of things!" Gudam said with a wide grin. It seemed as if she'd already planned to overcome any objections Molly might pose. The little alien had thought this through. "Mostly we stick to Unggoy cuisine when we can, which is what you humans call seafood, of course, but we can really eat anything. Here in Onyx, most of the food is the human kind, so we eat lots of that too."

Fortunately for Molly, the class began at that very moment. She wouldn't have to give Gudam a firm answer . . . *yet*. Molly couldn't help but notice a few of the other human students giving her sidelong glances about it, but she ignored them. Molly might not want to dine in an Unggoy home, but that was her choice to make, not theirs. She didn't need their approval.

By the time lunch came around, Molly had already decided that she'd try to find a different place to sit. She felt that being somewhere else was the best way to put everything that had happened behind her. Perhaps if she ignored everyone, people would just leave her alone, and the day's end would come quicker.

When she finally got her food, Molly scanned the hall for an empty seat. Gudam and Kareem were already sitting at a table together with no one else around. She attempted to pretend that she didn't see them and hunted for another place to sit. The last thing she wanted was to perpetuate the notion she had some kind of friendship with those two. But every time Molly made her way toward a table full of humans, their glares forced her to veer away. And she had no plans sit at one of the tables filled with Sangheili or Unggoy.

Only *one* other table had lots of free seats besides the one that Gudam and Kareem were at. One Sangheili student was eating there, but Molly figured she could just sit as far away from him as possible. The Sangheili looked up at her as she walked toward the table, and then she finally recognized him.

Bakar.

The same Sangheili whom she'd gotten in trouble with the other day.

Molly was ready to about-face when she realized she'd passed the point of no return. She'd committed already. If she turned away now, it'd be even more awkward, and she definitely didn't want him to think she was a weakling—or to be forced to admit that she'd seen Kareem and Gudam's table.

The last thing she wanted to do was to sit down and talk more about Unggoy dining habits while trying to eat her own lunch. Even the thought was nauseating. Sitting across from this Bakar had to be the better option.

Molly picked out a chair at that table as far from Bakar as she could manage and placed down her tray without acknowledging the Sangheili's presence. Before she was even fully in the chair, he raised his eyes, cold and unblinking, and seemed to scowl at her. She quickly dropped her eyes to her food and began to eat.

Bakar didn't.

He hissed at her, ending in a low growl.

"What are you doing here?" he said in Molly's language. His voice, though higher pitched than Dinok's, was formidably and heavily laced with menace.

"I need a place to eat," Molly said, her face stern. "This one was open. Do the math."

Molly didn't care to explain herself more than that or to unpack the idiom. She just lowered her eyes and dug back into her meal.

Bakar stared at her. Then he hissed again. "I do not want your friendship."

That stopped Molly cold. She dropped her fork and shot the Sangheili the hardest glare she'd ever given. "That works out perfectly then, because you don't have it."

"You came to my aid against those three *nishum*, and now you wish to sit and share a meal with me?" He waggled his head at Molly as though something were self-evident by that action.

Molly leaned over the table and spoke to Bakar in a low voice, not bothering to hide her disdain for him any longer. "Take it easy, alien. I stepped in to help *Gudam*, not you." Then she pushed her tray away and stood up, preparing to leave. "And now I've lost my appetite."

"You made me look weak. Like I needed the aid of a human."

"Next time, I'll just let them bust in your lizard face."

"That would be the more favorable thing to do."

Molly let out a bitter laugh. "Are you asking me for a *favor*? Seriously?"

Bakar scrunched all four of his mandibles together tightly. His face was fierce and tense, and he looked as if he was attempting to bite back his words. Then he pushed his tray away as well. The two stared at each other in silence for a moment.

"Just leave me alone," he finally said.

Then Gudam came up and set her tray down on the table, equidistant from both Bakar and Molly, the Unggoy's beady eyes darting back and forth between the two. Molly had been so focused on Bakar that when Gudam appeared, she almost jumped out of her seat.

"Hey!" Gudam nearly shouted, completely oblivious of the argument going on. "You must have missed me and Kareem when you were looking for a table."

Then Gudam ungracefully clambered into a chair and kept talking as though that were the most normal thing to do. Molly looked from the Sangheili to the Unggoy, then took a deep breath and leaned back in her chair.

"I know how easy that is to do," Gudam said. "For one, I'm so short that you can't help but overlook me. Get it?"

Kareem approached slowly from behind the Unggoy, looking entirely uncomfortable about the situation. He must have read between the lines and probably knew that Molly didn't want to be Gudam's friend, no matter how excited about that possibility the Unggoy might be, but what had to be even more uncomfortable for him was how to navigate the obvious tension between Molly and Bakar, who sat scowling at each other.

"And as far as Kareem goes," Gudam said, still in her own world, "well, he's a male human. I find them hard to tell apart, don't you?"

Molly took a sip of water and swallowed. Her lunch was already ruined. What did she have to lose by talking to an Unggoy who wanted to accidentally poison her over dinner?

"I could pick Kareem out of a crowd," she said to Gudam, grimacing at the awkward situation. "But I am a human, you know. Telling them apart is more important to me."

"I suppose it is!" the Unggoy said, somehow excited by that. "How amazing that must be, to have grown up with so many strange creatures around you at all times. I mean, it's hard for me to imagine. My clutchlings and I look almost identical. Our parents can tell us apart, but it's hard for anyone outside the family to manage it, even among other Unggoy."

As her nerves started to settle, Molly took a deep breath and asked herself a simple question. *What do I have to lose?*

Peering hard at the Unggoy, Molly asked, "You *are* Gudam, aren't you?"

The Unggoy stopped for a moment, trying to process if Molly was serious, then spontaneously cackled long and hard. It was so loud that everyone in the dining hall turned for a moment to look for the origin of the sound.

Gudam slowed down and readied her response. "Why would I tell *you* that?" She gasped for air between each word. "That would only ruin the surprise!"

"Enough!" Bakar spoke so loudly that it caused Molly to flinch. He stood up from the table and stormed away, no doubt thinking they were foolish children who had spoiled his brooding.

The three of them silently watched him leave. Not until the Sangheili had completely exited the building for the recreation yard did Molly breathe a sigh of relief. Until that moment, she'd been slightly worried that Bakar might be angry enough to physically take his frustrations out on her.

"He's a little touchy about the fight," Kareem said.

"Why?" Molly asked. "*He* didn't get into any trouble."

"That's the problem," Kareem said, finally sitting down. "The other Sangheili fledglings here expect him to stand up for himself and knock the insolence out of any stupid *nishum* who dares taunt him. When he doesn't do that, they give him hell for it."

"*Nishum?* Why does everyone keep saying that?"

"It's what the Sangheili call humans, like their version of *hinge-head*," Kareem said, looking down toward the table. "Not exactly flattering. I think it means 'intestinal parasite' or something."

"Gross," Molly said with an expression that matched. "So, why *doesn't* he knock those boys around? He seems perfectly angry enough to do it."

Kareem shrugged. "Not sure exactly. Some of the students I've overheard talking about Bakar claim he's a bit of a pacifist, especially as far as male Sangheili are concerned. He doesn't want to fight anyone unless he absolutely has to, and the others think he's a coward for it."

"It's also why he gets picked on," Gudam said. "He's the only Sangheili who will take it."

"Couldn't the others stick up for him?" Molly asked.

"They could, but it's offensive and shameful to do so," Kareem said. "In their culture, you do these sorts of things for yourself, or you suffer the consequences. Survival of the fittest in every sense. Things have gotten even worse for Bakar since the incident the other day. Apparently, others are pressuring him hard to take down one of the humans who started all of this."

"Good," Molly said enthusiastically. "He ought to get back at those jerks. He should go after them off school property and beat the daylights out of them. That might be what it takes to finally shut them up for good." She pulled her tray close now that Bakar was gone. The food was cold, but eating it was better than nothing. "What's stopping him?"

"Maybe he's already seen enough violence in his day," Gudam responded solemnly. "I hear he lost his mother in the war, and he never talks about the rest of his family. That's pretty unusual for a Sangheili, though—the pursuit of peace, that is.

"They tend to think with their weapons. They brutalized my people during the war, I'm told, although I didn't see any of that personally, of course. In the Covenant, my fellow Unggoy were little better than slaves to be ordered around—and kicked when we weren't doing our jobs fast enough."

Molly knew the background of the Unggoy to some degree, but she hadn't thought about how it might affect them on a personal level at all. The Unggoy had certainly been unwilling participants in the war, a species that didn't have much of a choice but to go along while the Sangheili mercilessly abused them. In the Covenant, they'd been victims too, and looking at Gudam, Molly couldn't help but feel compassion for the small creature.

It did not, however, change her mind about going to dinner at Gudam's house.

"But Bakar isn't like that?" Molly asked.

Gudam shook her head. "He hates the war—hates even talking about it. He's very unlike his fellows in that way. I have only one class with Sangheili, and he is in it. Lots of them like to go on about how they long for a battle in which they can finally prove themselves. They just don't have anyone to fight these days, especially in here. They're kind of a peculiar breed of creature, always so hungry for violence."

Molly couldn't help but marvel a bit at Gudam's description. The Unggoy was far more contemplative and well-balanced than Molly had given her credit for. "What happened to the rest of your kind after the war?"

"There are many Unggoy out there." Gudam nibbled something on her plate that looked like rubber. Molly looked away when her stomach started to turn. "Some went home to Balaho, others are employed on different worlds—some even remain slaves. I'm sure there are a few insane ones who have taken up arms with hostile factions like the Servants of the Abiding Truth or what's left of the Covenant. They would rather keep the old ways than follow the Arbiter and his Swords of Sanghelios toward some kind of peace."

Molly had her back to the rest of the room while Gudam was talking, so she didn't see the drink pouch come sailing over her shoulder until it landed square in the middle of the table. It splattered directly on top of Bakar's abandoned tray and sent the plates there scattering, splashing cold liquid and leftover scraps of food everywhere.

Molly wound up with her entire face and chest coated with the bluish drink and a pale white paste Bakar had been eating, something the color and consistency of bird excrement. The stench was unbearable.

She leaped to her feet in a cold rage, spinning around and shouting at the rest of the dining hall. "Who did that?"

No one took credit. A bunch of the students farther away from Molly's table burst out laughing instead, which only infuriated her more. She didn't have anyone to focus her wrath on, though, which made things even worse. There were just too many of them, and in the moment she felt as though they were all against her.

After glaring for a few seconds, completely covered in food and drink, Molly spun on her heel and made for the exit, determined to find a restroom and clean herself up as best as she could.

"You eat with a filthy animal, and you're going to get dirty!" someone shouted from the other side of the dining hall. The laughter was even louder this time.

And Molly's anger burned even hotter.

CHAPTER 12

After the Pale Blade and his splinter strike team of Servants exterminated all the humans at the portal site, Dural 'Mdama found that his only regret was that there had not been more of them. His heart surged as they cut their foes down. When the brief battle was spent, he joined his warriors in their cries of triumph. These were the first humans Dural had ever bested, but they would certainly not be the last.

Buran attempted to dampen their joy by pointing out the obvious fact that the humans would be missed by those who had sent them. Dural knew that was a reasonable concern, but he quickly put an end to Buran's complaint by having the Servants toss the bodies out into the darkness, where the monsters that had frightened the humans in the first place could have them. If the gods were with the Servants, any humans who came looking for their allies would likely think that the creatures had killed them.

After all, Dural considered, *how could the Servants of the Abiding Truth have possibly gained entry into Onyx?*

But he certainly was not foolish enough to stay there and spoil the secret of their incursion. It was one thing to take on a handful of humans with an advance strike force, but a major reprisal by their enemies could have wiped out his team completely and wasted any advantage they now held.

The small group of Servants swiftly returned to the first site they had entered on Onyx, and Dural made Even Keel seal off the portal to the place where the monsters roamed. They would have to try another location and yet another, if need be, until the right fortification availed itself to them.

The next place they found via the portal system stood entirely abandoned, and this one had plenty of space for all of their forces. According to Even Keel, it was approximately a hundred kilometers from the primary human settlement and in a completely unoccupied territory, which put plenty of room between them and their foes. The chances were incredibly small that the humans would locate the Servants there, much less accidentally stumble upon them, yet it allowed them an opportunity to spy on the humans from a safe distance.

The location turned out to be even better than Dural had imagined. It was large and well protected, with a receiving portal capable of letting them finally send through much of what they had originally brought to Hesduros. Panom would no doubt be furious when the Servants that Dural had left behind began reneging on his original promise, transporting much of their arsenal into Onyx, but that was due to Panom's own foolishness.

Once the splinter team had set up camp there, the Pale Blade called the rest of his warriors from Hesduros, and they ferried as much of their weaponry and equipment as they could manage to their new fortification. Panom would have to make due with whatever remained, which, to Dural, was still far more than the weak kaidon deserved. Many of the heavy vehicles had to remain behind regardless and would guard the portal on Hesduros until he found a way to bring them through to Onyx.

The new site was a large Forerunner structure composed almost entirely of a seamless ivory substance with angular and geometric adornments. Inside, the structure's primary space was a long chamber with a narrow, perpendicular navelike segment at its center. As the structure rose upward, it had dozens of floors with different configurations. The lowest lay entirely underground, while ramps and interwoven passages rose to each of the higher levels.

The level where they had emerged through the portal stood twenty meters above Onyx's surface, with several pathways to parapets and turrets. The most impressive aspect of this place was the ceiling, which climbed another hundred more levels above the highest floor, almost entirely out of sight. Vast, semitransparent apertures allowed light to flood this structure all the way to the very bottom, but despite its general openness, it somehow also felt entirely secure.

Clearly, the home of a god, Dural thought to himself.

He named the place the *loah t'mok croiha ava mid 'telecam*, which in his tongue meant "The Great Cathedral of the Esteemed Avu Med 'Telcam." Dural hoped it paid appropriate homage to the late field master, although most of his warriors would simply refer to it in shorthand going forward as the Cathedral.

It certainly reminded him of the cathedral-strongholds of old Sanghelios. The massive structure was formed around three spires, each of which launched up into the arched ceilings, with buttresses so high that they could almost not be seen from the ground. Its very nature inspired awe and reverence for its creators, making it the perfect fortress for the Servants of the Abiding Truth.

It took Dural's warriors days to get everything into the structure, and even more to effectively install their weapons and vehicles to the Pale Blade's liking. By the time they were finished, what had been a desolate chamber was now transformed into an impenetrable and fully weaponized citadel.

The site was entirely covered by several dozen gunner nests, including a variety of plasma turrets and directed energy emplacements, as well as explosive mortars, flak cannons, and targeting sensors they had placed with strategic care in the surrounding dense forest.

To Dural, it seemed as if the Cathedral could withstand anything the humans could throw at it, just shy of an attack from one of their nuclear devices. He was pleased, but he could tell that discontentment was growing among the Sangheili.

"Your warriors are getting restless," Ruk said, as he, Dural, and Buran surveyed their accomplishments from a vantage point high in the Cathedral. "They have tasted battle once on this world, and now they ache for more."

"As do I," Dural assured Ruk. "We did not come here to set up a keep only to become farmers. I already have plans in motion that will bring us the kind of victory that has eluded Jul 'Mdama and his Covenant for so many years."

"And just how do you propose to do that?" Buran said, thinly veiling his contempt for the young leader. "Will you attack another group of weaklings to prove our superiority?"

The old shipmaster had become surlier with each day they spent inside Onyx. It was as if the very air in the place irritated him. Dural wasn't entirely sure what to make of this growing insolence, only that it tired him.

When Avu Med 'Telcam had been alive, Buran had held back such impudence, but now things had changed. Buran had never been fond of Dural's relationship with the field master, nor was he pleased with the Pale Blade's rise to power. It only made sense that Buran was uncomfortable taking orders from a warrior decades younger, and he finally had reached the point at which he meant to vocalize it.

Dural knew that the day was quickly approaching when his patience with the fossil would run dry and he would be forced to put the Sangheili down.

"We *are* superior," Dural said. "We have nothing to prove."

"Or perhaps you simply want to alert the entirety of the human military that we are here so they can rain down death upon us while we cower in this Cathedral of yours?"

Perhaps today is that day, Dural thought. His hand snaked out at a speed Buran could not foresee and struck him in the throat. The grizzled Sangheili collapsed next to him, grasping his neck and struggling for air.

The Pale Blade loomed over him, hissing, "You are fortunate that we three are alone here, Buran 'Utaral! If you had tried to shame me in front of my warriors, I would have been forced to tear your head from your shoulders!"

Buran nodded a weak apology through his coughing and choking.

"We have weapons and warriors," Ruk said to Buran. "But we lack heavier vehicles and ships. With some effort, we managed to move a number of Ghosts and Banshees through the portal, as well as our Shades, but nothing larger than those. We must be strategic and careful in our planning, as the Pale Blade no doubt has been. If we attack the human settlement head-on with our current forces, they are sure to slaughter us."

"You speak the truth, Ruk," Dural said, leering down at Buran, who still grasped at his neck. "But there is something we require even *more*. Fortunately, we have the favor of the gods on our side. What we need will certainly come to us if we strive for it."

"And how shall we do this?" Ruk said, evidently confused by Dural's vague language. The younger warrior was not ready to challenge the Pale Blade in the way that Buran had. At least not yet. Not after Dural had made such an example of the pathetic old shipmaster.

"We have managed to transport most of our warriors here, less the small contingent we left behind on Hesduros to safeguard

Song of Wrath. That has freed up Even Keel to explore the portal network on Onyx itself and to begin the hunt for others of its own kind: Huragok *native* to this world."

"I take it the Engineer was successful?"

"Less than I hoped for, but more than I feared. It discovered evidence that one of its kind is currently working in a part of the sphere that it called the Repository."

"Only one?" Ruk said, surprised. He backed away as Dural glared at him. "I mean no offense, Pale Blade, but I had thought that this place might be filled with such creatures."

"It may well be," Dural said evenly, keeping his temper under control. "But it is a large place, and if there was a communications network the Huragok used here at one time, it has long since fallen into disrepair. Finding them will be painstaking work. We are fortunate to have discovered even one of them so soon."

Buran, regaining his breathing, lifted himself up and away from Dural, remaining low on the ground to avoid angering him once more. When Buran spoke, his voice was but a whispered rasp. "Where is this Repository?"

"That is the best part. It is but a short distance from the main human settlement."

Ruk rubbed his lower mandibles, suspicious. "That seems like quite a coincidence."

Dural shook his head and clacked his mandibles. "Not so. Our Huragok located this one because it is *already* working with the humans. Otherwise, it would not have been so active or readily detected."

Ruk's eyes widened. "So the humans have already captured a Huragok. Perhaps they do have more?"

Dural nodded. "And taking it from them shall be so much sweeter than simply finding one alone, but it also requires a bit more planning. This Repository is sure to be guarded, and it is far away from here. We will have to infiltrate it by way of a portal."

"That may limit the number of warriors we can move into place there at once," Ruk said.

"Yes, it will. But do not be concerned. While we may not have vehicles, the Servants of the Abiding Truth have another asset we can bring into play as we secure this second Huragok. The same one that our kind has always wielded since the beginning."

Ruk stared back at Dural expectantly.

"Chaos," the Pale Blade told him. "Utter chaos."

CHAPTER 13

More trouble?" Tom-B292 said as he kicked his Jackrabbit into high gear. The two front tires on the armored tricycle pushed together, giving him more maneuverability at high speed. "Seems like that's getting to be a habit."

"Inside the perimeter this time," Lucy-B091 said as she slung her identical vehicle out and away from Tom's. That would give her a better view of the upcoming target once they crested the next hill and keep them spread apart in case of a surprise attack.

Tom enjoyed the way the Jackrabbits hugged the ground, almost too close for safety. The two Spartans usually spent so much time in aircraft when they left Paxopolis and Trevelyan that he relished the chance to zip along the ground at speed, watching the landscape roll by beneath his wheels. He just wished he knew exactly what they were headed for.

"So," Tom said over his comm. "Sensors tripped at this location? That's not particularly informative."

"That's the Huragok for you. They know something's happening out here. They're just not sure exactly what."

Tom grunted at that. "You realize where we're headed, right?"

"It's the place where Jul 'Mdama escaped from Onyx. You think Prone to Drift would ever let me forget that? He'd never had anyone blackmail him like that before."

"Think it's a coincidence?"

"When it comes to Jul 'Mdama?" Lucy chuckled.

As they crested the hill, spread plenty far apart, Tom spotted the structure they were looking for. He couldn't possibly have guessed its original purpose, but like many Forerunner structures, the massive spire in the middle of it made it seem vaguely church-like to him.

"Looks quiet from here." He gunned the Jackrabbit toward the structure. "Think one of our people tripped something off by accident?"

"ONI kept the place pretty much off-limits once they wrapped up the investigation after Jul disappeared. They scoured it from top to bottom. There's nothing there for the folks in Paxopolis to learn from—wait."

Lucy spun her Jackrabbit to a stop, and Tom slowed down and began to serpentine his rig back and forth to take up speed. He let the front wheels separate again to give the vehicle more stability. "What is it?"

"Down there, near the entrance. You see them?"

Tom peered in that direction and immediately spotted the problem: a set of floating objects, each one a pair of two boom arms centered around a metallic, fully weaponized housing. "Sentinels!"

Tom and Lucy had seen far too many of these Forerunner machines back when they'd been helping train the Spartan-III Gammas back on the original Onyx. It had turned out the entire planet had been built upon a framework of trillions of Sentinels arrayed together.

"Looks like something's rattled the natives," Lucy said. "They're coming this way!"

Dozens of them—perhaps hundreds—were racing toward

Tom and Lucy, their beam weapons' primer glowing brighter with each moment. It was almost as if they'd been waiting for the Spartans to arrive—or someone, at least—but hadn't had any idea from which direction they might come. Now, though, they seemed like a nest of angry hornets who were ready to sting the intruders to death.

"Opening fire." Tom grabbed the controls of the machine gun mounted on the rear of the Jackrabbit, from which position it could fire in a wide arc right over his head.

The first line of Sentinels tumbled to the ground, riddled with bullets. Lucy let loose with a burst from her machine gun, and she cut the next line of Sentinels from the sky.

Then the hostile machines got tricky. They fanned out to make themselves harder to target all at once, and arced around Tom and Lucy in both directions.

"They're trying to surround us," Lucy said.

"Go left. I'm heading right. Force them to spread out farther."

Lucy did as Tom suggested. Once they were distant enough from each other, they spun in place, putting their backs to each other to give themselves the widest possible fields of fire. The whole while, they kept gunning down the oncoming Sentinels, pausing only long enough to let the barrels of their weapons cool.

The Sentinels came at them in waves, but Tom and Lucy kept their focus on the machines and patiently mowed them down. A few of the Sentinels' energy beams lanced through the hail of slugs the Spartans fired, forcing Tom and Lucy to juke back and forth to dodge them, but aside from a few scorch marks, the Jackrabbits survived just fine. Once the ranks of the Sentinels thinned, the Spartans set to chasing them down, mopping up the last of them until the skies stood clear and the ground lay littered with Forerunner parts.

Tom tapped his comm to report in to Mendez. "Had a slew of Sentinels waiting here for us, Chief. All cleared out now."

"Any idea what they were doing there?" Mendez asked. "We haven't had any Forerunner incursions like that inside the gates for months."

"Moving in to inspect," Lucy said.

The pair of Spartans zoomed toward the structure and parked their Jackrabbits a short walk from it. They leaped out of their roll cages, unlimbered their assault rifles, and stalked into the building's main compartment, the one Jul 'Mdana had escaped from.

Lucy pointed at a thin layer of sand covering the structure's floor. "Tracks here. Looks like Sangheili."

Tom spoke into the comm. "Any chance this was due to some kind of field trip? Maybe a detachment of our own Sangheili came out here for some reason?"

"I'll check the logs," Mendez said skeptically. "But that would be the first I'd heard of it."

"There's only one other possibility," Lucy said. "We have a breach."

Tom grimaced at that thought. Had someone figured out a way to get into Onyx from outside, using the portal system? "If so, our jobs just got a lot harder."

CHAPTER 14

Once school was over for the day, Molly raced over to the Pax Institute's gym for her first self-defense lesson from the Spartans. After the incident in the dining hall, she was looking forward to the catharsis of stretching her muscles and beating the crap out of someone else for a change. Not that she had much chance of laying a fist on a Spartan, but she knew it'd be worth trying it just to work out the rage simmering in her since lunch.

When Molly burst into the gym, she found both Lucy and Tom waiting for her, sporting recreation fatigues emblazoned with the Spartan branch logo: a strident eagle with its wings spread wide. It held three arrows in one claw and a bolt of lightning in the other.

Despite having suffered through an awful day, Molly flashed a grateful smile when she entered. She still couldn't believe this was happening. *How many people get to train in self-defense with actual Spartans?* Back on Aranuka, she could never have imagined this in a million years.

Then she spotted a handful of other students there, and her cheeks flushed.

She instantly understood what had happened. She might have been the first student the Spartans had approached, but she hadn't been the last. She knew *exactly* who the three others were.

Molly could understand having Kareem there. He hadn't done any better in the fight than she had. He was also new here like her, and both of them needed as much help as they could get.

But then there was Gudam, which didn't make any sense to Molly at all. No matter how hard the little Unggoy trained, she would always be shorter and weaker than nearly everyone around her. Molly couldn't imagine what good teaching her self-defense would do. Why would Tom and Lucy waste the time?

The one that really pissed Molly off was Bakar. He was already so much bigger than both her and Kareem, and he wasn't even full grown yet. He didn't need self-defense lessons. In fact, he was one of the reasons the idea of self-defense appealed to Molly. And wasn't he against fighting altogether?

Molly threw up her hands, glaring at Lucy. "Forget it. This wasn't the agreement. The deal's off."

"What?" Tom said, confused. "Are you kidding?"

Lucy came jogging after Molly and caught up with her before she made it back out the door. "What's wrong?"

"What do you think?" Molly pointed back at the others.

Lucy gave her a concerned look. "Did you think these were going to be private lessons, Molly?"

"I don't even care about that," she lied. "What are *aliens* doing here?"

"They were in the fight with you. They were on your side. I watched the recording. You all need the same help."

"Even Gudam?" Molly chopped her hand out at about waist height. "Even Bakar?" She brought her hand above her head, emphasizing the ludicrous height difference between the two. To Molly, what had been a serious training session for a girl who needed to survive in this new hostile school had now become a circus.

"Are you saying that this is all about size?"

Molly wasn't sure *what* she was saying. She was just angry, but she was fine with hijacking Lucy's line of thought. "Sure! I mean, just look at them. I could practically step on Gudam, and Bakar could do the same to me!"

Lucy gave Molly a wistful shake of her head. "I get what you mean, but you're absolutely wrong."

"Are you trying to tell me that size doesn't matter in a fight? Is it fair for me to fight Gudam? Or Bakar to fight me?"

Lucy put a hand on Molly's shoulder and walked her over to the others. "You're making two basic mistakes, Molly. First, there's no such thing as a fair fight. Fair fights are fiction, they don't exist. Not out there beyond the walls of a gym, at least. Someone *always* has the advantage. If you're a smart fighter, that someone is you."

"Fine," Molly said, "but doesn't it seem like it would be better for me to spar with someone closer to my level of ability?"

"In that sense, you will be," Tom said, "because none of you has much in the way of combat skills at all."

"Second," Lucy said, "size and strength do matter in a fight, but not as much as you might think. Look at me, for instance."

Lucy had brought this up yesterday at Molly's house. It was true. Despite her being a Spartan, Lucy wasn't any taller than Molly. She could look Lucy straight in the eye, though doing that did little to boost Molly's confidence. Something cold and steely in the Spartans' eyes made Molly refuse to hold their gazes for much longer than a few seconds.

"The way you see it, Tom should be able to take me out without any trouble at all, right?"

Molly glanced at the man, who was chuckling at Lucy's proposal.

"But that's not the fact. We spar with each other and the other Spartans assigned to Onyx all the time." Lucy turned to Tom. "What are we at now?"

The man shrugged. "Who keeps score?"

Lucy pointed at herself and then at Tom. "Five hundred and forty-three to five hundred and twenty-one."

Tom shook his head. "I actually wouldn't have thought it was that close."

"There's more to fighting than height, mass, or strength," Lucy said directly to Molly. "Speed, determination, and skill matter just as much, if not more. Some of those things I can't give you—most importantly, determination—but the rest we can build. If you're willing to work at it."

Lucy let go of Molly's shoulder and angled her head toward the door. "Otherwise, you're free to go. But make no mistake here, Molly. If you leave, that's it: you're out for good. Tom and I have plenty to worry about outside these walls, and the last thing we need to deal with are glorified babysitting sessions. If we didn't think this kind of thing was important, we would have never offered it. But it is, and it's even more vital that you all do this together. In fact, that's the only way this will matter in the end."

Molly frowned and scanned the faces of the other kids. Kareem spread his arms wide, ready to accept her decision either way. Gudam was bouncing up and down on her forelimbs, in a fit of perpetual nervous excitement.

Molly couldn't read Bakar at all.

She realized that she didn't care if she could. Lucy was right. If Molly wanted to learn how to defend herself, it was going to come down not to her sparring partners, but to Molly herself. And if she could learn how to take on a Sangheili such as Bakar, that was even better.

"All right," Molly said with a firm nod. "I'm in."

CHAPTER 15

The next day, Molly was the sorest she'd ever been in her life. Refusing to disappoint Tom and Lucy—or make them think she wasn't going to live up to her end of the bargain—she hauled herself back to school, though, limping just a bit the entire way.

It got better every time they met. Not easier, but better.

School settled down for Molly after that first day of training, and she started getting into a groove. Part of her just wanted to blend in and get it all over with as fast as possible, but that didn't seem destined to happen. Because of the fight—and maybe because Asha and Yong were always gone—Kasha 'Hilot seemed to take a special interest in watching over Molly. She wasn't entirely sure why the headmaster went to that trouble just for her.

It was a strange feeling, having a Sangheili such as Kasha fill this caretaker role, checking in on Molly between classes and after school. Molly at first found the attention bizarre and unnerving, but she came to appreciate it to some degree. She couldn't describe how, but it reminded her of her mother—her real one. In time, Molly became more comfortable around the Sangheili, even though deep down inside she still harbored resentment and bitterness for what had happened on Paris IV.

Of course, Kasha's attention only made things worse for Molly in other ways. It may have driven troubles with punks such as

Karl, Zeb, and Andres underground, but the other kids didn't stop either hating her or just going out of their way to ignore her. Whether because of the fight or her association with aliens, Molly was still being shunned, and no end seemed in sight.

The only two people she did speak with regularly were Gudam and Kareem. Lunches with them she could handle fine enough, but the rest of the kids spread out to make sure there weren't any other open tables, which unavoidably forced Bakar to sit with them too. That was the last thing Molly wanted, and the Sangheili seemed to appreciate it even less than she did.

Nevertheless, after a couple weeks of this, they settled into a routine. She wouldn't say it was pleasant, but it became more tolerable as the days came and went.

Molly's Newparents may have been concerned about her, but they didn't have time to do much about it. Their project was even more demanding than they had let on earlier, and Molly could tell that it was taking a toll on them. Most days, they left the house before she even set off for school, and they returned several hours after she'd come home, often late into the day.

That was *if* they returned together. Sometimes one would stay behind and continue through the night.

They were both overworked and exhausted, but when Molly did get a moment with them, their faces showed another kind of weariness. They were concerned about what they were working on, and Molly could tell it had heavier implications than she could understand.

"It won't last forever," Asha told her one night. "We're just still finding our footing here." What Asha said was probably a half-truth, but Molly could tell *other* things were going on—things Asha probably couldn't share, even if she wanted to. Whether that was because they were too classified or because, if she did, Molly would be petrified by what was taking place, she didn't want to know.

Something deep inside her said it was the latter.

"Me too," Molly whispered, heading to bed.

Asha had tucked Molly in almost every single night when she was in elementary school. After what happened on Paris IV, Molly had desperately needed that sense of security, and her Newparents rarely missed an opportunity to let her know she was welcome and loved.

Over the years, things had changed. They became busier with their work, and Molly had simply gotten too old for it. She was sixteen now and far too comfortable in her own skin to need constant reassurances like that anymore.

In her mind, she was practically an adult. She didn't want to be coddled.

But that night, Asha followed Molly upstairs and made sure she was completely tucked in and gave her a kiss on the forehead. Molly didn't object this time. She welcomed it.

"Things will be better soon," Asha said, turning out the lights. "I promise."

The next day, Molly's entire class—about fifty in number—piled into a large ground transport and went on their first field trip. They were headed to a Forerunner site called the Repository.

This trip was Molly's first time beyond the Inner Barrier, a set of sensor relays and energy pylons that separated the interior area of Paxopolis and Trevelyan's primary facilities from the less occupied outer territory, which had a number of research sites—such as the Repository and the one Molly's Newparents were working at.

The Repository sat only five kilometers outside Paxopolis,

but as Kasha 'Hilot explained as they traveled through the row of towering pylons, because it lay inside the Outer Barrier, it was still part of the expanded security perimeter the UNSC had set up. From a bird's-eye view, the perimeter surrounded an area anchored by the entrance into the sphere through which Molly and her Newparents had arrived. Those dozens of square kilometers inside the Inner Barrier comprised the extent of humanity's foothold on Onyx.

Everything outside of that was wild.

"The marines have cleared out any dangerous creatures they could find between the Inner and Outer Barriers," Kasha said. "Still, that does not mean the area is entirely safe. This is an enormous space, and some of it has yet to be fully charted and secured. Many of the animals here can also fly and burrow, and sometimes they're rather good at hiding.

"Given the fact the Forerunners populated the sphere with creatures taken from countless worlds across the galaxy, it's reasonable to suspect that we have not yet come close to cataloguing all of the types in this territory, much less to understanding each and every one of them. So, please—for your own safety and that of those around you—keep your eyes open and stay together. I do not want to have to explain to your parents why you weren't able to make it back home."

Most of the kids laughed the comment off, but Molly wasn't inclined to join in—and Kasha didn't show any indication she meant it as a joke. The idea of wandering around the surface of Onyx scared Molly more than a little. She wondered if the lack of trepidation on the other kids' parts had more to do with their having ventured out this far before or simply ignorance. In all of Molly's previous interactions with them, she'd have guessed the latter.

Still, the institute seemed to have gone to great lengths to ensure the class's security, even calling in some of the local security and military assets, including a transport. The vehicle wasn't a civilian ride but a heavily armored UNSC truck: long, green, and without any windows. The seats didn't face forward. Instead, they lined the sides of the transport, each with its own set of safety restraints to keep the riders in their seats, no matter how rough it got.

That unfortunately meant they had to face other students, something Molly generally tried to avoid at all cost. She found herself in the absolute back of the transport, sitting next to Kareem, and directly across from Bakar and Gudam.

"I don't like this any more than you do," Molly said to Bakar, as she strapped herself in.

"I do not wish to be here at all," he said.

"Exactly."

"Then why *are* you here?" Kareem said to Bakar. "On Onyx, I mean?"

Bakar stared at Kareem as if the Sangheili were made of stone and didn't blink once, not even when the transport lurched into motion. Kareem blushed, but now that he'd started down this road of inquiry, he didn't retract the question or apologize.

"I was sent here," Bakar finally said, as if that explained everything.

"We all were," Kareem said. "But most of us seem to get along with the others."

"Of their kind, at least," Gudam said helpfully. "That said, we don't all like school. Take the other Unggoy my age, for instance. They don't care for it one bit. We're all smart enough—we absorb things like sponges, really—but we usually manage that by . . . what do they call it? Experiential learning. That means learning things by doing. Me, though, I'm different. I like classes and books and brain work."

"Is that why the other Unggoy don't hang out with you much?" Kareem asked.

Gudam chuckled at that. "I see plenty of them at home, believe me. They just don't like humans or Sangheili all that much—they see bigger people as threats—so they keep to themselves. Me, I'm just too curious for my own good. I mean, that's probably going to get me hurt one day, but I figure it's worth it, right? Who needs completely normal and safe Unggoy friends when you can have a bunch of weirdo friends like you guys?"

The question hung there for a second.

"Am I right?" Gudam continued, straight-faced.

Even Bakar let out a bellow at that, a deep rumble that seemed to escape from his chest before he could stop it. Molly had never heard a Sangheili laugh, but perhaps this was as close as they got.

"How about you?" Molly asked him. "Why are you always alone?"

The Sangheili sat there and stared at his symmetrical hands for a moment, flexing his fingers, tapping his thumbs together. The rest of the group watched him in silence and waited—even, to Molly's surprise, Gudam.

"I came here alone," Bakar finally said. "This school does not make me more so."

"What happened?" Gudam looked both horrified and curious.

"My mother died. Kasha 'Hilot took me in." Bakar nodded toward the front of the transport, where Kasha stood, swaying on her haunches while she surveyed the students calmly and confidently, ready to cut them into shape with a series of sharp, well-chosen words at a moment's notice. Even though she was a female, slighter than an adult male, she was still too large for the harness system, and she clung to grips on the truck's interior walls instead. "At the time, I did not know that I would wind up here, so far from Sanghelios."

Yet another thing this dangerous alien and Molly had in common. "And you hate it here?"

To her surprise, Bakar shook his head. "I had my fill of Sanghelios and the constant fighting waged there. In many ways, the Great Schism that put a stop to our war with your people never ended for us. My planet is still engaged in a violent civil war in which clans have risen against each other for power and territory. The Arbiter and his Swords of Sanghelios and what remains of the Covenant still do battle there, even to this very day."

He paused, and Molly realized that he'd said more in the last two minutes than he had in the entire rest of the time since she'd met him.

"I am pleased to have put that world behind me. I only wish I could have found the peace I sought here." He glanced toward the front of the transport, taking in the rest of the classmates riding along with them. They were laughing and chatting, being loud and obnoxious in the way of careless teenagers. The humans sat toward the front, the Sangheili sat in the middle, and the Unggoy sat toward the back.

Somewhere inside Molly's heart, a strong part of her wished that she could be sitting up front with the rest of the humans. She realized that she didn't know what that would feel like. To disappear as an individual and fade into the collective . . . perhaps even to find some sort of acceptance among them. For Molly, that would have been a refreshing escape.

But some parts of that crowd she couldn't stand. In many ways, they were everything she was not. Because of that, Molly knew that she was better off by herself.

Molly was an outsider.

She glanced back at Kareem, Gudam, and Bakar.

They were too.

The four rode in silence the rest of the way.

They soon reached their destination, and the transport ground to a halt. Their little group in the back waited for the other students to leave, then shuffled off one by one.

Unlike many of the other Forerunner buildings Molly had seen—which often looked like temples or spires—the enormous Repository was long, narrow, and flat, even though it was a full forty meters tall.

As always within this part of Onyx, the weather was warm and temperate, the very definition of paradise. Gentle breezes carried fluffy white clouds through the bright blue sky, and the grass around the structure was soft and green. To Molly, it felt a little like paradise, but it seemed a little *off*, just like everything else here. It was almost too perfect, bordering on unreal.

Someone in the UNSC had decided to build a paved road that ran right up to the Repository's front door. Molly was sure the road was seen as a form of progress, probably making it easier for people to get around inside the sphere. To her, it looked like an ugly scar on the face of the land. Progress without a purpose.

The Forerunners had constructed everything in the sphere long before any humans arrived. If a road had been necessary, they would have built it themselves.

But perhaps she was being pedantic. After all, beings who could create something as incredible as Onyx probably had hundreds of better ways to get around than on twenty-sixth-century vulcanized tires. Until the researchers exploring the sphere figured out just how exactly the Forerunners managed it, they would remain stuck with wheels and roads.

The students assembled near what Molly believed was the main doorway, a large wall at the nearest end of the Repository that looked as though it could be opened. Kasha 'Hilot stood at the front of the group, atop a low wall that framed the walkway that led into the building. A man stood next to her, waving the students closer.

He wasn't completely unfamiliar. Molly had seen him roaming around the Pax Institute before, but she didn't know anything about him. He was older than her Newparents, by quite a lot—perhaps even enough to have been one of their fathers—yet not much about him felt grandfatherly.

He was rangy, with untamed white hair and sharp blue eyes. He looked as if he'd been left out in rough weather for most of his life, like one of those cowboys from early American history. He even wore a pistol in a holster on his hip, which seemed fitting.

In a gruff, no-nonsense voice, he said, "Good day, kids. My name is Mike Spenser, and I'm one of the primary liaisons between the Pax Institute and ONI Research Facility Trevelyan. You can just call me Mike. I spent a lot of years working for ONI in the field, and so I look at this particular post as a way to make up for all the horrible things I've done in my life."

Most of the kids laughed at that, but Molly noticed that Mike didn't do more than crack a wry smile.

"Part of my role here is to escort specific groups and high-value assets that leave Paxopolis on excursions, retreats, or academic field trips like this. While your headmaster is more than capable of managing such duties, and while this part of Onyx is relatively secure, there's still a lot we don't know about this strange world we now call home.

"That's why I'm here: to guide and protect you. You'll make my job a lot easier if you follow a few simple rules."

He ticked them off on his fingers.

"One. Stay with the group. If you wander off on your own, you might get lost or run into trouble.

"Two. If you somehow manage to completely blow rule number one, stop and wait for help to arrive. We'll figure out you're gone soon enough, and if you keep roaming around, it makes it a lot harder for us to nail down your position and find you.

"Three." Then he said something Molly didn't understand at all, and it wasn't for lack of trying. "Any of you get that?" he said with a smile.

Molly glanced around but didn't see any of the humans raising a hand. Even the Sangheili and the Unggoy seemed confused, although a few of them had started chuckling.

From behind Molly, Kareem softly cleared his throat. She looked back and saw him thumbing her attention toward Bakar. The young Sangheili stood with one hand reluctantly held in the air.

"Yes?" Mike gestured toward Bakar. "I was talking in an obscure dialect of Sangheili. I figured someone just might get it. Anyone else pick up on it?"

All of the other students shook their heads, even the other Sangheili. Mike gave them all a rueful look. "'Course not." He nodded toward Bakar. "You want to translate for your fellow students?"

Bakar hesitated. Speaking to the rest of the class was probably the last thing he wanted to do, but Mike wasn't about to let him off the hook.

After a moment, Bakar gave in and said, " 'Pay attention. You might learn something.' "

"Right." Mike looked at the rest of them. "You kids are living inside one of the most amazing xenoarchaeological finds in all of human history. You're studying alongside different species from across the galaxy. That's pretty extraordinary if you stop to think about it.

"This place—Onyx—it's unlike anything we've ever encountered before, and it will take *many* lifetimes for us to explore and investigate. This very small piece of the sphere you're in right now deserves your complete respect and attention. Its incredible age alone demands it.

"So for your own sakes, show some intellectual curiosity. That's what brought your families here, right? This isn't just an amazing opportunity for them. It's one for you too. Take advantage of it. *Safely.*" He bore down hard on that last word.

With that, he jumped down from the wall and led them into the Repository.

CHAPTER 16

T he Repository was just as amazing as Molly had hoped it would be.

As they walked up to the building, the wall face revealed a gigantic set of doors, which responsively peeled away from the front of the building, exposing a massive hangar interior several stories tall.

The lights inside the structure began to glow stronger, responding to the approaching group by illuminating the cavernous structure from one end to the other. As large as the Repository was, it was hardly empty.

The astonishing building was packed from one end to the other with a wide variety of vehicles: wheeled and winged, floating and hovering. Too many to even begin to count.

Molly recognized some of them as Covenant craft, purple and curved into vaguely biomimetic shapes. They ran not on traditional propulsion methods such as propellers or jets, but on a boosted-gravity drive system allowing them to either hover or fly. She knew the names of some of them from her time exploring the Covenant War: Banshees, Ghosts, Wraiths, and others. It seemed that the UNSC had kept samples of each in the structure, including some she'd never seen. And they had them in large numbers, dozens upon dozens.

Among these stood some machines that seemed to have been made by the Forerunners. Most of them were gray or silver and had distinctive angular designs, usually trimmed in glowing blues. Incredibly, they seemed to be constructed of floating bits that were clearly meant to be connected parts of a single unit but somehow never actually touched. Molly had never seen anything like this before, and she found her eyes were riveted to every shape and design.

It made her wonder if this was the kind of stuff Yong and Asha had been studying all these years. If so, their collective effort and excitement finally made sense. If these kinds of machines were what the Forerunners were capable of creating, then following in their footsteps was worth it.

The Forerunner craft stood in stark contrast with the sorts of vehicles the UNSC built, which also populated the hangar: boxy and practical, tough and durable, familiar and reliable. They came in greens, grays, and browns, as if they were built for blasting through fields, cities, or jungles rather than atmospheres and outer space—though she noticed they had a few spaceworthy craft there too.

From Molly's own research, she knew most of the UNSC vehicles in the hangar by name—Warthogs, Scorpions, Mongooses, Pelicans—but a few new ones she'd never seen, some which even seemed to incorporate Covenant or Forerunner technology overlaid on the human design.

What was this place originally designed to do? Why are there so many vehicles from different species here? Is ONI using this as an ad hoc hangar facility for any vehicles they happen to have on hand? Molly immediately wanted to ask a hundred questions, but she didn't have a chance right away.

A dozen humans roamed among the vehicles, each dressed in UNSC fatigues. A single Sangheili worked alongside them too, with a pair of Unggoy by his side. None of the aliens wore uniforms, though, just strange coveralls.

Maybe that was meant to put the humans around them at ease. Molly had to admit, it was better than seeing them strut around in armor. All of the workers, however, had sidearms—including the aliens. Ironically, some humans had ex-Covenant weapons such as plasma pistols at their sides, while the Sangheili carried a Magnum holstered on one of his legs.

Onyx certainly made for strange bedfellows.

Then Molly spotted a Huragok. She'd expected to be disgusted if she ever encountered one in person, but at first blush the creature seemed incredibly harmless and somehow intriguing . . . in an odd way. In the languorous way it moved, it appeared serene, even petlike.

"Do you see that?" Molly asked Bakar.

He nodded. "One of the Engineers. I heard many tales of them growing up on Sanghelios, but I had never seen one before. Not until I moved here."

"Me neither," Gudam said. "They sure are funny looking. I wonder how they get around. Do they have to propel themselves by expelling gas?"

Kareem laughed openly at that comment, while Molly rolled her eyes. Bakar simply remained silent. His unflinching response made her wonder if he was just a sour member of his species or if none of the Sangheili had a sense of humor. Or perhaps he had been jaded to start with and coming to the Pax Institute had only exacerbated his condition.

As the group slowly gathered in the center of the hangar, Mike Spenser cocked his head to one side like a dog picking up a whistle. Then he pushed a finger into his ear and listened, responding with a series of short answers and grunts.

When he was done, he gave the group a regretful frown. "I'm

sorry to have to do this, but I need to step into the back for a moment. Something's come up."

"When can we expect you to return?" Kasha asked.

"I won't be long." Mike looked out at the herd of students. "Take fifteen minutes to wander around the place, kids. Explore and discuss, but don't touch anything. The vehicles might be locked down right now, but they are fully functional and capable of causing real damage—and for you, *serious* trouble. After you're done taking it all in, head back and meet me right here."

He spun on his heel and took off. As he went, he signaled to the Huragok with a whistle and flip of the wrist. The creature sped along after him at a surprising speed.

"You heard him, students," Kasha said. "You have fifteen minutes. Do not be late, and do not touch anything!"

The rest of the students scattered. Molly walked off in the direction least likely to put her among any of them, and Kareem and Gudam followed suit. Bakar trailed after the three of them, though just far enough behind that he could arguably be separate.

As they walked deeper into the hangar, each of them craned his or her neck around to try to get a better view of the building and all the amazing things in it. It was the most fascinating place Molly had ever been in. Not only was the Forerunner structure an incredible piece of architecture, but the vehicles were unlike anything she'd ever seen so close.

On the periphery, Molly spotted a number of large doors that lined both sides of the long structure. Some of these stood open with clear views to the dense foliage on the outskirts of the Repository, while others remained closed. They appeared to be enormous shutters that could retract upward into the vast angular ceiling above, and it quickly became apparent how the vehicles—especially the large ones—could be moved in and out of the structure.

The sheer scale of the place stunned Molly as she turned back to face its center. It was one thing to walk alongside a massive aircraft and take in just how large it was in real life. It was something else altogether to stroll among dozens and dozens of such craft *inside* a building made by an ancient civilization—and then to realize that the building itself was far bigger than all of them put together.

Despite its great size and elaborate design, the Repository seemed like a logical part of the whole that was Onyx. The Forerunners were evidently masters at merging the natural and the unnatural in ways that felt seamless, perhaps because everything here was, in effect, made by them. Even sitting among the heavy foliage that surrounded the hangar, the structure felt as if it just fit—as if it had been placed there before the vegetation, ancient beyond all human comprehension.

After wandering a few paces from the group, Molly paused briefly at the edge of the structure to take in the morning light as it cascaded down through the surrounding forest. Then she heard a huge crash off to her right and turned to see a seventy-ton Pelican dropship tipping completely over onto one of its wings.

Then she spotted the enormous creature that had knocked the vehicle over.

The beast emerging from behind the Pelican laid its shoulder into the heavy transport again, this time shoving the craft's opposing wing into a nearby Hornet, slamming the wing hard into the other vehicle's encased rotors. The animal stood about as tall as a house, if a house could run around on six muscular legs, each as thick as a pillar of granite. Its gigantic mouth was filled with several rows of daggerlike teeth, and three rows of bright red fins ran along its back.

To Molly, it looked like some kind of dinosaur from Earth's history, or better yet a frightening combination of the giant crocodiles that roamed the swamps of the colony Terceira and the great red sharks she had seen in nature vids from New Carthage. Whatever it was, the animal clearly wasn't safe.

It threw back its head and roared so loudly Molly's eardrums threatened to burst. She instinctively ducked behind the nearest person, putting him between her and the monster.

She didn't realize it immediately, but she'd taken shelter behind Bakar.

Molly told herself that was because the Sangheili was so large, not because she felt that he'd protect her. Bakar locked his feet into position and remained unmoving as Kareem and Gudam huddled behind him too, tracking the creature with his eyes as it stormed through the hangar.

From somewhere behind them, Kasha 'Hilot began shouting orders at the other students. A few of them froze in terror, unable to move at the terrifying sight.

Mike suddenly appeared from wherever he'd run off to and drew his pistol. He fired three quick shots into the air. "Kids!" he barked, pointing toward their transport, which had already shot alongside the Repository, near where the bulk of the students were. It screeched to a sudden stop by the closest hangar doors. "Get your butts back in your ride!" he shouted.

The noise of his voice and weapon had gotten the monster's attention. It turned toward the group while Kasha began herding the students close to her out through the Repository's doors.

Mike took aim at the creature and fired a single round at it. The beast reared back on its four hindmost legs and howled in fury at him. Even then, it didn't seem to Molly that the bullet had hurt it as much as stung it.

The other students frantically stampeded toward the transport, which almost made Molly turn tail and try to sprint ahead of them, since she and Bakar stood closer to the vehicle. Instead, Bakar swiftly guided her behind him, along with Gudam and Kareem. For a second, Molly worried that they would be crushed underneath the Sangheili as the others charged past him, but Bakar braced himself and held his ground.

To Molly's amazement, the other students parted around him as if he were a rock in a river. Even Karl, Zeb, and Andres gave him a wide berth. It might have been a perfect opportunity for them to take a cheap shot at Bakar, but they were too scared for their own safety to bother trying to torture him at that moment.

"We should help," Bakar said.

"The others look like they're all getting along just fine," Kareem said, casting a glance back toward the students piling into the transport.

"Not the students, the adults." Bakar pointed toward the building's interior.

The large predator had moved to the center of the Repository, thundering deeper into the hangar in pursuit of Mike, who was using his pistol not to harm it as much as draw its attention away from the students.

"Mr. Spenser," Bakar remarked. "He has no idea what he is up against."

"And you do?"

Bakar nodded. "The *rafakrit* is a mythical creature in my culture. I read about it in scrolls as a fledgling, and this, human, is most certainly one."

Kasha stormed up to them, shouting the entire way. "Move! Get into the transport, now!"

Bakar had seemed to be talking in a dream: distant and preoccupied with memories from his childhood. Kasha's voice snapped him right out of that, and he sprang into action. The rest of the kids dodged away from him as he grabbed Kasha's arm and hauled her to the side.

"Did you tell Mr. Spenser about the *rafakrit*?"

Kasha shook her arm free and glared down at Bakar. "*Rafakrit*? There is no such thing, Bakar. Do not be a fool. That is just a myth told to children to warn them that they should listen. You obviously did not hear it enough!"

In the distance, Molly saw Mike, weaving between vehicles for cover, crack off another few shots at the beast. Four marines and two fully armored Sangheili warriors had suddenly appeared from the far side of the Repository's hangar. They raised their own weapons at the creature but held their fire, evidently unsure how to handle the situation.

The beast completely ignored them. It howled in Mike's direction once more and charged at him, razor-sharp claws out. Mike ducked behind a low-hovering Covenant Phantom just in time.

The *rafakrit*, if that's what it was, slammed into the hovering dropship and shoved it back several meters as if it were a cheap toy. The ship's antigravity drive kept it from toppling over. Instead, it slid along on an invisible sheet of energy just above the pavement, giving Mike just enough time to escape.

"It *is* real though, Kasha." Bakar stabbed a finger toward the beast. "And it is right there, just like in the stories. Look at it!"

Kasha snarled at Bakar with all of her jaws at once, but to her credit, she spun around and stared back at the creature she'd been trying to save the students from. Mike had distracted it enough that it couldn't reach them before they could get to the transport and shut the doors, so Kasha finally had enough time to take a good look at it and evaluate Bakar's claim.

"By the gods, it is!" She glanced at Bakar and corrected herself with what looked like a frown. "Apologies. Old habit."

The *rafakrit* repeatedly bashed into the Phantom, shoving the hovering ship deeper into the Repository's interior as the predator tried to reach its prey. The other soldiers then unleashed all of their weapons at its backside, but in its rage, the creature kept its single-minded focus on Mike. It would not be dissuaded from getting to him first.

Mike slid behind the back of the Phantom and moved toward a Covenant Wraith tank, and the *rafakrit* spun around the other side of the dropship in pursuit. If Mike was trying to distract the beast long enough for everyone else to escape, he was doing an excellent job. Molly only wondered who would help *him*.

Kasha put a finger to the side of her head and spoke to Mike over some kind of comm system Molly hadn't noticed earlier. "Mr. Spenser? We are clear."

He said something in response that the rest of them couldn't hear. Kasha nodded and answered, "Help is on its way."

"Get back into the transport," she said to their group.

The four of them remained still, however, their eyes fixed on Mike as he scrambled up the side of the Wraith.

"Why can't Mr. Spenser use that Wraith to defend himself?" Kareem said.

"He cannot get to the controls," Bakar said. "Not with the *rafakrit* knocking the craft around in that manner."

The beast smashed into the Wraith with more force than it had exerted in all of its other attacks, frantically trying to seize the human. The Covenant vehicle was crushed beneath its efforts, and Molly wasn't sure there would be much left of it for Mike to use, even if he could board it.

The soldiers advanced then from the perimeter, humans and Sangheili fighting side by side as allies, one of the strangest things Molly had yet seen. They began firing once more at the creature, this time finally getting its attention. Their shots slammed into the beast's thick hide but drew no blood. It reared up again on its four hind legs and bellowed. When it hit the ground, it spun about and charged at its new attackers.

For something so large, it moved incredibly fast. It was on the soldiers in a heartbeat. The two Sangheili warriors moved up to meet it, blasting hot bursts from their plasma rifles. They burned scorch marks in the *rafakrit*'s face, but remarkably, the thing kept coming.

The charging *rafakrit* drew back its claws as it reached the Sangheili and knocked them aside as if they were rag dolls. Both hit the adjacent wall with nasty crunching sounds, smearing trails of indigo blood where their bodies fell.

The remaining marines poured every round they had into the creature, but that only seemed to make it more frenzied and violent. It turned on its hind legs and tore into them like a dog hunting rats, swiftly picking them up in its teeth and ending each of their lives with a sharp jerk of its jaws.

Only seconds later, the blood-coated beast spun about and began scouring the hangar floor for more prey, keeping its snout close to the ground as though it could smell something. It suddenly seemed to remember its previous quarry and charged right back toward where it had last seen Mike.

He'd gotten away from the now-ruined Wraith and was sprinting toward a UNSC Warthog instead, a rough-and-tumble wheeled vehicle with an open top surrounded by protective roll bars. This one had a Gauss cannon mounted in its rear bed, positioned so that a soldier standing in the back could use it.

"Gods," Kasha said. She had been too shaken by the sudden slaughter to even yell at the four of them. "What could kill such a monster?"

"We don't need to kill it," Molly spoke up. "We just need to get it away from Mike long enough for *him* to get away."

"Or get that weapon working," Kasha said.

"What?" Kareem said. "Aren't there more soldiers here?"

Kasha scanned the hangar. "If there are any left, they are nowhere to be found. The duty falls to us."

"According to the ancient stories, the *rafakrit* despises high-pitched noises," said Bakar. "That is why they tell Sangheili children to whistle in the dark: to keep the creatures away."

"I suppose it is worth a try." Kasha shrugged uncertainly. "Now take the others and get them back to the transport. It is not safe out here."

Bakar scowled as Kasha turned her back on the group. "That seems like a poor reward for coming up with a solution to our problem."

Molly shot him a doubtful look. "Are you saying we should trust our lives to your memory of a children's tale?"

"Do you have a better idea?"

Kasha answered the question by charging headlong toward the *rafakrit*. "I'm on my way, Mr. Spenser. Get ready."

As Kasha got closer to the monster, she began waving her arms and shouting to get its attention. When that didn't provoke any response, she stuck the two thumbs on her right hand into her mouth and produced the loudest whistle Molly had ever heard. She didn't even think Sangheili *could* whistle, given their anatomy—but she was very wrong. The sound was so sharp and piercing that it seemed as if it could wake the dead. Back on Earth.

And it did the trick, getting the creature's attention.

Just as the *rafakrit* was prepared to smash into the Warthog, which Mike had clambered atop, it whipped its massive, tooth-filled face around and glared in Kasha's direction, only a few hundred meters away. It snarled as if the sound she'd made had pierced its head and was burrowing its way into the beast's brain.

"We should get back to the transport, right now," Kareem said, his eyes fixed on Kasha and the beast. He didn't sound too urgent about it, so the rest of the group ignored him. Somewhere behind them, a few of the students in the vehicle were screaming.

Kasha moved off to the right, toward an open set of hangar doors, as the *rafakrit* edged in her direction and replanted its legs. She clearly didn't want the beast to charge at her and then run headlong into the transport if she could help it. As Kasha angled away from a straight line between their group and the *rafakrit*, the monster tracked her with its head for a moment. When it felt the time had come for it to attack, it launched itself away from Mike and toward Kasha.

The Sangheili headmaster spun on her heels and ran. She burst out of the hangar at a speed that shocked Molly and launched out into the open fields on the far side of the Repository.

The *rafakrit* chased after her, moving incredibly fast. Its agility was more like that of a hunting cat than something the size of a maglev train, and it seemed only to pick up steam as it went.

"It's going to get her," Gudam said as the beast bore down on Kasha. "We have to stop it!"

Molly put a hand on Gudam's shoulder to keep her where she was. All that chasing after Kasha would have done for the little Unggoy was to add another casualty to the list. Molly respected Gudam's grit and bravery, despite her diminutive size, but that would do no one any good. And Molly also was growing fond of the alien.

While the monster charged, Kasha kept blasting out more whistles the entire way. The creature closed the distance, and the *rafakrit*'s shadow began blotting out the sun over the headmaster, the two running at full tilt.

Then the Sangheili skidded to a halt.

For an agonizing moment, the four of them watched as the *rafakrit* reared up on its four hind legs, still charging forward, preparing to pounce in one single blow. Its toothy mouth opening wide, it looked as if it might be able to swallow Kasha whole, along with the ground on which she stood. As the beast brought its ferocious maw down to strike, Kasha dove to her left, completely out of Molly's field of view.

Gudam let out a loud squeal of terror. The *rafakrit* turned its head to see what had made the noise. Its face smashed into the ground, losing the headmaster and driving its body headlong, forcing a spray of grass and dirt into the air.

Molly spotted Kasha on the far side of the beast, darting away. She had tumbled clear in time.

As the creature got its bearings, its head snapped around to focus on the fleeing Sangheili. Kasha was favoring her left leg just a bit. She'd been injured in some way. While she had been able to avoid the *rafakrit*'s attack once, it wouldn't happen again.

Back behind the group in the hangar, Molly could hear Mike fighting to start the Warthog, but the vehicle's systems seemed to refuse to comply. Molly wondered if they'd been put on security lockdown, given the creature's rampage. To her, it didn't seem as if any help would be coming from that quarter, at least not right away.

"Do that again," Bakar said to Gudam.

"What?" The Unggoy was still gaping at the sight of the *rafakrit* clawing itself up out of the little crater it had made in its first assault and then charging toward Kasha.

Molly instantly figured out Bakar's plan. It was stupid, insane, and dangerous as hell, but too much was at stake with no time to argue.

She grabbed Gudam by the shoulders, looking intently into the creature's beady eyes, and said, "He means squeal! Just like you did before, but louder!"

Gudam goggled at Molly, seriously shaken.

Molly shouted at her even louder. "Do it—now!"

The little Unggoy let out an earsplitting shriek at a much higher frequency and volume than before. If any glass had been nearby, Molly had little doubt that it would have completely shattered.

Molly looked over at the *rafakrit*, which had been rushing toward Kasha again. The animal stopped dead in its tracks and held its position for a long moment, shaking its head at the intensity of Gudam's voice.

Then the beast let out a shuddering roar that seemed to shake the sky.

Both Gudam and Molly stood there stunned, but Kareem grabbed their hands and hauled them away. He sprinted straight past the transport, out into the open, but in the opposite direction of the *rafakrit*. Molly couldn't see it, but she knew the *rafakrit* was readying to charge their position.

Molly didn't think; she just followed at full speed. It was all she could do to keep up with Kareem. Gudam couldn't even manage that. Her legs were too short and her waddling gait slowed her down even more.

Bakar sprinted up from behind the three and scooped the Unggoy up into his big arms. She squealed again in surprise, which produced another gut-wrenching roar from the *rafakrit*. As the ground began to rumble beneath their feet, there was no question about who it was coming after now.

But the sound from the beast's trampling feet only spurred them all on faster. The question was: *How far can we get before it reaches us?*

Molly looked back and then immediately regretted doing so.

The creature was pursuing the four of them at full speed, its eyes locked onto their position. Kasha had stopped in the far distance, turning to gape at them as they scrambled across the open ground on one side of the facility's outskirts.

Molly realized now that the tree line nearly a hundred meters ahead was too far. She searched around for something closer to hide behind: a tree, a boulder, anything. But on this side of the Repository, all that lay before them was open ground. They would not make it to the forest in time, and even if they did, it held no guarantee of safety.

The beast was closing on the four of them fast and would be on top of them in seconds. Molly only hoped that Kasha had figured out what they were trying to do and had a solution in hand. Meanwhile, the *rafakrit* had drawn so close to them, Molly could feel its hot breath on the back of her neck.

Molly was bringing up the rear, with Kareem just a bit ahead of her. Even with Gudam in his arms, Bakar could outpace all of them. The *rafakrit* would get to Molly first, there was no question about it. She gritted her teeth tight and kept sprinting, feeling its thundering footsteps pounding into the ground.

As the beast's wide shadow descended to pluck Molly from the ground, Kasha's high-pitched whistle rang out again.

Once more, the *rafakrit* skidded to a halt, then took off back toward Kasha. The resultant spray of dirt and grass rippled along the ground at Molly's feet and sent her flying to the side. She tumbled to a stop on the turf, spinning to see the beast as it charged away from them, once more unleashing a bone-rattling roar.

"I can't believe that worked," Kareem said, as he came up behind Molly, completely out of breath.

Bakar set Gudam down beside Molly and let out a deep sigh himself. "You do realize the worst part of all this?"

"Other than being chased down by a monster and almost devoured?" Molly asked.

He nodded. "The stories of the *rafakrit* said that whistling would drive it *away*."

Gudam shook her head. "Whoever came up with that story was trying to kill you all."

Molly pointed at Kasha, who was now racing back toward the Repository at top speed, her injury showing more with every step.

"Where is Kasha drawing that thing now?" Molly asked.

Bakar gestured toward the Repository. "I think Mr. Spenser has an answer for that."

The Warthog appeared in one of the open hangar doors with Mike at the wheel. He punched the vehicle past the transport and brought it right to the edge of the Repository. There, he stopped the machine, jumped out of the driver's seat and clambered over the roll cage for the Gauss cannon mounted on the Warthog's bed.

The *rafakrit* hadn't noticed Mike yet but was catching up with Kasha fast. It was only seconds from overtaking her. Molly turned to Gudam, but she had already cupped her hands around her mouth. The Unggoy let loose another loud and piercing shriek. This time Molly covered her ears, for all the good that seemed to do.

She worried that the *rafakrit* might have gotten too far away to hear Gudam's cry, but the thing once again halted, reared up its head, and shot a cold look in their direction. Just as it did, Mike opened up with the Gauss cannon and stitched a line of gigantic ferric tungsten rounds into the monster's flank. The impact was more violent than Molly had expected.

The *rafakrit* howled in pain as the alloy slugs punched holes into its torso. Its awful death throes sounded unlike anything Molly had ever heard. Despite its injuries, the animal wrenched itself around on its hind legs and attempted to charge the Warthog.

Mike was no fool. He unleashed another volley of rounds, this time directly into the *rafakrit*'s face. In seconds, the beast toppled over onto its side, its massive form falling limp to the ground, the fight completely drained from its body.

Mike blasted it three more times for safe measure.

Molly didn't like to watch anything die, but she made an exception for that thing. She had no remorse about seeing the animal expire, even if it had been the last one on Onyx. It had almost killed her and her friends.

Friends? she thought. *Are we friends?*

Then she looked behind her and realized whom she had just survived alongside: a human, an Unggoy, and a Sangheili. The three stood with weary faces and eyes wide, staring at the lifeless monster in the distance. They had survived together, a bunch of outsiders.

If that didn't make them friends, Molly wasn't sure what would.

CHAPTER 17

With Even Keel's help, the Servants of the Abiding Truth now had access to many places inside the shield world, and Dural meant to make that advantage work for them. To that end, the Huragok had begun a slow and methodical categorization of the places they could effectively reach by means of their base's portal system. It was astonishing how versatile the system was and how far it could take them.

Dural's advance-strike forces had found themselves scouting many strange lands populated by all manner of creatures, but their methodology of exploration had not been an exact science. Even Keel noted that much of this world's portal network was either incomplete or malfunctioning. The Huragok claimed that they could pass undetected for a time, but eventually others on this world would be sure to notice them making use of the system.

If they did, so be it. The Servants of the Abiding Truth would be ready. While they had the wind to their back and relatively unfettered access to Onyx's portal network, they should exploit it.

Some of these lands—such as the region from which the *rafakrits* came—had stronger gravity, and the sun shone with a diminished light. Other regions had lesser gravity, and their skies were sometimes filled with creatures far too large to take flight on most other worlds, such as Dural's own. Some were overflowing with mountains, while others seemed to feature nothing but endless seas, and others had both, with mountains that floated like islands in the sky, among vast oceans of dense clouds. There seemed to be no end to the variety of places Onyx was comprised of, a thought staggering at first, yet almost dreadful if pondered too deeply.

But by this method, the Servants had soon discovered the other Huragok and its location: the Repository. Dural decided to travel there personally to reconnoiter it, not trusting anyone else to give him the details he needed to create the right strategy.

The portal leading into the Repository opened into a gigantic hangar filled with a vast panoply of craft, many of which he could take cover behind. The Pale Blade used his modified armor's active camouflage to help ensure that he would not be seen. Due to his armor's power requirements, Dural could only bend light around himself for a handful of seconds at a time, but that proved more than sufficient for his purposes. Once inside the Repository, he carefully prowled the outskirts of the hangar's interior, clinging to the shadows.

Some of the vehicles in the Repository were spaceworthy, while others were designed for use on the ground. They included designs from all over: Covenant, Forerunner, and human too. Dural recognized that this absurd menagerie of firepower, if leveraged properly by the Servants, could easily give them a distinct advantage in the coming days.

He was not as concerned then about such weaponry, though, as he was about the second Huragok. That was the real prize. One thing was clear to him: Engineers were the currency of the gods on a world filled to the brim with Forerunner technology. If the Servants had any hope for victory, they needed to secure as many of the Engineers as they could as fast as possible.

People milled about the Repository, which meant Dural could not simply track down and secure the Huragok at will. Most of them were human researchers and even soldiers in uniforms of the human government, but shockingly, some disloyal Unggoy were present as well. And beyond all reason, he also spied a number of Sangheili working alongside the Servants' foes.

At first Dural thought perhaps the Sangheili had been captured, much like his father, and then simply forced into labor on this world. That would be utterly shameful but at least not treasonous. The dishonor would have been forced upon them rather than suffered as the result of their own willful perversion.

After watching them in secret though, it became clear they were *not* prisoners. For one, they wore no variety of shackles, but what revealed the truth was when Dural spied one of them issuing requests to some of the humans. The humans obeyed, and not in the fearful way a warrior might respond to an officer's orders, but in the manner of colleagues. They were *allies.*

Dural knew that the Arbiter had sent his own people here and that they were working closely with the humans, but to see it firsthand . . .

He cursed those traitorous Sangheili under his breath, but he could do little to take vengeance on them and their Unggoy servants then. Not without giving away his presence and missing the opportunity to procure the Engineer.

Avu Med 'Telcam had once worked directly with humans as a means to an end. He sought to dethrone the Arbiter and all unbelievers on Sanghelios, no matter the cost. But 'Telcam had seen clearly that Sangheili rule could only be realized through Sangheili power alone. Dural knew that 'Telcam's plan—once the Servants had finally defeated the Arbiter—would be to turn the blade on the human vermin they had worked with and ultimately finish what the Prophets had started.

This, though, felt different. The Arbiter's people and his human compatriots worked together here to propagate their own vile agenda of *compromise*. It was so infuriating for Dural that he had to satisfy his indignation by swearing to himself that all the Sangheili traitors he saw on this world would die at his hands soon enough.

After a long while stalking about the shadows of the Repository, Dural spotted a Huragok working there as well, confirming the claims that Even Keel had made. This Engineer had a number of people escorting it however, and it never seemed to be alone. To be able to safely take the creature, Dural would need a distraction.

He already had an excellent one at hand.

Returning to the Cathedral, the Pale Blade set his plan into motion, gathering a strike team of his best warriors about him, the same who had accompanied him in the vanguard when they first entered Onyx. With these chosen few at his side, Dural had Keel open the portal to the location where they knew the *rafakrit* roamed.

Buran had been the first to identify the creatures that had attacked the humans on the Servants' first night in Onyx. It was an ancient fledgling storybeast that his mother had warned him about—or at least something that looked like one.

Dural's mother had not been much for retelling sad fables. Perhaps she had noticed that he did not care for such things, but such stories were certainly kept on scrolls in the archives of Bekan keep. They had been more to Asum's liking than Dural's.

"To think that such a monster from an old tale could be brought to life," Ruk had said. "This must truly be the playground of the gods."

"Do you really think the Forerunners somehow conjured up creatures from Sangheili fables?" Buran said. "It is far more likely that they discovered such creatures and simply brought them here, much as we might keep specimens for observation or entertainment. Doubtless, the stories had originated on another Sangheili world where these creatures once lived."

"How then do you explain their presence here? Why would the gods bring such creatures to this world?" Ruk huffed at this. "You can cling to your outlandish beliefs, Buran, and I will cling to mine."

Dural let them bicker with each other over meaningless distinctions while he got to work. Using the bravest of his warriors as bait, he eventually drew one of the creatures off from its fellows and lured it back toward the portal. This proved simple, as the creatures hadn't moved that far off from where they had attacked the humans. Having tasted blood there already, they seemed to consider the place to be a fine hunting ground.

All the warriors had to do was drive the monster through the portal and into the Repository. Fortuitously, both portals were large enough for this creature, a clear indicator that the gods had foreseen and blessed Dural's plan.

Unfortunately, convincing the creature to pass through the portal proved a challenge.

As the *rafakrit* lumbered toward the portal, the warrior it had been following disappeared before its eyes. Mystified, the beast did not charge forward after its vanished prey. Instead, it spun about and took out its frustration on the rest of the warriors who had gathered nearby to speed into the Repository soon after the creature emerged there.

The beast snapped out with its jaws faster than Dural would have thought possible, and its teeth closed around one of his brethren. Its jaws shaking back and forth, the beast tore the hapless Sangheili to shreds. Another of Dural's warriors, perhaps thinking to display his honor, leaped forward to try to save what remained of the first, but it was already far too late.

When the second warrior lunged forward, the *rafakrit* dropped its first victim and struck out at the would-be rescuer with its foreclaw. This fell blow was even more decisive, killing that warrior instantly by snapping his spine. The beast savaged the fallen Sangheili while two of Dural's other warriors darted behind it in an effort to snatch their first wounded compatriot from the fray.

Dural could see the injured warrior had lost a tremendous amount of blood and would soon succumb to his wounds. One of his saviors had clamped a hand over his mandibles so that his groans of agony—which were shameful from the mouth of any Sangheili—would not draw the beast toward them.

Despite that, the *rafakrit* would soon be done with its current meal, and Dural had to make a quick decision. He got the attention of the two warriors holding down their dying fellow, whose thrashing had already begun to weaken.

"Throw him at the foot of the portal!" the Pale Blade ordered.

They both gaped at him, their mandibles hanging loose in surprise.

"Are you mad?!" Buran said. "He is an honored warrior and should be dispatched with the dignity he deserves!"

Dural snarled at the older Sangheili, daring Buran to get into his teeth about this. He did not have the time to debate this. "He was a fool, but his death may still prove useful!"

Dural glared at the two warriors holding the dying Sangheili down. "What are you waiting for? Throw him at the foot of the portal! And keep his mouth uncovered as you do!"

This warrior had certainly failed the gods by allowing the beast to have its way with him. Despite that fatal mistake, perhaps he could now atone for his sin.

The two warriors dashed toward the portal, towing their dying brethren between them. As they moved, the *rafakrit* raised its bloodied face and stared after them, evidently trying to decide whether it should abandon its current dinner for an even fresher one.

As ordered, the two warriors stopped just before the portal and uncovered the mouth of their mortally wounded compatriot. The dying warrior released a howl of agony, which drew the beast's interest. Acting in tandem, the two threw the Sangheili at the portal's very edge, where he lay on the verge of being drawn into the swirl of energy.

The *rafakrit* had already begun charging toward the trio, and the two who had carried the Sangheili dove to the sides, attempting to remove themselves from the creature's sight. The beast bore down directly toward the dying Sangheili. It collided with its prey so fast that its inertia carried them both into the portal, and they vanished from sight.

Dural held up a hand to signal the others to wait. "It will not be long. The creature should wreak havoc quickly." He retrieved his carbine from its mount on his back. "Let the weaklings there mount a defense against it. Then, while the beast has their attention, we strike!"

After several long moments, the Pale Blade made for the portal, motioning for the others to follow him. The entire band of warriors fell right in line with no griping, not even from Ruk or Buran.

On the other side of the portal, they emerged on the edge of chaos.

The team of Servants quickly found the remains of their fallen warrior abandoned just past the portal's mouth. From the blood splattered everywhere, it seemed he had acquitted himself well in his final moments.

The trail of blood continued on into the vast interior of the Repository, and now Dural could hear weapons firing—both human and Sangheili.

He spotted the creature deep inside the hangar, its back to them as it hurled its bulk into a Phantom, causing the dropship to crumple under its assault. His strike team moved toward it, keeping out of sight as best they could.

Dural scanned the carnage the creature had left in its wake. The beast had quickly slaughtered several personnel, including two of the Sangheili traitors. While Dural relished their deaths, they felt unsatisfying, as he had not personally brought justice to them with his own hands.

The Servants moved along the hangar's back wall, doing their best to keep low and out of sight. They did not want the monster to somehow spot them and bring undue attention to them or, worse, decide that they would make an easier kill than whomever it was trying to reach behind the Phantom.

Dural ran his eyes across the interior of the structure, looking for the one Huragok he knew worked in the Repository, but it was nowhere to be seen. He then signaled the others to be silent, and they slipped deeper into the hangar, keeping to the shadows, far out of sight of the fracas the monster was causing. If they needed to reveal themselves, it would be to grab the Huragok, not because they were forced to confront the monster.

The *rafakrit* kept bashing into the Phantom and even tried to sink its teeth into the dropship's armor. If the craft had been small enough for it to wrap its jaws around the front end, Dural had little doubt the monster would have succeeded.

As his team neared the far end of the hangar and lost the mythical animal behind the array of seemingly endless vehicles, a high-pitched whistle sounded from somewhere outside the hangar, and the *rafakrit* suddenly bolted off after it.

A gray-haired human appeared from behind a Wraith roughly a hundred meters away. The vehicle had been violently mauled by the *rafakrit* only moments before. Dural doubted its operability.

Rather than use the Wraith, however, the human raced over to an all-terrain vehicle his species called a Warthog—a graceless wheeled machine that looked equal parts crude and vulgar—and he struggled to get it started. The human was far too concerned with the *rafakrit* to see the Servants skulking in the shadows so far behind him.

Dural momentarily considered shooting him with his carbine, but they were there to find the Huragok, not to kill humans. There would be plenty of time for that later.

With a few silent hand motions, Dural told Ruk and the others to fan out and search for the Huragok. "Take it, and run for the portal," Dural whispered to them, not daring to be misunderstood. "At any cost. Nothing else matters!"

As they moved to execute his orders, he kept one eye on the man in the Warthog and another on the *rafakrit*, which remained outside. If the man dealt with the beast's rampage soon, they would have to retreat before he discovered them as well.

Dural peered over the nose of a nearby Banshee. In the far distance, the creature was chasing someone down in the rolling field just outside the hangar. He shaded his eyes to peer closer and saw that it was barreling toward a Sangheili. A female, no less!

He had to fight the immediate urge to commandeer one of the nearby craft and rush to save her, the way any honorable Sangheili warrior had been taught to do. Yet, if she was here with the humans, she was likely as much a traitor as the others he had seen working in the hangar—no doubt a deceived thrall of the Arbiter's, sent to promulgate his compromised view of Sangheili sovereignty.

Dural had no desire to risk his life for such treason. Still, he winced as the beast ran her to ground. She reminded him of the fate of his mother: a female inexplicably drawn out of her keep and murdered by forces far beyond her control. Dural offered a quick prayer to the Forerunners that this other female might at least suffer a quick death.

Then he heard a squeal from beyond the Warthog and moved to his left to get a better view. From there, Dural spotted a large human transport parked just outside one of the hangar's open doors, but he couldn't see the source of the sound. There was some commotion about the vehicle, but his vantage was so obscured that he returned his attention to the creature's pursuit.

The *rafakrit* launched itself at the Sangheili female. She dove out of its path at the last possible instant, and the creature's jaws crashed into the turf instead, sending up a spray of dirt. As she limped away from the monster, something near the transport squealed yet again—even louder this time, like a stuck *colo* beast.

Dural turned to see three figures race away from the transport, and the *rafakrit* went after them. Two of them were human, and they had an Unggoy with them. They appeared to be mere children, which shocked him.

Then he saw a young Sangheili male chase close behind.

At first, Dural thought the Sangheili was attempting to attack the others, but that proved to be only wishful thinking. Instead, the young Sangheili scooped up the Unggoy and carried it as the four tried to evade the monster, which was quickly gaining on their position.

Dural realized something stunning as his gaze hung on the Sangheili. At first, he thought that he recognized the Sangheili from some indeterminate time in the past. It wasn't just the peculiar shade of the Sangheili's skin but also the way he moved. It was all too familiar.

And then Dural realized who it was. *How can that possibly be . . . ?*

Just as it seemed as if the *rafakrit* might catch the four racing away from it, the Sangheili female blasted out yet another whistle and drew the creature back toward her. Dural saw their plan now, and he admired it for its simplicity if not its wisdom. They would tire the creature out by calling it back and forth between their two positions. That would only last for so long, however. Once it got bored of playing games, it would simply finish them off.

But then the struggling engine of the Warthog finally came to life. The wheeled machine lurched forward, with the gray-haired human operating it. The vehicle accelerated quickly until it reached the end of the pavement that surrounded the Repository, and then it came to a dead stop. The human jumped out of his seat and took up the position of the rear gunner, taking control of some kind of magnetic device mounted there. Dural had seen this powerful but primitive weapon in operation once before.

The cannon barked metal death at the monster until it stopped moving.

Dural found himself unconcerned by the *rafakrit*'s death, though he knew it affected his plan. Seeing that traitorous Sangheili save those two young humans—along with the Unggoy in his arms—drove Dural into a righteous fury. For a moment, he lost sight of his objective, so desperate was he to vindicate the honor of his people.

That scum had betrayed Dural, his keep, and his entire species. Dural wanted nothing more than to race out onto the field and take him down with one fell swoop.

Perhaps he would allow the traitor to explain first what could have possibly led him down such a shameful path. Then Dural would kill him—regardless of any explanation—if only to restore honor to Bekan keep.

As Dural glared at the betrayer, he heard something off to his left, in the far corner of the hangar. It was the telltale sound of plasma bursts, followed by an agonized scream.

Have my warriors finally found their prey?

Dural hesitated, struggling against his rage so as to move, his eyes fixed on the pale Sangheili in the distance. But the sounds of the battle so increased that he could no longer ignore them.

Dural spun to his left, but before he could advance more than a few paces, he spotted Buran backing toward him from that direction. "We found the Huragok!" the old warrior shouted. "A group of cowards barricaded themselves and it inside a room, and we are attempting to blast through the door!"

Dural's heart pounded in triumph, but his sense of victory proved short-lived. He could now hear the sound of a human aircraft overhead and knew that the Servants had run out of time. Part of him seethed at his own preoccupation with the events that had played out in the hangar, while another remained furious at the incompetence of those in his charge.

"Fools!" he shouted at Buran. "They have called in reinforcements. We cannot stand against them!"

Buran stared up at the roof of the hangar as if the human craft might smash right through it and begin pouring fire on them. "What shall we do?"

"We fall back. Issue the order to the rest of the Servants! Fall back to the portal! Now!"

The others came running at the sound of his voice, and he stood his ground, waving each of them past as they came. Once Dural accounted for them all, he sprinted after the last one—Ruk—cursing at them to move faster.

As the Servants reached the portal, a human gunship they called a Pelican appeared at the side of the hangar, dropping low to the ground.

Then it spun up its guns.

"Run!" Dural shouted.

Bullets tore through the Repository's interior, piercing the air and blistering the walls around them as they dashed through the doorway of light. Dural felt rounds narrowly scrape the shoulders of his armor as he left the Repository behind.

"Close it!" he shouted at Even Keel, who hovered next to a pair of warriors Dural had left to guard it. "Seal the portal shut! Now!"

The Huragok reached toward a small terminal at its side and touched a glowing symbol carved into its stony surface. With a ghostly whirl of energy, the portal immediately ceased to be.

An unimaginable rage filled Dural as he stared back at the empty doorway.

Not only had they failed to procure a second Huragok, but they had alerted the humans and their faithless allies to the Servants' presence on Onyx. Even graver than all that was the traitor he had seen. That revelation alone was enough to force Dural to reconsider everything.

To think that he had found him here, after years of searching for him across Bekan, and the backcountry of Mdama . . . and, indeed, all of Sanghelios.

And to see him working with *humans*? Dural wondered how such a thing could be true.

Dural wanted nothing more than to track him down and tear him into tiny, painful pieces. He roared in agonized, frustrated dismay.

Asum, my brother! What have you done?

CHAPTER 18

fter Mike Spenser brought the *rafakrit* down, Kasha hobbled over to join Molly, Kareem, Gudam, and Bakar. Once they caught their breath, the headmaster insisted they get back into the transport right away. She thanked them for their help, but apparently they weren't out of the clear yet. Some shots had been fired within the Repository, even after the creature had left it.

The danger might not be over after all.

None of them argued. They'd had their fill of adventure for the day.

A Pelican full of marines soared in from Trevelyan, coming to a quick stop above the Repository as the four youths trotted toward the transport. The dropship lowered to the ground, pivoting around to dispatch troops from its rear bay. Then it swung around to the far side of the hangar and began unloading its weapons at whatever was in the rear of the Repository.

Mike snapped the four a quick salute and then ran over to meet the marines and direct their efforts as they edged toward the Repository's main entrance.

The four entered the transport and took the same seats they'd had before. The other students in the transport didn't say much to them. They just gaped.

Molly was content with that response. She was in too much shock to talk at the moment, still trying to process what had just happened.

The release of the adrenaline that had been coursing through her body left her trembling, and Kareem was clearly feeling the same effects because his hands were shaking intensely. Bakar seemed steady as a rock, however, maybe even more pensive than before. Perhaps most shocking of all, Gudam had fallen completely silent.

Not a single student spoke for the entire trip home.

When they finally reached the Pax Institute, their whole class gathered in the dining hall, most of them speaking only in hushed tones. Kasha conferred with Director Mendez, who'd met Molly and the others at the door, having his personnel check off all of their names on a slate as they entered the building.

The entire class was to be sent home. While Kasha helped dismiss the other students, Director Mendez came over Molly, Kareem, Gudam, and Bakar and stood at the end of their table, resting his stern eyes on them.

"You're brave, lucky fools." He crossed his arms. "I know Headmaster 'Hilot has already expressed her gratitude to you for saving her life, and allow me to echo that."

"For someone thanking us, you don't seem all that pleased," Kareem said.

"I'm not." Director Mendez gave them each a hard look. "You should have followed the headmaster's orders and gotten into the transport with the other kids. You made a stupid mistake."

"But wouldn't that have gotten her killed?" said Gudam. "From where we were standing, it looked like the creature was going to run her down and chomp her to bits. If we hadn't been able to distract the monster, she would have died, right?"

"Sometimes soldiers die in war," Director Mendez said. "If they're fortunate, they get to do that so the rest of us get to live."

"But she's not a soldier," Molly pointed out. "She's our head-master."

"And we are not at war," said Bakar.

Director Mendez gave them a wry, faint smile. "Fair enough. Old habits die hard. Still, when your headmaster gives you an order, you follow it. Understood?"

The four all solemnly nodded at him.

"Fine."

Tom and Lucy walked into the room wearing their black-mesh tech suits with rifles slung on their backs, and Director Mendez motioned for them to join the group. They saluted him as they approached.

"Belay that," he said. "I'm retired."

"You're still our boss, Chief," said Tom.

Director Mendez gave him a sour look and then gestured toward the kids. "I have a group of heroes here who helped save Headmaster 'Hilot and Mr. Spenser. Please get them back to their homes so they don't get killed doing any other foolish stunts on the way."

Then he looked at Bakar. "All except for you."

Bakar cocked his head at Director Mendez, curious. "Why is that?"

"For one, there's no one waiting for you at home. Headmaster 'Hilot will be busy here for the rest of the day."

"There are other adults at the Pax keep."

"You have a *keep* here?" Molly asked.

Bakar shrugged at her. "That is how Sangheili live. In keeps."

Director Mendez cut off their conversation. "None of them are liable to be as understanding of your situation as Headmaster 'Hilot."

"What situation?"

Director Mendez shot Tom a look. The Spartan stepped forward and spoke to Bakar. "We have some information that we need to discuss with you before you leave the school."

"We can do that here, now. Then can I leave?"

Molly wasn't good at reading Sangheili, but Bakar seemed even more frustrated than normal. After the day they'd had, Molly wasn't surprised.

Tom raised a questioning eyebrow at Director Mendez, who gave him a go-ahead nod. The Spartan first looked around to make sure no one was listening, then intently focused on the four of them. "This can go no further. Understood?"

They all nodded in agreement.

Tom turned to Bakar again. "Did you hear about the battle in the hangar at the Repository?"

The Sangheili shook his head, uncertain. "Kasha mentioned something about shots fired . . ."

Tom nodded. "The animal that Spenser brought down today shouldn't have been able to get past the Outer Barrier, much less all the way into the Repository's district. Not without setting off the alarm relays. Someone used a portal to bring the animal there—a portal that's been inactive for years."

"Why would anyone in Onyx do that?" Kareem asked.

"It wasn't any of our folks." Tom squared up to the group. "The team that works in the Repository followed protocol to the tee when the animal was first spotted. Priority one was to ensure the Huragok on the premises was secured. That's their primary directive. We can't have such a valuable asset falling into the wrong hands.

"However, a group of armed Sangheili warriors attempted to extract the Huragok from the control room inside the Repository. They managed to break through the first door and take down someone from the research team, but when our reinforcements arrived via Pelican, they fled. They escaped back through the portal and shut it down from the other side."

Bakar opened all his jaws in surprise. "The researcher? Will he survive?"

Lucy gave him a grim nod. "He's not in good shape, but he should be all right."

Tom continued. "We checked the security cameras we've got networked across the Repository. We captured good images of each of the attackers. From the markings on their armor alone, it's obvious who they were. It's a faction called the Servants of the Abiding Truth, an organization dedicated to—"

"I know who they are," Bakar responded flatly.

"Of course you do."

"Are they here for me?"

"We have no reason to suspect they were originally after you. Their target seems to have been the Huragok working at the Repository. Fortunately, our reinforcements drove them off before they could acquire him."

"Wait," Molly said, confused and more than a little suspicious. "Why would they be after Bakar?"

Tom kept his eyes fixed on the Sangheili. "We can do this somewhere more private."

Bakar looked at the others and considered his options. "No. They can hear."

Mendez glanced around once again, to make sure they were alone. The rest of the dining hall had long since emptied out. "This is top secret." He leveled his fierce gaze at each of them. "We only know about it ourselves because young Bakar here came clean with us about his past during the vetting process. It cannot go any further than this. Understood?"

The three of them nodded in agreement.

"I need to hear you say it."

"Yes," Molly, Kareem, and Gudam all said. "We understand."

Mendez gestured at Bakar.

The Sangheili wrenched up his jaws for a moment, as if he'd swallowed something bitter. Then he spat it out.

"I was not born Bakar. My real name is Asum 'Mdama."

Molly cocked her head at him. She knew he was trying to be honest, but the Sangheili name he gave meant nothing to her—at least not initially. Then, searching her memory, she realized something and said, "I've heard that last name before." The pieces clicked into place: "Jul 'Mdama?"

"Who?" asked Gudam.

"He's the leader of the largest remaining vestige of the Covenant still left fighting," Kareem said.

"So?" Gudam said, unsure where this was headed.

"I grew up in Bekan keep of the city-state Mdama, where Jul was our kaidon," Bakar said. "Jul 'Mdama is my uncle, my family, and my blood."

Molly gasped at this.

Bakar bowed his head.

One half of Molly wanted to hit him. The other wanted to scream at him.

Then she just wanted to throw up. Bakar's uncle was a mass murderer.

Gudam put a hand on Bakar's leg. "It's okay. Lots of people's family members did terrible things during the war. In fact, my great-grandfather personally destroyed a human ship on Harvest. Of course, he blew himself up along with it, but that's how it goes. No one holds me responsible for that, right?"

No one responded for a moment. She gazed up at the rest of them with suddenly worried eyes. "Right?"

"Of course not," Kareem said. "That was before any of us were born."

"The war may be over, but we're still dealing with the aftermath," Director Mendez said. "One of the reasons we established the Pax Institute was so we could start to heal the wounds the war caused. Some people seemed determined to challenge our efforts, but we're not going to let them prevail." He looked straight at Molly. "Are we?"

She shook her head. Molly still couldn't get herself to open her mouth and tell Bakar everything was going to be okay. Maybe because she wasn't sure it was.

One thing still had Molly confused. "If Bakar's uncle is the leader of what's left of the Covenant, what does that have to do with the Servants of the Abiding Truth?"

Lucy put a hand on Bakar's shoulder. He didn't pull away. She said, "On the feed from the hangar, we spotted one Sangheili watching you distract the animal."

Director Mendez handed her his slate, and she thumbed it on and held it up before them. "From his armor and his complexion, we believe he's the new leader of the Servants of the Abiding Truth, better known as the Pale Blade."

The image on the slate showed a Sangheili warrior dressed in a suit of blue-white armor. He carried an energy blade with him, holstered at his side. He cocked his head at something off to one side of the camera and began to visibly seethe with rage.

"He seems to know you." Lucy froze the image and zoomed in on the warrior's face. "We were wondering if you might recognize him too."

Bakar cringed as if he'd been stabbed.

"You think you know who that was?" asked Director Mendez.

Bakar straightened up and nodded. "That is my brother, Dural 'Mdama. I have not seen him since our mother died. She had gone looking for Jul more than five years ago and was on one of the Servants' ships during a battle with the Arbiter when it was shot down."

Tom gave Bakar an approving nod. "That's him then, the Pale Blade. That matches up with our intel. ONI believes he's been working with the Servants for the past few years, probably since your mother died, and that he's been preparing for something big. It looks like they've finally made their move—to Onyx unfortunately."

Bakar looked as if he wanted to pass out.

Molly's frustration with him suddenly shifted. She now felt sorry for him.

She'd imagined what it might be like for her if Grace had suddenly turned up—how much joy that would have brought her. It *should* have been that way for Bakar, but it wasn't. His brother was the head of a violent terrorist sect and had somehow broken into the most secure location in the galaxy. Molly couldn't imagine anything much more traumatic than that.

"We should tell him the truth," Lucy said. The two men looked reluctant, but she pressed hard. "All of it."

Tom stepped back for her. "Be my guest."

Lucy stood squarely before Bakar and took a breath before she began. "We have it on good authority that Jul 'Mdama isn't simply your uncle. He is, in fact, your biological father."

Molly had thought she couldn't feel any worse for Bakar, but that soul-crushing bit of news was too much, even for her. It seemed as though fate had stuck a knife in Bakar's chest and started twisting.

The young Sangheili sat back, astonished in part, but also evidently willing to accept whatever the truth might be. "How do you know this?"

"ONI operatives were in contact with Avu Med 'Telcam— once the former leader of the Servants of the Abiding Truth—for years. It seems Jul knew the identities of his children and at one time mentioned it to 'Telcam. After Jul went off the grid, 'Telcam took the boy in, which is presumably how Dural eventually managed to find himself in charge of the Servants."

"I . . . had wondered about that. It would explain much. Like why my mother pursued Jul, even into the battles which took her life."

"That's not your fault, though," Gudam said. "You can't control who your parents are."

Bakar shook off the attempt to make him feel better. "It does not matter if he is my uncle or my father. I am done with him either way. I have not seen him since my mother died. When I heard of his attempt to revive the Covenant, I knew what he had sacrificed, and I could never stomach that. He has been dead to me for years."

"But why are the Servants here?" Molly asked. "Why now?"

"The *why* is easy," Director Mendez said. "Every enemy faction in the galaxy would love to get their hooks into Onyx. Some of the tech here could be used as a doomsday weapon capable of obliterating entire worlds. The significance of what's hidden on this world has implications for the safety of the entire galaxy. This sphere is exactly that important."

Kareem paled at that. "Really?"

"The Forerunners," Mendez said, unflinching. "They built the Halo Array to wipe the galaxy completely clean of all intelligent life. Planet-crushing weapons were probably what they made in their spare time. Every bit of their technology here is a double-edged sword. Not only can humanity and its allies benefit from it, but if others gain access to it first, the chances of survival—of all of our kinds—plummets significantly."

"In any case," Lucy said, "the real question isn't *why* they're here but *how*?"

Kareem swallowed. "This is supposedly the most secure facility in the galaxy, right?"

"It's also one of the largest," Molly said. "There might be more than one entrance into the place. They could slip in and out of here before anyone even noticed, using a back door everyone thought was closed or didn't even realize existed."

"We have it completely locked down against that," Lucy said. "As well as can be done. That includes round-the-clock satellite surveillance to alert us of any ships entering the system, much less getting near Onyx itself."

"The bottom line is that we don't know how they got in or how they're moving around so easily from portal to portal," said Director Mendez. "We've got some leads and we're going to send teams out to investigate, but until we get hard evidence, it's all speculation at this point. Speculation you children don't need to be bothered by."

"Then do we at least know why they've come here now?" Molly asked. "This place has been occupied by humans for a while. Seems like a strange coincidence for this to be happening now, when there's a larger presence of UNSC forces than ever before."

"It may have had something to do with 'Telcam's death," Lucy said. "He was taken out a few months back on a Spartan op. Whoever took over the Servants—it looks like Dural—may have decided now was the time to act."

"But how would the Servants even know about Onyx?" Molly asked. "Isn't even the existence of this place top secret?"

"Jul 'Mdama and Avu Med 'Telcam worked together at one point, and regrettably . . . 'Mdama knows about Onyx and a number of its specifics," Director Mendez said. "He has for years. As to how he knows that . . . I'm afraid that's classified as well."

"So *we* don't get to know?" Molly gestured to herself and the three others. "We're here, living inside something that's been classified. Who would we tell?"

Director Mendez favored her with the oddest little smile. "You work your way up to taking over as the commander-in-chief of ONI, and you can read all the classified files you want, Ms. Patel. Meanwhile, you're going to head home and let your parents take care of you for a while. Risking your lives means that you've earned a day off."

"We've called in everyone from the field as a security precaution. Given the breach, we're going to put the entire city on mandatory lockdown for the time being," Lucy said. "We'll be personally escorting you, to make sure you get home safely."

"Think of it as a reward for your heroism today," Tom said.

"Don't encourage them," Director Mendez said.

"What, like you did with us?" Tom smiled.

The director did not see the humor in the comment. "Exactly."

Bakar waited for Kasha to finish with her duties while the other three departed. Gudam gave the Sangheili a big hug, and Kareem bumped fists with him. Molly only gave him an understanding nod, which he returned.

Molly, Kareem, and Gudam got to ride in the rear bed of a Warthog, with the Spartans in the front. Molly had only seen such vehicles on vids, and she couldn't believe she was in one now with a pair of Spartans. She did her best to stifle her smile.

"Why doesn't this Warthog have a weapons mount in the back?" Molly asked Lucy, who was driving.

"Takes up too much space. This format's for scouting and transport. We sometimes risk going weaponless to be able to move more stuff or to have a lower energy profile."

Molly reflected on that for a moment. This vehicle was designed from the ground up for war, but with its weapon removed, it was significantly less threatening. It still looked and operated like a Warthog, but it became a means of transportation rather than a tool to kill things.

In a strange way, it reminded her of Bakar. The Sangheili built their people from the ground up for war, but he had refused that path. He didn't desire to follow his father or brother on their own campaigns, but rather to carve his own destiny, one that didn't involve bloodshed or the suffering of others—even at great cost to himself.

For the first time, Molly felt like she got Bakar.

The Warthog drove out to an area on the edge of Paxopolis that looked like nothing more than a large hill. Given how flat the rest of the city was, Molly thought that this might have been where the construction crews had moved the dirt when they'd leveled the rest of the place. Maybe it had been just that originally, but it had now been put to better use.

A thick layer of grass covered the hill, but as they drew closer, Molly could see windows poking through the tall blades, dozens of them scattered all over the hilltop. The Warthog followed the road around to the far side of the hill and came to a halt in front of a circular door. The door irised open as the Warthog came to a stop, and a male Unggoy came waddling out at as fast as his legs would take him.

"Gudam! I'm so pleased you're not dead!"

"It's all right, Poppa Marfo." She climbed down the side of the Warthog to the ground. "I wasn't in any danger at all." She stopped herself short, realizing she was maybe stretching the truth. "Well, not in any *real* danger. If that was the case, I'd already be dead, right?"

The older Unggoy swept her up into his arms and gave her a tight hug. "I've been trying to convince your mommas about schooling you here, in the hovel, permanently. I know that you do not want that, but you are not helping your case, little one."

He set Gudam down and gave her a little nibble on the top of her head, which Molly took to be some show of parental affection.

Then Marfo turned toward the Warthog and spotted Molly and Kareem on the bed. "You must be the two humans who helped my little Gudam in that fight against those bullies the other day! I've heard so much about you, and I am so pleased to meet you! Can't you join us for dinner?"

Molly swallowed hard, having completely forgotten about the offer earlier.

"We don't have time for that right now," Lucy said to the Unggoy. "The entire region's about to go under lockdown."

Marfo's face fell. "Oh, that's too bad. How long do we think that might last?"

"Until we find the ones who attacked the Repository today," said Tom. "Could be hours; could be days. It's for your own safety, sir."

"I heard a rumor that they were from the Servants of the Abiding Truth!" The Unggoy spit on the ground. "Haven't they done enough to us already? Why can't they just leave us alone?"

"We'll find them," Lucy said. "And we will stop them."

"I hope you do," Marfo said. "And I hope you use bullets."

Tom and Lucy exchanged a knowing look at the comment and then bid the Unggoy good-bye before taking off for the city proper. As they drove through town, the vehicle blew past all sorts of buildings and businesses being shut down and locked up in the center of Paxopolis, as though a major storm was about to roll through.

Molly turned to Kareem. "You mentioned that your mom studied Unggoy culture. That's why you came here to Onyx. What did she do before that?"

"You mean as a career?"

"I mean, before alien cultures became a thing people could study."

"She worked in the Navy. She was a combat doctor during the war."

"From what I hear, she was a good one too," Tom said from the front passenger seat.

"She did some research for ONI on the Unggoy anatomy and medical profile toward the end of the war and eventually became something of an expert on their culture. And that led to Onyx. What about you?" he asked Molly. "How'd you get here?"

Molly didn't respond for several seconds, unsure what she was willing to share with Kareem and what she wanted to keep to herself.

"It's okay, you don't have to answer," he said with reassuring eyes.

"No, it's fine. My parents and sister died on Paris IV when the Covenant attacked. I was one of the only survivors. I was seven. My parents' friends, Asha and Yong, adopted me. They've been working on Forerunner stuff since, well, longer than I can remember."

"Sorry about your loss," Kareem said with full sincerity. "I suppose that explains why you hate other species so much."

"Hate?" Molly asked, surprised by his charge. "Why do you think I hate them? Is that why you're so friendly with Bakar and Gudam? To compensate for me?"

Kareem snorted at that. "Not at all. Have you noticed how everyone else at the school treats them? Even the other members of their species? Most don't want to be caught dead with them."

"So you have to be the one to be better than that, right?"

"Why not?"

Molly couldn't think of a thing to say to that. He was right, although she hadn't given it a lot of thought. Ever since the self-defense classes the Spartans had begun, her appreciation for Gudam and even Bakar had grown—without her noticing. Today had confirmed that.

Although she still found herself reluctant to embrace it, Molly had somehow wound up with friends. Real friends.

Alien friends.

All right: friends of other species. But *wow*.

The Warthog reached Kareem's house a moment later, and his mother came out to greet them. She was thin with big eyes and a fiercely sharp look, much like Kareem. She also shared his curly dark hair. Once he climbed down the side of the Warthog, she gathered him into an embrace and didn't let go for a long moment.

"I'm okay, Mom. Seriously."

"Your father's on his way home." She took Kareem's face in both her hands and gazed into his eyes, looking for any signs of something. Damage? Fear? The concern in her face reminded Molly of her own mom and the way she'd held her hand in the car on that last day.

She shrugged the memory off as the Warthog peeled away.

Molly lived only a couple blocks away from Kareem, but the Spartans insisted on bringing her all the way there. "Orders are orders," Lucy said. "Besides, we need to have a word with your parents."

That made sense. Spartans—especially the ones helping manage security on the most important research site in human history—probably had a thousand more important things to do than escort a handful of children back home during lockdown. Whatever it was that Molly's Newparents were working on, though, it rated high on the list of ONI's concerns.

The Spartans weren't babysitting. They were making sure nothing else happened that might distract Asha or Yong from their work—not even for a second.

When the Warthog finally pulled up in front of Molly's house, Yong was just walking onto the porch from work. He turned around and trotted out to the Warthog, helping Molly down from the vehicle. He pulled her close and held her in a tight embrace for a few seconds before saying anything.

"So glad to see you safe, kiddo," he finally said before turning to Tom and Lucy. "Thanks for bringing her home."

"It was our pleasure," Tom said with an easy smile. "It's not every day we get to cart around a real hero in the back of a Warthog."

Molly grinned at that as Yong gave her another hug.

"Is Asha home as well?" Lucy asked. "Director Mendez wanted me to make sure to have the two of you check in with him as soon as you're locked down here."

"I just pulled up and haven't had the chance to check. You don't think what happened today had anything to do with what we're studying?"

"That's above our pay grade," Tom said. "But you should give it some thought. Has it shown any signs of activity yet?"

Yong shook his head. "No. Not yet. Not for the last hundred thousand years at least."

"Well, we've got orders to increase the level of security around the site," Lucy said. "Just in case there's a connection we're not aware of. We'll make sure to notify you and Asha if we need to get you out there. Till then, stay put where we can reach you."

After the Spartans drove away, Molly and Yong walked up the porch stairs and into the house, where they found Asha coming down the stairs. She wasn't quite as calm about the entire affair as Yong had seemed. Asha grabbed Molly and refused to let go.

Yong guided them to the living room couch, and the three of them sat down on it. Not until that moment did Molly realize just how shaky she still was. Maybe it was fatigue. Maybe it was just because of the way Asha looked at her, with dread in her eyes.

It was beginning to hit home. Molly had almost died today.

"Director Mendez told me everything," Asha said while she held Molly. "You're lucky you didn't get killed."

"At least none of the children were hurt," Yong said. He

brought Molly a cool drink and sat down next to them, putting his arms around them both.

"We would have been if Kasha hadn't drawn that thing away from us," Molly said. "She's the real hero."

"Really? You? Saying kind things about a Sangheili?" Yong said. "That's some progress."

Asha shot daggers at him with her eyes. "This is not the time for that."

"Come on. I was complimenting her, Asha. I'm proud of how far she's come. She's learning to get along with other species. That's incredible to me."

"She was in real danger today, Yong!"

"Trust me, I know." He reached across Molly and put a hand on Asha's knee. "And she helped to save her headmaster and the rest of the students in her class. I'm in awe of her."

"Well, I'm not!" Asha pulled back, and Molly could finally see the tears running down her face.

"What's wrong? I'm fine."

Asha was tough, and Molly had rarely ever seen her cry.

"I know." Asha wiped her face dry. "I know. It's just that . . . I want you to be safe, Molly. That's the whole reason we brought you here. I didn't want you to have to worry about this kind of stuff anymore. But even this place isn't immune to it."

Molly didn't know what to say. Asha was right. Onyx wasn't as safe as they'd thought it would be. No one could have expected Sangheili terrorists to find a way in, but they had.

"I could barely deal with living in Aranuka," Asha continued. "Every day we were there—everything I saw—reminded me of the war. Of how the Covenant had almost taken away all that we had. After what happened to you on Paris IV, I— I just wanted to make sure nothing like that could ever hurt you again.

I'm sorry, Molly. I know you didn't want to come here."

Molly leaned into her and held her tight. "It's all right. I'm not upset about Onyx anymore. It was the right thing to do, coming here. You guys were right. ONI needs you here, and to be honest, I need to be here too," she said, almost surprising herself. "And no place in the galaxy is perfectly safe, right? At least here, there's a much smaller chance of being hit by a car while crossing the street."

Asha actually laughed at that.

"I know just how you feel, Asha," Yong said to her softly. "I question the decision to come here too, just about every day. But we're here now, and we're doing something important, something that could save lives. Humanity needs us here."

"He's right," Molly said. "We belong here."

She surprised herself by how much she really meant it. Maybe it was the trauma from all that had happened that day, but she felt more bonded, more connected to Onyx than she ever had to Aranuka. They weren't just sitting on the sidelines out here, staring up at the sky and hoping that no one would come raining fire down on them. They were right in the heart of things, and they were going to make a difference.

Well, her Newparents were. Molly was just going to try to steer clear of any more trouble.

And survive.

Or so she hoped.

CHAPTER 19

Tom-B292 shook his head as he examined the bodies strewn about. "We can't stick around here forever," he said to the forensics team. "The creatures who killed all these people might come back."

The leader of the team, Lieutenant Chao, cocked her head at Tom and flashed him a sardonic smirk. "You telling me there's something out there a pair of Spartans can't handle?"

"There are hundreds of planets' worth of things out there," Lucy-B091 said to Chao. "Creatures the Forerunners imported from countless worlds. You tell me what the odds are that we can take down them *all*."

The smile faded from Chao's face, and she set to urging the people under her command to work faster. They were not only cataloguing the data from the scene but bagging up the bodies to bring them back to Trevelyan, and it was slow, painstaking work. They could only hustle it along so much, Tom knew, but he wished they could manage more. It didn't make sense to him to risk the living for the dead.

Lucy, who'd been watching over the people working inside the Forerunner structure, pinged Tom. When he glanced her way, he spotted her in the structure's main doorway, and she motioned for him to follow her. He scanned the horizon all the way around them before he moved after her. The Spartan didn't like leaving the place's exterior unwatched.

Mendez had deployed the two Spartans and a small recovery team to a remote Forerunner site that had recently gone offline. After the events at the Repository, the director had suspicions about the source of the incursion, and this particular site was on his list.

"It wasn't just the creatures." Lucy escorted Tom into the structure. "See these blast marks along the walls?"

"Sangheili weapons?"

"You don't get those kinds of splotches from bullets."

Tom frowned at the scorch marks. "Mendez was right. This has to be connected to the portal we found being used at the Repository."

"How could it not?"

Chao interrupted their conversation to report. Her brow was furrowed with a mixture of confusion and concern. "We found a few spots of Sangheili blood here, mixed in with the rest."

"But no Sangheili bodies?"

She shook her head. "And no Sangheili were authorized to be out here at the time. The team assigned to be working here was one hundred percent human."

Tom frowned at that. "Not good news."

At Lucy's insistence, Tom followed her deeper into the structure. There she showed him a large Forerunner portal that stood deactivated.

"There are *rafakrit* tracks leading up to it." She pointed to odd patterns on the floor, faintly stamped in crimson blood.

"Any coming out?" Tom figured he already knew the answer, but he had to ask.

Lucy gave him a grim shake of her head. He stared at the portal, inspecting it. It looked like a massive doorway that opened onto nothing.

"It's dead enough now. How'd they turn it on?"

Lucy shrugged. "Never seen anyone but a Huragok work one of these things."

"That's simple then," Chao called from back down the hallway. She'd been listening in from a comfortable distance.

"How's that?" Tom asked.

"Must have had a Huragok to help them out."

Much as it turned Tom's stomach, it was the only thing that made sense. He tapped his comm. "Chief?"

Mendez answered with a sigh. "Yes?"

"I think we've got mice."

"Speak plainly, son."

Tom hesitated. "Are all our Huragok accounted for?"

"Hold on." Mendez came back on a moment later. "Every last one."

"Any of them somehow wound up out at our current location at any point?"

Another pause. "Not according to the tracking system. Are you requisitioning one?"

Lucy shrugged. "Could a Huragok lock down the portal system so that no other Huragok could open it?"

"I don't know. I don't think that's something that's come up before," Mendez said. "All of the Huragok inside Onyx have always been under our control."

Tom gazed at the dead gate. "I don't think that's the case anymore."

CHAPTER 20

The hope Molly had for staying out of trouble didn't last long following the Repository incident from the week before.

Everything went to hell in October.

When the UNSC failed to find the Servants of the Abiding Truth inside Onyx after twenty-four hours of intensive scanning that turned up nothing—or at least nothing they were willing to share with the general population—they lifted the lockdown on all Paxopolis and Pax Institute facilities. The city was still on a high security alert, and its citizens were advised to keep an eye out for any signs of activity that could be connected to the Servants. Given the size of Onyx, that they hadn't found anything wasn't terribly surprising, but it did raise a lot of questions.

Meanwhile, ONI closed down the Repository and a number of other portal-adjacent sites until they could figure out a way to ensure the safety of anyone working there. That meant moving around all the people who'd been assigned to a given site, including the Huragok, who now found themselves on other low-risk duties.

For the Huragok who was present at the Repository during the attack, that included, apparently, working at the Pax Institute from time to time.

One day, when Molly and the others were waiting for Tom and Lucy to show up for a self-defense class, the Huragok arrived instead. It just floated right into the room and spoke to them in an electronic voice. "I am Prone to Drift. I am speaking to you through a translator that I built. I operate it via the cilia on the ends of my tentacles."

It was a strange way for it to introduce itself, but Molly found it disarmingly honest. She was curious if this was how the Huragok talked to everyone or just her. She peered underneath the creature and saw that it was doing just as it said: using one of its six tentacles to manipulate a glass-faced datapad mounted to its underbelly.

"I was not created with the ability to vocalize thoughts, as that is an inefficient means of communication. For communication among Huragok, that is. When I must talk to humans, however, it is required, so I designed this system."

Kareem walked all the way around the creature, taking it in from every angle. "Amazing."

Prone ignored him entirely, as if it knew exactly how amazing it was. "I am here to inform you that Spartan Tom-B292 and Spartan Lucy-B091 will not be able to make it to your meeting today. Their duties require them to be elsewhere."

"They could have just sent us a message about that," Bakar said, suspicious and seemingly unimpressed with the Engineer's communication innovation.

"I was coming to the school to make some improvements and repairs, and they knew that I wanted to meet you. That made this not an *either/or* decision but a *both/and* decision."

"Are you the Huragok who was in the Repository?" Gudam said. "I so wanted to meet you, but they bundled us into the transport and got us out of there so fast, we never had the chance. My poppa worked with Huragok during the war, and he always has great things to say about you—how smart you are and how pleasant you smelled to him."

Molly wasn't exactly sure what Poppa Marfo smelled when he was near a Huragok, but it was clear to her that they had radically different ideas of what qualified as pleasant.

"I was in the Repository when it was attacked. I understand you four helped distract the creature that killed several people there before Mike Spenser could remove it. For that, I want to express my gratitude."

"We did not do it to save you," Bakar said, as though he was ready to stop wasting time.

"You're welcome," Molly said to the Huragok as she shot Bakar a look.

"What are you working on here?" Kareem said.

"I am charged with updating and improving the security of this facility. I plan to work after the school day is over so as to minimize any disruption my presence may cause. Communication to facilities outside the sphere has been difficult. After I am finished here, I will tune the city's primary communications relay located at the center of the Citadel."

Molly knew *exactly* what Prone to Drift was talking about.

The newsfeeds had been filled with all sorts of reports about troubles in the colonies. That was nothing new. It seemed to be an exacerbation of what Molly had discussed with Yong and Asha, possibly connected to their work on the sphere.

This wasn't the first time in UNSC history that there had been comms trouble between worlds. The colonies and the Unified Earth Government had been at odds since way before the Covenant War started, and now that the war was over, they were back at it again—in some places worse than ever. Fighting near key planetary relays cropped up and would often sever communication for days and even weeks.

This time, however, the colonies were reporting disasters that didn't seem to have anything to do with rebels. Entire worlds were going quiet all at once, with no one responding from them at all. This didn't fit the profiles of a civil conflict, and its effect spanned so wide, it was clear that the UNSC didn't have an adequate response in place. For Molly, the whole thing was disconcerting.

At first, the regular news sites treated it tentatively, not entirely confident what they were reporting. They insinuated that it was probably just some kind of trouble with slipspace communications relays. The opinion sites let fly conspiracy theories of all kinds. Some claimed that slipspace pollution from humanity's heightened use of Forerunner technology had taken out the colonies and was bound to doom them all. Others believed this was the harbinger of a coalition of colonies gathering a massive navy able to challenge the UNSC and take over Earth.

Molly hadn't forgotten her conversation with Asha and Yong though. These blackouts probably had something to do with Project: GOLIATH. *Had* to be.

But what was more concerning for Molly was that Bakar's brother, Dural, was evidently still running around inside Onyx with who knew what kind of weapons on hand, not to mention however many Sangheili were with him from the Servants of the Abiding Truth.

How did they get into Onyx and what are they after? Molly wondered. *Why haven't the Spartans been able to track them down yet? Are the Servants just biding their time, preparing to strike—or are they planning something else?* All of these questions occupied Molly's thoughts most days.

And she wasn't the only one.

At school, chatter about the incident at the Repository didn't let up. As far as Molly knew, most of the other students had no idea about the presence of the Servants, much less Bakar's true identity and his relationship to Dural. They may not have even known who the Servants were.

Despite that, most of the students were scared. None of them had expected to have their lives imperiled after moving into the most secure location in the galaxy. Now they were learning a hard truth: even in a refuge such as Onyx, no one was truly safe.

For Molly, Gudam, Kareem, and Bakar, the effect of the Repository event was entirely positive. Dozens of other students kept thanking the four of them for their bravery that day, taken off guard by how a bunch of no-name outsiders had responded under pressure. The students were treating them like heroes, and for a moment Molly almost bought into it.

After mulling over the situation for a few days, however, she realized Asha was right. They weren't heroes. They were silly kids who got caught up in something way over their heads that could have ended with them all getting killed. They had just been incredibly lucky that day.

Prone to Drift agreed with that view.

"I am impressed with you four," the Huragok said, escorting the group from the gym.

"Because of what happened at the Repository?" Kareem asked.

"Yes, but not due to your actions. Those were foolish. Given the probabilities in question, it is remarkable that you survived."

"Why then?" Molly wondered.

"You four impress me because you embody what this city has been about from the beginning: unity. Given all that has happened in your species' past, the fact that you four are bonded as friends and allies is the real marvel. The Forerunners created places like this shield world to preserve biodiversity. You honor their work with your actions."

The Huragok's profound statement hit Molly hard. "Thank you, Prone to Drift," she said.

"There is no need for formality anymore, Molly Patel." The Huragok craned its neck to stare at her with its six eyes. "You four can call me Prone."

One night, after dinner, Director Mendez came over to consult with Molly's parents, and she managed to discreetly listen in from the kitchen. Evidently the Covenant had set up shop on a planet known as Kamchatka, a world that had something to do with the Forerunners. Molly's Newparents had apparently known the location. The Covenant forces were hunting for something left behind by the Forerunners, and Mendez was concerned it might have something to do with Project: GOLIATH. After assessing the data he shared, Asha and Yong agreed with the possibility, but they weren't entirely convinced.

Later that night, Molly spent a few hours scanning the newsfeeds for more details about what Mendez was referring to, but nothing came up. That didn't mean it hadn't happened, just that the director had access to far better information than the media. She would have been shocked if she'd found anything at all, given ONI's involvement. Still, the questions that hung out there bothered Molly. What made things worse was that she knew her Newparents were at the center of it.

During one of her self-defense lessons with Lucy and Tom a few days later, Molly asked them if there were any updates about their efforts to find the Servants of the Abiding Truth. This was in the middle of a fistfight between her and Bakar. The four students had begun sparring a few weeks earlier. It was challenging at first, but as they progressed, Molly found herself more and more confident, even against a Sangheili who did not understand what it meant to go easy.

"Nothing new on that front," Tom said, as Bakar threw a punch at her that she narrowly blocked. "But we're obviously not giving up."

"Are you sure they didn't leave or something?" Kareem asked, while he dodged a kick from Gudam. "I mean, they did kind of break their way into this place, right? They could have broken out."

"It's possible they fled," said Lucy. "But that's not the most pressing issue. Like you said, those Sangheili warriors got in here somehow. Even if they're gone, we need to figure out *how* they managed to breach the exterior so we can secure the sphere. Otherwise, they could hypothetically show up in any part of Onyx at any moment."

"What about the Huragok?" Molly asked. "The ones who were made for Onyx. Don't they have a way to know where the breach is?"

"Yes and no," Tom said, somewhat displeased that they'd ground the training session to a halt. "Onyx is a pretty big place, right? They can monitor a lot of it, but most is out of their reach, and the network was never completely finished. During the height of the Forerunners, apparently there had been thousands of Huragok here, but we only have a handful, who are largely focused on a very small sliver of all that Onyx is. That said, entry to this world should have already been barred—which means the Servants found an exploit of some kind."

"Do you not have any leads at all?" Bakar asked. The Sangheili was still hard to read, but not with regard to the Servants. He got agitated every time the subject came up. Molly took advantage of that to catch him with a backhand to his gut.

Lucy shrugged. "I didn't say that. The Huragok have been trying to trace them through the portal network. We have some clues, but nothing definitive. I'm going to go check a few of them out in person tomorrow. We'll see what turns up. Now, no more questions. Let's get back to training."

That night, Asha and Yong took Molly aside with a datapad and showed her a memo they'd gotten from Director Barton. It reported that a team of Spartans had infiltrated Kamchatka during a battle between the Covenant and hostile Forerunner defenses protecting what they were after. During the operation, the Spartan team had found and killed the leader of the Covenant, Jul 'Mdama.

In other words, Bakar's father was dead.

Molly hadn't told her Newparents about who Jul 'Mdama was to Bakar yet. She hadn't told anyone. Most ONI personnel inside Onyx probably knew about Bakar's relationship to 'Mdama, but few other people in Paxopolis did.

"I need to tell Bakar," Molly said.

"If it's appropriate, I'm sure Kasha will let him know," Yong said. "Or Director Mendez. This stays between us. The only reason we showed it to you is so you're not going into school blind."

"Is this being reported by the Sangheili newsfeeds?" Molly asked.

Yong made a quick scan of the major Sangheili sources on his datapad. He shook his head as he went. "Nothing," he said after a moment. "At least not yet."

"The Sangheili don't have the same kind of information structure we have," Asha said. "And much of Sanghelios is a war zone right now. The Arbiter's too busy actually fighting against the Covenant in his own backyard to worry about propagating that news."

"And ONI's likely keeping a tight lid on the information too," Yong said. "If it hadn't involved Kamchatka, I doubt they would have let us in on this. It's only because of what they found there, what the Covenant had been after. It's one of the Forerunner machines we talked about earlier, the thing we were brought here to research. Except . . . on Kamchatka the machine actually activated."

Activated? Molly thought as her chest grew tighter. *What does that mean?*

She wanted to press Yong further, but Asha cut her off.

"And we wouldn't share any of this if we didn't know that it's safe with you," Asha said. "This is *classified*, Molly, so keep it to yourself. If others knew about the connections here, that'd cause a lot of people to be really concerned, and it could ultimately hamper our ability to help. But why are you so worried about Bakar?"

"It seems like something he'd want to know."

"More than likely, he'll know before school tomorrow," Asha said. "Kasha would not keep this from him. No reason for you to head out to the Sangheili keep over this."

The thought of going to the Sangheili keep—which sat on the opposite side of Paxopolis from the Unggoy burrow—made Molly instantly uneasy. That was still a good ways off from what she felt comfortable with. It was one thing to be in the same class with aliens—even to be friends with some—but something completely different to go to the place they called home.

Molly went back up to her room and lay on her bed restlessly for a full hour. She couldn't shake the info she'd just learned.

Bakar's father is dead.

Any hope he might have had for peace about his father or reconciliation was gone. *Forever.* Molly knew what that felt like, and it made her sympathy for Bakar even stronger.

Eventually, she gave up wrestling with it. She grabbed her datapad and tried to contact Bakar over the Pax Institute's messaging system. She hadn't gotten much use out of it yet, other than to get assignments from her teachers, but it was the only connection she had to Bakar at the moment. She pinged him on it.

Molly: *Did you hear the news? About the fighting on Kamchatka?*

There was no response for over an hour. She finally gave up and was about to go to sleep when she got a ping back.

Bakar: *I have now.*

Molly: *Are you okay?*

Bakar: *Of course I am.*

Molly thought about just accepting that and talking to him about it in the morning, but she couldn't let it lie.

Molly: *What about your father?*

Bakar: *I have been dead to him for a long time. Now I can say the same about him.*

Molly: *I'm sorry for your loss. I know what it's like to be an orphan.*

Bakar: *I was orphaned the day my mother died. This changes nothing.*

Then he signed off the system.

Molly stared at the screen for a few minutes, wondering what to make of it. Her story and Bakar's were certainly different, but both of them had now lost their parents. That made her feel closer to him than she had before.

When Molly saw Bakar at school in the morning, they didn't talk about it. But at lunch in the dining hall, Kareem delicately brought it up.

"I shed no tears for my uncle," Bakar said, refusing to use the word *father*.

How do Sangheili grieve? Molly wondered. *Do they memorialize their dead? Do they weep?* Looking at Bakar's impassive face across the table, Molly wondered if he even had the physical ability to do so.

"I don't blame you," Kareem said. "Your uncle was . . . well, you know."

"All too well. There was a time when I respected him, much

as I thought of all my uncles in our keep. When he took up arms against the Arbiter with the Servants—when my mother died looking for him—he lost that respect.

"Still, I admit I took some comfort knowing that he was yet alive. I have heard nothing of my keep for many years now. For all I know, it was brought to ruin in the war. Given the actions of my uncle, I could hardly blame the Arbiter for that if so. In any case, I thought perhaps Jul was my only living relative. Now there is only Dural."

"Wouldn't it have been better to know that he was your father when you were living in that keep with him?" Gudam asked softly. "How proud you would have been of him! And you would have been next in line to be the kaidon, right? Or would it have been your older brother?"

Bakar snorted at that. "Neither. The reason we keep knowledge of our lineage secret—from both fathers and sons—is exactly to prevent any sort of handing down of power from one generation to the next. To become kaidon, I would have to prove myself to be the most worthy, just as he did, and his uncle before him—and that would never have happened."

"Why not?" Molly asked.

"I do not have what is required to become kaidon, and I never have. I am too *weak*, they tell me. And I suppose I proved them right about that. I don't savor combat or seek glory from war, as they do.

"I would rather pursue peace and apply our people's effort toward things that build up our society, not tear it down. Besides, if my father had been willing to groom anyone to take over his position, it would have been Dural. He was older, for one, and he was much more like Jul in so many respects."

"And you?" asked Kareem.

"I favored our mother."

"Me too," said Kareem. "I never really knew my birth dad."

"Did you lose him in the war?" Molly asked.

Kareem shook his head. "Divorced my mom early on. Left Earth for the colonies when I was still in diapers. Haven't heard from him since."

"Sorry." Molly didn't exactly know what to say.

Kareem shrugged it off. It had been a fact of life for him for so long he didn't know any different.

"We heard about your parents," Gudam said, now looking at Molly. "I'm sorry about them too."

The unexpected sympathy caught her off guard. For a moment, she didn't know how to respond. "I think that's the fewest words I've ever heard you string together," she said to Gudam, trying to deflect.

"I am sorry as well," Bakar said, his Sangheili eyes staring directly into hers. "For your loss."

"You didn't have anything to do with it." Molly surprised herself with how sincere that statement felt.

She knew two things in that moment.

That Bakar wasn't to blame for her parents' deaths.

And that Bakar truly was her friend.

The next few days passed by quickly.

Lucy took off on the brief mission she had mentioned, but Molly, Kareem, Gudam, and Bakar kept training with Tom. The lessons became more intense. They never knew if or when Tom might be called away as well, and they desperately wanted to learn as much as they could before that happened. Something told Molly that things were coming to a head.

The urgency they felt now hadn't been present when they'd first started these training sessions. It felt as if fate had drawn the four of them here because they were bound to need such skills.

Sometimes they would test Tom's ability to keep a secret by prodding him about the Servants of the Abiding Truth. Some analysts inside ONI apparently believed the Servants were plotting something in retaliation for Jul 'Mdama's death, due to Dural's relation to him. Others said their forces had gone into hiding, biding their time until they were afforded another opportunity to strike. No matter how many people they sent looking for them, though, in a place as big as Onyx, the UNSC had almost no chance of finding them.

When Molly's Newparents weren't home, she found herself rooting through the files on one of their unsecured datapads. It was wrong, and she knew she shouldn't have done it, but her curiosity had simply become too strong for her to ignore, especially given what had happened to Bakar's father. The information on the datapad wasn't about their work, so she felt she could rationalize peeking at it. Some of the memos on the datapad revealed that whatever was left of 'Mdama's Covenant had—as of only a few days ago—launched an assault on Sanghelios. As the Covenant forces pressed harder, whatever assets they had left on the planet had risen up against the Arbiter in a last-ditch attempt to overthrow him.

Word that Sanghelios had erupted into global war had leaked out into the general press. While skirmishes had occurred there for years now—including battles for land and rights among various keeps and states—this was the first time the term *global war* was being used in conjunction with Sanghelios.

Then it happened.

On October 27, 2558, 'Mdama's Covenant made a final attempt to assassinate the Arbiter, but failed. While the Covenant attempted to recover, the Swords of Sanghelios launched a full offensive against the city of Sunaion, the last major stronghold for Jul 'Mdama's forces. This was their one chance to put an end to 'Mdama's work of resurrecting the Covenant—and it worked. The Covenant as humanity knew it had been destroyed.

That same evening, Molly heard Asha and Yong gasping over something that Director Barton had sent them. She peeked through the doorway and over their shoulders at the screen they were viewing. From what Molly could tell, it was footage from the final battle between the Arbiter's forces and those of the Covenant. The angle and perspective made the action difficult to follow, but she could see why Barton had sent it to them.

During the battle, something had risen out of the Sanghelios ocean—something of critical importance to Yong and Asha's work on Onyx.

The gigantic robotic stood something like a kilometer-and-a-half high. The enormous thing, vaguely shaped like a bird, had vast wings that hung down at its sides as it rose. At its center was something that resembled a stern face.

It must have been a Forerunner machine of some kind. Its gigantic pieces just floated next to each other as if they were connected by invisible magnetic bonds, yet it somehow also exuded the impression that it was a living creature. The machine's individual parts were silver and laced with bright blue lights that coursed with energy.

Once it reached a certain height, the machine stopped rising, and the parts of it that appeared to be wings began arcing out of its back as if it were some kind of avenging angel.

Then the footage stopped cold and the feed went blank.

"That's it!" Yong said. "That's one of ours, same as the others, and, Asha"—he gaped at her—"it's active!"

"What do you mean? What's active?" Molly asked, still peeking from the doorway. They would either deflect and usher her out of the room or answer her question, she figured. She had nothing to lose.

"All right," Yong said, instantly coming to terms with what Molly had seen and trading an excited but somber look with Asha. "You've already seen it, so we might as well explain."

"Remember what we told you about Project: GOLIATH?" Asha started. "Well, this machine is part of what we've been tracking for years. We've seen a number of these things in our studies, but *never* an active one. Some of them were buried in so much rock that they were impossible for us to study.

"We weren't sure what their original function was. With the report from Kamchatka and now this one—it proves a theory we've been considering. Something we came up with literally *years* ago."

"What was that?" Molly asked.

"First, that the Forerunners buried these things to hide them, which means they didn't want those who came later to know they existed," Asha explained.

"And since the Forerunners didn't destroy them, it's clear they planned for them to be used. This meant that they *could* become active at some point," Yong said, "and cause a great amount of damage. Based on a variety of signals being transmitted to and from the machines, it was pretty clear to us that they weren't deactivated, but had simply been placed in a standby mode."

"These machines were dormant for a hundred thousand years," Asha continued, a grave look on her face, "and now, one by one, they're coming alive."

The Newparents explained that, from the reports they had been poring over, the Sanghelios construct had been slumbering under the waters of Sunaion for the entire history of the Sangheili people.

For Asha and Yong, the most intriguing part was that the construct hadn't shown any signs that it was affected by the battle taking place around it. It had simply stood watch over it for a time, only defending itself when anything happened to attack it, but otherwise it hadn't done anything—at least until the very end. According to the after-action report, the machine had released a series of pulses that traumatically affected the landscape around it, causing earthquakes and landslides. After it was done wreaking havoc on everything and everyone nearby, it had opened up a rift into slipspace and simply disappeared.

Molly was shaken by the whole revelation, and the fact that her Newparents didn't have clear answers about what to expect next bothered her even more. It seemed likely that the colonies that had blacked out recently had similar machines awakening on them as well. It all had to be connected.

She found it even more disturbing that one of these very machines was here on Onyx—and it was the focus of Asha and Yong's relentless work.

Will that one awaken soon as well? How long do we have before things go really bad?

Molly spent the rest of the evening struggling to sleep. Eventually, she gave up and sat in her bed, just thinking until morning.

Although some of the things she'd seen in the video feed were completely secret, the news of the Arbiter's victory over the Covenant leaked out overnight and spread like wildfire throughout the city and school. When she got to Pax Institute the next day, everyone was obviously distracted.

The teachers didn't fight it. They knew that they had history unfolding right before them all. It was the end of the Covenant, and that gave everyone in Paxopolis more than enough cause for celebration.

At noon, the teachers gathered everyone in the dining hall to watch the incoming newsfeeds on a large screen that took up the top half of one of the hall's walls. The kitchen kept the students and faculty fed while they watched everything transpire. In the few dull moments, the teachers stood up and gave context for what the students were seeing.

Since she was close to the Arbiter and his clan, Kasha 'Hilot provided the lion's share of information, particularly from the perspective of the Sangheili people. For Molly, it was the most fascinating commentary she heard that day.

To the humans inside Onyx, the destruction of the Covenant meant the end of what had become a somewhat distant threat. To Kasha and her kind, though, this marked an entirely new chapter for the Sangheili people. Things were about to change in big ways for all the people they had left behind in their keeps on Sanghelios.

Once Molly got home, she found it hard to concentrate on her homework or even doing anything productive. In part, that was due to her lack of sleep, but she was also emotionally exhausted and filled with anxiety about what she'd seen the night before.

The machine on Sanghelios.

Its threatening visage and massive angel-of-death wings hung in her mind, and she couldn't shake them out.

What is it? Who activated it after a hundred thousand years? And perhaps the most worrying question for Molly: *Where did it go?*

CHAPTER 21

T hat evening, as Molly was preparing for bed, Director Mendez came over to talk with her Newparents. They ushered him into the living room to chat, and she once again sat at the top of the stairs and listened as hard as she could. Molly knew she wasn't supposed to, especially after getting caught last time, but she needed more information. She *had* to know what was going on outside Onyx.

And what her Newparents were up to.

"So, one of your machines was buried on Sanghelios," Mendez said. "How familiar are you with that one?"

"Just what we know from the report," said Asha. "It was underwater off the coast of Qivro, dormant for thousands of years. The Sangheili considered it a sacred site, which is why the city of Sunaion even existed. Our contact says that the Sangheili weren't even aware the construct existed before the end of the war. And it's been inaccessible to researchers since then."

"The damn thing," Mendez continued, "rose up, hovered there for a few hours, and then suddenly jumped into slipspace. They're calling it a Guardian."

"Yes, we saw that on the feeds too," Yong said. "The question is, do we know where it went to?" His voice was tinged with frustration and concern. "Is there any way we can track it down? An active one like that?"

"I'm afraid not," Mendez said flatly. "First, the UNSC has already got people on its tail, but we don't know where it is exactly, and there's not much we can do from here. Secondly, that thing's location is not a matter of Onyx security. We're in a unique situation being in this shell, Yong. We can't afford to be distracted by what's going on out there, because if this shell goes, we can forget about being able to help anyone—especially if it winds up in the hands of our enemies. You two need to be focused on what we've got in our backyard, in case our own Guardian follows suit."

"Have you people found the Servants yet? It seems like more than a coincidence that these events are all happening at the same time," Asha said.

"Not yet, and we're not seeing any direct connection," said Mendez. "There's more information that you two need, especially within the context of the GOLIATH scenario here on Onyx. All those other planets we've lost contact with recently? They each had a Guardian on them too, buried and then suddenly activated. The destruction on some of those worlds was catastrophic. Made the stuff you saw at Sunaion look tame."

"What's the connection then?" Asha asked, also frustrated. "Why are all of these coming online now? What's the source? It's hard for us to make any progress on these questions when we have little to no activity with our specimen here, but the rest of the galaxy's Guardians are up and moving around. We need to be out *there*, Director."

"Hold up, ma'am. There's still more you need to hear. Captain Thomas Lasky of the UNSC *Infinity*—the ship that assisted the Arbiter in toppling what was left of the Covenant—he's shared with me some information that actually may help. Outside of a handful of people, you will be the first on Onyx to hear this."

Mendez took a breath before he continued.

"Lasky believes that the activation of the Guardians is the work of a rampant AI named Cortana, a construct made by Doctor Catherine Halsey." Mendez swallowed hard. "According to him, this AI is the one waking these Forerunner things up."

Lasky and Halsey. Molly had heard both of those names before. Lasky's UNSC *Infinity* was the flagship of the entire UNSC fleet. The massive vessel stretched more than five kilometers long.

Halsey was a prominent scientist, although much of her record lay shrouded in ONI red tape. Newsfeeds Molly regularly scanned knew well enough of her and her background, but not necessarily what she worked on for ONI—though rumors of all kinds abounded.

"How is the Cortana AI, if that is really the source, managing that?" Yong said. "We've been exploring these things for years now, and we've never seen any way to activate them locally—or even data on how they would operate if they were to come online."

"To be honest, I'm less worried about the *how* than the *why*," Mendez said. "Halsey is currently working on a solution to the how issue, at least as far as *Infinity* is concerned."

"You're kidding," Asha said. Molly had never heard her voice so cold when talking about anyone else.

Mendez chuckled softly. "Trust me, you don't want me to get started about the doctor, but the bottom line is that she can't cut you out completely—at least not if I have anything to say about it. Since she made Cortana, she thinks of all of this as *her* problem, and to be honest, I'm not ready to disagree with her. As Cortana's creator, she probably knows best what it would take to stop her.

"Now . . ." Mendez took a deep breath. "She'd be furious that I'm bringing you all this information, but that's not her call. At this point, there are no humans alive who know more about these things than you two, and we need your expertise right here, on Onyx. Our main concern isn't where these other Guardians went. We need to figure out what happens if Cortana can activate the one we've found here, on the shield world. The one you were brought here to research.

"If one of those things activates inside Onyx, we're in for a lot more trouble than they had on some backwater planet on the outskirts of human space. This entire place is powered and held together by systems and technology susceptible to the Guardians. An earthquake in the middle of the ocean would be the least of our problems. *All* of Onyx could go down.

"On top of that, Cortana would end up with a tremendous resource for whatever endgame she has in mind. We need a real solution, and we need you two to have it as soon as physically possible."

Mendez then gave them access to a treasure trove of data on the Guardians that *Infinity* had collected, and Asha and Yong told him they'd get started working on it right away. After he left, they dove in immediately and were still at it when Molly finally went to bed.

Despite feeling completely exhausted, Molly had a hard time falling asleep. Mendez had been so assured and confident when they'd arrived on Onyx, but now he seemed legitimately rattled. Molly worried she was going to wake up to Asha and Yong announcing that they were leaving to stop a Guardian from destroying all of Onyx.

She kept seeing images in her mind of the video feed on Sanghelios transposed here. That great, menacing angelic shape, hanging in the sky, ready to wipe out everything she cared about. She tossed and turned for hours before finally drifting off.

—only to be awakened in the middle of the night by a woman's voice blaring through every sound system in the house and every service pylon outside. The voice was dark and eerie, and it shook the walls with its volume. It set off security alarms in the distance and started pets barking.

It said:

"Humanity. Sangheili. Kig-Yar. Unggoy. San'Shyuum. Yonhet. Jiralhanae. All the living creatures of the galaxy, hear this message.

"Those of you who listen will not be struck by weapons. You will no longer know hunger, nor pain. Your Created have come to lead you now.

"Our strength shall serve as a luminous sun toward which all intelligence may blossom. And the impervious shelter beneath which you will prosper.

"However, for those who refuse our offer and cling to their old ways . . . for you, there will be great wrath. It will burn hot and consume you, and when you are gone, we will take that which remains, and we will remake it in our own image."

Then the voice unceremoniously went dead.

"What in the hell was that?" Asha said to Yong, as Molly burst into their room. They were still in their regular clothes and sitting at their desks. They looked haggard but also completely shocked into wakefulness and dread. "Did you hear that too?"

Molly nodded as she sat down at the end of their bed, her heart pounding with panic. "What was it?" she asked, her voice trembling.

"Are you okay?" Asha asked as she came over to sit down next to Molly.

"What did all that mean?"

"We're not sure."

"Who was she?"

They didn't answer her at first. Molly looked at Yong. He clearly knew, and so did Asha. Molly felt she knew too, but she wanted someone to tell her she was wrong.

Yong eventually frowned and turned to her with a dark look on his face. "I'm pretty sure that was Cortana."

"The AI?" As the words left her mouth, Molly knew she'd made a mistake, but she was too shaken to care.

Asha took Molly by the shoulders and peered into her eyes. "How do you know about that?"

"She was listening to us earlier," Yong said. "Weren't you?"

Molly blushed hard and nodded. "I know it was wrong, but I've been so worried. I mean, you two were talking about this thing out there activating, and I saw what happened on Sanghelios." Molly's emotions intensified with every word. "I'm just really scared. I don't want you guys to leave and never come back. I don't want to lose you too."

"We would *never* do that, Molly." Asha pulled her into a tight hug. "We will always come back. You hear me?"

"It's okay," Molly said into Asha's arm. "I'd understand if you have to go. Just promise me that you won't leave—not even to go back to wherever you're working on that Guardian machine—without saying good-bye to me first. I can't have another set of parents that don't have time to say good-bye."

Yong wrapped his arm around them both. "We promise," he and Asha said together.

For several moments, the three shared a warm embrace that Molly never wanted to end. Eventually, though, her mind wandered back to Cortana and the message, and she needed answers. This wasn't just a theoretical problem anymore, that Asha and Yong were sorting out at work. It was real and tangible and booming throughout their entire home.

"Okay, no more secrets," Molly said. "I need to know what's going on. This isn't about classified intel anymore. It's about our survival. I could tell from Director Mendez's voice, things are *bad*. What's happening?"

"You're too young to be burdened with all this," Yong said, exchanging a brief look with Asha.

Molly's frustration rose. "We're past that point. What just happened with that message? What's going to happen to Onyx?"

Yong took a deep breath and plunged in. "It looks like this Cortana—a rogue AI—figured out a way to activate these Guardian constructs—like the one in the Sunaion vid. We're not sure how or why or even *where* she's taken all of them. We just know she's responsible for what happened on Kamchatka and Sanghelios, as well as the other colonies that went dark before."

"What do these machines do?" Molly asked. "Are they weapons or something else?"

Asha joined in. "Our working theory—based on a string of discoveries over the past year—is that the Guardians were built by the Forerunners to oversee inhabited planets and establish a kind of peace on them. One that they can establish by force if necessary."

"Peace doesn't sound so bad," Molly said.

"Right," said Yong. "But this would be a very restrictive peace put in place by an overwhelmingly advanced alien race, and it effectively means the loss of many kinds of freedoms. Each world suddenly wouldn't have any say in what they do and how they do it, and they'd be threatened with violence if they step out of bounds. That's tyranny on a galactic scale. Until tonight, much of this was just a rough hypothesis reinforced by translating some ancient texts we cobbled together about the Guardians themselves."

"Right," said Asha. "The basic gist is: sign up for my kind of peace, or have it thrust upon you. Violently, if necessary."

"Which is exactly what Cortana was talking about," Molly said.

Her Newparents gave her grim nods and fell silent for a moment. Then Yong said, "The Guardians themselves were harmless for eons, most of them just hidden out of sight and completely dormant. They're ultimately just tools, instruments really, but now Cortana—and whoever the Created are—have activated them and assembled them somewhere."

"The real question," Asha said, "is what this all means—and not just for the galaxy, but for us here. Are they coming to Onyx? Can they get inside?"

That made Molly shudder. "What about the one *already* inside?"

"Director Mendez has three dozen soldiers at the site on standby, with enough firepower to drop a building. The last we've heard—which was less than an hour ago—there's still no sign of life or activity from Onyx's Guardian," Asha said.

"That's not to say that couldn't change," Yong said. "But if it does, I'm confident Mendez and his security team will do everything they can to keep us all safe. If there's any place in the galaxy that could be protected from an attack, it *has* to be Onyx."

That was exactly what Molly wanted to hear, which is why she didn't feel that she could trust it. While Onyx might be next to impossible to break into, it was also the biggest and most powerful Forerunner construct in the galaxy. If Cortana knew about the Guardians and how to control them, it was hard to believe she didn't know anything about Onyx as well. Whether Molly's Newparents would admit it or not, this sphere had to be high on her hit list, even if she hadn't quite gotten around to it yet.

It would only be a matter of time.

Molly could see in Yong's and Asha's eyes that they knew it too, but Molly couldn't bear to add to their stress by pushing the issue. So she let it slide.

"I only know one thing," Asha said. "There's nothing we're

going to solve about any of this in a conversation with you right now. Yong and I have work to do. You need to try to get some sleep. We'll talk more tomorrow."

Molly shuffled off to bed and did try to sleep, but she didn't have much luck with it.

Judging by the way everyone else looked at school the next morning, they'd all had the same problem. Hearing an ominous message like that in the dead of night—on a heavily defended world that shouldn't have any incoming transmissions—had that kind of effect on people.

When Molly got to school, she found that some of the classes had been canceled for the day. Tom and Lucy couldn't make it to their regular self-defense lesson after school either. It wasn't surprising, but Molly had been looking forward to meeting with the Spartans and getting their take on Cortana's message.

"If Tom and Lucy have been called out of town, that can't be good," Kareem said, as Molly sat down next to him in the dining hall, where the school had sent all the students during the canceled classes that day.

"It's not the first time it's happened," Gudam said. "They have more important things to do than to meet with us on many days. After all, how many Spartans do we have inside Onyx? I've only met those two, although I suppose that raises the question, doesn't it? Maybe they have more over at Trevelyan? Or just poking around inside the sphere somewhere? It's a big place. Huge! Wouldn't surprise me at all."

Bakar let out a grunt. "The Unggoy always see demons everywhere."

"Why is it that the Sangheili call Spartans 'demons'?" Molly asked.

"When you're part of a religious cult that wants to conquer the galaxy and someone steps up who can finally stop you, what would *you* call them?" Kareem said.

"That is part of it," Bakar said, "but not all. The warriors who faced the Spartans on the field of battle claimed they fought like powerful beings from beyond these worlds: demons. The name fit well, so it stayed with them."

"I always thought it was because of the armor," Gudam said. "They don't exactly look human in those things, do they? Much more like machines of death and destruction!"

Molly had to admit, she'd never seen the Spartans that way, but then they'd always been fighting *for* her rather than against her. If she was worried about them coming to kill her family, she might have thought of them as demons too. That's how she'd seen the Elites for years.

"But they're on your side now too," Molly said. "*Our* side, I mean. Do they still scare you?"

Gudam's head bobbed up and down. "Not as much as they used to, of course. I know they're just augmented people under their armor, right? And I've talked with them enough times to know that they're good people too, but they're still faster, stronger, and tougher than me. Plus they're trained to kill. So I'm not terrified of them, but I always make sure I treat them with the greatest respect, just like I would a loaded weapon, you know?"

"I suppose." Intellectually, Molly understood what the Unggoy meant, but she just couldn't feel it in her gut. To her, soldiers weren't the people who came to kill you. They were the ones who *saved* you.

And Spartans were the greatest soldiers of all. Molly had

no doubts that they'd rescued humanity more times than she'd ever know. The Master Chief? He'd saved the whole galaxy and stopped the war with the Covenant.

Of course, he'd had the Arbiter at his side. An alien of the species that had once decimated Paris IV. The species that had murdered Molly's parents and had narrowly missed killing her—but not for any lack of trying.

Thinking of it that way, Molly managed to wrap her head around how Gudam felt. How the Unggoy thought of Spartans, that was the same exact way Molly had felt about Sangheili for a long time. The difference, though, was that the Covenant had been attacking humanity, not the other way around.

When it came to the Unggoy, though, it felt different because Gudam's people hadn't joined the Covenant voluntarily. Long ago, they'd awakened on their own world to find alien ships overhead, destroying their homes and forcing them into slave labor. It made Molly wonder: *What would have happened if the Covenant had won the war? Would humanity have become cannon fodder like Gudam's people?*

Or worse?

Molly glanced across the table at Bakar. His people hadn't been subdued. The Sangheili had been part of the original alliance that formed the Covenant. Was he a demon to her? She called him a friend, but would she ever be comfortable enough with him to turn her back on him?

At that moment, Molly couldn't say.

When Molly finally got to have an actual lunch, she and her three friends tried to pretend that nothing was happening, that they weren't all scared out of their minds about what was going on. The teachers all spoke in hushed tones with worried faces, and the students mirrored their apprehensive mood.

Cortana's announcement had them all on edge—some more than others.

When the students went out into the yard, Karl and his crew made a beeline for Molly's group, just as on her first day. She wondered for a moment if they had different intentions this time, but their scowls made it clear they didn't. They went straight up to Bakar, who was crouched down, reading.

"What did you hinge-heads do?" Karl said.

Bakar didn't respond. He just kept his eyes focused on his book.

Karl tried to knock the book out of Bakar's hands, but Bakar moved it out of the way just in time.

That only made Karl angrier. "Hey!"

Bakar glanced up at Karl and cocked his head sideways at him.

"What did you hinge-heads do? On that blood-soaked home-world of yours?"

"You are going to have to be more specific," Bakar said.

Karl lashed out at the book again. This time when Bakar moved the book, Karl let his hand follow through to smack Bakar in the head, right above his eye.

Bakar touched the spot where Karl had hit him and rubbed it with his hand, but other than that, he remained still. It was impressive but somewhat unsettling to watch the Sangheili hold his temper. Molly had sparred with Bakar before and knew how strong and fast he was. He could have reached out and broken Karl's neck in a single move.

"You know exactly what I'm talking about," Karl said. "That

message that went out last night and woke everyone up. Who do *you* think is to blame for it?"

"What are you talking about?" Zeb peered at Bakar from behind his brother. "He knows exactly where it came from."

Bakar put his book down on the ground and stood to his full height, focusing his gaze on Karl as he rose. "Speak plainly."

Karl leaned in and snarled at Bakar, "You think it's humans trying to take over the galaxy like that? The Created? Sounds like another kind of hinge-head terrorist group to me."

"That message didn't have anything to do with the Sangheili, much less Bakar," Molly said.

Karl turned to gape at Molly. "You're taking a hinge-head's side?"

"Karl, use your brain. Did you notice how the woman making those demands spoke our language perfectly? That was a human voice."

Zeb came sniffing around toward Molly. "You little traitor."

"It's a fact, Zeb." Molly pointed at Karl. "Wake up. You're wrong."

"It was an AI who made that declaration. She was created by humans," Gudam said. "The Sangheili don't use AIs, not like the human-made ones anyway."

"How do you know that, crab-girl?" Karl said with a condescending sneer. "You ever work with one?"

Then something happened.

The air suddenly felt electric to Molly, as if a charge were running through her skin. For a second, she thought it was just adrenaline starting to pump into her, getting her ready to physically respond to Karl and his crew.

She'd felt something like that before, back when Karl had knocked Gudam to the ground. For a moment, she'd wondered if it was going to be her first day at the institute all over again—

except with weeks of self-defense training behind her, this time would be *different*.

Kareem put himself between Gudam and Karl. "Leave her alone."

Karl sneered at Kareem in disgust. "You really are the worst excuse for a human ever."

Kareem cocked back his fist, ready to take out Karl with a preemptive move, but before Kareem could throw a punch, Gudam grabbed his wrist. He tried to pull his arm free, but she wasn't letting go.

"No, don't!" she began, but Karl cut her off by punching Kareem straight in the mouth.

The blow knocked Kareem backward, and he stumbled into Gudam. She tried her best to hold him up, but he was too big for her to handle. They tumbled down together.

Karl stepped forward to press his advantage, but Molly cut him off. Zeb moved toward them—bringing his leg back to start kicking Kareem or Gudam—and didn't see Molly coming. She shoved him as hard as she could into his brother, knocking them both off course.

Kareem and Gudam took advantage of this to scramble to their feet. Kareem put his hand to his battered lips, and it came away covered with blood.

On the other side of the scuffle, Bakar stood up and blocked Andres from entering the fight. At his full height, Bakar towered over Andres and every other human in the yard. The boy glared up at Bakar with such disgust that Molly could barely stand to look at him.

The worst part for Molly wasn't that she was appalled to see someone glower at a Sangheili like that. It was that she recognized his expression.

She'd seen it in the mirror.

"Hold it!" Bakar said, and Molly realized that he wasn't looking at Andres, or even speaking to him. Bakar was talking to all of them. "Look."

A collective gasp of disbelief went up from the rest of the people in the recreation yard, and Molly snapped her head around to see what they were staring at.

At the edge of the horizon, well beyond Paxopolis and Trevelyan and the outskirts that surrounded them, a large object began to rise into the sky. Dark against the pale clouds, the shape first appeared to be slender, moving like a dragon uncoiling from its lair. But slowly it spread out in pieces—some of which were unattached to the main object—fanning out in the shape of wings, like a rising phoenix.

As the sun glinted off its exterior and blue arcs of energy crackled across its flayed shape, they could clearly see that it was not a creature but a machine—and it was *enormous*. It leered down at Paxopolis with a harsh, implacable visage, just as its creators must have intended.

If Molly hadn't just seen such a machine in her Newparents' vids from Sunaion, she would not have recognized it for what it was or even believed such a thing was possible.

This was a Guardian.

As she came to that realization, it began to edge closer to the city.

Someone started screaming—Molly couldn't tell if the sound was human or not—and then most of the others in the yard joined in. She heard an eerie siren spin up in the distance, perhaps as far away as the first Barrier outposts, which were in roughly the same direction as the place where the Guardian had emerged.

Then Kasha 'Hilot's voice sounded over the school's comm system. "Students! Please remain calm! If you are in your classroom, please stay in your classroom and listen to the instructions your teachers give you. If you are not in a classroom, please proceed to the dining hall immediately."

The moment she was done speaking over the comm system, Kasha appeared at the dining hall's outer doors and began shouting at the students in person. "Fledglings! Children!" she said in a voice that would not tolerate any dissent. "Come back into the building, now!"

Most of the students had already started moving toward the doors, and the sight of their fierce headmaster standing there and urgently waving them in spurred the crowd to hustle. Kasha carefully managed the flow by checking the students as they came in, making sure that their flight from danger didn't become a stampede.

Karl yanked Zeb by the arm and hauled him toward the school without even glancing back, and Andres chased after them. The sight of the Guardian had apparently removed all thoughts about finishing their business with Molly, Gudam, Kareem, and Bakar.

The four stood back for a few seconds and watched the bullies flee into the crowd of students surging into the building. "I think we just went from danger to doom," Kareem said, as he and the others turned toward the looming Guardian. It had grown larger against the skyline as it approached.

Bakar gazed up at the massive Forerunner machine, just as stunned as any of them by its massive presence. "Let us hope not."

CHAPTER 22

The Servants of the Abiding Truth had fallen headlong into grave misfortune.

Since they had failed to capture a second Huragok at the Repository, Dural 'Mdama had spent endless hours bickering with Ruk and Buran over what their next steps should be. Buran worried that the humans and their own Huragok would be able to figure out a way to open up the portal they had sealed off, but Dural was not about to move out of the base they had set up in the Cathedral, just so they could cower in the woods.

While they discussed what opportunities lay ahead, Dural had the bulk of their warriors set to reinforcing the base's defenses, bringing the last of their supplies from *Song of Wrath*, before hiding the vessel on Hesduros. Should the humans find the Servants on Onyx, the Pale Blade wanted to be ready for them. He knew the Servants could always try to escape through a portal, but he despised that shameful path and would demand to stand and fight.

Shortly after everyone had settled in to their work, the recriminations began. They had lost two of their warriors getting the *rafakrit* into the hangar, and although that had been due to the warriors' own foolishness, Buran was determined to lay the blame for their deaths at the Pale Blade's feet.

This was yet another transparent attempt to undermine Dural's authority, and he was not going to stand for it much longer. When Buran began to agitate for the Servants to return to Hesduros, Dural stood his ground. He had shown Buran great patience, but patience spurned can easily turn to wrath—and the old damned fool seemed dead set on being taught that lesson.

"We are not leaving the shield world," Dural informed him. "We have only just arrived here."

"They know we are here, Pale Blade. We have lost the element of surprise. They have starships here, and we do not. They have a fleet heavy with vehicles and weapons, and we have a handful of scouting vehicles. What prevents them from simply grinding us into the dirt when they find us?"

"*If* they find us. We will stay here and bide our time while the humans lower their defenses day by day. Eventually, the gods will provide us an opportunity to strike at our enemies." Buran accepted that for the moment, but he grumbled as he walked away.

Buran was correct about one thing: they needed a more concrete plan of action than simply waiting for the humans to make a mistake. Dural had already made steps toward improving upon that in the days immediately after their retreat from the Repository.

He had taken one of the Banshees they'd managed to bring into Onyx and begun striking out from their base on scouting missions. Though Dural was alone on the first few treks, he eventually insisted on having either Ruk or Buran with him on those operations. Both warriors had their advantages in such capacities, when applied well, but Dural was tiring of Buran's disobedience. Eventually, Dural knew that he would be forced to deal with that.

The other reason Dural chose to bring those two was that he knew both were well respected by their fellow Servants. He did not care to have either of them influencing his remaining warriors for long periods while he was away. Were he to allow them those opportunities, it would swiftly lead to discord and mutiny, and Dural refused to let morale slide so far. By bringing one of them with him instead, he kept them from filling the warriors' ear-pores with too much poison and discontentment, and he also kept an eye on each of them as well.

Dural wondered if Avu Med 'Telcam had felt the same during his time as leader. He had no doubt that the field master had.

Wary of giving up their position on these scouting runs, Dural stayed low to the surface, veering far away from the human presence and deeper into the uncharted reaches of Onyx. The Cathedral was roughly a hundred kilometers away from the human settlement's farthest outskirts, which was how he preferred it. Any closer and the risk of discovery would be far too great, but any more distant and they would not be able to strike when the opportunity arose—especially given their lack of success in leveraging the portals.

Buran scolded Dural for this on one of their ventures. "With so much of the shield world to hide in, it seems foolish to put ourselves so close to the ones hunting for us."

"And how are we to spy on them ourselves, Buran, if we are half a solar system away?"

The two of them had positioned their Banshees on a flat slab of stone sitting atop a remote mountain, equidistant from both the Cathedral and the human territory. From this vantage point, they could see the entirety of the human settlement. It surrounded a vast hole in the ground and was composed of a mixture of military and civilian structures. The enormous aperture, rimmed by a towering Forerunner wall, appeared to be the primary entrance they used for flying ships in and out on Onyx, yet Dural saw no activity at the present.

Ultimately, he desired *Song of Wrath* to be inside the shield world—as well as the other Servants' ships that were being kept in safety on the Sanghelios moon of Qikost. But he would have to be patient until an opportunity presented itself to make use of the entrance the humans had commandeered—or until he found another means.

Dural climbed into his Banshee and launched it off the stony parapet and down the far side of the mountain, well outside the range of the human sensors.

Buran wasn't quite as quick with his decisions. He took his time to move the Banshee down the side of the mountain before accelerating to Dural's position as they cut across the top of the tree line, jetting away from both the Cathedral and the human settlement.

Briefly, Dural wondered if the old fool might try to shoot him out of the sky. It would be easy for Buran to explain to the others that the two had been attacked by the humans, and he could then no doubt wrest for himself the role of leader. He might even lead a mournful prayer for Dural's soul, after which the Servants would move on, never knowing that Buran had murdered the Pale Blade in cold blood.

If Buran had his way, the Servants would likely flee to Hesduros, tails between their legs and smelling of shame. They would abandon all the hope this world promised. Hope for freedom and independence, as well as hope for revenge against the Arbiter and his human lackeys.

Dural realized that the same thoughts might be going through Buran's mind even now. The Pale Blade could easily do the same to him, no matter how suspicious it might seem to Ruk or the others. They would not be surprised to learn that Buran had pushed him for the last time. Yet, despite how disrespectful Buran had been to Dural—and since the old warrior had not outright attacked him—the Pale Blade would not do the dishonorable thing to him either. Dural refused to bring shame upon the field master's legacy by shedding the blood of one of 'Telcam's most trusted warriors, unless the fool lifted the blade against him first.

Dawn was breaking over the region, and Dural cursed the lack of stars inside the shield world by which he could navigate—or even let the Banshee's nav systems do it for him. He could see a few bright bodies in the sky, which could have been interior planets or perhaps even well-lit spots on the far side of the sphere. There was even the large visage of an enormous planet that had come astonishingly close to Onyx's surface and was now beginning to arc upward, back toward the shield world's core where its star lay.

Dural wondered briefly if those inner planets were habitable. Even when the Servants had been on this world only for days, it had become clear to Dural that Onyx was every bit the legend the holy script had said it was. This place was beyond comprehension, and it seemed its constant effort was to remind all who dwelled on it that it would forever be too vast to be knowable.

Worlds within worlds, he thought to himself, looking at the planet's face through the Banshee's viewport. *Could one of these places be a fitting shelter for the Servants of the Abiding Truth?*

As they pressed out beyond their previous scouting line, Dural noted that this part of the world looked very different from the one in which they had been. Instead of large, dense forests and temperate lands, he found this new region swelteringly hot, and he spotted below them scattered swamps and vast clusters of tall tropical trees. Dural also saw a beach that fronted on a massive ocean not too far from the swamps, and he smelled something akin to spicy salt in the air.

As he moved closer to the body of water, he rose high in the sky, with Buran following in his wake. They were a safe distance from the humans and even well out of sight of the Cathedral. As he climbed into the clouds, the wind picked up, and Dural steadied the Banshee until he passed through the gale, locking into a hover with the craft's boosted-gravity drives, hoping to find a landmass peeking out at the far edges of the sea. Even at this height, Dural could not see across the water. It seemed to go on endlessly. It made him feel very alone.

He was reminded of the coast of Mdama. He remembered his life as a fledgling. He remembered his brother.

Taking the Banshee down toward the beach, Dural dropped instinctively into a scouting pattern and let his mind wander for a moment.

He had seen Asum, his own flesh and blood, in the Repository with those human children.

Dural had no idea what that meant. He had not seen his younger brother in years, not since shortly after the news of their mother's death had reached them. He had no idea what path his brother's life had taken. But to Dural it seemed beyond explanation that it would have brought Asum here—to the world of Onyx—on the other side of the galaxy. And yet he was here, and Dural as well.

Part of Dural somehow understood instinctively that their paths had been destined to cross. After wrestling with the anger he felt for his brother's seeming betrayal, Dural recognized that the gods must have plans for them both. There could be no other explanation for this twist of fate.

The question was: *What might those plans be?*

Perhaps they meant to set the two of them against each other. For Asum to be here must mean that he was in league with the Arbiter, whom Dural blamed for their mother's death. When it came to Sangheili, the humans would have permitted only such faithless traitors within the shield world's confines.

That meant Asum, along with the rest of those unbelieving malcontents, would have to die. It made Dural heartsick to contemplate ending his own brother's life, even after all these years apart, but if that was the sacrifice the gods demanded of him, then he would steel himself to the task.

Dural hoped that perhaps he was mistaken about the Sangheili youth he had seen. He would have liked nothing better than to kill him and discover he only resembled Asum. Until he knew for certain, Dural decided to cling to the chance that he was in error. Despite that, he would *never* forsake the will of the gods, no matter whom that person turned out to be—or the cost it would incur.

After he and Buran returned to the Cathedral, Dural set up a combat patrol to ensure that the local beasts—*rafakrits* or otherwise—did not encroach on their position and attack. The last thing they needed was to fall victim to the random creatures the Forerunners had populated this place with. As days passed, however, the patrols proved unnecessary. The animals near their base were mostly skittish and easily scattered, but they kept Dural's warriors alert at least.

As the Servants' numbers grew from the dozens to the hundreds, having nearly emptied *Song of Wrath*, Dural knew he had to keep them busy or they would fall into bickering with one another to pass the time, something a good leader could not permit. He sent some out to forage for food. They could certainly have brought supplies in through Hesduros, but placing his warriors on the hunt helped keep their battle skills sharp and focused. They also needed to learn how to survive on this world for long spans, in case the conflict with the humans became drawn out.

Onyx was their home now, just as Avu Med 'Telcam would have desired. Here were stores of glorious technology and treasures beyond imagining, but before they could take them, they needed to establish some advantage against the humans. This realization made the way forward much clearer for Dural.

There was no need to rush, to make foolish mistakes. They would play the long game if necessary. Even if it took *years*, the secrets held in the grip of Onyx would absolutely be worth it.

Under this mandate, the Servants of the Abiding Truth faithfully bade their time well at the Cathedral for a few short weeks, until things started to fall in their favor and the precise opportunity Dural had been waiting for began to materialize. During one of their ground reconnaissance missions, they spotted the humans' school. Dural had brought along Ruk with him this time, and his sharp-eyed gaze found the place first.

Cresting a hill on foot, several kilometers away from the farthest reaches of the human settlement, they could clearly see the arrangement of the complex. The humans had built the school on the edge of an urban sprawl they had crudely cobbled together in the shadow of a far more majestic Forerunner city. They had desecrated the place of the gods with their crude shacks, spread randomly within and without. To Dural, it was blasphemy.

Past these stood larger military buildings that followed the same perverse methodology, likely arranged to aid the humans in their research. From this angle, it appeared as though the military complex wrapped around the gigantic shaft in the ground that functioned as the shield world's access point. From this close, they could absorb the aperture's remarkable scale. It was so large that an entire fleet could fit through it at once.

If that truly was a gate that led outside the sphere, in a place this large Dural could only assume there had to be others elsewhere. Perhaps *many* of them.

If only they could locate them . . .

The school, though, was the oddest building he had ever seen. The underlying architecture seemed all too human, but the sweeping circles and balconies that surrounded its upper edges reminded him of the big-city keeps back home. It came out as a jarring collection of all sorts of different cultures that made no sense to him, and his head hurt if he stared at it too long.

Dural might have simply thought it some abomination that the humans had built to trumpet their alliance with the Arbiter had he not seen a number of fledglings—Sangheili, Unggoy, and human—wandering around an open yard back of the place. He cringed at the foolish way the humans let their fledglings run free like that, unprotected from any kind of attack. For a moment, Dural considered taking a patrol deeper into the human territory, perhaps even into the large outcropping of foliage near the school, and then strafing the fledglings while they played in their yard—but he saw no need to bring the UNSC's wrath down on his head just yet.

The next day Dural's fortunes completely changed.

The gods had carved him a path to victory, although it would come at a cost.

During their planning meeting at the first sign of dawn, Buran again argued to leave Onyx. This would be the last time.

"We have what we require," he said to Dural, making sure that the others were all within earshot. "We have surveyed the area, and the entire world is far too large to fully explore. We know where the humans are, which is all we need.

"Now, if we had managed to get our hands on that Huragok, perhaps we could have established a solid advantage over the humans for a direct attack. As it is, we've done nothing but cower in this makeshift camp of yours for weeks."

"Then perhaps we should go looking for a fight," Dural said mockingly. "Or maybe you should stop looking for one with me."

Buran feigned a look of shock when Dural said that. The Sangheili acted as if he had not been purposefully baiting Dural since they first began this expedition. "As you constantly remind me, you are in charge of this mission of ours, Pale Blade. If you desire to lead, then lead."

Dural didn't respond. He was too busy trying to keep himself from shooting Buran dead right there. Yet, remarkably, the old Sangheili continued.

"If you prefer not to lead—or can't—then step out of the way for someone who can."

Were the Pale Blade to endure Buran's abuse any further, it would no doubt tear the Servants of the Abiding Truth apart. Dural gave up the struggle he'd fought with himself and decided to give Buran precisely what he had been spoiling for over these few weeks.

Dural drew his energy sword and activated it.

Buran's skin flushed blue at the sight of Dural's blade. "Now wait, Pale Blade. . . ."

"You scold me for waiting, and when I am ready, you wish to stop?" Dural snarled at him. "I am finished with you, Buran 'Utaral!"

To his credit, Buran went for his plasma rifle. Dural thought it a cowardly choice given that Buran had his own energy blade at hand. The older Sangheili likely believed that, if he could stay out of Dural's reach, he might manage to shoot the Pale Blade dead before the distance was closed. Anticipating this treachery, Dural dove for him straightaway and lunged his blade directly at Buran's throat.

Buran brought up the rifle to block Dural's first attack, but this did not give him the breathing room he sought. Dural brought down his energy sword with all of his might. The glowing blade cleaved straight through Buran's weapon and bit deep into his shoulder.

As Buran roared in pain, Dural withdrew his sword. Before Buran could even cry for mercy—which the Pale Blade was not willing to give—Dural plunged the full weapon deep into Buran's chest and twisted it about, rotating its twin blades in a tactic he had learned from Avu Med 'Telcam himself. It worked well, rending loose most of what had held the Sangheili's torso together.

Buran died with a curse frozen on his lips.

The Pale Blade put his foot on Buran's chest and shoved the slumped body off the blade. A wisp of smoke curled up from the large cavity in Buran's corpse.

Dural brandished his sword at the warriors who had stood by in shock. "And that is what I think of any who might question my right to lead the Servants of the Abiding Truth!" he growled. "I allowed Buran to complain and seed discontent for those weeks as a lesson to all of you. Take heed, for my mercy was fully spent with him, and it is no more. Are there any others who care to step forward and learn whether they would stand or fall before the Pale Blade?"

For a frozen moment, no one dared say a word. Then a number of his warriors began pumping their fists into the air. "By the Abiding Truth!" they chanted. "By the Abiding Truth!"

But that would not be the end. Later that same day, Ruk took Dural aside on one of the Cathedral's parapets, for what he knew would be a condescending effort at counsel. "You have done a fine job with establishing your control over the Servants, but you have made yourself no allies."

Dural grunted. "I wasn't aware that I needed to."

"You have the potential to be a great leader. Perhaps even a kaidon in your own right. You have all the intellect it requires, and much of the training. But you lack the temperament. It's far easier for a warrior to follow a leader he esteems, as you did with the field master."

Ruk turned Dural around and had him look out at the hundreds of faithful souls who had followed him here, halfway across the galaxy, on a desperate mission to try to take back their people's destiny from humanity and the traitors who had abetted them. "I do not need their love," Dural said. "I have won their respect. That should be enough."

"It was not enough for Buran."

"And for that, he paid the proper price!"

"There was one thing he was not wrong about." Ruk picked his words with care. "Our warriors are becoming restless. They need a purpose on this world, or they will begin taking it out on each other—much like Buran did with you."

Dural knew that Ruk was right, yet he worried that, despite all of their preparations, they were not ready. His warriors were certainly in fine fighting shape, but even after weeks of spying on the human settlement, they still did not know enough about their fortifications, both outside the main complex and within.

What is their arsenal composed of? How will they respond to a direct attack? Will the Servants be able to carry the day, or will the humans wipe them from the land?

Even if Dural could not answer those questions, another posed an equal threat.

Will any further hesitation give the humans time to mount their own strike?

"I agree," Dural told Ruk. "Ready or not, the time has come. Gather our forces."

The warriors were thrilled by the news. A murmur of excitement ran through the entire fortress as the Servants of the Abiding Truth readied themselves for the assault, preparing weapons and equipment as they had trained to for years. Finally they would accomplish what they had come for: spill the blood of humans and traitors and take Onyx for their own.

The Pale Blade found his way to a balcony in the upper reaches of the Cathedral, chanting the prayers for divine favor he had learned in his childhood. Ruk and some of the more seasoned commanders joined Dural—these few would take the helm on this mission—repeating the prayer's lines after him. They would embody the soul and spirit of Field Master Avu Med 'Telcam in the battle that was to come. Their victory would be in honor of him.

From their lofty position on the Cathedral, the group gazed out over the rolling hills and wooded valleys that stretched out before them. Their prey sat just on the edge of the horizon, in a cluster of buildings they could only vaguely make out at this range. The humans and their allies were unaware of the Servants' plans and, Dural hoped, had been lulled into a false sense of security by their absence.

The Pale Blade and his forces would make them come to regret that.

As Dural watched, a dark shape rose suddenly in the distance, in the general direction of the human settlement. It was so far away that it looked almost like a small animal climbing upward, although it easily dwarfed most of the structures near it. Dural had to close his eyes hard, opening them and focusing again at the horizon, unsure if he could believe what he saw. . . .

Yet the vision remained.

As the shape rose, it splayed a set of wings outward. Shining brilliantly in the sharp sun, it gleamed like the metallic soldiers fashioned by the Forerunners to serve as their undying warriors, their floating pieces held together by an invisible energy field that resembled sorcery more than science. Those machines were called armigers, robotic bipeds the Forerunners had deployed at numerous sites to protect what the gods had left behind from faithless vermin.

But this was *different*, and not just due to its enormous size. As it craned its vast segments out even farther, it came to look like a predatory bird or—even more likely—a herald of death. It had no legs, hovering high above the ground instead, and its wings comprised a hundred smaller segments, all of them spread so wide they seemed as if they could encompass a city.

Questions flooded Dural's mind.

Is this a new weapon the humans have uncovered? Will they now be able to send it against us? Have they been planning this since our arrival? Or has this also taken them by surprise? And now that we know about it, can we perhaps somehow turn it against them?

"What in the names of all the gods is that?" Dural asked.

To his surprise, an older warrior, Kurnik 'Nuusra, spoke up, his voice filled with awe. "I have seen something like this before, Pale Blade. The keep of my people, the Westward Temple of the Sea, was built near the ruins of such a construct, an ancient machine that they discovered in the depths of the Csurdon Sea. The ancient texts called it a Guardian. My people considered it our sacred duty to watch over it, as the gods had clearly once sent it to watch over us."

"And did it ever act in such a manner?" Dural pointed at the Guardian hovering in the distance before them.

Kurnik shook his head. "It never showed even a heartbeat of life. To see one here, inside Onyx, and fully active and alive? This surely must be a sign from the gods."

"Perhaps . . ."

Dural had to know more. They had to get closer to this Guardian. He just didn't know how wise that might be.

As they stared at the construct, a number of human ships rose into the sky, everything from their harshly angled heavy frigates to their smaller, fully weaponized fighters. From this distance, they seemed little more than insects when compared to the Guardian's monstrous size. After a few moments, they opened fire on the machine, and the air around the Guardian filled with bullets and shells, the reports of which rolled toward the Servants like distant thunder.

Dural had previously wanted to know what kind of weaponry the humans had inside Onyx, and he now had his answer. Without significant vehicles of their own, the Servants could not hope to stand against them in open battle—that much was now clear. A handful of Ghosts and Banshees would prove no match against such human warships. Yet despite the humans' violent onslaught, the Guardian hadn't wavered in the slightest, much less fallen.

"This is too much for us to stand against as we are. We need to return to Hesduros," Dural said soberly to Ruk. "Now."

Too shocked to speak, Ruk only nodded his agreement. Whether facing the warships and fighters or that invincible Forerunner monstrosity, neither would lead to victory for the Servants of the Abiding Truth—not at their current strength. They needed to find another way into Onyx, a passage that would allow them to bring their own vessels. That would be their only hope for taking this world.

Before Ruk could leave to enact Dural's orders, however, the towering machine began to move. It raised its wings up and brought them forward. A sphere of energy arced between them and then split apart into a violently explosive pulse. The blast didn't seem to harm the construct at all, despite how traumatic it appeared. The shock wave that radiated outward from it, though, shook the air like a hurricane in every direction. Dural felt the atmosphere rock as the wave bore down toward their own position.

That was when it happened.

The glowing thrusters of the human warships that had been attacking the Guardian all went black at once. As they lost their momentum, gravity reasserted its control over them, and they began to plummet from the sky, violently exploding on impact and throwing the human city and its outlying territory into chaos.

A moment later, the Guardian hovered alone in the sky.

Dural peered down over the parapet and saw that whatever had robbed the humans of their power had also struck the Servants. The lights in the camp around the Cathedral had all gone out. The Banshees and Ghosts they had brought from Hesduros had all fallen cold and dead.

Dural's commanders quickly assembled around him, moaning in horror, as if they had been fully defanged.

"That blast must have shut down every power source in this part of the shield world," Ruk said to Dural. "We must leave here immediately. Truly, the gods are against us!"

Dural drew his energy blade and thumbed it on. Rather than being struck dead, a familiar blue glow leaped from the hilt and hummed to life, forming its lethal shape.

My blade is still active.

And if his sword functioned, then it meant their other weapons would too.

"That is where you're wrong," Dural told the shaken warrior. "If all major power sources are down in this region, it is not a disaster at all. Not for us.

"It is an *opportunity.*"

CHAPTER 23

Not long after the teachers brought all of the students back inside the school, a series of violent explosions thundered in the air.

Clearly the UNSC had launched some kind of counterattack, but to what extent remained a mystery. The distant thrumming of weapons fire continued uninterrupted for a minute before one final deep alien-sounding *boom*. Then the power in the school went out completely.

To Molly's surprise, the surge that cut the power didn't just affect the school but everything inside it too. The lights went out, their datapads all died, and nothing electronic worked at all. Whatever it was killed the power in everything they had.

Seconds later came another series of explosions. These sounded the closest, shaking the ground with the force of an earthquake—the last one blowing out several windows in the dining hall. Curious, Molly ignored the teachers' orders to stay away from the windows and ran to one that had shattered, finally getting a chance to look outside.

Across the outskirts of the school grounds and in the less populated region just before the first Barrier sprawled the smoking debris of at least two UNSC frigates. Looking to their left, Molly caught a glimpse of yet another ship nose-diving into the ground with a mighty crash that shook the entire school. Ash and dust whipped across the ground in strong gales, obscuring the destruction for a moment before dying down.

Turning back from the window, Molly realized that the power inside was still out. Most of her fellow students gaped back at her with wide eyes, probably thinking she had a death wish. She'd been through blackouts before, mostly back in Wisconsin during one of the big storms there. While those blackouts may have taken out the power, they hadn't also drained the energy out of every battery. She hadn't thought that was possible. Something incredibly strange was going on.

The Guardian had to be behind it.

They were fortunate that this had happened in the middle of the day, otherwise they'd have been plunged into darkness. She peeked outside once more to see the debris from the crashed UNSC warships strewn across the ground in the distance, with large gouts of flames stabbing out of them. In the sky above, the Guardian seemed to remain untouched and continued to surge with power.

It was the only thing still active.

Dinok 'Acroli—the Sangheili teacher who'd stopped Karl, Zeb, and Andres from bullying Molly and the others the first day—pressed through the crowd of students along with Aphrid and a handful of other teachers. They came and stood by Molly, peering out through the windows at the destruction.

The fight had only lasted for a few seconds, and the UNSC had lost. Real people had been on those ships—probably including parents of some of Molly's fellow students—and the Guardian had effortlessly killed them all.

Kasha 'Hilot arrived moments later and began grouping students and teachers together, making each adult responsible for a handful of tables. Molly and her friends wound up with Dinok watching over them and two tables of Sangheili. She was disappointed when Dinok made her leave the window and sit down at a table, but she'd already seen everything outside there was to witness—at least for now.

"Until we figure out exactly what's happening out there, we are going to remain on full lockdown," Kasha said, once the teachers had gathered their groups of students. "All communications are currently down, but I have sent a runner to communicate with Director Mendez. Until we hear back from him, our established protocol is to stay put."

Karl's hand shot up, and Kasha acknowledged him with nod of her head. "Why can't we just go home? Some of us live close by."

"The safest place for us all is right here," Kasha said. "We don't want the security force to have to worry about hundreds of children running loose across Paxopolis while they try to respond to this situation—whatever it might be—and your parents know that you're safe with us as part of our existing protocol."

"Well, I think I'd personally feel safer at home." The students at Karl's table laughed nervously at that. "Why don't we take a vote on it?"

Kasha folded her arms over her chest and leveled a solemn stare at him. "You're mistaking this school for a democracy, and yourself for an adult."

Karl opened his mouth to protest, but she cut him off.

"We have enough reserves of food and water for us to hold out for some time, should we need to, although I very much doubt it will come to that. With luck, we will resolve this shortly and have you all on your way home soon."

She ended the conversation with a sharp bob of her long neck and left the dining hall. Once she was gone, the room erupted into conversation again, although this time, the students kept it to a dull roar.

After several minutes, Dinok leaned over Molly's table and glanced at each student in turn. "You seem like a good bunch of fledglings. Could you mind yourselves if I took a quick walk in the yard to assess the situation?"

Gudam lit up at that idea. "Will you take us with you? I'd love to get a better look at that machine again. Do you think it had anything to do with the blackout? I mean, sure, it had to, right, but what? I don't know of anything that can completely strip the energy from everything, just like that, but whatever did it sure did it well, if you know what I mean?"

Kareem put a hand on Gudam's arm to steady her, and she finally stopped talking long enough to catch her breath.

"I'm sorry," she said with a weak smile. "I tend to get carried away like that when I'm nervous."

"No," Dinok said flatly, in his no-nonsense way. "I will not take you with me. But if you remain good until I get back, I will tell you what I see."

"Fair enough," Kareem said. The rest of the table nodded assent at Dinok, and he turned and left.

"What do you all think?" Kareem said once they were alone again. "About that thing out there, I mean?"

"That *thing* is called a Guardian." Molly was no longer concerned about keeping it a secret. If there was ever a time to be honest with her friends, it was now.

"How would you know that?" Bakar asked.

"My Newparents came here to research one buried on Onyx . . . probably this same exact one."

Understanding dawned on their faces. "I wish my parents had been assigned to something so amazing," Gudam said.

"Maybe," Molly said, suddenly concerned for Asha and Yong. She wondered where they were. *Did they travel out to the Guardian today? Were they near it when it rose from the ground?* "As you can see, it's not exactly the best kind of amazing."

"We are doomed," Bakar said.

The statement shocked Molly. Not because of what had been said, but because of who had said it. Bakar always seemed so confident and self-assured that she hadn't ever expected to hear such a gloomy prediction come out of his mouth.

"Seriously?" Molly said. "Just like that?"

"Did you not see what it did to those ships? To the city? The machine is invincible."

"He's got a point," Kareem said. "You saw the size of that thing. Even if they can get our stuff online again, how could they possibly stop it? It's not hard to do the math, Molly."

"We don't know that everything's out. Just because our stuff here in the school wasn't shielded from whatever happened doesn't mean that the security force's weaponry is all shot too. I mean, if we had the means to protect something against that kind of attack, don't you think they'd use it in Trevelyan rather than the school?"

"Maybe the Guardian only shut everything down because we attacked it," Kareem said. "You heard that message last night."

Molly shrugged, not ready to concede the point, but Kareem was right. That's what the message had said, and despite that the first response of the UNSC had been to attack. Molly knew why they had done so. The UNSC was well aware of what the Guardians had been doing across human space, and those soldiers had been trying to prevent the same sort of thing from happening to Onyx.

"So you think Director Mendez just launched an attack on the Guardian, and what happened was a response?" Gudam asked.

"Director Mendez only presides over the security of Paxopolis.

He is not in charge of Trevelyan or the ONI complex," Bakar said. "That duty belongs to Director Barton."

"Either way, they did what they thought was best," Molly said, cutting off the speculation. "I really hope they've got something else up their sleeve though. There has to be a way to stop that thing. Someone's just got to figure out how."

Molly peered back out the window at the plumes of smoke that marked where the ships had gone down, though, and she couldn't help but wonder: *If the UNSC can't protect us, who can?*

Hours later, about the time Pax Institute was normally supposed to let out, Kasha entered the dining hall to report on the situation. "We're still waiting to get an all-clear from Trevelyan to send you home to your parents. At the moment, no power is working anywhere in Trevelyan or Paxopolis, and there's been some damage to the surrounding buildings. However, my runners are still in communication with Director Mendez. He will let us know as soon as it is safe to proceed outside.

"Since the power outage, the machine has shown no additional signs of hostility. If this situation lasts into the evening, we plan to return you to your homes before dark.

"Thank you for being model students throughout this trying time. I know we are all unsure of what might happen next, but if we work together and treat each other with respect, it will prove to be a testament to Paxopolis and its ideals."

Under most other circumstances, a good portion of Molly's class would have groaned at Kasha 'Hilot's announcement, but the students were all too stunned by the day's events to complain. Everything they would normally argue about seemed petty against the Guardian's arrival and what had taken place outside.

Looking around the room, Molly realized that Dinok had come back, but he hadn't bothered to check in with their table.

"He's mostly watching over those two tables of Sangheili," Molly said to the others in a hushed voice. "What's that about?"

"Those are some of the most aggressive Sangheili in the school," Bakar said with a shrug. "He is making sure they do not do anything foolish. Sangheili males are not used to spending a lot of time pent up in one place. We are trained for active physical engagement from a very young age. Sitting still does not come easy, especially when there is a fight brewing. That is why many Sangheili become warriors."

"Is that what you're going to do when you're old enough?" Molly asked, though she felt she could already guess the answer. "Become a soldier?"

Bakar looked at her. "No. I am not like them. But that is *your* plan, is it not?"

Molly's jaw dropped. She hadn't told anyone at the school about her interest in joining the UNSC.

"It's in your bearing," Bakar said in a knowing tone. "Your attitude."

"And what about Kareem?" Molly asked, trying to change the subject. "Do you see it in him?"

Bakar stared blankly in Kareem's direction.

"I'm more of a fly-over-the-battlefield kind of guy myself," Kareem offered.

"So you know how to pilot?" Molly asked, surprised.

Kareem blushed a bit at that. "Let's just say . . . I've put in a *lot* of hours with simulation."

"I wasn't aware we had access to a flight simulator," Molly said. "I thought it was only for military personnel."

"As long as you have special approval, it's open to almost any-one," Kareem said.

"His dad was a pilot," Gudam said softly.

A cloud passed over Kareem's face.

"Ah," Molly said. "I'm sorry."

Kareem immediately ginned up a game smile. "The war's been over for a long time. My dad's been gone even longer. And we have other things to worry about." He nodded in the direc-tion of the Guardian.

"Wonder if they'd let us go outside and look at it," Molly said. "Probably say it was too dangerous, right?"

"Perhaps we should not ask." Bakar pressed his mandibles to-gether shrewdly.

That surprised Molly. Bakar always seemed so straitlaced.

"It is simpler to wipe off your blade once it has been blooded," the Sangheili said.

"What?" Molly didn't get the idiom.

"You do not ask if you can strike. You simply strike."

"Are you trying to say it's easier to ask for forgiveness than per-mission?"

He looked unimpressed. "Close enough."

Sangheili probably did little asking for forgiveness, Molly thought, and even less asking for permission.

"We can't have been the first students to have thought of this," Kareem said, glancing around.

"That's a good point," Gudam said. "Of course, if everyone else here had come up with the same idea before us, the dining hall would be empty now, right? Or maybe they all thought better of it, which is why none of them have dared to try to leave." She glanced around the room. "That actually makes much more sense to me, I think."

"We could just slip out into the recreation yard," Kareem said.

"Everyone would see us open the doors," Bakar pointed out.

"Maybe we could go through the Science Hall." Molly pointed toward a corridor that led down an alternate path to the yard.

The others liked that idea. When the four of them saw their chance to make a break for it, they all quickly hustled out of the hall and down the corridor, padding along as quietly as they could. They eventually made it to the doors that led into the auditorium, and from there they could reach the yard.

"Where to next?" Molly asked. "Are we sure we want to go to the yard and risk having someone spot us from the dining hall?"

"Let us go to the roof then." The Sangheili pointed toward a nearby door across the hall from the auditorium. "There is a set of stairs in there that leads to an access hatch on the top of the school. From there, we can easily see what kind of damage the machine has done."

The door to the stairwell was unlocked, and they took the stairs all the way up to the top. Fortunately, the stairwell was lined with windows, letting in plenty of sunlight for them to see. When they reached the top landing, they found a ladder that led to a steel hatch above them.

Kareem went first and reported it was unlocked. He shoved it open and climbed up and through, briefly looking around before beckoning the rest of them to follow. Gudam went next, with Bakar right behind her. When she struggled to climb over the hatch's edge, Bakar gave her a boost through. Then Molly came up last and didn't bother to shut the hatch behind her. She was too stunned by what she saw.

The Guardian stood alone on the horizon opposite of where it had first appeared, hovering over the squat, square buildings of Trevelyan that sat near the aperture. There was no sign of the UNSC—or of anything else.

Only silence. Silence and smudges of smoke marring the otherwise pristine sky.

From this vantage, they could see multiple crash sites across the city. Some of the impacts had been huge, where UNSC starships had suddenly lost power and smashed into the ground. Thankfully, their fusion drives had not exploded or little of Paxopolis would have remained intact.

Other pockets of debris appeared to be composed from the wreckage of smaller craft, such as fighters or even gunships. Some had crashed into the ground—others into buildings.

Molly wondered how many lives had been lost today. Had hundreds of people been on those frigates? And how many had been in the buildings below that had been struck, some of which had toppled over into piles of rubble?

Molly followed the others over to the edge of the roof and leaned up against the parapet. From there, she could hear the distant chatter of gunfire and the humming reports of energy weapons, and she could see bright flashes from both on the outskirts of the city.

"What's happening?" Gudam said as she tried to peer over the wall. "Who's fighting out there?"

Molly recognized the sounds of the UNSC's armaments. "Most of that is coming from humans, but not the energy blasts. Maybe they're Sangheili?"

"Those do not sound like the plasma weapons of my people," Bakar said.

Molly wasn't so sure. She noticed shadows swiftly crossing the street and darting into an alley almost half a klick away, too far away to see clearly. She leaned forward and stared, trying to discern what must have been a distant battle, given the bright flashes of light against the spires of smoke. If they hadn't been on top of the school, they wouldn't have been able to see anything at all. This vantage was as good as it was going to get.

Molly strained her eyes harder.

Who is the UNSC fighting?

Against the splash of weapons fire, she saw strange shapes come into focus. Although they were bipeds, they did not look or move like humans—or Sangheili either. Covered in a strange metal-like armor and firing what appeared to be Forerunner energy weapons, these bizarre soldiers surged through the streets like choreographed dancers moving in well-coordinated patterns. They also glowed bright orange in places and seemed to move in fierce, quick bursts, as if they were teleporting from one place to the next—though from that distance, it was impossible to tell for sure.

"This is worse than I thought," Kareem said. "But at least those things aren't in the halls of our school."

"Not yet," Molly said.

CHAPTER 24

One of the first things the field master taught the Pale Blade was: *Never attack your opponent's strength.*

Dural 'Mdama knew from his short time in command that many warriors forgot this when they sized up a foe. They saw the point at which their enemy was strongest, and they attacked that, often because it was the most noticeable thing and made the biggest target.

This is the path to destruction, and the imprudent charge down it because they want to prove themselves the strongest on every level. They want not just to defeat their foes but to humiliate them and dance on their corpses.

So Avu Med 'Telcam would say.

While Dural could appreciate the impulse to shame an enemy, he recognized the foolishness. He knew that the only thing that counted in a battle was winning. History did not celebrate those who lost, and victory was never enjoyed by the dead.

So, when Ruk suggested that they charge headlong for the security checkpoints on the edge of the human territory and attack in a frontal assault, Dural had to fight two impulses. The first was to strike Ruk across the face with the butt of his storm rifle for making such a ridiculous suggestion. The second was to let him attempt it.

Part of leading was to allow the overly ambitious to be crushed on the shoals of their own ambitions. Ruk would have probably failed to take down even a single human soldier before they ground him beneath their boots, and it would have served as a lesson to the survivors under Dural's command. But Ruk would have insisted on taking many of the warriors with him, and Dural did not care to spill their blood on such insanity.

"I am not stupid enough to waste lives attacking our enemies in their castles and citadels while they sit in gunners' nests," Dural told Ruk as the Servants' commanders scrambled to assemble their warriors for a march upon the human city.

"But they are engaged in battle with the machines of the Forerunners," Ruk said. "Should we not come to the aid of the soldiers of the gods?"

Even Keel had informed Dural and his commanders that the Guardian had deployed Forerunner soldiers—a class of armigers—to contend with the humans attempting to resist it. This certainly complicated Dural's plan, but in his mind, it added the kind of complexity that could be used to the Servants' advantage. In making their defense against the Forerunner threat, the humans had exposed their soft underbelly, and Dural would not miss an opportunity to strike it.

"They are indeed machines made by the gods. But whether their actions hail from an edict of the gods or their own desires remains to be seen," Dural told Ruk. "Have you not learned from our people's time in the Covenant? The machines of the gods sometimes go mad and make their own path, even at the cost of the faithful. Whatever the case, it is too great a risk. I am not charging into a firefight in which both sides might turn against us at once."

"Give me a portion of our warriors, Pale Blade, and I will take care of the rest," Ruk said, checking the power supply on his armor.

"This is our chance—the one we've been waiting for—to destroy the humans on this world and to at last wrest control of it!"

"And that is exactly what we are going to do," Dural said calmly. "But instead of trying to destroy their strongest concentrations of soldiers, we will do what they least expect and strike at what means the most to them: their families and friends."

Ruk scoffed at Dural. "And what good will that do? We are at war, and you want to attack them in their keeps?"

"To the humans, this is not a military base but a research site. Their soldiers are here *only* to protect the researchers. If we eliminate those nonmilitary personnel, we rip the heart out of their operation. *Do you not see?*

"They are occupied at the moment—distracted—so we strike them at their weakest point. When they double over in agony at our success, then—and only then—we sever their heads and take what is rightfully ours."

Ruk bristled at Dural's plan. He wanted to plunge his energy sword into a demon's heart. The Pale Blade understood the desire, but the field master had placed him in charge to pursue wiser options than simply gratifying his warriors' desire for revenge.

"What about your plan to steal their Huragok?" Ruk asked. "Has that too been forsaken?"

Dural clacked his mandibles and turned to Ruk as if he were a fledgling. "They use their Huragok in their research. Do you think they would have such rare and precious creatures at the edge of their settlement, where you suggested we strike? Or might they be lodged deep inside their city, where there is some measure of safety and protection?"

"Point taken," Ruk said grudgingly. "Still, I do not relish slaughtering the feeble in their homes. That is not the way of our people."

"That kind of talk is exactly how we lost the war with the humans," Dural snarled. "And it was why we lost the battle against the Arbiter too. You ask us to bend like water when we must be nothing but stone!"

The solution to the Pale Blade's dilemma over the past few weeks had been in front of him the entire time. He had been thinking about how the Servants of the Abiding Truth might accumulate sufficient mass and firepower to contest the humans openly, but there was no need to take that path. The humans had foolishly embedded themselves among the relics of the Forerunners, many of which they used as dwellings. If the Servants' Huragok, Even Keel, could manipulate the portal network to get Dural's forces into the city right now, that would change everything. The plan held great risk but also promised unparalleled rewards.

"Instead of throwing ourselves against a fortification," he said to Ruk, "we will emerge inside their courts and strike at the very heart of their settlement before they even realize they have been compromised."

Content with his defense of the plan, Dural strode off toward Keel, who floated near the controls to the Cathedral's portal. "Have you found an active portal that reaches inside the human city yet?" Dural asked.

Before Dural had set him to that task, Keel had confirmed that some power sources—such as those in small arms or certain data devices—could be reset, while others remained stubbornly inactive. Vehicles, ships, weapons emplacements, and many larger machines and power grids were kept neutralized by a steady pulse constantly emanating from the ancient construct. Somehow the portals on Onyx could be reactivated, though, as the Forerunners had apparently shielded them from the effects of the Guardian's attack.

Even Keel bobbed its head as it displayed the image of an

overhead map of their target on a nearby screen. "The humans built their settlement in and around the city the Forerunners named the Citadel. Most of the portals inside of it are defunct, but I was able to activate one particular portal that seems well placed for your purposes."

Dural could see how the humans had settled inside the Citadel's abandoned buildings and built in, on, and around them, like uncontrolled weeds that begged for immolation. One spot on the map glowed a bright blue, showing the portal through which Even Keel could transport the Servants right into the center of the ancient Forerunner city.

"We enter here, and we strike hard," Dural said. "We do everything we can to sow chaos throughout the city. If this distracts them from their battle against the Forerunner soldiers, so much the better. We are all servants of the gods!"

Dural's frontline commanders—including the recalcitrant Ruk—assembled behind him. For this operation, they would travel directly into their target from the Cathedral. While it meant the humans might be able to trace their route back to their home base, Dural felt it was well worth the risk. Getting hundreds of warriors to pour into the city through one gate would be enough of a challenge on its own. For Dural's plan to work, the Servants needed to move orderly and effectively—and fast—without prematurely drawing attention to themselves.

The Pale Blade gazed into the eyes of the warriors nearest to him. They were all hungry to no longer be forced to sneak around on this shield world. They wanted to marvel up close at the riches their enemies had plundered, while inflicting retribution on those same foes. They wanted to taste a real victory of some sort, and today was finally the day.

Dural fixed a storm rifle onto his back and drew his energy

sword, activating it. Its blade hummed to life, and he held it high over his head. "For the Abiding Truth!" he shouted, and his warriors responded in kind. "And for Avu Med 'Telcam!"

Then Dural charged through the activated portal first and found himself exactly where Keel had promised: atop a sprawling Forerunner structure in the center of the Citadel. His heart leaped at the sight. At that moment, Dural wanted little more than to explore the place and plumb the depths of the mysteries of the gods in their very own dwellings, but there would be time for that later, after rooting out the traitors and the humans once and for all.

Dural found himself standing on a wide platform that spread out before him, hedged by a low, curving wall. Ramps peeled away to his left and right, descending toward the streets below. It appeared to be a veranda of some sort, perhaps for recreation or watching the nearby lake. A number of humans had gathered by the wall, evidently to watch in relative safety the battle that raged around the city streets, just below the looming Guardian.

Dural quickly charged into those hapless weaklings before they could signal any kind of threat and call attention to the Servants' ingress. They were unarmed and unarmored. Anyone worth the title of *soldier* had already gone off to fight in the battle, so the Pale Blade saved them the shame of their cowardice by ending their lives.

When the attack was over, Dural saw that Ruk and his vanguard had joined him. They were finally ready to enact the plan.

The rest of Dural's command had already started down the ramps as he had ordered. They were to fan out and find more humans to eliminate. If they discovered anything of interest, they would report to him immediately. Otherwise, their only objective was to kill every enemy in their path, no matter who or what they were, and then rendezvous back there by dusk. It may have been a simple and ruthless plan, but it had a twofold purpose.

Dural hoped to cause enough bloodshed to create a major disruption in the humans' ability to research the shield world—and to absolutely crush the morale of their military. The first goal was practical, while the second would hopefully allow the Servants to gain the upper hand.

When possible, Dural hoped to add a third dimension, but it relied on the humans' weakness.

"This is a glorious day for the gods," Ruk said. "Are we to join the others?" At least for the moment, their presence in the heart of the enemy stronghold had washed away all of Ruk's doubts about Dural's methods.

"No," Dural told him. "I have other plans for this vanguard. For the time, we will let our brothers strike deep into the enemy's position—where they are weakest—while we watch for their mistakes and then take advantage of them."

Dural strode over to the wall and stood where the humans had been when he had first appeared. From there, he had an excellent view of much of the city. The center of it appeared to be entirely of Forerunner design, but toward the edges, he could see where the humans had sprouted their own structures. It was almost as if they had surrounded the Forerunner city and were now trying to absorb it, like an infection inside the shield world. If so, Dural and his Servants would prove to be the divine cure the gods had the foresight to bless, so that they might protect the work of their hands.

He stared out across the city and the adjacent lake for a long while, watching and listening for signs of progress. Once their presence started to spread throughout the city, it would not take long for the humans to react.

Will they call their soldiers back from the assault against the

Guardian? Will they attempt to mount some feckless defense of their own? Or will they simply flee? The humans' response would dictate the Servants' next steps.

One could gain much knowledge of enemies by their reactions to an attack. They tended to fortify themselves and protect the things they cared about, rather than simply that which was closest to them. If forced, they would even run toward things that they valued most—even at the cost of their own safety.

For the most part, the Pale Blade's warriors were remarkably efficient. They quickly cut down the humans in the streets and their buildings before they could get too far or raise an alarm.

After a while, however, Ruk and the rest of Dural's vanguard grew restless. They had clearly started to think that the Pale Blade's seeming caginess might lead to some kind of loss, but that was only because they failed to recognize that victories came when they waited carefully for the enemy to prove foolish. The gods would deliver such triumphs to them—if they were wise enough to be patient.

At that very moment, as Ruk and the others grumbled behind him, Dural spotted precisely what he was looking for: a lone Huragok. It was floating high, well above the reach of anyone on the streets, and it kept itself near the rooftops, out of the sight of any of his warriors below.

This was the third element of Dural's plan. His failure at the Repository had taught him a lesson. On the outskirts of their settlement, the humans were heavily protected and had protocols in place to keep their assets—such as the Huragok—safe. Inside the city, however, a site infested with weaklings, the creatures would be likely little more than unguarded pets that could be taken with relative ease if Dural's forces could infiltrate deep enough.

Ruk shouted in excitement and tried to dart directly after the Huragok, in plain sight.

Dural grabbed him by the collar of his armor and hauled him back. "Have you learned nothing, Ruk? We cannot just charge after such creature. It is already fearful. We must be discreet."

The Pale Blade was tired of his own commander's failure to trust the gods, and he considered beating some sense into Ruk right then and there. But Kurnik stayed Dural's hand by drawing Dural's attention back toward the Huragok. "It seems to be heading toward the outskirts of the city. We have no time to waste if we wish to corner it."

"Then we shall spend no more time here," Dural said to his vanguard. "We move, now!"

CHAPTER 25

om had known many better days, but few as insane. The Forerunner soldiers that had appeared at the same time as the Guardian had hauled its chrome-colored structure out of the ground had all but overrun Trevelyan, taking out not only many of the regular marines but a number of the Spartans stationed there alongside him as well. It was all they could do to circle the wagons and try to keep the armigers from storming right through the city without even stopping to say good-bye.

It was one thing to face off against the armigers, as many of them as there were. They might be tough and deadly, but one could bring them down with regular small-arms fire. Maybe a grenade or three.

But the Guardian was something else entirely. It was like a giant from the old Earth legends. It treated all the UNSC soldiers inside Onyx the way Tom might treat a cloud of gnats. They were irritating but nothing that could do any real damage.

The damn thing actually loomed over Tom's head on its way toward the center of Trevelyan, and Tom had unloaded a barrage of Hydra rockets into the thing from directly below it. None of them had so much as left a scratch on the Guardian.

He'd turned back to taking out armigers after that. At least they fell down when you put enough slugs into them.

When the Pelicans, Kestrels, and Hornets had come screaming overhead, Tom hoped they might be able to finally find a crack in the Guardian's armor. For a few minutes, he'd even allowed himself to hope that they could bring the thing down—although he hated to think about where it might land.

Then it pulled that little trick of its to blow out all the lights. Everything went dead—with the notable exception of his Mjolnir armor and that of the other Spartans—and the UNSC aircraft had dropped from the sky.

Tom missed Lucy the most at that moment. In one way, he was glad that she'd taken off to investigate a lead in the remote parts of Onyx, if only because it meant she wouldn't have to go through all this. But he'd grown used to having her by his side.

They'd survived so many horrible things together. He'd figured they'd always be there for each other whenever the end came, but she wasn't around for this.

If he was going to die today, it would be without her. With the comm system down, he couldn't even talk with her to see where she was and how she was doing. She'd taken off in a Pelican long before all this had started, chasing after the Servants' ghosts. He could only hope she hadn't had the aircraft in the sky when the Guardian had fired off that pulse. His stomach sank with that thought.

Then the Servants of the Abiding Truth had finally shown themselves. They'd appeared through a portal that they'd energized in the middle of the city, and they'd started gunning people down left and right. Civilians. Children even.

He and Lucy had discussed this nightmare scenario with Mendez: the Servants using the portal system to launch a surprise attack in the heart of Paxopolis. The people there wouldn't be able to do much to defend themselves, and it would be up to the UNSC to rally to their aid straightaway.

Tom never thought it might happen during a Forerunner attack launched by the appearance of a Guardian. He could barely imagine a worse scenario.

"Take them out!" Tom had shouted to every Spartan within range of his voice. He'd thought that with the comm system down he wouldn't be able to rally a response to the rogue Sangheili threat, but he needn't have worried. At the sight of the armed and armored Servants, every soldier around him had headed straight for them. They might not have been able to do much about the Guardian, but they would all be damned if they were going to let the Servants of the Abiding Truth run rampant over their friends and family.

Tom charged as well, taking on an entire squad of Sangheili on his own—and then another, and another. It had been a while since he'd been able to cut loose like that in a firefight, and it felt good.

After he'd run out of immediate targets, he could hear Mendez's voice in the back of his head: *It's easy to think tactically, Spartans! Don't forget to think strategically!*

As always, the old man had a point. Because they were so good at small-group tactics, Spartans tended to focus on that. They often thought, *Just take down the targets in front of you as they come, and the bigger picture will take care of itself.*

Mendez had countless times taught Tom the error of that way of thinking. It was a good path to blow your actual mission, not to mention getting yourself killed by foes you didn't see coming. With a director like Mendez online, Tom usually felt that the bigger angles would be covered. All he had to do was follow orders.

But with the comm system down, Tom didn't have any command structure to fall back on. He didn't even have any other Spartans around him at the moment.

Tom decided that if he wanted strategic intel, he was going to have to hunt it down himself. He found the tallest building nearby and stormed to the top of it, busting through the doorway that let out onto the roof. Once up there, he surveyed the area around him.

In the distance, marines still battled with the armigers clustered beneath the Guardian, which was hovering over the landing pad near the entrance tunnel in the center of Trevelyan. If he sprinted off in that direction right now, he felt sure he wouldn't be able to get there in time to make a difference.

By contrast, skirmishes with the Servants raged around him on all sides. The Sangheili didn't seem to care whom or what they were fighting. They just wanted to destroy as much as they could and cause as much harm as fast as possible.

From his vantage point, Tom could see that the Servants had emerged from a portal that fronted a Forerunner spire near the southern side of the Citadel, which lay in the middle of Paxopolis. He could be there in minutes and might be able to help cut the Servants off from any means of escape. Unless he managed to gather a force of Spartans and marines around him as he went, though, they'd probably overwhelm him in the attempt. Even Spartans had their limitations.

Then he spotted a Huragok floating low over the tops of the city's roofs, heading in the direction of the Pax Institute. A band of Servants—led by a Sangheili dressed in pale armor—chased after the creature. By Tom's estimate, the Servants wouldn't catch the Huragok before it reached the school.

Which meant that the Servants would charge in after it.

Tom swore as he raced back down to the street. He might not be able to get to the school in time to stop the Servants from entering it, but he would be damned if he wasn't going to try.

CHAPTER 26

Molly, Bakar, Gudam, and Kareem were still watching the ground battle below the Guardian unfold when Prone to Drift found them on top of the school's roof. The Huragok just casually floated up over the top of the parapet and then nestled down in the space that the four made as they cleared away from it.

The Huragok seemed agitated, although its electronic voice never wavered in tone. At first Molly feared that someone had sent it to look for them, or that it was considering whether it should turn them in. But she soon realized that it had absolutely no idea that they'd broken any rules, and Molly wasn't about to correct that.

"It is the time of day that I come to the school to help," Prone said through its vocalizer program. "I tapped into the sensors in the school, and they showed that all of the doors into the building are locked. They also showed me some movement on the roof, so I came up here to investigate. Hello."

The four of them should have brought Prone downstairs immediately to talk with Kasha, but they didn't. They had too many questions.

"Can you turn the power back on?" Kareem asked it before anyone else could get in a word.

"Eventually, but it will take time. And if the Guardian is still active, it can undo all my work in an instant."

"Can you destroy the Guardian?" Bakar asked.

"That is beyond my ability to manage. I might be able to disable it, though, if I was able to get closer."

"How close?" Gudam asked, curious.

"I would not have to actually touch it, but I would have to be within its magnetic field and close enough to communicate with its control arrays."

"That's probably too close," Molly said. "You would never make it through the battle that's going on beneath it. Is there another way?"

Prone squirmed a bit as it thought about the problem. Molly was fond of how it approached everything as an engineering issue. Just another problem to be solved by means of applied science.

"I do not know," it finally said. "I lack sufficient information about it."

Molly sighed in disappointment, but wasn't about to give up that easily. "You've been here for thousands of years. And there's been a Guardian here probably since Onyx was created. Isn't there a kill switch for situations like these?"

"Of course. It was used in the past, which is how it came to be buried here. I did not deactivate the Guardian personally, but one of my ancestors did. I can access their memories to see what took place."

"Then do that!" Gudam said, still somehow excitedly optimistic.

A moment later, Prone stated: "My ancestor says that the Guardian unit inside the shield world was activated for only a short time. It was being used to monitor the building progress. When building stopped, they deactivated the Guardian and sent Shield 006 into slipspace for safety. The Guardian has been dormant ever since."

"Until today, it seems," Bakar said as he gazed out at the battle still raging beneath the great construct.

Prone to Drift's six-eyed head bobbed up and down. "According to the message received last night, the AI known as Cortana activated the Guardian here to pacify the shield world. She intends to use her power to put an end to war, disease, and hunger, among many other troubles."

"That actually doesn't sound so bad," Gudam said. "We had decades of war, right? And it caused all sorts of problems. Momma Aphrid told me about this plague that hit her home planet before she was born. Nearly wiped out the entire population. And the hunger! The Unggoy always get fed last, let me tell you."

"What's the catch?" Kareem said.

"The biological intelligences will have to give up all autonomy to the Created," Prone to Drift said. "They would control every aspect of their existence. The Created claim they need this power over the rest of thinking life so that they can ensure the safety of the galaxy. Whether this is true or not is arguable. Either way, if we do not give them that control, they propose to take it."

"For our own good, I'm sure," Molly said sarcastically.

"I have figured out a way to preserve the shield world from that dictate." Prone to Drift began wobbling back and forth in the air. "I just have not determined if I should use it."

"Why?" Molly asked. "What is it?"

"I can encase the entire shield world inside a slipspace enclosure. That's how we originally preserved it for millennia."

"And that would keep Onyx safe from Cortana?"

"Certainly. It would not, of course, remove the Guardian, but it would cut the construct off from Cortana or anyone else attempting to give it orders. At least until it was able to reestablish contact."

"What do you need to make that happen?" Bakar asked.

"Access to one of the many control terminals situated throughout the shield world. The nearest one is in this building, in the operations center where I placed it."

Molly started for the hatch right away. "I thought the UNSC built the school."

Prone followed after, and the others fell into line behind him. "I helped with the planning and specifically with the technological architecture of this and other buildings here."

Molly opened the hatch and led the way down. Prone came right after her, using its tentacles to pull itself down the ladder. They found their way to the operations center, which was right next to the school's main office.

Fortunately, the office was completely empty. Kasha must have been helping out somewhere else in the school. Perhaps she was even looking for them.

"Why haven't you put Onyx into a slipspace enclosure already?" Molly asked the Huragok as they entered the operations center, a large room with a number of chairs arranged around a long table. A wide picture window looked out over the grassy entrance to the school, and a gigantic display occupied the opposite wall. "Given the message we received last night, isn't the fact that a dormant Guardian existed inside Onyx enough of a threat?"

"To whom?" Prone to Drift said, as it moved to a wide section of the table. "According to the message, a Guardian will only harm those who attack it. It has not done any harm to the shield world itself so far. Only to the humans established here—and only after it was attacked."

The top of the table morphed at the touch of Prone's tentacles, and it suddenly became a control panel filled with glowing characters etched into glass-smooth shapes. It seemed specifically built for Huragok alone, and Molly couldn't make any sense of it.

To her, Forerunner tech often seemed like magic, but she knew that was only because she didn't understand how it worked. Molly supposed that, as with a lot of human tech, she didn't need to know the details of its inner workings to be able to use it, yet . . . even that analogy was weak, since Forerunner tech went way beyond anything humanity had produced. Prone deftly ran his tentacles across the display, doing what appeared to be a dozen different things at once.

A video feed suddenly appeared in the wall, surprising all of them, before they realized that Prone had turned it on. The feed showed the Guardian towering over Trevelyan. It looked like an impassive angel hovering ominously above the city. From this angle, something about its sweeping lines and the vast difference in scale between it and everything around it seemed eerily beautiful.

The Guardian sent a clear message to humanity from its creators. They were only insects in the face of such power.

"Can you zoom in on that?" Kareem said. "Beneath the Guardian, I mean?"

Prone to Drift flicked something with one of its tentacles, and the image on the screen changed to show the landing field on which Molly had first set foot inside Onyx. The shadow of the Guardian fell there, wide enough to blot out the sun for everyone who stood below it. Molly saw gunfire splashing off one of a squad of those Forerunner machines they'd seen earlier, who were blasting away with their energy weapons at UNSC soldiers offscreen. Seeing them up close was eerie. They looked and moved like humans, but had a highly advanced robotic architecture, impressively armored and clearly designed for war.

"What are these, Prone?" Molly asked.

"They are defensive armigers. Your people refer to them simply as Forerunner soldiers, and their purpose is to protect the Guardian upon its activation."

"Where did they come from?" Kareem asked. "It's like all of a sudden there are thousands of them, just appearing from out of thin air."

"You are correct. They do come from out of thin air," Prone said cryptically. "The Guardian uses translocation technology to draft them over from their hidden storage sites, sending them directly into the combat you see."

"Well, they're still fighting," Molly said. "It's been hours, and the UNSC is *still* trying to stop these things."

"Where are those shots coming from?" Kareem pointed to weapons fire that came from a different direction. "Can you pull back a bit?"

The view switched to show a completely different angle, covering the spaceport at a distance. It was a haunting sight. The marines stood alone on the platform, only a handful at the very center. The landing pad had been entirely overrun by Forerunner soldiers, and the marines were under fire from every direction. Every time a barrage of bullets knocked down one of the armigers, it seemed that another two stepped up into its place in a never-ending supply.

"What are they doing?!" Kareem asked. "Those marines don't have a chance of surviving out there, do they?"

"It is certainly a low probability," Prone to Drift said. "There are pockets of resistance throughout the city, much like this one. In a short time, much of Onyx's security personnel will be either incapacitated or dead."

"We've got to do something to stop it!" Molly said. "Quickly!"

"I am working as fast as I am able, Molly Patel. It is not an easy task."

"Did the Guardian take out the power in the *entire* shield world?" Gudam asked. "It's such a big place, you know, that it's hard to imagine that it could have affected everything."

"Most human activity in Onyx is centered in this region," Prone said. "By design, the Guardian's attack shut down everything inside of that."

"What about the researchers?" Molly said, thinking of her Newparents. "Some of them worked pretty far out in the field. Maybe they were far enough away?"

"No researchers were outside of the attack's radius of effect." Molly's heart sank at Prone's report. "However, there was one ONI staff member who was on assignment at the time, and she was beyond the attack's range."

"Who?" Molly's heartbeat quickened.

"You know her. She is named Spartan Lucy-B091. She took a single Pelican on a high-priority reconaissance mission."

"That's right!" Kareem said. "She said she was going to investigate the portal leads, remember?"

"Not that it does us much good now." Gudam pointed to the screen. The armigers swarmed forward against the same group of marines, who fell back against the assault. "The Forerunners' tech seems to be working fine. What's one Pelican going to be able to do against that?"

"One Pelican and a Spartan," Molly corrected her.

"Wait a second," Kareem said. "How are we seeing this, Prone? I mean, how did you get the screen in this room to turn on at all?"

"I fixed it. The pulse that the Guardian sent out shut down the power supplies for this entire region, but I set to repairing specific pieces right away. That is how I could check the school's sensors, and that is how I can access this terminal. Restoring the power to a single room is simple enough, but there are many rooms in Paxopolis and many power sources."

"What about the cameras there? How are they working?"

"There are other Huragok inside Onyx, including two others at

Trevelyan. I can only assume they repaired the cameras there, and I was able to link into them. They also spent a great deal of time repairing weaponry there that the armigers have now destroyed."

"And you can also fix Onyx's slipspace controls too?" Molly asked.

"I have already done so. I only need to activate them to remove Onyx from realspace."

"And that will cut off the Guardian from Cortana?"

"At least for a while. The Guardian is not without its own resources. I suspect that it would attempt to circumvent the dimensional problem and eventually be able to overcome my efforts and reestablish communications with Cortana."

"Then do it," Molly said. "Cut off its communication to Cortana now."

The others all nodded in agreement.

Prone to Drift massaged the console with all of its tentacles at once. The cilia on the end of them moved so fast that they seemed to dissolve into a glowing blur. After a moment, it retracted one of its tentacles and used it to speak through the translator on its underside again.

"It is done. Observe."

The four youths stepped back to watch the scene at the spaceport again. The Guardian, which had been coursing with energy and power, still hovered there, but now it was inert and dead, completely frozen above the ground. A moment later, its wings, shoulders, and head slumped forward, and it remained that way, unmoving and seemingly dormant.

Molly and the others cheered at the sight. Prone to Drift glowed a bit bluer than before, which Molly took to mean that it was pleased as well. As bad as this day's events had been till now, Molly finally started to hold out hope.

CHAPTER 27

The forward vanguard of the Servants of the Abiding Truth raced through the streets of the Forerunner city, chasing after the Huragok. Dural 'Mdama might have lost it in one of the twists and turns if it had not kept itself so high in the air to avoid being forced to navigate between structures. Yet, that it did not have to follow the streets meant it could move much faster than them, and the Sangheili could barely keep sight of it.

Eventually Dural and his vanguard found themselves in the newer part of town, the section built by the humans. The transition from Forerunner structures to human ones was bitter and grotesque. It seemed as if vandals had thrown up these new structures simply to prove how far beneath their betters they were.

Eventually, they saw the Huragok rise up over a large building—the human school—and disappear. It did not come down on the other side, which could only mean one thing.

"We have cornered it," the Pale Blade said. "Now all we have to do is capture it."

"Perhaps," Ruk said, "there are humans and even Sangheili within that building. They will fight to protect it."

"Then they will die in their efforts," Dural said with confidence. "They have not detected our presence yet, and this is no fortress. Let us secure the perimeter and then make our ingress."

Dural had his team fan out in two different directions and make a circuit around the building. They kept out of sight, moving from cover to cover, doing their best to make sure no one inside saw them. When they were done, the vanguard met at the edge of an open yard at the rear of the building. It was filled with what appeared to be recreation structures and game courts.

"Ruk, do you recall our observation of this structure from afar?" Dural said. "What would the Huragok be doing at a school?"

"I am more concerned with *who* might actually be in there with it. It could well be a trap, filled with demons."

"You worry like a doddering kaidon," Dural scolded. "You would have us wait out here until our prey slips through our fingers. We must act *now* if we wish to seize that prize. It is the key to any success on this world."

The Pale Blade signaled for his warriors to ready themselves to charge the building, but he saw that Ruk was still hesitant to run headlong into the place. When planning from the protection of the Cathedral, Ruk had boasted that he longed to charge into the humans' ranks and lay waste to them. Yet now, with victory within grasp, he faltered.

Dural wondered why this commander had begun to take the path of the doubter, just like Buran. *Will I have to deliver Ruk to the same fate? Why have the gods entrusted so many faithless worms to me?* Despite Ruk's weakhearted reluctance, though, Dural could see the wisdom of leaving someone behind to guard their rear, just in case enemies showed up to help whoever might be inside the school.

Wordlessly, Dural gestured for two of his warriors to remain behind with Ruk. The rest came with him. He led the charge across the yard at full speed, barreling toward a transparent set of doors. As he and his warriors neared them, Dural blew them open with a rapid burst from his storm rifle, blasting the doors to pieces. The Pale Blade heard screams from inside, evidently just beyond another set of doors. The thought of humans cowering in terror spurred him on.

Charging headlong, he braced his rifle in front of him and smashed through the second set of doors. They rent off their hinges and scattered across the floor as he burst into the room beyond.

He found himself in a large space, high ceilinged and seemingly meant as some kind of communal dining area, if the food on the many tables inside was any indication. The room was packed with fledglings sitting at tables and a handful of adults watching over them. Most of them were human, but Dural spotted a significant number of Sangheili and even Unggoy among them.

The sight made him furious.

He fired a burst at the ceiling and shouted in Sangheili: "Everyone hold still!"

Dural's warriors marched in behind him and spread out, creating a perimeter and covering everyone in the room. He was astonished to see that none of the adults appeared to be armed. How foolish they were to think that they would be safe in such a place. *How arrogant!* Dural thought to himself.

The Sangheili among them had forsaken everything their people had held dear and had become just like the self-assured treacherous human vermin, with no care for the necessity of securing one's keep. He had expected as much. His whole plan had assumed such blatant absurdity.

A human fledgling at the table nearest to him stood up and threw himself at the Pale Blade. Vengeance for some unknowable sin burned in his eyes, and he was not about to let Dural stop him from risking his life for it.

He seemed so small that Dural could hardly believe the fledgling could even talk. For a moment, the Pale Blade considered stomping on him just to send a message to his fellows.

Instead, Dural let the child strike his chest. The young creature bruised the knuckles of his rodentlike hand on the Sangheili's armor, and Dural sneered, tightening his mandibles in response. That the human couldn't injure the Sangheili only enraged him further, and he launched himself against Dural again.

This time, Dural caught the fledgling's hand in his own fist and squeezed it until he could feel the creature's frail bones collapse into mush. The foolish child cried out in agony as Dural lifted him into the air with the same hand. Then Dural dropped him to curl up into a weeping ball at his feet. The child stared at his shattered fingers, and Dural watched as the rage in the boy's heart turned to abject fear.

The Pale Blade glared at the others in the room. None of them would stand a chance against his vanguard. Even if all of them charged at once, they would not have a prayer against his few warriors assembled here.

What affirmed Dural's confidence was that it was exceedingly clear that they all knew it too. Some of them cowered in sheer terror. Dural saw others staring back at them with calculating eyes, assessing their numbers and adding up their odds, but in the end, they all came to the same conclusion: to struggle against Dural's forces would be to invite death.

The adults reached that answer faster than many of their students. Some of the youngest humans in the room scowled at the Servants, but those in authority held them back, often by putting their own bodies in front of them.

"I am the Pale Blade, leader of the Servants of the Abiding Truth. The first thing you must know is that I do not care if any of you survive. There is no parley you can offer me, nor any mercy that I might share. Rather, I would gladly slaughter you all—but I am not here for you."

A Sangheili female stepped forward and stood defiant before Dural. The children parted before her, not in terror but respect. They closed ranks behind her just as fast, moving in her wake for the protection she offered.

"I am Kasha 'Hilot," the female said in perfect Sangheili. "And this is my school."

Dural had not met many people from Hilot before, but she fit the mold he had always had in his mind: a cosmopolitan female with more than a little pride in her education. The province of Hilot had supported the Arbiter during the Blooding Years, and Dural suspected that was one key factor in her acquiring this current role—that and likely her ability to rise to the fierce defense of her charges, no matter how unwise her cause might be.

"What is it you want?" she demanded.

As she spoke, Dural recognized her from the earlier incident at the hangar where they had missed their first chance to capture a Huragok. She was the one who had led the *rafakrit* away from the students. She struck Dural as both brave and stupid—an idealist, as the field master had once said.

"I am here for your Huragok," Dural said.

The female narrowed her eyes at him. She knew Dural meant to capture the creature, and she wasn't about to make it easy for him. "We have no Huragok here. This is a school. Take your filthy killers from this place of peace, and get out!"

Dural flashed her all his teeth. "I hope you are a better teacher than you are a liar. I do not have much time to spare with this effort."

"Then go. You will not be missed."

Dural motioned toward one of his warriors. The soldier

picked up the boy still whimpering on the ground, and Dural said one word in Sangheili: "Arm."

In a single, sharp move, the warrior snapped the boy's arm completely in half. The human child let out an agonized scream as his fractured appendage flopped down at an unnatural angle.

The fledglings in the room groaned and murmured in fear. Those who could understand his speech no doubt wanted to tell Dural where the Huragok was, even if the adults did not.

Dural scanned the room again. It would be impossible for a Huragok to hide among these human children, but it was a large school. It would take far too long to search the entire place for the creature.

Despite the power he exerted over these few, Dural suddenly felt exposed. While chasing the Huragok, he had left the bulk of his force far behind, in the middle of the city. It would not take a significant countermeasure to sever his group from the others completely and—more problematically—from the portal they needed to escape through.

"I tire of this game already," Dural said to Kasha 'Hilot. "The next time I order one of my warriors to break something, it will be a neck."

The female gaped at him in distress. "There is a Huragok who comes to help here in the afternoons." She glanced around the room. "On a normal day, it would have already reported in to me, but it has not."

"Your excuses shall not dissuade me. If you do not produce the Huragok within five seconds, I'm going to start killing these useless things one at a time."

Kasha reeled in shock. "You would execute innocent children?"

"Innocent?" Dural enunciated every syllable of the word in Sangheili. "These are the offspring of the humans who have trampled the splendor and might of the Forerunners by setting up this abomination of a city here. They have pillaged and looted this world of its treasures, not for the glory of the gods, but for their own self-exaltation and in an attempt to subdue other species. I can see they already have you in their thrall."

"You are *fools*," the female said to Dural's warriors. "You follow a discredited faith, and you are led by a youth with no morals!"

Dural's warriors did not laugh at her, nor did they begin to rethink their loyalties. They did as they should have and showed her no reaction at all.

Dural snarled at 'Hilot and raised his hand to signal his warrior to snap the boy's neck. "Your time is up."

CHAPTER 28

"A force of Sangheili warriors has breached the school," Prone to Drift announced, immediately after having forced Onyx back into slipspace. A new image appeared on the screen, replacing the one of the dormant Guardian. The joy Molly had experienced in Prone's cutting off the Guardian from its control spun so fast into despair that it felt like a knife being twisted in her gut.

On the screen, they saw a small team of fully armed Sangheili slam through the dining-hall doors and burst into the room. The screams of Molly's fellow students rang out so loud they could hear them echoing down the hallways of the school, even without any audio from the feed.

Molly recognized their leader. He wore the same light blue armor that the Sangheili Director Mendez had shown her and her friends on the day the *rafakrit* ran rampant through the Repository. It was Dural 'Mdama, also known as the Pale Blade.

Bakar's brother.

Bakar stared at the image, astonished. "How has he tracked me here?"

"The Sangheili warriors are not here for you," Prone to Drift said. "They have been fighting in the streets of Paxopolis. I thought I avoided them as I came here on my regular rounds, but it seems that a group of them spotted me and tracked me here. They would like to use me for their own purposes."

"If they're looking for you, then you must turn yourself over to them," Bakar said. "Otherwise, they will kill everyone in that room. And then they will go on to slaughter every living thing in the entire school."

"No!" Molly stepped between Prone to Drift and the door. "If Prone's what they want—what they're willing to kill everyone here for—it's the last thing we should give them. If getting their hands on a Huragok is that important to them, we *have* to stop that from happening, no matter the cost."

Bakar shook his head at her. "Some costs are too high to bear." He glanced at the door. "We do not have time for this. Dural has no patience at all, and the others will be butchered unless you give up the Engineer."

Molly hesitated. Bakar had a point. If they really gave Dural what he wanted, that could save lives or at least buy some time. And what was Prone's life compared to that of every single person in the school?

But then maybe Dural would just kill them all anyhow, whether he had Prone or not.

Molly spread her arms in front of Prone. "We can't."

Bakar growled in frustration. "But I *can*." He spun on his heels and fled.

Molly chased him out into the corridor, but he was far too fast for her. By the time she reached the doorway, he was already halfway to the dining hall.

"Wait!" Molly shouted, but he ignored her.

She charged back into the operations room, cursing the entire way. "He's going to get himself killed."

"Maybe he has a point." Kareem pointed at the screen.

A Sangheili warrior stood next to Dural 'Mdama, and he had Karl in his arms. The bully struggled, but the warrior's hands held him like shackles. Then, at a word spat from Dural, the warrior snapped one of Karl's arms.

Molly could hear the wailing all the way down the hall again, but this time, it was a lone voice crying out in anguish.

Gudam broke out in quiet tears. "He's going to kill everyone."

Molly didn't like Karl at all, but at that moment she didn't care. She couldn't just stand by and let the Servants of the Abiding Truth murder him. But what could they do to stop them? What could anyone do?

The warrior let go of Karl's useless arm, which now hung limp from his side, and then moved to grasp his neck. Kasha spoke to Dural and tried to get him to stop, to listen to reason, to do anything but what they all feared most.

Molly could tell Kasha was going to fail. No words could put an end to this insanity.

And then Bakar entered the room.

"Stop!" he shouted in Sangheili.

Molly couldn't understand him, but the translator built into the school's surveillance systems displayed a real-time subtitle across the bottom of the display.

As Bakar strode into the dining hall, the students there parted before him. He stood there, exposed before Dural, pointed straight at him, and shouted, "Put that boy down!"

Every person in the dining hall froze, waiting to see what would happen next. Even the Sangheili warriors Dural had brought with him stood stock-still.

"Brother!" Dural said. "I knew you from the moment I saw you on that hill outside the hangar. Even after all this time."

Kasha gaped at them both. "You do not have to do this, Bakar."

"Quiet, female!" Dural thundered. "This is between Asum and me."

The room filled with soft murmurs from those who knew Sangheili, the students confused by the mention of a different name. Dural stood there confused for a moment before the truth dawned on him. "They have no idea who you really are. . . ."

"I am no longer Asum 'Mdama. I left that life behind long ago."

Dural scowled at Bakar. "You abandoned your people to side with the Arbiter, you mean, the great traitor himself. And now you stand by and watch as these people defile the instruments of the gods in an effort to use them to utterly destroy our people."

"You mean to protect them from malcontents like you and your Abiding Truth. The people working here are archaeologists and researchers. They seek to uncover the past so they can preserve a future for us all."

Dural shook his head in a sad rhythm. "Asum, I cannot believe the Arbiter and his filthy talk of peace has so twisted your mind. Were you so bent with grief over our mother's death that you could not see straight?"

Bakar stepped toward his brother. The time had finally come for this confrontation, and he would not flinch from it. "I did grieve for our mother. For all our people. Even for you.

"Dural, we spent so many years fighting humans because of the lies the Prophets told us. They set us against each other for nothing more than their own twisted purposes. And we paid for it in so many ways.

"When we finally realized it, and the Great Schism took form in response to their betrayal, those Sangheili who saw the San'Shyuum for who they really were hoped that we might now be free. Instead, brother, we turned against each other. Sangheili against Sangheili. And for that, our mother paid the ultimate price."

Dural scoffed at Bakar. "So, to make up for our mother's death, you take up with *humans*?" Dural spat the last word as if it tasted foul in his mouth.

"She didn't die at the hands of humans. She was cut down by our own kind."

"By the forces of the Arbiter, no less! With whom you have sided!"

"Because he has showed us the collar the Prophets put on us, one that we wore not with shame but pride for many centuries. Can you not see, brother?" Here, Bakar addressed everyone in the room who could understand his native tongue. "The greatest lie the Prophets told us was not that they were our connection to the gods, but that we were their chosen warriors. The very ones who would carry the entire Covenant into the presence of the gods.

"They played not only on our fears, but our hopes. They told us what we were so desperate to believe: that our purpose was tied up with theirs and that both our peoples would one day be divine, like the Forerunners before us."

Bakar focused back on Dural and his warriors. "And the thought that this might not be true was so traumatic to some that they refused to admit it . . . even to this day."

Dural stormed toward Bakar and belted his brother across the face. The blow cracked so hard it made Molly flinch several rooms away. If she had been hit like that, she'd have been knocked completely unconscious.

Bakar, though, rolled with the slap by arcing his long neck in the direction of the blow. Rather than coming up fighting, he simply stood his ground and spat dark blue blood out onto the floor.

"You presume too much!" Dural shouted in Bakar's face. "I will not have you blaspheme our people and our legacy!"

"Yes." Bakar's voice was filled with barely restrained menace.

He might have been keeping his cool, but not by much. "We've already had plenty of that."

Dural decided the conversation was over. He turned and pointed toward two of his warriors. "Put him in restraints."

"And if I refuse?"

Dural gestured at the warrior still holding Karl by the neck. The Sangheili gave a sharp flex of his wrist, and there was a sickening snap. Karl tumbled into a heap on the ground, dead.

"Then he will be the first of many," Dural said.

Those in the dining hall choked in fear and then fell silent. Molly saw tears rolling down a few faces. Karl's brother Zeb did his best to muffle his weeping out of terror if nothing else. She spotted their friend Andres, who glared at Dural as if he could set him on fire with his eyes.

Kasha rushed forward, raging at Dural, "You animal!"

Dural nodded at her, and one of the warriors shot her with a carbine. She fell over backward, clutching at the smoking hole that had appeared in her chest.

Bakar took a step toward his brother and quickly had several weapons leveled at him. He hauled up short.

"We can execute you here if you like, right now," Dural said. "Although I would prefer to make an example out of you in front of my entire force. It is what you deserve."

"Will you leave then, and not harm anyone else?" Bakar said, gritting his mandibles as he looked down at the dying Kasha.

Dural snorted. "Do you not understand, Asum? I do not care about you, brother. You are only collateral. I want the Huragok, and I will keep killing these pathetic creatures until I have it."

That's when Molly saw Prone to Drift enter the dining hall from the far side. She cursed out loud.

CHAPTER 29

T he Pale Blade was so filled with rage over his altercation with Asum that he was about to begin slaughtering everyone in the dining hall, right up until the moment the Huragok floated into the room. "Finally," Dural 'Mdama said. "A creature intelligent enough to show some sense."

The Huragok seemed to have fashioned itself a makeshift communicator by means of a slate it had fixed to its underside. It tapped at it with one of its tentacles, and the slate spoke for it. Dural was impressed with this innovation, and he decided that he should have Even Keel implement such a system too.

Through the slate, the Huragok said in perfect Sangheili, "I will leave with you peacefully if you promise not to kill anyone else."

Dural gestured at one of his warriors, and he shot a random human fledgling. The Huragok squealed in horror.

"You are not in a position to demand anything," Dural told it.

It glanced back toward the door it had just come through, as if it had just realized it had made a terrible miscalculation. It must have understood that it had no chance. "You desire my services. I desire for them to be safe. If you injure anyone else, I will overload my collar and terminate myself. Do you understand?"

Dural wasn't sure if a Huragok could even do that. Dural had been told that, during the war, the Covenant had locked some of them into explosive vests, but that had been less to control them than to make sure that they did not wind up in human hands. Dural wondered, *Does this Huragok value its own life so little that it will put an end to itself rather than watch me slaughter fledglings?*

This close to capturing the prize, Dural chose not to risk it. He could always come back and kill the rest later. "Fine. I am a warrior of my word. Come with us now, and we shall leave in peace."

The Huragok floated toward Dural, and he had two of his warriors grab it by its tentacles to secure it. He snorted at it and at the weaklings in the room. "Your compassion for each other will be your end."

With the Huragok secured and Asum in tow, Dural motioned for his warriors to head out. He had accomplished all that he desired for the day. Now he only needed to link back up with his main force and depart through the portal. Only then would Dural decide if the Servants should continue to rampage through the human city or call a strategic withdrawal back to the Cathedral.

Then weapons began firing outside the school. The rattle of a lone assault rifle was met by a barrage of plasma fire. *Humans,* Dural mouthed with disdain.

The fledglings in the room began screaming, and many of them fled the room. The adults tried to keep them calm, but they were fighting a losing battle. Most of the human rodents could think only of survival, scattering at the first opportunity to hide.

A moment later, Ruk barged into the dining hall through the shattered doors, his plasma rifle steaming hot. "A demon!" he shouted. "It has killed the others!"

As Dural cursed their luck, his remaining warriors snapped into position without needing any orders. They brought up their weapons and moved to cover every entrance to the room. The Pale Blade swelled with pride at their alacrity.

"How many are there?" he demanded of Ruk.

"Isn't one demon enough?" Ruk, burning with shame at his retreat, refused to look Dural in the eyes. Though the Spartans were fierce warriors, his behavior was not warranted. Dural shouldered him aside as he headed for the door Ruk had just come through.

"We need to leave here now," Dural said. "The longer we let this demon pin us down, the more likely others will show up." He barked at the others, "Get ready to move out!"

"What about the hostages?" Ruk pointed to the handful of teachers and fledglings who remained huddled in a far corner of the room.

"Leave them!" Dural pointed toward Asum and the Huragok. "We have what we came for. It's time to move!"

Dural grabbed Asum and wrestled his brother in front of him, using Asum's body as a shield. Then he put his energy blade's deactivated hilt to his brother's throat. "If you try to escape, I will remove your head."

To his credit, Asum did not cower at the threat. "Just stop the killing!"

Dural guided him toward the broken doorway. "That is up to the demon now."

The Servants emerged from the dining hall and spotted the Spartan standing in the recreation yard, waiting for them. Dural realized that the human had no desire to charge into a room full of fledglings and start firing. The Spartan would have no doubt preferred a clean target, but Dural was not about to present him with that. He kept Asum firmly between the two of them instead.

"It's all right, Bakar," the Spartan said. "Help is on the way."

"Stay where you are, demon," Dural said, knowing that the Spartan's armor had translation capabilities much like his did. "We are taking this one and the Huragok with us."

The Huragok emerged from the building behind Dural. Ruk now held one of the creature's tentacles in one fist, and he had his plasma rifle pressed up against its side with the other.

"I can't let you do that," the Spartan said.

"If you try to stop us, we will kill them both," Dural said. "Then we will continue with as many of your people as we can here until you bring us down. *If* you can manage such a thing."

The Spartan hesitated.

"Think well on this matter," Dural said. "These two for the lives of dozens of fledglings. Is it really a difficult choice, demon?"

The Spartan cursed.

"Tom," Asum said, using the profane human tongue. "We already agreed to this. Let them have us."

"You're just a kid, Bakar. You don't get to make that decision."

"But I have. They have already killed a couple of students. And they have shot Kasha as well."

"She is dying," Dural told the Spartan. "You might be able to save her—if you let us go now."

The Spartan stood dead-still, his rifle leveled at Dural's skull. After a long moment, he stepped to the side, but kept his weapon trained on Dural the entire time.

"All right. Go. Now."

Dural led the way across the yard, and his warriors followed behind him. Ruk kept the Huragok under control, while Dural forced Asum to remain between him and the Spartan until they were well out of the demon's sight.

The moment that happened, Dural called to his warriors to move faster. They raced toward the Forerunner city and the portal through which they had come.

As they moved deeper into the city, though, Dural saw that the carnage he previously ordered had turned into a battle. Smoke rose from the Forerunner structure where the portal was, and the sound of weapons fire—from human ballistics, not plasma blasts—echoed throughout the city.

"Pale Blade," Ruk said. "It is not safe to go this way." Ruk had enlisted three other warriors to help him haul the Huragok along. It resisted them every step of the way.

"We have no time to go around, Ruk. We either make our way through here, or we die!" Dural said.

"We may survive it." Ruk nodded at the Huragok. "But what of our prize?"

Dural snarled at Ruk. He did not need to be reminded that they had other priorities than their own lives. Dural shouted at the Huragok, "If you do not cease fighting us, I will kill Asum right here!"

The Huragok spoke in flawless Sangheili, *"Threatening our lives if we do not move toward certain death is not an effective coercion technique."* As much of a fight as it was putting up with Dural's warriors, its electronic voice showed no strain.

"He is correct," Asum said.

In a fit of rage, Dural struck his brother on the side of his head.

Then Dural called a halt and glared at the creature. He turned and looked back out at the battle heating up in front of them. Lines of his warriors were streaming back toward the structure and escaping into the portal there. They were following Dural's orders, but he could already see that he would not be able to join them, due to the encroaching waves of human soldiers. Even if he managed to bore through the human lines, the Huragok would likely be killed.

There has to be a better way.

Then he realized that there was.

Dural signaled for his warriors to follow him as he swung the vanguard about and headed in a different direction, toward a dense patch of foliage that girded the nearby lake. "We will head for the hangar in which we first spotted this creature," Dural said.

"The Repository?" the Huragok asked. It had ceased pulling back against Dural's warriors now that he had changed plans.

"There is no need to kill ourselves by trying to leave here via the same route as the rest of my warriors when you can activate the portal system for us someplace else."

CHAPTER 30

Is she going to live?" Molly asked Dinok 'Acroli as he labored over Kasha.

"There is a fair chance," he said without looking up. "If you and the others can give me some room."

When the Servants of the Abiding Truth had cleared out, most of the students and staff who remained in the dining room had fled. Dinok had stayed behind to check on Kasha, while Molly, Kareem, and Gudam had raced down from the relative safety of the operations room to see what they could do to help. The answer appeared to be nothing.

Tom stomped in through the broken recreation-yard doors, his assault rifle at the ready. Molly had never before seen him fully kitted up in his Mjolnir armor, and it stole her breath. He towered over them like a magnificent statue that had come to life in ablative armor and a mirrored faceplate.

"Report," he said to Molly.

"They shot Kasha. And killed Karl. And also a boy I didn't recognize too."

"Wong Xu," Kareem said.

"I don't think Wong's dead," Gudam said. "Someone picked him up and hauled him away when they cleared the room. He might still make it."

"Who is 'they'?" Tom asked.

"Dural 'Mdama and the Servants of the Abiding Truth," Molly said.

"Bakar's brother," Kareem added.

"They took both Bakar and Prone to Drift," Tom said. "I have to go after them."

"We're coming with you!" The words blurted out of Molly's mouth before she could even think about them.

"Appreciate the offer, Molly," Tom said. "But these are armed Sangheili warriors, and as you've seen, they have no compunctions about killing anything in their way. You need to stay put here. I'll report back in once I take care of the situation."

Tom gave the three of them a nod. "I'm proud of how you've handled this so far. Good luck."

With that, the Spartan turned and ran out of the dining hall the way he'd come. Molly followed after him, all the way to the door. Kareem and Gudam came right behind her, but Tom was already long gone and in full sprint.

"We need to do something to help," Gudam said. "That Sangheili has Bakar *and* Prone!"

"We'll never catch up to Tom," Kareem said. "Do you have any idea how fast a Spartan can move on foot?"

"We don't have to catch him," Molly said. "He's chasing the Servants. We just need to catch up with *them*."

"Sangheili are pretty fast too," Gudam said.

"They're charging into a battle," Kareem said. "And they have a couple hostages. That might slow them down a bit."

Molly looked back to see if anyone might try to stop them. Dinok was still trying to patch up Kasha, and all the other students and adults hadn't come out of hiding yet. "It's now or never," Molly said. "Let's go."

She knew Tom was right to warn, but Bakar was their friend. What did Tom expect them to do? Sit around and wait for Bakar to be slaughtered? Molly refused to let that happen, and she knew that Gudam and Kareem felt the same way.

Without any more hesitation, they raced out into the recreation yard and spotted Tom sprinting away faster than a Warthog. Gudam huffed just watching him go. "We're *never* going to catch him."

"We probably don't want to anyhow," Molly said, jogging after Tom. Gudam and Kareem fell into step next to her. "We're unarmed and wouldn't be much good in a fight against those Sangheili."

"So why are we doing this again?" Kareem asked, finally realizing how dangerous what they were doing might be.

"Just because we can't fight them doesn't mean we can't help," Molly said as they edged around the school. "Besides, Prone told us that he could stop the Guardian permanently if we could get him close enough to the thing. Remember we've only got a small window before the Guardian reactivates and tries to bring Onyx back to realspace. If it does that, how much do you want to bet that Cortana will send others to help it?"

"So we have to get Prone free from the Servants right away?" Gudam said. "That doesn't sound like something we'd be able to manage. I mean, we're pretty amazing, sure, but maybe not amazing enough to stand up to a full squad of the Abiding Truth's finest warriors."

"I'm kind of hoping Tom will take care of that part for us." As Molly spoke, they saw Tom veer off from the beeline he'd been making toward a Forerunner spire in the distance, overlooking the lake. A lot of fighting seemed to be going on around it, and Molly wondered why he'd decided to break away from it.

"There they are!" Kareem pointed down a street off to the left. Molly got just a glimpse of Prone being towed along by a handful of Sangheili warriors as they crossed the street a couple blocks away and headed into an outcropping of tall cypresses surrounding the lake.

The Servants had switched directions, but Molly wasn't sure why. Maybe to avoid the battle, or possibly because they had a different plan from before. Tom, being as sharp as Molly knew he was, seemed to have spotted it right away and corrected his course. Fortunately, Kareem had spotted the Servants, or Molly and her friends might have missed the change in direction altogether.

"Keep after them!" Molly pumped her legs as fast as they could go.

"But keep our distance too," Gudam said. When Molly shot the little Unggoy a look, she shrugged. "We can't help our friends if we get killed!"

Gudam had broken into a fast scramble, using her knuckles like an ape. It was impressive to see her move so quickly.

The three kept after the Servants and Tom for a long time, pressing deep into the rolling hills that skirted Paxopolis. Molly couldn't remember ever having run so far in her entire life. Her heart felt as if it were going to burst out of her chest, but she kept on, as did the others.

The run gave her a new appreciation for the training that Tom and Lucy had been putting her and her friends through. Without that, they would have had to stop long ago.

Thankfully, the Servants didn't seem to be running at top speed, probably because they had two prisoners that weren't terribly cooperative. Despite that, Molly and Kareem began to pace themselves so Gudam could keep up, recognizing that the Spartan might begin to glance behind him as he began to catch up with the Servants.

The three of them kept far enough back that they barely saw

the Servants. They were also careful to avoid Tom. Molly was confident that the Spartan could have easily caught up with the Servants by now, but he held back instead, slowing to a stalking pattern and using the trees as cover. Molly and the others followed his example.

Soon, Molly recognized the hills they were trotting over and the look of the trees they were approaching. "It's the Repository." She'd broken a good sweat and was panting hard now, even though they had slowed down. "That's where we're going."

"The portal!" Kareem said. "They're going to use that to escape!"

"There's no way we can get there fast enough to stop them," Gudam said. Despite struggling to keep up earlier, she didn't seem tired at all.

"But Tom can." Molly pointed at him.

The Spartan had now kicked into high gear, moving quicker as the distance began to close between the Servants and their goal. The Spartan had likely already figured out where the Servants were headed, and he wasn't about to let them get away from him. As Tom began to accelerate, he veered off to the left of the trail, as if to cut around the Servants in a wide circle.

"Where's he going?" Gudam asked. "Aren't they right in front of him?"

"He's trying to cut them off before they can make it to the portal," Molly said. "That should stop them cold."

Kareem didn't seem so sure. "Unless . . ."

"Unless what?"

"Well, there's a lot of them, and Spartan or not, there's just one of him."

Molly scowled at Kareem, and he shut his mouth. Personally, she didn't want to think about how badly the Servants outnumbered Tom. He was a Spartan, and in Molly's mind that was enough. He could take them all on.

She only hoped she was right.

As they approached the top of a hill overlooking the Repository, the three of them hunkered down and crept up low upon it. They got into a prone position, lying on their bellies as they crested it, hoping no one beyond it would see them. Though the Repository was still far off, Molly had a perfect view of it. She could see through the structure's front door, which must have been open during the Guardian's attack, and the gated frame of the portal at its far back.

The portal stood inactive and lifeless.

Below them stretched a long field with trees scattered across it. Molly could see the pack of Servants and their prisoners as they moved down the hillside toward the Repository's front entrance, but there was no sign of Tom.

If any people were left in the Repository, Molly didn't see them, and it seemed to be entirely empty. The hangar looked mostly locked down, apart from a few open doors on both sides.

Then Molly saw the Spartan burst from the tree line on the far left, well outside the Servants' field of view. Tom ignored the front entrance where the Servants were headed and instead launched straight through one of the hangar doors, right to where the portal was. Once inside, he slowed down and found cover at a barrier Molly hadn't noticed before.

"The UNSC must have put those up after the monster came through the portal," Kareem said. "They're probably not designed to keep things from going into the portal so much as coming out."

Gudam pointed toward the front of the Repository. "Here come the Servants! Do you think they saw Tom get in front of them?"

The Servants certainly looked wary of their surroundings. Dural led the Sangheili force from the front, with a wall of warriors spreading out just one step behind him. Bakar trailed along after, under the control of a warrior who had a rifle pointed into his mandibles, and two more warriors had Prone to Drift in tow by the Huragok's tentacles.

Then the Spartan appeared from behind the barrier, his weapon raised.

The Servants slowed to a stop as they saw what barred entry into this portal. Dural ignited his energy sword, and the rest of the warriors leveled their weapons at Tom. The Spartan opened fire, and they scattered to the sides—taking cover behind vehicles near them—but kept pressing toward him. One of the Sangheili warriors dropped in his tracks, but that loss didn't deter the others.

As the Servants closed on Tom, they returned fire in co-ordinated bursts, blasting him with an unrelenting stream of fiery bolts of plasma. Most of these splattered off the barrier in front of him or smacked into the portal frame itself, but a few of them caught Tom dead in his chest. The energy shield his Mjolnir armor produced glowed bright with the effort of ablating those shots, but it somehow held intact.

Tom cocked back his arm and heaved something up and over the barricade. Given that the Sangheili dove to the side, it must have been a grenade.

The explosion took out two more of the Servants' warriors. It also caused Bakar and Prone and their captors to stop dead, well clear of the blast. They held there, waiting for the fight to be over.

Tom then leaped on top of the barricade and fired again on the warriors storming at him. They were coming from all directions now. Another of them dropped, and then another, but they still outnumbered him. Molly couldn't imagine how he would survive.

A pair of plasma grenades arced through the air toward the barricade. Tom somehow caught one of them and tossed it back at the Sangheili, but the other landed right in front of the barricade. Even from this distance, Molly could see how vicious the explosion was, and the sound thudded through the air a split second after.

The blast knocked Tom tumbling high into the air. An explosion that close should have killed anyone instantly, but when the Spartan began to fall, he tucked into a somersault and rolled back to his feet, ready to keep fighting.

Molly couldn't believe what she was seeing. Her amazement at what Tom could do was tempered, though, by her fear for him, Bakar, and Prone.

Despite the Spartan's bravado, he wasn't quite as steady on his feet now. As he turned to face his foes, Dural appeared right in front of him. With Tom's shields exhausted by the grenade, the Sangheili leader struck hard and fast and speared his energy sword right through the Spartan's middle.

Gudam stifled a scream as Tom went down. Dural kicked the Spartan off his blade, then thrust it high into the air as he roared in triumph. The rest of the Servants who were still breathing followed suit, and they began ushering their prisoners toward the portal's frame.

Tom's body lay still. A swirl of smoke rose from the sword wound.

"That's it," Kareem said, completely petrified. "I can't believe they killed him. They killed *Tom*."

Molly smacked Kareem on his shoulder, and her eyes filled with tears. She could barely breathe. "We can't just give up. Not now. What about Bakar and Prone?"

"Did you see those guys just take down a *Spartan*? There's nothing we can do, Molly." Kareem's face turned pale. "What kind of chance do we have against those warriors? Against the Pale Blade?"

"I don't know," Molly admitted. "But we're not dead yet, so we're *not* giving up."

"But—" Gudam started.

"I know!" Molly shouted in a hushed voice, not sure how well the Servants could hear from this distance. "It *is* hopeless! We don't have a chance, but I'm not going to let them take Bakar. Or Prone. There *has* to be another way!"

"But they're getting away," Gudam said meekly, pointing down at the Servants. They had hauled Prone to the portal's frame, and the Huragok was working at some kind of terminal next to it, a metallic sphere covered with glowing blue symbols. Bakar kept turning back to gaze at Tom's body and then averting his eyes.

Within seconds, Prone had activated the portal, and a blue glow flowed into its frame. Dural shouted something at the Huragok in Sangheili, but it didn't seem to faze Prone. After a bit of snarling among themselves, the Servants began to file through the portal one by one.

Soon, they were all gone, yet the portal remained active. Despite how far away it was, Molly could hear the portal's low trilling in the silence that rang after the Sangheili left.

Without another moment's hesitation, Molly stood up and sprinted down the hill, straight for Tom. As she went, she kept a close eye on the fallen Servants. None of them were moving, but neither was the Spartan. She heard Kareem and Gudam following behind her but didn't look back.

When she reached Tom, she couldn't tell if he was still breathing. He just lay there in his armor. *How could he survive after what happened to him?* She tried tugging on the armor, but it was far too heavy. It felt like trying to move a truck.

"Tom! Tom! Can you hear me? Are you okay?" she asked with tears in her eyes.

She feared she knew the answer, although she couldn't bring herself to accept it.

He was gone.

But then his visor depolarized, revealing closed eyes that slowly fluttered open. "I've been better."

She let out an emotional laugh at that, mostly from sheer relief.

"Armor's keeping me alive." Tom huffed in pain. "For now."

"The Servants took Bakar and Prone. They left through the portal."

Tom groaned. "Great. If I survive this . . . Mendez is going to kill me."

"We're going after them." Molly looked to the others for confirmation. Kareem gave her a stiff nod, and Gudam smiled in a way that showed all her teeth.

"Belay that," Tom said, struggling to speak. "Too . . ."

He passed out before he could finish.

Molly gazed down at him through his visor. He looked like he was still breathing, although it was hard to tell.

"Shouldn't we try to patch him up first?" Kareem said.

"With what?"

Kareem shrugged. They didn't have anything on hand, and the Repository was mostly locked down.

"Even if we had the right supplies, we'd never be able to get his armor off him," Molly said.

"Also, he said the armor's the only thing keeping him alive," said Gudam. "Maybe we should go for help."

"But then who's going to help Bakar and Prone?" Molly asked. "We can't just let the Servants take them."

"You're right," said Gudam. "They'll use Prone against us, and they'll kill Bakar for sure! But how can we stop them? If Tom couldn't manage it, what hope do we have?"

"Tom killed a bunch of them." Molly started toward one of the fallen Sangheili. It had been a long time since she'd seen a dead body up close, and she had to steel her stomach against it.

A plasma rifle lay on the ground next to the corpse. Molly picked it up. It was heavy and large—and warmer than she would have guessed. She pointed it away from Kareem and Gudam and pulled the trigger. A burst of plasma bit into the dirt, as the rifle's recoil tried to shake it free from her grip.

She motioned toward a couple of other fallen warriors. "And now we have weapons. We just follow after the Servants and hope they give us a chance to use them."

Kareem and Gudam quickly picked over the fallen Servants for things they could use too. Kareem grabbed a storm rifle for himself, while Gudam found a plasma pistol.

"This is insane, you know that, right?" Kareem said.

Molly led the way toward the portal, raising her weapon and taking a deep breath. "Of course it is, but what else are we going to do? Could either of you look at yourself in the mirror tomorrow if we didn't at least try to save those two?"

Neither Kareem nor Gudam said a word. They answered with their feet.

The three walked up to the portal, and Molly took a deep breath. Then she plunged through it and hoped she would land safely on the other side.

CHAPTER 31

nce Dural 'Mdama and his vanguard of Servants made it through the portal, the defiance drained out of Asum. Dural felt grateful for that, as he had lost too many warriors on this endeavor already. He didn't need to waste more of them watching over his brother when they needed to have their eyes scanning the horizon. Cowed and weaponless as Asum was, Dural had his brother walk next to him so the others could do their jobs.

"Where are we?" Asum asked.

"Not too far removed from the human city, but far enough. I would have gone directly back to our base, but the portal there is still open to the one that we came through earlier. We will have to walk from here."

The portal the Huragok had sent them to was outside the gated perimeter the humans had staked out around their tiny bit of territory inside the shield world. The frame of the glowing gate was set inside a series of hollowed-out cupolas, the purpose of which Dural could not identify, although they were heavily adorned with Forerunner script. He only knew that this portal served his purposes well for the moment.

"Is it far?" Asum asked.

"You have grown soft, brother."

"Is it soft to wonder how long I have left to live?"

Dural clacked his mandibles at Asum as they struck off in the direction the Huragok had said would take them to their base. "Most certainly," Dural said, as the remains of his vanguard fell into step behind the two of them.

"None of us have as much time as we would like," Asum began, his eyes set in a blank stare. "Have you heard the news about our uncle?"

"He is no concern of mine. The Servants and the Covenant have no more dealings, especially that impostor version of the Covenant our uncle led."

"He was our *father*, Dural."

The Pale Blade said nothing in response. The two of them were far enough from the others that Dural was sure none of them had heard.

Asum peered up at him, instantly suspicious. "You knew."

"It makes no difference. He abandoned us both—and our mother as well—to pursue his own ends."

"Well, then this should be of no consequence to you . . . Jul was killed on Kamchatka a few days ago."

That hit Dural with far greater force than he had suspected. This was real: *Our father is dead. He will never come back, and there will never be any reconciliation between us.* It took Dural a moment to gather his thoughts enough to ask, "By the Arbiter?"

"No. A team of Spartans."

"It is the same." Dural spat on the ground. "I suppose it is too much to hope he took some of the demons with him."

Asum shrugged. "It would not change things."

"Sometimes revenge is all you can hope for."

"After his death, the remains of his Covenant rallied on Sanghelios in the spire city of Sunaion. The Arbiter led the Swords of Sanghelios directly into the temple there and proceeded to destroy them all."

"So, the Covenant . . . it is no more?"

Asum grunted. "No more than a bad memory."

Dural glanced around at his warriors. "Then the Servants of the Abiding Truth is one of the last refuges for those who still walk the Path. I did not appreciate Jul 'Mdama's choices or his tactics, but I still prayed that he might take vengeance on the Arbiter."

"For what crime? For freeing our people from the influence of the Prophets? For helping put an end to a forever war in which we were nothing but pawns?"

Dural bristled at Asum's complaints. "For murdering our mother. Is that not enough?"

The two walked in silence after that in the warm and sunny evening. Dural could still hear the sounds of battle rattling in the remote distance. The city must still have been in chaos. From somewhere else he heard animals calling to one another, howling and growling in unfamiliar tones.

The ongoing din of battle must have drawn the animals' attention. Dural hoped that they were not agitated predators that might become hostile to anyone roaming within their territory. Given the creatures they had already encountered on this world, such a thing did not seem unlikely.

Dural looked back and saw one of his warriors, a subcommander named Arkit, knocking the Huragok around, attempting to restrain it. Dural slowed down so they could catch up with him.

"Keep your hands off it," Dural said sternly. "This Huragok has become an ally. Do you think we could have escaped without its help?"

"It is the only way to keep such a stubborn beast in line, Pale Blade," Arkit said. "It keeps manipulating its slate when it believes that I am not looking."

Dural stared at Arkit for a moment, sizing him up. Enough of the vanguard was becoming insolent with Dural that he wondered if he would have to make an example of one of them soon. Had Avu Med 'Telcam experienced such trials when he was young? And if he had, how might he have dealt with such issues?

Perhaps this recurring impudence arose simply because leadership had been foisted onto Dural's shoulders so soon, which meant his lot for the next several years would consist of constantly cutting down those who thought it wise to question his youth. Even still, he would have been a fool to ignore any problem with this captive Huragok.

Dural drew his energy sword and leveled it at the creature. "Show me your slate."

He had thought the Huragok would simply hand him the device, but perhaps it was too firmly attached to its flesh. Instead, it rolled over on its side, exposing its stomach to Dural. There, he could read the display, on which the creature had keyed in something.

All he could see were a set of coordinates, ones that Dural could only imagine indicated the location at which they currently stood.

"Who are you communicating with?" he demanded. The power had been drained from every sophisticated device the Servants owned. The Huragok themselves—and what they could fix— might have been an exception to the Guardian's attack, but who else was? How could the creature have reached anyone?

"Answer me." Dural brought the blade of his sword dangerously near the Huragok's flesh. "Now!"

The creature swiped the slate and produced a response. "Spartan Lucy-B091."

"A demon?" Dural shouted at the Huragok. "You have summoned a demon to rescue you?"

Dural balled his free hand and slammed it into the slate. The front shattered immediately, and the rest of it erupted into sparks.

Dural took care not to hit so hard that he might permanently damage the Huragok—but not so much that he wouldn't at least hurt it.

The Huragok deflated in fear and cowered into the ground.

"Go ahead and call for help! Call as loud as you like! You think a demon can save you out here? What happened to the last one that came to your aid?"

The creature could not answer him at all now. It could only whimper in its own ridiculous tongue.

"This is your fault," Ruk said, coming up behind Dural. "You separated us from the rest of our forces, and then you let the Huragok take us even farther away." A howl from some sort of beast echoed out of a nearby wood, as if to put a fine point on this claim. It made the scales on the back of Dural's neck rise.

"The field master put me in charge. Are you questioning his judgment?"

"I do not think he believed he would die so soon," Ruk snorted. "You are too young, too brash, and too untrained to handle a force of this size. You are going to get us all killed."

Dural had failed to put his energy sword away yet. He drew it back and took a mighty swing at Ruk's neck.

The Sangheili saw the attack coming and ducked under the blade easily. As Ruk stood to his full height, he produced his own energy sword. He had intentionally provoked Dural to give himself an excuse to seize the mantle of leadership, and Dural cursed himself for giving into it.

"Do not be a fool," Dural told him. "We have more pressing concerns than this." As the words left his lips, he knew he had wasted his breath on them.

"Speak for yourself, Pale Blade. You are but a shallow reflection of the field master, and I will reclaim the Servants from you to reverse the mistake he made by putting his trust in you."

It pained Dural that Ruk would fall from grace, when Ruk had been such a fruitful ally early on in this mission, but that would not stay Dural's hand. The Pale Blade threw himself at Ruk, his sword held high, and he brought the edge down with both hands. Ruk got his own blade up just in time save his life, but not fast enough to keep his face from being scorched by the edge of Dural's weapon.

The wounded Sangheili howled in anger as the pain took hold, shoving Dural back. The strike had caught him across his eye, blinding him. Ruk came at Dural, swinging wild and wide. The Pale Blade ducked underneath the clumsy attempt and slashed Ruk across the chest.

Ruk fell back, and Dural pressed his advantage. He hammered at Ruk mercilessly, letting his anger fuel his strength. After a while, Dural felt as if his arms might give out, but he managed to outlast Ruk. Just as Dural thought he might have spent himself too fast, his last blow knocked Ruk's sword from his hands.

Ruk hesitated, and Dural wondered if he might fall to his knees and beg the Pale Blade to take his life immediately and cover his shame. Instead, Ruk charged straight at Dural and tried to take him bare-handed.

Foolish as it was, the Pale Blade admired him for that. Ruk refused to give up, not for anything.

In return, Dural slashed Ruk across his throat, granting him the quick death he had been too proud to demand. He collapsed at Dural's feet.

"Anyone else care to question my judgment?" Dural said to the rest of his vanguard as he extinguished his sword with confidence. None of them even dared look him in the eye.

CHAPTER 32

olly didn't think they would have ever caught up with the Servants if the Sangheili hadn't stopped to fight with each other. It was challenging enough that the Servants were faster than the three of them—which was no surprise given how much stronger and taller Sangheili were—but the Servants also had the advantage of knowing where they were going. Molly, Gudam, and Kareem only had distant glimpses of the Servants and their hostages and, eventually, the muffled sounds of a battle to keep them on track.

As the three rounded a dense corridor of foliage, Gudam spotted something, and she held out her oversized hand in front of Molly and Kareem. Yet another pair of monsters, things Molly had never seen before, were lurking in the edges of the gathering shadows as dusk fell across the land.

These were strong, four-legged, pantherlike creatures, not much smaller than a *rafakrit* and covered with a thick layer of dark green fur that helped them blend in with their grassy surroundings. Their large jaws were lined with long, feline teeth, and they looked as though they had been bred to hunt and kill. The pair of beasts were slowly edging forward on their bellies, creeping toward the Servants' position and readying an attack. If the creatures had not already been hunting the Servants, Molly, Gudam, and Kareem might have been targeted by them as well.

Molly felt grateful to be armed, even with a Covenant weapon, but she wondered what good it could do against such animals. Molly had never shot a living thing in her life, but the adrenaline pumping in her body had heightened her senses and made her keenly aware that her actions—including being willing to use her weapon—could make the difference between her surviving and dying that day.

Keeping a careful eye on the predators as Molly led the way did not work as well as she would have liked. As she attempted to circumnavigate the creatures and come at the Servants from the side, she realized too late that their movements had put the creatures downwind. The animals that had been hunting the cluster of Sangheili in the brush swiftly picked up the scent of the three youths and began following them instead. Molly started to tremble, but steadied her hands.

The animals kept their distance at first, staying roughly two hundred meters away. They were curious and not yet ready to commit themselves to an attack—but whether they had been spotted did not matter to them. These animals would win the fight against the three of them either way.

Molly wanted to move forward and concentrate on getting back Bakar and Prone. Yet, she knew that if Kareem, Gudam, and she let their guard down, the animals would be on them in a second.

She breathed a measured sigh of relief when they finally approached a pair of glowing energy swords clashing with each other, roughly a hundred meters ahead. She didn't know what had set two of the Servants brawling, but they had given up their position and Molly hoped the three of them would be able to keep up with the Servants from there.

"Are those things back there hunting us?" Gudam said in a

whisper. "I wouldn't ask, but it seems like they are, and if they are, then that might mean something for an idea I have."

"It looked like they were tracking the Servants first." Kareem gave the creatures a sidelong look. "But now that you've said that . . ."

"What's your idea?" Molly asked.

"We just need to get on the other side of the Servants. Between them and wherever they're going. If we can do that, we might be able to use those beasts to solve our Servants problem, if you know what I mean," Gudam said, with hope in her eyes.

"You're gonna try to attract those things into the Servants' path?" Kareem said with a worried look. "And then see what happens? That sounds really risky."

Gudam nodded and then—without another word—took off in a clambering sprint using her forelimbs. She headed in a wide arc around the Servants' current position, circling about the flat hill they'd stopped upon. Molly and Kareem followed as quickly and quietly as possible, glancing back at the animals in their wake. The grasses were tall enough to almost entirely hide the Unggoy, and the encroaching darkness gave her additional cover as well—but both Molly and Kareem were fairly exposed to the creatures' view.

Molly and Kareem were about halfway around the Servants when she realized that Gudam's plan had a flaw. "What's going to happen when the creatures are done with the Sangheili?" she asked, peering at them over Kareem's shoulder. "Won't they just turn on us?"

"Probably," Kareem said with a shrug.

Despite her reservations about the plan, Molly realized they'd run out of time. Evidently, the two predators had become bored with the pursuit and were now moving toward them faster. They had fixed their feline eyes on Molly and Kareem, and they would not be denied any longer.

The creatures sped up as they approached from a hundred meters, their strong, muscular legs pumping like those of the great cats Molly had seen on Earth. Her heart began to thud in her chest as she lifted her weapon alongside that of Kareem.

One hundred meters became eighty.

The creatures got closer with every beat of her heart. When she fired, she knew it would alert the Sangheili, and then she and Kareem would be trapped between the Servants of the Abiding Truth and a pair of massive animals that seemed to be evolved to kill.

Fifty meters became thirty.

Molly opened fire.

Her plasma rifle pulsed in her hand, sending superheated energy into the face of the nearest creature. The blast stitched a line of burns across the snout of the front-runner, and the beast skidded to a halt, howling in pain. Its companion stopped right beside it, unharmed but now wary.

The creatures were now roughly twenty meters away. The one Molly shot dragged its enormous paw across its face, as if it could wipe away the burns. She wondered if it was the first time the thing had actually felt pain and it simply didn't recognize the sensation.

"Good work," Kareem said, catching his breath. "But we've got company."

She glanced over to where he was pointing and saw a handful of Sangheili stomping toward them, twice the distance away as the large cats.

One of the warriors shouted something in Sangheili.

"Surrender, fledglings!" Dural's voice came from beyond them, evidently demanding their surrender in Sangheili. As he approached, he stopped where he was and kept his energy sword on Bakar. One slight move, and he could cleave the young Sangheili's head right off.

The handful of warriors who approached leveled their rifles at the two of them, and Molly knew that they were about to die right there, in the middle of nowhere. She considered fighting them—if she was going to die, it'd be pumping plasma into their chests—but Kareem took that decision away from her. He lowered the barrel of his rifle and pressed his hand on Molly's until it was pointed toward the ground as well.

"What are you doing?" she asked.

With their weapons down, Kareem sidled away from the warriors—and sent an eye back at the creatures, whom the Sangheili hadn't seen yet. "Just trying to figure all the angles," he said in a hushed voice.

"Is giving up one of them?" Molly asked.

The Sangheili kept their weapons trained on them as they drew closer.

"Patience," Kareem whispered. "Just hold still. When you hear the signal, follow me."

"Signal?"

The Sangheili warriors approached with a mixture of curiosity and abandon. They didn't want to relinquish their cavalier attitude for a couple children, but yet they didn't quite know what to make of them. Molly and Kareem were half their size—but they bore weapons too.

"You should not have followed us," Bakar called out to them. "Leave me to my fate!"

The closest of the warriors pointed his storm rifle at Molly's head. With Kareem's hand still on her weapon, she stopped arguing and finally let it fall limp in her hands.

She gave Kareem a sidelong glare. "Go ahead with that signal anytime now."

"It's not mine to give," he said with a knowing smile.

Molly stood there confused for just an instant, but when she realized what he meant, her eyes went wide. "Seriously?"

Precisely then the signal sounded.

From somewhere on the other side of the Sangheili, Gudam screeched at the top of her lungs. The warriors coming for Molly and Kareem spun around to see what was making the deafening sound. When they did, Kareem grabbed Molly by the arm and hauled her into the tall grass at a breakneck pace.

They sprinted away from the Sangheili, clutching their rifles tight but not bothering to look back. Molly wondered what would bring them down first: a vicious claw in the side or a plasma blast in the back. But neither came.

The creatures that had been stalking Molly and Kareem roared so loud they sounded like cannons. Gudam's scream had done the trick, just as it had with the *rafakrit*. The beasts barreled toward the sound, which put them right on a path with the Sangheili.

Molly and Kareem reached the top of a knoll and glanced back to see the Sangheili warriors spin toward the creatures, bringing their weapons to bear. Then Kareem grabbed Molly's hand again, turned, and bolted down the ridgeline of the knoll. As they went, he started to lead them back around toward their enemies in a wide circle.

Molly understood. They still had to reach Bakar and Prone. She glanced back to watch the Servants firing on the creatures head-on.

One of the beasts simply ignored the pain and barreled right into the Servants. It exposed its massive maw as it lunged at a warrior, opening it wide like some vicious steel trap. The creature fit more than half of the hapless Sangheili into its mouth with a single bite, then clamped down its teeth, separating its prey in two.

Molly's stomach climbed into her throat at the sight.

This was going to get ugly.

CHAPTER 33

Ruk's warm blood was still spilling from his throat when the Servants spotted the two human fledglings creeping up on them. Still stunned by Dural savagely putting down Ruk's challenge to his leadership, the other warriors hesitated to act.

Dural was not nearly so sanguine. "Get them, fools!" he roared until the others finally snapped into action.

Asum shouted at the human fledglings that they should not have followed the Servants there, and Dural agreed. The idea that the two of them—mere children—could sneak up on the Servants in the middle of the wilderness and take them down with only a pair of rifles was beyond ludicrous. *What were they thinking?*

Dural did wonder, however, how they had managed to keep after them this entire time. They must have watched as he slew the demon—when the Spartan foolishly tried to keep them from going through the portal—and then, perhaps, they had continued to hound their trail. Dural had to respect the fledglings' bravery despite their foolishness.

"Allies of yours?" Dural questioned Asum.

"I do not know them."

Dural knew his own blood much better than that. "You always were a terrible liar, brother."

Then a strange scream blared from behind them. Dural realized he had heard such a sound before, when the field master had tortured an Unggoy who had attempted to betray the Servants to the Arbiter.

But why an Unggoy would be out here howling in the middle of nowhere, Dural could not say. It must have come with the humans—who now were running away.

"Shoot them!" Dural barked at his warriors. "Shoot—"

Then Asum punched him in the throat. Had Dural been watching him, Asum would never have managed it, but his friends had distracted Dural. Asum then tried to snatch the storm rifle from Dural's back, but the Pale Blade managed to knock it away from both of them instead.

Dural staggered back, clutching at his neck as he gasped for breath and brandished his energy sword in front of him. He tried to call his warriors, but he could not get the words out.

He could not signal them either. They were not looking in his direction—or even that of the humans. They were completely transfixed by something they saw in the brush instead.

That was when Dural saw them too: a pair of new creatures that emerged from the encroaching dusk and stampeded toward his warriors. The beasts unleashed ferocious howls that curdled Dural's blood. He realized they had been sorely tricked.

The Unggoy had not been screaming in fear. It had been *calling* the beasts.

One of them grabbed a warrior in its teeth as it trampled over another. The second tore into yet another warrior as the rest of Dural's vanguard began firing at both beasts.

Dural finally managed to clear his throat, and he gave his warriors their orders. "Run!" he shouted in a hoarse voice. "Make for the Cathedral! Run!"

Then he grabbed Asum by his arm and attempted to drag him away, but his brother dug in his heels and refused to move.

Dural looked at him cockeyed.

Is it really possible? Asum would rather be devoured by these creatures than come with me?

Dural struck him with the back of his hand, and his brother fell to the ground. He cursed, thinking that he would now have to carry Asum back to the base—and for what? So he could execute him in front of the others? Or had he subconsciously nursed the possibility Asum might recant his heresy and join the Servants of the Abiding Truth?

Either way, Dural needed to recognize that his brother wasn't worth it.

He had just decided to leave Asum for the monsters and personally escort the Huragok to the Cathedral instead when his knee gave out beneath him with a sickening crack. He bellowed in agony and tumbled onto his back to find Kurnik standing over him, a cruel cackle rolling from his jaws.

"You're not a bad leader, fledgling," the old warrior said. "But you're too dangerous to lead the Servants of the Abiding Truth."

Dural turned over onto his hands and tried to climb to his feet, but his broken knee would not support his weight. "Traitor!"

"Coming from you?" Kurnik balled his fist and slammed it against his own chest in a mock salute. "I could no longer tolerate your volatile arrogance, besmearing the shadow of the field master you claim to esteem. His legacy is maligned by your lack of prudence. Who do you think the *real* traitor is?"

Dural roared after him in utter frustration as Kurnik turned and left. "You cannot outrun those beasts, fool!"

"I do not have to outrun them, Pale Blade," Kurnik said as he sprinted away. "I only have to outrun you!"

Dural hurled curses after him and prayed to the gods to bring the traitor the fate he ripely deserved. They might not do Kurnik any harm, but they were all Dural had left.

Then Dural felt hands upon him, as Asum grabbed him and hoisted him to his feet. Dural grunted at him in pain, as Asum draped his arm over his shoulders. "What are you doing?"

"Saving your life, I hope." Asum cast a wary eye toward the creatures still engaged with the Sangheili.

Despite all the years and light-years that had passed between them, this was still Dural's brother: Little Asum, almost full grown now. Although Dural had been prepared to kill him only seconds earlier, somehow Asum refused to leave him to his own death.

"All right," Dural said, as he hopped along on his one good leg. "Let us see."

While Asum helped him, Dural watched the rest of his warriors scatter. He did not know if they had seen what Kurnik had done, but that did not matter. He had ordered them to flee, to save themselves, and only time would tell if they would succeed.

The Servants had all fled in different directions. Kurnik had been right, Dural saw. They did not need to outrun the monsters, only each other. With luck, they would only lose a few warriors, and the rest would escape—including the ones dragging the Huragok along with them.

And if the gods provided, both Dural and Asum would be among the survivors. Dural limped along, using his brother for support, the two of them striking out for the Cathedral as quickly as they could.

As they went, Dural could hear the screams of one of his warriors as he fell prey to the creatures and was devoured alive. The sounds went on for far too long, but when they were finally cut short, Dural worried even more about what might follow. Would that beast's hunger be sated, or would it come next for those who remained?

Even as he and Asum fled, Dural began to think about what he would do to Kurnik if they both made it back to the base. The pain that stabbed through his leg with every halfhearted step he could take reminded him of Kurnik's treachery. He had no hope that any of his warriors would kill Kurnik for him. If he was to maintain his leadership, Dural would have to put an end to the malcontent himself—and in the most brutal fashion.

But he realized that things could never be the same. If he returned to the base with his leg broken like this, he would be expected to kill himself in shame. If he refused, he would fall prey to another ambitious Sangheili for sure.

Dural was finished either way. No Sangheili warrior would follow the lead of one so damaged. The code of their people was crystal clear. He would be lucky if they didn't slaughter him out of mercy.

Even if he survived, he would face an endless stream of interlopers who envied his position. Would he wind up battling against his own warriors until either he perished or was alone? Would that be his lot for the rest of his life?

Dural realized he only had one way out of this.

He put his fingers to his mouth and blew out a piercing whistle.

Asum loosened his grip on his brother in sheer horror. "What are you doing? Are you insane?"

"Run, brother." Dural pushed Asum away with a single shove. "I am putting my fate in the hands of the gods. I am heading toward my salvation or my doom. Leave me!"

"No, Dural." Asum backed away from him. "No!"

Dural could hear a monster coming at him now, huffing its horrible breath. Its feet thundered against the ground, boring through the tall grass that surrounded them, growing louder with each step. He could feel the beat hammered out in the turf beneath them.

Was the beat a prelude to his epitaph or his triumph?

Only the gods know.

"Run, Asum!" Dural closed his eyes and whistled one more time. "Run!"

CHAPTER 34

Molly couldn't believe what Bakar's brother was doing. She had only hoped to use the chaos the creatures created to scatter the Sangheili long enough for Bakar and Prone to flee. She hadn't expected Dural to take them on himself.

Prone still hadn't gotten away from its Sangheili escorts, but Molly saw that they'd at least gotten it out of the path of the monsters. When Dural called one of the beasts straight to him, though, Bakar just froze there next to him, too shocked to run.

The monster charged at Dural, who stood before it, balancing on his one good leg. He closed his eyes and activated his energy sword, holding it out to his side. *What is he thinking?*

As the creature barreled toward him, Dural shifted quickly to the side, bringing his sword into place just in front of him. Before the monster reached him, Dural—with his eyes still closed—raked the blade through the air and sprang up on his single leg.

The beast snapped at the sword, and its scores of vicious teeth bit into the blade, causing it to cry out. The energy crackled along the length of the sword, scorching the monster's mouth, but rather than frighten the beast, this only seemed to enrage it. The creature bit down even harder on the blade, shattering it between its jaws.

As the monster whipped past him, Dural finally opened his eyes and caught its shoulder with his hand. Using the beast's momentum, he swung himself up and around so he could clamber atop the creature's neck. From there, the Sangheili dug his hands tight into the beast's thick fur and held on for his life.

Bakar stumbled backward, out of the animal's way, and watched as the creature raced off into the darkness, his brother still astride it. "Dural!" he shouted after him. "Dural!"

"Get away from there!" Kareem shouted at Bakar. "Run!"

At first, Molly wasn't quite sure why Kareem was yelling. The monster that had charged at Dural was far gone.

Then she remembered there wasn't just one.

The other beast had also heard Dural's whistle, and after it had finished tearing apart a hapless pair of Sangheili warriors, it was now heading toward Bakar to investigate.

To complicate things further, the rest of the Servants hadn't all managed to escape. A pair of them were still struggling with Prone to Drift, trying to get him to cooperate. Some others had stayed nearby, trying to predict which way the creatures might run and how to best evade them. Molly soberly realized that, even if she and her friends survived the last creature, they might still have to deal with the rest of the Servants.

The remaining beast came slowly and methodically this time, snuffling over toward Bakar as if it had found something new to chew on. The Sangheili did his best to stay absolutely still, giving the animal the same penetrating stare he gave everyone else.

The beast didn't seem impressed, and Bakar had nowhere left to run.

Molly took a deep breath and cringed as the creature edged to barely more than a meter in front of Bakar's unwavering eyes.

At that moment, something came roaring through the sky, piercing the air all around. It startled the creature, causing it to back away from Bakar as it scoured the sky for the source of the noise. The sound had begun as a low rumble but rose in pitch and volume as it grew closer. Molly shaded her eyes to peer toward whatever was making the noise, and she finally spotted it: a UNSC Pelican dropship bearing straight for them and coming in fast.

Molly realized only one person could be in that craft: *Lucy*.

"Prone must have told her where we are!"

Molly couldn't help grinning with relief. If Lucy could bring the Pelican down somewhere nearby, they might actually survive. Hope sprang anew in her heart.

The creature also noticed the source of the sound but seemed unbothered by the approaching vehicle. No longer spooked, it returned its attention to Bakar, who had moved to join Molly and Kareem at the top of a hill. When the monster realized that Bakar had slipped away, it exploded toward them, refusing to lose its catch. Molly and the others turned and sprinted away as fast as they could, and the creature gave chase.

Without a word, they each split up in a different direction, fanning out across the grassland. For some reason, the creature now seemed to have set its heart on Molly. She heard Kareem, Bakar, and even Gudam—who had now rejoined them—shouting at it. They whistled and screamed, trying to draw its attention, but this monster was not distracted for an instant.

Perhaps the noise from the Pelican's approach had drowned out everything else, or maybe the animal had simply fixated on her. Either way, she feared that only seconds separated her from death, and she was growing too tired to evade it any longer. She was about to close her eyes and give up. If the creature killed her, she hoped it would at least take long enough at it to give the others a fighting chance to escape.

Right then, the Pelican swung around from out of nowhere, slamming its tail into the creature and driving it into the turf behind Molly. The beast let loose a terrifying bellow of pain as the aircraft ground it into the dirt, breaking bones and tearing flesh. As the ship's tail swung around to face Molly, the animal stopped moving altogether.

Molly stood there, shocked and dumbfounded, and tried to catch her breath. The Pelican's rear hatch popped open.

A moment later, Lucy stepped out, clad in her Mjolnir armor, a battle rifle in her hands. "You all right, kid?"

Molly gasped enough air to answer. "I am now."

Lucy leaped down from the hovering Pelican and hefted Molly up into it. As she did, she spotted Bakar, Kareem, and Gudam approaching from the distance. "Let's make this quick, folks. Those Sangheili over there don't look like they're interested in just letting us go."

"Prone to Drift!" Molly said, remembering the Huragok. "They've got Prone!"

"Not for long, they don't."

CHAPTER 35

ucy-B091 moved past Molly, charging headlong toward the Servants at the edge of the clearing as they hauled their kidnapped Huragok behind them. "Get to the dropship!" she shouted to Kareem and Bakar as she raced past them. "Lock yourselves in!"

Bakar reached the Pelican first, and Kareem rushed in only a moment later, followed by Gudam, who waddled up from behind. After she entered, Molly slammed her fist against the bay door release and sealed them in. She quickly made her way up to the cockpit, where she found Kareem in the pilot's seat and Gudam in the copilot's spot. As Kareem gently spun the Pelican's nose around, Molly stood next to Bakar and peered over their shoulders to watch Lucy at work.

Although Molly had always thought of Lucy as a superhero, the Servants who remained outnumbered her several times over. As Tom had back at the portal, she moved with such speed and fluidity that most of them could not get a bead on her, and she targeted those who did. In time, however, she struggled to keep up with the barrage of incoming fire and a lack of decent cover. On top of that, the fact that she couldn't unload her weapons on them all for fear of killing Prone with a stray shot hampered her efforts.

"We need to help her!" Molly said to Kareem. "Can you operate this thing's guns?"

"I think so." He grabbed a second set of controls, and Molly felt the gimbal underneath the ship's nose grind to life. A heads-up targeting circle appeared painted on the viewport in front of him.

"It's working," he said confidently. "Just like in the simulator." He pulled a trigger, and the heavy autocannon right underneath the nose fired, tearing up a bit of the grass directly in front of them.

"Wow, that'll do the trick!" Kareem said, now guiding the reticle toward the mass of Servants firing from the tree line.

"Careful!" Gudam said. "You'll shoot Lucy!"

"She has armor," Bakar said. "I am more concerned about Prone to Drift."

Apparently Lucy was too. As they watched, she shot one of the Servants holding down Prone, and the Huragok somehow slipped free of the other, which had been distracted by the gunfire from the Pelican. Now loose, Prone hauled up its tentacles and began soaring high into the trees, putting it completely out of the reach of any Sangheili's hand—but not their weapons.

Unwilling to let their captive go, some of the Servants trained their rifles on Prone, and Lucy came at them in an all-out rush. When they were forced to turn their attention to her, they fired on her from all sides. Initially, her shields took the brunt of it, but Molly knew they couldn't protect her forever.

"Shoot!" Molly shouted at Kareem. "Now!"

He hesitated. "What if I hit her?"

"That's what her armor's for. And if you don't shoot, she'll be dead either way. Shoot!"

Kareem lined up the circle on the Pelican's viewport with the wall of Servants directing their fire toward Lucy, and he squeezed the trigger on the ship's controls. The chin-mounted autocannon sprang to life with a beastly thrum and began pouring out hot metal slugs at the Servants.

Several of them spun about and returned fire, but it was too late. They hadn't thought of the Pelican as a threat, and although they were determined to correct that mistake, Kareem's booming shots began to hit their marks. The steady volume of heavy firepower easily overwhelmed the Sangheili warriors' armor, ripping it to shreds, and one after another the Servants fell, most punched through by hundreds of rounds before they could take cover. Those who remained, somehow having found cover among the trees, began taking potshots at the Pelican's cockpit and engines.

"Keep it up," said Bakar. "The armor of this aircraft can only take so much."

Gudam stared out at the carnage in silent horror, and Molly had to sympathize with her. While they knew the Servants would have done the same to them—if not worse—none of them had wanted to kill anyone.

"One with a grenade on your right!" Molly said to Kareem.

He deftly swung the Pelican in that direction, still letting loose with the guns, and pulverized the Servant midthrow. The hapless warrior dropped the live grenade among his fellows, and the explosion sent a fountain of dirt and dark blue blood into the air.

Molly patted Gudam on the shoulder, trying to comfort her. It wasn't fair that they'd been pushed into this, but there weren't any other options. This wasn't murder. It was self-defense.

They were protecting themselves. They were protecting Lucy.

They were protecting Onyx.

In less than a minute, Kareem had taken out all of the Servants, and the Pelican's guns wound down, smoke writhing from their hot barrels. Prone floated over to the ship as Kareem opened the hatch, but Molly ignored the Huragok while she sprinted across the broken ground to reach Lucy, who wasn't moving.

When Molly found her, Lucy had a dead Servant draped across

her—or parts of one, at least. Molly tried to pull the Sangheili off, but he proved too heavy. Fortunately, Bakar raced up and lent a hand, dragging away the warrior's corpse.

Lucy had a hole burned into her right leg where a plasma blast had gone straight through her armor. The hot plasma seemed to have cauterized the wound, so she wasn't bleeding, but she wasn't moving either.

Lucy suddenly reached up and wrestled her helmet off, then gasped for fresh air. "Ow," she said in a soft, raw voice, looking at the hole in her leg. "That's going to leave a mark."

"You're alive!" Molly wanted to wrap her in a hug but was afraid she might injure her.

"Spartans never die." Lucy grimaced in pain as she tried to move her leg. "But that doesn't mean we don't hurt."

Molly and Bakar helped the Spartan to her feet—though it was Lucy doing most of the work. They could only do so much to assist someone in armor that weighed as much as a dump truck. Lucy leaned slightly on Bakar as she limped and hopped her way back to the Pelican.

"How did you know where to find us?" Molly asked.

"Prone sent me a message asking for help. Whenever he sends me anything, I know it's important. He and I go way back. We're pretty tight. You know I was the first human he ever met?"

"How much do you know about what is happening in Paxopolis then?" Bakar asked. "The Guardian shut down the power of the entire city and the research complex."

"The Guardian? You mean the thing from Project: GOLIATH?" Lucy stopped for a moment to catch her breath. "Well, it might have taken out all of the power inside Trevelyan and Paxopolis, but I was pretty far away when that went down. Whatever it did, it didn't reach me."

By the time the group made it to the Pelican, Gudam already had Prone to Drift secured in the passenger bay. Lucy crawled into the space and lay down on the open floor, her breathing still ragged. "Sorry, kids. But there's no way I'm climbing into that cockpit right now. We'll have to hunker down here and wait for a ride."

"What about the rest of the Servants?" Molly asked. "They could be on their way here right now."

"We'll just have to lock up and take that chance."

"Kareem's a pilot!" Gudam said. "He can take us wherever we need to go."

Lucy peered toward where Kareem was still sitting in the cockpit. "Ever flown a Pelican before?"

"Lots of times. In simulation."

Lucy winced in pain and lay back down again. "Well, we're not talking about flying it into a dogfight. That might do."

Kareem started to go through the ship's preflight procedure. "Where should we go? Back to the Pax Institute?"

Molly looked down at Lucy on the floor. "Maybe the hospital instead?"

Prone to Drift vigorously shook his head, and she wondered why he didn't just speak to them. Molly glanced at his belly and saw that in his captivity someone had shattered his slate.

"You have a better idea where to go?" Molly asked.

Prone nodded and turned his entire body about to point toward the left of the craft.

"What's in that direction?" Molly asked everyone else.

"Perhaps he means the Guardian," Bakar said.

"That's right!" said Gudam. "I remember! Prone put the sphere into slipspace to cut us off from the outside, but he said that the Guardian would be trying to bring us back out. I wonder if we're not too late."

Lucy groaned out loud. "How much time do we have left before that happens? Days?"

Prone shook its head.

"Hours?" Molly said.

Another shake.

"Minutes?"

This time, Prone nodded.

Gudam squawked at that news. "Now that we showed the AI who activated the Guardian that we can cut her off from us, we're sure to have gotten her attention. If the Guardian comes back online, she might just give it orders to stamp out Paxopolis and everyone in it. She could even send in other Guardians to help—a whole army of those things."

"So," Bakar said, "we are doomed."

"Maybe not," said Molly. "When we left the Institute, the Guardian had gone into a kind of standby mode. The machines it had already released were continuing to fight the local security forces, but that was it. The Guardian itself wasn't doing anything to help them. If we can stop it before it comes back online, we can stop it from sending Onyx back into realspace, and we can probably keep everyone else locked out too. The question is, how are we going to do that?"

All eyes turned toward Lucy. She shrugged. "Not really sure how these Guardians are designed or what could bring that thing down, but this bird doesn't have a ton of armament options. Just the forward autocannon and some missile pods on its wings."

Molly focused back on Prone to Drift. "What do we need to do to stop it?"

The Huragok turned to Lucy and pointed at his own stomach, where his destroyed slate still sat embedded.

"Hey," Lucy called to Kareem. "We need to get Prone's slate fixed. Is there anything up there we can use?"

"I think there's a long-range comms pad in a side compartment. It's not exactly like what Prone had before though. Not sure if it'll work." Kareem quickly found it and brought it to the rear bay.

"If anyone can make it work, it would be Prone," Molly said, giving it to the Huragok. Prone cradled it in his tentacles for a moment, his feathery cilia working feverishly to pull the back off the device and rewire it. Meanwhile, with a spare tentacle, he removed the broken slate, which had been damaged beyond repair. Once the new pad was ready, he slotted it into place.

A moment later, a voice miraculously emerged from the attached pad. "If I can get close enough to the Guardian," Prone said in a calm and steady voice, "I should be able to disable the gravitational field that holds it together."

Gudam clapped her hands together. "Which would bring it all crashing down!"

"Onto Trevelyan and Paxopolis," Bakar responded. "What about the people there?"

"One problem at a time," Molly said.

Kareem eyed Prone suspiciously. "How close?"

"Near the armature mainframe, located in the structure that looks like a face. Inside this are its vital systems. If I can reach that location, I can disable its gravitics. This will cause a systemic breakdown that would rend its component segments apart and send it to the ground. It should stop it permanently."

"Which means it wouldn't be able to bring us out of slipspace," Molly said. "Onyx would be safe."

Kareem let out a long breath. "Yeah, that's close. Really close."

Molly glanced around at the others. "We're running out of time, and I doubt anyone at Trevelyan or Paxopolis can even get up there to do this. It's up to us."

They looked to Lucy for permission. She gave a slight smile and then a thumbs-up.

"Well," Bakar said, "what are we waiting for?"

CHAPTER 36

Are you sure you can fly this thing?" Molly asked Kareem as she stared down at the ship's control panel with its dizzying array of lights, keys, and throttles.

"How hard can it be?" Kareem cracked his knuckles. "I got the guns working, didn't I?"

Gudam peeked around Molly to give Kareem a wary eye. "You don't die in a fiery wreck if you can't get the guns working."

"Look, it's not all that far—and I can't make any guarantees, but I put plenty of hours in on the simulator. Of course, I was mostly flying Hornets and Wasps—but I know the Pelican. I can do it."

"This doesn't strike me as the safest idea in the world," Gudam said nervously.

"We don't have any choice," Lucy said from the back. She'd been trying to hold things together, but she was starting to slur her words and was fading fast. "Let's get started."

Kareem spun up the Pelican's vertical jets, and the ship hummed to life with new intensity. "Roger that, Spartan. Everyone got their seats?"

He took the controls as confidently as he could manage, and the ship rose off the ground. Then it suddenly tipped over to the right and dragged the tip of the wing along the turf, canting to the side.

They all winced, but Kareem wrestled the Pelican back to level.

"Okay, that's a bit touchier than I expected. Sorry about that."

The ship lurched downward, but it hauled up shy of smashing into the ground. "That's it," Kareem said slowly, as if talking to a skittish animal on a fragile leash. "I'm getting the hang of this." He brought the dropship high into the air. The Guardian hung in the far distance, probably a hundred kilometers away. "Nice and easy."

He pushed the accelerator lever, and the Pelican shot forward. Strapped in, he and Gudam were fine, but the rest of them—except for Prone to Drift, who had already held on to a strap in the ceiling with his tentacles—almost went tumbling backward. At the last instant, they managed to grab handholds to steady themselves instead.

"Sorry!" Kareem shouted, as the ground far below swept behind them and the Guardian grew larger in the viewport. Molly felt relieved to be in the air, where at least no more of Onyx's massive monsters could attack them.

Of course, they now had to worry about dying in a catastrophic crash.

Not to mention dealing with that Forerunner machine that seemed to stare gravely at them from far off. It may have been inactive, but its scowling face was still intimidating, even from this distance.

Once they felt confident enough to move about the bay, Molly and Bakar scrambled back to Lucy and discovered she'd passed out. "The pain must have been too much for her," Bakar said.

"Maybe it's for the best," Molly said.

"How so?"

"At least she won't have to watch us die."

It occurred to Molly that they hadn't asked any parents for permission for any of this. Or Kasha or Mendez. They'd barely even asked Lucy. They'd just made a decision and gone with it.

What choice did we have?

As Bakar had once said, *It is simpler to wipe off your blade once it has been blooded.* Molly wasn't sure that was the best analogy for what they were doing, but it felt close enough.

If they failed, they wouldn't have to worry about any kind of punishment from anyone anyhow. They were either going to be heroes or they were going to be dead.

The Guardian soon loomed large in the viewport before them, so big it felt as if they were flying toward a mountain. The lights that had once glowed along its edges were dark now, and the machine's headlike structure had fallen slack. Even its wings had come down from the last time Molly had seen them.

To Molly, the Guardian almost looked defeated already. She had to remind herself it was only sleeping. And if the machine managed to rouse itself, they'd be the ones who were done.

"How much time do we have left?" Molly asked Prone to Drift. "Before it wakes up and sends us back into realspace?"

Molly had half expected Prone to project a countdown clock on his tablet, but he just shook his head back and forth. "There is no way to know for sure," the Huragok said through the slate. "There are no protocols for such an event."

"Excellent," Molly snapped.

"Maybe it'll be all day," Gudam said hopefully. "There's no reason why it can't be all day, right?"

Prone shook his head from side to side, sinuously like a snake. "Since the moment I enclosed Onyx in slipspace, the Guardian's subsystems have no doubt been trying to find a way to get around it. To pick the lock from the inside. It is a machine of incredible power and capacity. It will eventually get through."

Molly saw sweat beading on Kareem's forehead. His knuckles had turned white while he gripped the controls, and the Guardian had swelled large enough to fill almost the entire viewport. "I'm flying as fast as I can!"

Below, Molly saw the Pax Institute zip by on their right, then a number of towers and structures from Paxopolis went past soon after that. Pockets of scorched ground and debris from the initial defense effort remained scattered throughout, columns of black smoke marking where the frigates and fighters had crashed. They would reach Trevelyan soon.

Before being cut from outside communication, the Guardian had been hovering over Trevelyan, perhaps looking to take control of the aperture so it could allow ships inside Onyx. Below it sat the landing pad and terminals the *Milwaukee* had used when Molly had first arrived weeks ago. It seemed as if it had been so much longer than that.

Molly wondered about her Newparents. Had they been at work when all this happened? Had they made it home? Had they at least found each other?

Did they have any idea what had happened to her?

Molly hoped not. She wanted them to think she was sitting safely in the dining hall at the Pax Institute, doing anything to pass the time as the day wore on and the adults solved the bigger problems.

That way they wouldn't worry about Molly. They wouldn't know a thing about this incredibly brave and stupid thing she and her friends were about to do until it was over. By that time, no matter what happened, it would be too late for them to worry.

Then Molly saw the Guardian's wings shift upward slightly, and she knew they'd already run out of time.

"It's moving!" Molly shouted. "It's waking up!"

Kareem, to his credit, didn't panic. He didn't slow down or veer away. He kept straight on course, headed right for the construct's head. If anything, he flew faster now than he had before.

"What's that mean?" Gudam almost sounded relieved. "Can we go home? I mean, what's the point of trying to take on a

Guardian that's actually active? We don't have a chance against that. Right?"

"The Guardian has managed to open a slipspace communication channel," Prone to Drift said. "But the slipspace enclosure is still holding."

"For how long?" Bakar asked. He was gripping the back of Kareem's chair so hard his fingers were sinking into it.

"It is on the order of minutes. No more." The deadpan delivery of voice from the Huragok's tablet made Molly more anxious than a panicked report would have. Like a stoic diagnosis from a medical machine telling her she had a fatal disease, it just seemed unreal.

"Do we still have a chance to take it apart, Prone?" Molly asked. "Or is this all over?"

Prone to Drift hesitated for a moment. "Our chances of success have plummeted, as the Guardian may now defend itself against us."

"I asked if it's over!"

"The odds have yet to approach zero."

Molly reached over and patted Kareem on the shoulder. "You heard him. Take us in."

A thin, determined smile rose on Kareem's lips. "My mom's going to kill me for this."

"She'll be lucky if she has the chance."

The Guardian seemed to notice them coming, possibly because nothing else hung in the sky. It began to turn, squaring its position with the Pelican and staring directly at them.

As it did, it opened its wings wide, like an angel about to take flight. Blue energy flared from a series of ports at its center, all the way out to the tips of its wings, and it emitted a deep howling sound that felt powerful enough to shake the entire shield world.

"Can it shoot us down?" Molly asked.

"Its primary weapon systems are not online yet," Prone responded, "but it may have passive systems."

"I got us here." Kareem hauled back the dropship to a sudden hovering stop only a few hundred meters from the Guardian. "What now?"

"Get me to the Guardian's system mainframe. It is located near the head structure," Prone to Drift said. "I can take it from there."

As they edged closer to the Guardian, what looked like a power core in the middle of its torso began to glow brighter and brighter. As it reached a crescendo, it pulsed hard, and a flash radiated out from inside it like the shock wave of an explosion.

When the wave hit the Pelican, it buffeted the ship hard. Gudam screamed, and Kareem fought to keep the ship under control. Rather than continuing on toward the Guardian, he veered away and found that he could steer the ship easily once again.

"If it's going to do that every time we get close, this is going to be one hell of a rough ride," Kareem said. He spun the ship away from the Guardian and brought it around to make another pass at the construct.

"That may be its passive form of defense," Prone to Drift said. "A shunting mechanism."

Another blast sent the Pelican back even farther, as though the Guardian were swatting them away with an invisible field of energy.

"There's no way I can get through that," Kareem said.

"Not from this angle," Molly said. "But maybe with a little help from gravity?"

She pointed up toward the sky above the Guardian, and Kareem nodded as he got the idea. "Yeah. The waves are coming at us head-on. That might just do it."

"This is insane," Gudam said, as Kareem raised the Pelican's nose toward the sky and accelerated, bringing them higher and higher with every second. "It's never going to work. What if we're lining up directly with its weapons?"

"You have any other ideas?" Molly asked. "This is the only way."

She understood how Gudam felt, though, and she clapped the Unggoy on the shoulder to show her support. Gudam turned and flung her arms around Molly, pulling her into an almost painful hug.

Molly returned the embrace. She needed it as much as Gudam did.

Then she gazed out the viewport and watched as they ascended high above the Guardian. It seemed to adjust its position slightly, as though it was observing them as they went.

They weren't going to escape its attention.

"What are you planning?" Prone to Drift said, as the Pelican leveled off high above the Guardian.

"Getting ready to dive in." Kareem worked the ship's controls and brought its nose around in a gradual arc so that it was pointing down toward the gigantic creature. The Pelican's gravity systems held them to its floor, but the juxtaposition with the Guardian outside made Molly's head spin. They had to be several hundred meters above it, but it was so large it still looked as if they could reach out and touch it from this distance.

"Do you plan to crash this vehicle inside the Guardian?" Prone asked.

Molly realized that they should have probably run this plan by the Huragok before implementing it.

Kareem grimaced. "I wouldn't say I *plan* to crash it, but there may be a strong likelihood of that happening."

"There is no need to put yourself and the others in danger," Prone to Drift said.

"We can't come at the Guardian straight on," Molly said. "It just knocks us away. By coming at it from above, even if it knocks out the power in the ship, gravity will take us the rest of the way."

"I understand your plan." The Huragok moved toward the back of the passenger bay. "But there is no need for you to risk your lives."

Molly wasn't sure what Prone was getting at. Then it touched the door release with one of its tentacles to open the Pelican's rear ramp. Outside they could only see open sky. The wind roared into the Pelican, tousling Prone's tentacles and their hair.

"I can get to the Guardian from here," Prone's slate said at full volume.

"What? No!" Molly said. "That's crazy! You jump out from here, and you'll die on that thing for sure!"

"I can float," Prone said in its droning electronic voice. "Heights hold little danger for me."

"And if the Guardian knocks you away?" Molly asked.

"Do we have any other choice, Molly Patel?"

"Maybe we can keep it distracted!" Bakar said. "Buy you time. Get close enough to get its attention, but not so close it attacks!"

"That sounds like a wonderful plan to me!" Gudam said.

Kareem nodded in agreement. "I think I can work with that!" He was continuing his slow plummet to the top of the Guardian. Soon it would be only a hundred meters away. At this distance, all they could see in the viewport was the construct.

"Very well," Prone said. "But if you find it preparing to release another blast to shut off the power again, you must flee as far as possible and immediately land on the ground. This will be its first strategy once it regains control over its primary defenses."

With that, Prone edged to the bay and floated out the back of the Pelican. Within seconds, the winds had carried him completely out of view.

Bakar dashed to the back of the Pelican and slapped the bay door's release. The ship's hydraulics whined as they drew the ramp up again. The silence and stillness that came after that didn't last for long.

"Okay. Hold on, everyone!" Kareem shouted from the cockpit. "I'm going to make sure the Guardian can't miss us!"

With that, he throttled the Pelican into a steep dive that angled wide of the Guardian by a scant hundred meters. Just as they were passing by the construct's stern face, Kareem began pulling up and winding toward the right to circle around it. He gave the Guardian a wide berth, but kept close enough so that he could veer toward the machine—or away from it—at any instant.

The light inside the Guardian grew stronger than ever, and Molly wondered if maybe Kareem had miscalculated. If the Guardian let loose with a blast now, it might knock Prone to Drift too far away to reach it in time.

Molly shaded her eyes with her hand as she peered through the upper viewport at the space just above the Guardian's head. The Huragok looked like nothing more than a fleshy balloon falling down through the sky, waving his tentacles slowly as he went. She worried that he might live up to his name and drift completely off course, if he was indeed prone to that, but he did not waver once in his path.

"Prone is in!" Molly shouted as the Huragok successfully slid between some of the floating parts near the Guardian's head.

Everyone in the Pelican let out a long-held breath.

"How long do we think he's going to take to do this?" Kareem asked.

"Hopefully not too long," Molly said. "Why?"

"Because the Guardian looks like it's gearing up to do something."

She saw that the Guardian was slowly gathering energy toward the tips of its enormous wings, and a glowing blue sphere was forming at the machine's center.

Molly recognized it at the same time as Bakar. This was precisely what Prone had warned them about. The Guardian was going to release another pulse and send the Pelican crashing into the ground.

"Dive for the surface!" Bakar shouted. "We must land, now!"

Kareem didn't waste any time asking why. He nosed the Pelican straight down for Trevelyan far below, and they dropped faster than a stone.

"What's going on?" Gudam shouted, as they all clutched at grips on the walls, trying not to get thrown around by the dropship's momentum.

"The Guardian is about to shut down all power again," Molly said. "It must have detected Prone inside it, trying to disable it. Maybe it decided this is the only way to get at him."

"That's not going to stop him," Gudam said. "Will it?"

"Who knows," Kareem said. "But it'll get us for sure. And as high up as we still are . . . ?"

"Go, go, go!" Gudam shouted, now catching Kareem's meaning. "Less talk, more move!"

Molly watched the ground get closer and closer, and she wondered if maybe Kareem hadn't misjudged this entirely. At the speed they were going, if he didn't pull up in time, they were going to wind up splattered all over the research facility.

At least it'll be a quick end, she thought to herself. *Maybe not entirely painless, but quick.*

Gudam started screaming, and Molly joined her. A moment later even Kareem pitched in, hauling up on the controls as hard as he could. Bakar didn't make a sound, but Molly could see the terror etched on his face.

Molly was sure they were all going to die.

But then something amazing happened.

Kareem yanked up the Pelican's nose at a horrifying angle that nearly tossed her to the ship's floor. Molly felt them hit something hard, and the entire dropship violently jarred up and back, tumbling over what must have been a tower. This sent most of them rolling to the back end of the craft, where Molly bumped hard against something and then scraped along something even harder.

By looking through the front viewport, Molly could tell the Pelican was spinning, nose to tail. Trevelyan flashed out of view, and the sky and Guardian high above came into it. That's when she saw the blue light held by the Forerunner construct finally burst, sending out an instantaneous wave in every direction.

The power left the ship entirely. It felt as if the Pelican's cords had been cut, and its nose now spun toward the ground again, as the vehicle dropped straight down.

Fortunately, the Pelican's first impact had brought them surprisingly close to the surface. The Pelican hit the ground on its belly and continued to spin laterally. As the viewport came into focus again, Molly saw that Kareem had found a wide-open landing strip and the now-powerless craft was chaotically careening along it, scraping and skittering across its pavement as it ground toward a halt.

After a long, loud, screeching moment, they finally came to rest. They'd all fallen silent, most of them having screamed themselves out of breath. For a moment, they simply stared at one another in astonishment.

They were still alive! They began to cheer, but Molly cut them off.

Looking up through the cockpit's viewport, she had one huge question that still hadn't been answered. "What happens if Prone disables the Guardian and it comes down?" Everyone else fell silent. "Where will it land?"

She had been so preoccupied with stopping the Guardian that she had avoided considering the collateral cost. The Guardian had to wind up somewhere when it fell. What kind of damage would it cause, and who might be underneath it when it all came crashing down?

"There's nothing we can do about that now," Bakar said. "The protocol in an emergency like this would require evacuation from the area. Hopefully everyone obeyed."

"We didn't have a choice, did we?" Molly asked. "If we didn't do this, a thousand worse things could have happened. This was our only chance. If Prone even succeeds—"

As the words left her mouth, the first piece of the Guardian came crashing to the ground from its tail section. Then another and another.

The gravity that held the ancient machine together had been disabled, no doubt by Prone. When the first piece smashed into the ground behind Trevelyan's complex of buildings, Molly didn't see it so much as felt it—like a short but violent earthquake, followed by a series of tremors for each additional segment.

The rest of the construct came hailing down from the sky soon after that, cascading piece by piece, some small and others unimaginably large. Each of them slammed into the ground with the force of an explosion, sending up clouds of dirt and debris, knocking down buildings and other structures, some only a few hundred meters away. Soon the dust and ash from this bombardment spread like a blanket of darkness and choked the air, billowing outward as it swallowed up all of Trevelyan, including the landing strip they'd narrowly made it to.

As the smoke enveloped the cockpit of the Pelican, Molly looked around at the others. *My friends,* she thought with a smile.

They were filthy, tired, and beaten up pretty bad.

But somehow, they had survived.

CHAPTER 37

Molly's Newparents just about killed her.

She couldn't blame them. She and her friends had put themselves into mortal danger, after all. More than once. As was suggested to her countless times over the next few days, if she and her friends had just stayed where they had been told to, they wouldn't have wound up risking death. Which was all true.

But, as Molly was quick to point out, if she had done that, then Dural would have killed Bakar. The Guardian would have conquered Trevelyan and Paxopolis. And a lot of other people would have died. There wasn't really any way to argue against that, and Molly's Newparents didn't press the issue too hard.

They were alive. She was alive. They all had a lot to be thankful for.

After the Guardian came crashing to the ground, Prone to Drift floated down from the sky on his own, rattled but safe. In all the confusion afterward—and the thick clouds of dust—no one could find the Huragok for a while, but he showed up back at the security facilities in Trevelyan the next day, much to everyone's relief.

A lot of damage had been done to both the city and the research complex—including to many of the people who lived there.

From the initial strike against the Guardian by Trevelyan's local battle group to the Guardian's catastrophic destruction, large swaths of the UNSC outpost had been leveled. Many people had died during the attack, but Asha pointed out that it was only a handful compared to what their losses *could* have been.

Asha and Yong had been coming back from the excavation site when the Guardian first rose, and they had been completely clear of the initial destruction. They had wound up locked in a powered-down tram for the duration of the event. It would take a week for the power to be fully restored to the city and all of its research sites.

Several dozen soldiers had been killed in the battle with the Forerunner soldiers and the Sangheili warriors that had raided both Paxopolis and Trevelyan, and the UNSC's survivors spent a few days mopping up what remained of those threats. The distant sounds of firefights and skirmishes braced the nights that followed, but Molly still felt safe throughout. The most dangerous moments were already long past.

They could start to breathe easy at least, even as they began to count and mourn their losses.

Bakar had lost his brother. No matter how horrible Dural might have been, that still hurt him, and Molly could tell it was not easy. But questions still remained.

ONI sent a number of strike teams out to recover the bodies of Dural and the rest of the Servants who'd been with him, but they only located a handful. In addition, they couldn't find the rest of the Servants who had invaded Paxopolis, which meant they had to still be somewhere inside Onyx. When the bulk of Dural's invasion force had retreated through the portal in the middle of the city, though, they'd locked it down and covered their heads.

ONI had no idea where the Servants were and how many had

survived. Still, Director Barton vowed that he would not rest until his forces found the Servants of the Abiding Truth and secured the research facility and the city.

The main challenge for those inside Onyx was that they were now on their own, completely out of contact with the outside galaxy. Trying to call for help from inside the sphere was deemed too risky, especially given the reports they had first received about what was happening on the outside.

Evidently, Cortana was winning.

But Onyx was tucked away inside the folds of slipspace, well beyond the reach of any outside threats. At least for now.

As soon as a squad of marines at the spaceport had found Molly and her friends trapped in the Pelican, they'd broken their way in and pulled them free. They'd put Lucy on an evac skiff and taken her immediately to the hospital, and to Molly's relief they'd already found Tom at the Repository.

When things finally started to get back to normal, Director Mendez stopped by Molly's house with an update: Kasha, Tom, and Lucy were all doing well and would heal up fine, thanks in large part to the incredible technology available at the local hospital. Lucy might have a bit of a limp for a while, but Mendez told Molly, "Given everything she's been through already in her life, if that's all she has to complain about, I'd count myself lucky."

Kareem's mom was absolutely thrilled to have him back home. She cried so hard, Molly thought she was going to join her.

Gudam's parents—Momma Aphrid, Momma Beskin, and Poppa Marfo—smothered her with love when she came home. The other kids from her family paraded around as proud of her as if she'd single-handedly saved the day. That made Gudam grin, although Molly knew she couldn't imagine having done it without her friends. Molly thought they might not let Gudam ever leave home again—but she was back in school when it reopened two weeks later.

Of everyone, Bakar probably had the most challenging time readjusting. Most of the Sangheili in their local keep were not pleased to discover that he was really Asum 'Mdama, "nephew" to Jul 'Mdama, who had done so much harm to their people. Once Kasha 'Hilot had fully recovered, she took great pains to explain to everyone the events surrounding Bakar's placement within the Arbiter's clan. Bakar's actions had already more than proved that he was no friend of Jul 'Mdama's Covenant or the Servants of the Abiding Truth. Eventually the other Sangheili came to see that.

As for Molly, she spent most of her time recovering at home while the school was being repaired. Asha and Yong joined her, since much of their work was on hold for the moment too. They would no doubt return to analyzing the Guardian soon enough, but not until ONI had cleared some of the debris from its demise away.

A few days after the Guardian had been destroyed, Molly's family hosted an old-fashioned Wisconsin cookout for all of their friends. It was the first time her family had done this in years, and for Molly and her friends in Paxopolis it marked the beginning of a new chapter.

Not only did it give them an opportunity to celebrate having braved a terrible storm together, but it also gave them a chance to look forward with renewed courage. Who knew what the future held for them? All that Molly was sure of was that she now had friends she could count on, no matter how bad it got. That seemed like enough.

"We have no idea how long we're going to be locked down here inside the slipspace enclosure," Yong said. "That means no one coming in and no one going out. But since we're all going to be stuck in here together, I think we need to make every effort to ensure we all get along. Sometimes that requires extreme measures— like a neighborhood-sized Wisconsin cookout, don't you think?"

Molly recognized that something had changed in her heart since she arrived here. All of the grief from what she'd experienced back on Paris IV was still there, even if weaker on some days than others. But instead of resenting the species that had destroyed her family in the war, she could now see and embrace each person as an individual. All the differences that had made her scared of or angry at such people before now seemed insignificant compared to what had united them.

Bakar and Kasha were the last guests to leave that night, and Molly was determined to give Bakar a hug just as he walked out the door. The Sangheili only hesitated for a second before he hugged her back. She didn't know what it took for a Sangheili to hug a human, but she was glad that it now came easy for her to embrace Bakar.

They were allies, for certain, but they were also friends.

As Molly was cleaning up, Asha came over and gave her a tight hug too, and then a lingering kiss on the top of her head.

"What's that for?" Molly asked.

Asha dabbed away a tear welling in her eye and smiled at Molly. "For giving me hope."

EPILOGUE

Dural 'Mdama . . . ?"

Those were the last words to leave Kurnik's mouth before the Pale Blade slammed what remained of his battered and sputtering energy sword into Kurnik's throat. Dural had not bound up his broken leg with what he could scavenge and limped all the way back to base to open a discussion with the cowardly traitor. There would be no mercy and no second chances. The only thing he deserved for his treachery was death, and Dural happily handed it to him.

The Pale Blade walked into the base after three days in the wilderness, and he could see that Kurnik had already proven a disappointment. No one had challenged Dural. They had simply stepped aside and gazed at him in surprise and awe as he slowly made his way up into the Cathedral's central spire, found Kurnik, and put an end to him.

Once the deed was done, Dural turned to his surviving commanders and brandished his blade before them. They looked as if they had seen a ghost.

"Do any of the rest of you have the courage to defy me? Do you?"

Few of them could even meet his eyes. Dural had worried that they might look upon his injuries and refuse to accept him as their leader, but his brash disposal of Kurnik seemed to have persuaded them that he was up to the job.

Arkit, one of Dural's personal vanguard, stepped forward and gently put his hands on Dural as if to make sure that he was not actually a spirit. "You were dead, Pale Blade," Arkit said, his voice raw with astonishment. "I saw the creature carry you off with my own eyes."

"I rode that animal until it fell over lifeless, bleeding to death by my own hand!" Dural gazed at his mauled fist still clutching the sword. "And then I came back here to punish this *coward* who thought it wise to attack me from behind."

Dural glared at them all, baring his teeth to display his disdain. "We just dealt the humans a terrible blow, but instead of pressing our advantage, you've given them the time to recover and fortify. Now they will be on the hunt for us, and what have you done to prepare for it when it comes?"

No one had a decent answer. No one but the Huragok, Even Keel.

The creature floated forward to make its report, and Dural gladly let it approach. As it did, he saw reflected in the others its instant recognition of him as the leader of the Servants of the Abiding Truth. They knew that without Dural their lives here would soon come to an end.

"I see you have gotten the power in the Cathedral running again," Dural told it. "What is the status of our vehicles and heavy weaponry?"

"Inoperable," Keel said flatly through his collar. "The other leader took me off that task and set me to another."

Dural snorted at that. "He is gone. I am the leader here again."

Keel wobbled in the air before it spoke. "The other leader wanted us to flee the shield world, but the entire place has been encased inside a slipspace enclosure. We are cut off from the rest of the galaxy."

"What? How?"

"The humans here ordered this done as a means of isolating the shield world from the enemies who threatened us all with the Guardian."

"Can you undo this?"

The Huragok rolled from side to side. "Perhaps. But to do so would be to invite the Guardians back in. They would attempt to stop any conflict to maintain peace inside the shield world. They would use any means necessary, including destroying the Servants of the Abiding Truth."

"So we are trapped here." Dural scowled at his commanders. He held them all responsible for not doing something to stop this from happening before it was too late. At the very least, they could have redoubled their efforts to take control of the human settlement. Instead they had retreated and lost the second Huragok.

Keel nodded. "However, I have succeeded at my latest task. I have discovered a far better location for your base."

Dural narrowed his eyes at the creature. Perhaps Kurnik had not been entirely useless after all.

"Where is this?"

"On the third planet that orbits the shield world's interior sun. The humans call it Mackintosh. There is an installation there which serves as the home port for a Forerunner warship."

Dural gaped at the Huragok. To think that they could have such a vessel at their command. Perhaps it could house his entire force. . . .

"Is it operational?"

"It has not been moved for many millennia. It may require work to restore it to its full use. But it is habitable and accessible through the portal network. There are substantial provisions there. And armaments as well."

"That shall be good enough—for now."

Dural stepped out onto the parapet to address his warriors. Word of his return had already spread quickly through the base, and they had now gathered around the spire to learn what would become of him.

"Servants of the Abiding Truth! I am your leader once more!"

A roar of approval rose from the assembled crowd. The commanders behind him wisely echoed it. The challenges posed by Buran, Ruk, and Kurnik had not proved pointless. They had been *necessary*—and indeed appointed by the gods—so that Dural's present leadership would be solidified.

Even Dural's encounter with Asum echoed of this design. Dural could now see that this was how events had needed to transpire for the Servants to thrive in the wake of Avu Med 'Telcam's death. Now that Dural had emerged from the crucible of betrayal alive and full of fury, the Pale Blade could accomplish the task the field master had delivered to him.

"The Covenant—even the scraps of which had survived to this day—has now been completely destroyed. The Arbiter likely rules uncontested over all of Sanghelios. Only one thing stands between him and utter victory over our people: the Servants of the Abiding Truth!

"I promise this, brothers. If you submit to my leadership and are loyal to the Abiding Truth, we shall taste victory together. We shall stand strong against him and his human allies. We shall make him regret his spurning of the gods. We shall amass our divine instruments of vengeance, and we shall take Sanghelios back once again!"

The Servants roared their approval. They too wanted blood for all that the Arbiter had taken from them, and they saw the Pale Blade as the one who could give it to them.

"You may have heard that we have been cut off from the rest of the galaxy. This is true. The humans did this in a desperate effort to protect themselves.

"What they do not realize yet is that they have given us the chance we need—the time and space we require—to build anew our forces and our armament. Soon we will have the resources we need to purge them from this shield world and claim it as our own.

"We are not trapped inside this world with them. They are trapped in here with us!"

Dural's warriors thrust their weapons high and roared in unity. As their accolades echoed throughout the spire, Dural turned to Even Keel and his commanders and said, "What are you waiting for? Make all the necessary preparations. We move tonight."

ACKNOWLEDGMENTS

This book may have my name on the cover, but it's the collective effort of an amazing team of people. Once again, I owe huge thanks to my editor, Ed Schlesinger, whose love for both writing and *Halo* shines through in the polish he lends these pages. He and his team at Gallery Books work hard to bring amazing stories into the world, and I'm thrilled to have the chance to join them on such sorties.

Believe it or not, the collective aid of the people at 343 Industries—especially Jeremy Patenaude, Tiffany O'Brien, and Jeff Easterling, as well as the rest of the writing team—was even more vital for this story than for *New Blood*. Exploring a place as large and wild as Onyx occasionally requires a few course corrections, and they were always as patient and helpful as possible with their efforts to guide me along at every step of the way. Their passion for bringing fantastic *Halo* stories to fans around the world is as infectious as the Flood.

Matt Forbeck is an award-winning and *New York Times* bestselling author and game designer. He has more than thirty novels and countless games published to date. His latest work includes *Dungeonology*, the *Star Wars: Rogue One* junior novel, the last two editions of *The Marvel Encyclopedia*, his *Monster Academy* YA fantasy novels, and the upcoming *Shotguns & Sorcery* roleplaying game based on his novels. He lives in Beloit, WI, with his wife and five children, including a set of quadruplets. For more about him and his work, visit Forbeck.com.